MW00785982

the
DUCHESS
and the
ORC

FINLEY FENN

ALSO BY FINLEY FENN

ORC SWORN

The Lady and the Orc

The Heiress and the Orc

The Librarian and the Orc

The Duchess and the Orc

The Midwife and the Orc

The Maid and the Orcs

The Governess and the Orc

The Beauty and the Orcs

Offered by the Orc

Yuled by the Orcs

ORC FORGED

The Sins of the Orc

The Fall of the Orc

THE MAGES

The Mage's Maid

The Mage's Match

The Mage's Master

The Mage's Groom

Visit www.finleyfenn.com for free bonus stories and epilogues, delicious orc artwork, complete content tags and warnings, news about upcoming books, and more!

To my fabulous friends at Finley Fenn Readers' Den, with my deepest gratitude for all the laughter, kindness, and encouragement. Thank you!

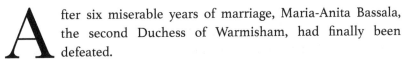

1

fter six miserable years of marriage, Maria-Anita Bassala, the second Duchess of Warmisham, had finally been defeated.

"I need to see my husband," she told the tall, armed man standing before the gilded bedroom door. "*Please.*"

Gerrard didn't move, though Maria was sure she caught a flash of pity, sparking through his blue eyes. "I'm sorry, Your Grace," he replied. "Duke Warmisham ordered me not to let anyone in."

And especially not you, was the unspoken meaning, and Maria dragged in breath, shoved down the steadily swelling panic. She had to stay calm. She had to think. She was losing *everything.*

"This is an emergency, Gerrard," she said, through gritted teeth. "I need to speak to my husband at once. *Please.*"

The pity again flicked through Gerrard's eyes, and he crossed his arms over his broad chest. "I'm sorry, Your Grace, but the Duke was *very* specific in his orders. And look"—he grimaced, his voice dropping—"you don't want to go in there now, all right? He's... *busy.*"

Of course he was, the utter bastard—and for an instant there was the wild, reckless compulsion to fight her way past Gerrard, to knock that odious, sickening look out of his eyes. It was the way everyone looked at Maria these days, from the scullery-maids to the grandest ladies of her acquaintance, and she could almost hear his thoughts aloud, grating down her spine like a dozen raking claws.

Difficult. Frigid. Barren. *Hysterical.*

"If you're suggesting," Maria said, voice clipped, "that I'm too irrational to accept how my husband prefers to spend his leisure time, I assure you, you're quite mistaken. I could not care less who he takes to his bed, providing it isn't me."

The words rang of truth, heavy and bitter, sparking yet more pity in Gerrard's watching eyes—and Maria had to force her body to stillness this time, her hands in fists at her sides. Gerrard was just doing what he'd been told, like every other horrid lackey in this horrid hellish household. And truly, for her husband to reduce one of his top generals to the post of bedroom doorman was surely an insult in itself, and Maria needed to think, gods damn it, *think.*

"I'm sorry, Your Grace," Gerrard said again, and he did even look sorry, the wince tightening his mouth. "I'm sure he wasn't expecting you."

But wait. *Wait.* That was it, good gods, and Maria felt her eyes squeezing shut, her shoulders sagging. Not a mistake, then. Not an oversight. No, it was another play. Another fucking *game.*

"Oh, I assure you, Gerrard," she said, far flatter than before. "He's most certainly expecting me. Now could you please stop this farce, and let me in?"

And maybe it was something in her voice, or her eyes, because Gerrard huffed a heavy sigh, and rapped on the door. And after an unintelligible reply from within, and then a moment's irritated-sounding discussion through the crack, there was the distant sound of a nearby door shutting. And finally, Gerrard stepped aside, opened the gilded door, and waved Maria in.

And while she should have thanked him, or something, she could only seem to stare straight ahead as she passed. Her hands still clenched in fists, the panic pounding a furious thunder-beat in her ears.

She was losing everything. And of course, it was all thanks to *him.*

Duke Warmisham, the ruler of Preia, the head of the realm's far-reaching Council. Rich, handsome, experienced, obscenely powerful. And currently sitting up in a mass of rumpled silk sheets, his chest bare and glistening, his silver-streaked hair boyishly tousled. And beside him, tossed casually on the bed, was a stoppered bottle of oil, and what looked like an army-issued pair of trousers.

Typical. So damned typical, from the man who just last month had upheld a law condemning such things. And the man who was currently smirking at Maria, as though he'd just accomplished the realm's cleverest coup.

"What in the gods' names is so important, wife?" he asked, his voice affable and cool, betraying not even a trace of its underlying malice. "You've worked yourself into a mania again, I presume? Sit down, before you hurt yourself."

He'd flicked his hand toward the nearby damask chair, and Maria choked back the surge of rebellion, of sheer overpowering rage. She'd had years of practice dealing with this man, enough to know that losing her temper would just play into his snide, slippery hands. Difficult. *Hysterical.*

"As you know, I met with Lakewood today," she made herself say, as she strode toward the chair with stiff steps. "And he informed me that my inheritance has recently been... *misplaced.*"

Her voice had come out smooth, rational, without the faintest whiff of so-called *hysteria,* and as she sank into the chair, her gaze on her husband was calm too, despite her shallow breaths. "My inheritance was protected," she continued, "by my late father. Of all the money you gained from our marriage, that was to remain mine, in perpetuity. You knew that. You *accepted* that."

Her husband didn't immediately reply, but only kept gazing at her, smug, amused. And looking back at his odious, handsome face, it felt laughable—laughable!—to think of all Maria's stupid, starry-eyed delusions of six years past. That she'd fallen into a deeply romantic tale, in which the dashing, worldly, recently widowed duke had swooped in to rescue the damsel in distress. That he'd desperately longed for an eager, capable new partner—someone to confide in, to share his busy political life with, to build a new family with. Someone to stand by his side against the world.

Laughable. Because in truth, Duke Warmisham had had no interest in a partner, political or otherwise. No interest in more family, either, thanks to the three hideously expensive adult offspring he already possessed. And he'd *certainly* had no interest in a wife with opinions, or emotions, or ambitions—or, most humiliating of all, with needs or expectations in the bedroom.

No. It had all been about the money. And also, perhaps, about Duke Warmisham's assumption that his devoted, naive new wife would surely be another weak, docile minion to fawn over him, and leap to do his bidding, and sweetly host his dinner-parties. Someone to look the other way while he freely indulged his true desires, none of which had ever included her.

"Oh, settle down, wife," he said now, with a casual wave of his hand. "It's likely due to the new bill the Council ratified last month. Protected personal funds can now be appropriated by the proper parties, providing it's in the deeper interest of the realm's public safety."

Good gods. Maria had vaguely heard about that new bill—her husband's awful Council had a regular habit of creating loathsome new laws—but he'd meant to use it against his own *wife*? To steal her inheritance? To make her *destitute*?!

"That money was *mine*," she heard herself say, her voice very far away. "It was *not yours* to take!"

But her husband only shrugged, and gave her a chilly, satisfied smile. "*I* didn't take it," he replied. "It's being used for the betterment of the realm. And you're perfectly well cared for here, aren't you? So what use did you have for it, anyway?"

What use did she have. Maria stared at him for an instant too long, as her clammy hands clutched compulsively in her lap, crushing the costly silk of her skirts. As the panic crept higher, closer, rattling against her ribs.

She needed the money to run.

She'd been formulating the plan for the better part of a year. Researching her options, mapping routes, purchasing supplies. Planning, secretly, for a new life. A better life, all the way across the realm, where she could start over. Find freedom. Escape this man's clutches, for good.

Because by this point, Maria knew very well, the public demise of her marriage was only a matter of time. And of how thoroughly—and how permanently—her husband would decide to dispose of his irrational, inconvenient liability of a wife.

She had to run. She *had* to.

"That money," she managed, far too late, "had sentimental value. It was meant as a gift from my father, for my *children*."

But she winced even as she said it, and once again, her husband didn't bother trying to hide his smirk. "I'm afraid I can't help you there, wife," he said. "Sentimental doesn't cut it anymore. Not when the entire realm is fighting for its very *survival*."

Wait. Maria felt her forehead furrowing, her head tilting. "It is?" she asked. "Good heavens, *how*? Against *who*?!"

Her husband's brows slightly rose, the smirk curling tighter on his lips. "Against the *orcs*, wife," he drawled at her. "You know, the cruel, cunning, bloodthirsty beasts, wreaking terror and havoc across the realm? Wielding their deadly black magic, and stealing away hapless women like *you*, so you can bear them their foul killer *sons*?"

Maria stared at her husband, while the incredulity jolted higher, hotter. Gods, not this again. This man had stolen *her* money, so he could throw it away on *orcs*?!

"But—the war with the orcs is *over*," she protested, her voice rising. "They signed that comprehensive *peace-treaty* with their neighbouring provinces last year. A treaty *your* Council publicly *ratified*, and which both parties have adhered to ever since. You have no remaining responsibility toward the orcs *whatsoever*."

But her husband only kept gazing at her, brows lifted, as Maria battled down the rapidly rising urge to leap up, and hurl her chair straight into the fire-grate. Those blasted orcs were a distraction, a *waste*, a dwindling pack of wild *beasts* who squatted under a single mountain half a continent away. And her husband's ongoing obsession with them was utter ludicrous *absurdity*, on a level with railing against a feral passel of *monkeys* who lived beneath the fucking *sea*.

"My father's inheritance has *nothing* to do with *orcs*," Maria tried again, over the pounding in her skull. "There must be *something* you can do to restore it to me. *Please*."

But she hated the words even as she heard them, because surely this was exactly the game her husband had meant to play today. His irritating, hysterical wife reduced to begging for his mercy, while he lounged comfortably in his bed, and smiled. And while a respectable, reliable witness listened to every word, just outside the half-open door.

Difficult. Overwrought. Too out of control to tolerate any longer...

"Despite your delusional opinions, *darling*, the orcs still pose a significant threat," Duke Warmisham countered, his voice rather flatter than before. "Perhaps you'll enjoy hearing that those ugly green beasts are *very* interested in women like you? Women with money. With *standing*."

They were? Maria blinked, and desperately forced her raging brain to follow, to *think*. Yes, she supposed, there *had* been a few isolated, rumour-ridden incidents out west, in which the orcs had reportedly seduced several wealthy, high-profile women. Unfortunate, to be sure—but it had all still transpired half a continent away, and paled in comparison to all the far more pressing priorities Duke Warmisham should be addressing here at home. Problems like hunger, poverty, disease. *Injustice.*

"That still doesn't explain why *my* inheritance was taken," Maria said, fighting to keep her voice even. "Surely you don't expect *I'll* next be seduced by orcs?"

She'd meant it as sarcasm, as an utter laughable impossibility—but something, something new, had flicked across her husband's face. Something that deepened the lines around his thin mouth, darkened the shadows under his cool grey eyes.

"Those orcs are vile, cunning bastards," he snapped. "They've been blatantly targeting nobility across the realm. And I'm well aware that they'd love nothing more than to publicly *ruin* me, just like they did to Norr."

Like they did to Norr. In truth, that one *had* hit closer to home, despite the distance—Lord Norr had been a longtime friend of Duke Warmisham's, and his supposedly barren wife had indeed been stolen away by orcs last year. The messy matter had ended with Lord Norr's untimely demise, as well as Lady Norr's permanent disappearance, and an ongoing feeding frenzy for gossips throughout the realm.

Norr's better off dead, the whispers went. *His legacy is destroyed. A lord, in the prime of his life, cuckolded by an orc.*

But to Maria, who was now far too inured to busybodies' whispering, the whole business had still reeked of distraction, of utter absurdity. Yes, it had been a targeted attack by the orcs, and probably even a clever one, because it had ultimately led to the peace-treaty the orcs had wanted. The peace-treaty her husband's Council had publicly *ratified*. Which should have been the end of the entire ridiculous matter, for good.

Maria's head was pounding louder, and she rubbed at her temples, drew in breath. "Lord Norr lived on the orcs' *doorstep*," she said, "and he was notoriously cheap with his security. He was an easy target. That kind of attack would *never* happen here."

It was true—beyond the far greater distance, Duke Warmisham was also a far more calculating man than Norr had been. He was a man whose fortress of a house was so well staffed, so well guarded and protected, that it had taken Maria all these months to plan her escape. And now it was *ruined*.

"Warring against the orcs is a *waste*," Maria continued, her voice cracking. "It's like raging against the *wind*. It gains you *nothing*. It's a massive drain on our province's already-strained resources, and on your very valuable time. Many of your advisors have repeatedly warned you against it. Even your cleverest *son*."

But she was treading deadly ground now—her husband loathed dissenters, and any reminders thereof—and she could see his mouth thinning, his eyes angling narrow toward her. "Kaspar and my advisors were targeted and compromised, *briefly*, by the orcs' devious propaganda campaigns," he countered. "And I am not warring against anyone—*yet*. I only protect the safety of my provinces. My *people*. My own dear *wife*."

That was truly ludicrous, on all counts, and Maria ground her teeth, fought down the words that were clamouring for escape. "I will *not* be kidnapped by orcs," she insisted. "I want my money back. *Please*."

But her husband didn't even look at her this time, and drummed his gold-ringed fingers against his bare chest. "No," he said. "But rest assured, wife, that it will support a noble cause."

Maria's throat barked out an unfamiliar noise, her hands gripping painfully at her chair. "Warring against orcs isn't *noble*!" her mouth hissed, on its own, before she could stop it. "It's utter foolish *absurdity*, a useless vanity project to make yourself seem powerful. And likely also some kind of deep-seated terror that some day, women will decide they'd rather risk the realm's most barbaric *beasts* than stay with the likes of *you!*"

Shut up, shut up, *shut up*, her distant brain was hollering, but it was far too late, and her husband snarled a mocking, satisfied laugh. "Ah, there's the hysterical woman I married," he said coldly. "You want to be kidnapped by orcs, is that it, wife? You want to be used and brutalized by a giant green *beast?*"

And for a screeching, dangling instant, there was the wild, almost uncontrollable urge to scream. To shout, *Yes, actually, at this point, being kidnapped by orcs would surely be an improvement on this hollow husk of an existence, trapped here in this horrible house with you—*

The truth of that seemed to strike Maria all at once, hammering deep into her soul, firing streams of fury and terror in its wake. Without her money, she was well and truly trapped. She had no other income. No living family. No friends who wouldn't betray her to their ruling Duke. And even her own personal servants were all in the palm of her husband's hand, united in their eagerness to closely monitor their frigid, unstable young duchess, ensuring she didn't fall into melancholia again, or suffer another of her hysterical spells, or worse...

She'd finally been defeated, for good.

"Well?" her vile husband asked her, cool, amused, mocking. "Shall I set you out upon a plain, wife, and wait for an orc to come and ravage you?"

Maria swallowed hard, her wide blinking eyes trapped on his—and catching, for an odd, dangling instant, upon that faint flare of *emotion* across her unfeeling husband's face. The distaste, the revulsion, perhaps even—the *fear*.

He's better off dead. A lord, in the prime of his life, cuckolded by an orc. They would love nothing more than to publicly ruin me...

And even as the idea flashed through Maria's thoughts, she knew it was no doubt the hysteria, come home to roost for good—but it still held there, gripped there, sank its teeth deep into her churning gut. The orcs had money, from those wealthy women they'd seduced. They desperately craved women and sons. That would *never* happen here...

But surely, Maria could run—*there?*

Her heart was wildly flailing, suddenly, her clammy hands clutching at her skirts, her eyes still blinking at her husband's smug, obnoxious face. She could do this. Good gods, she could do this. She could seek freedom, and justice, and *revenge*.

"Is that what you want, wife?" repeated her husband, taunting, vicious. "You want to be ripped away from your pampered, privileged existence as a *duchess*, so you can be ravaged and broken by an *orc*?"

And somehow, somehow, Maria found the strength to shake her head. To give the odious man before her a small, wan smile. To be defeated. Until...

"Of course not, my lord," she said. "To want such a thing, a woman would have to be truly *insane*."

2

Six weeks later, Maria silently slipped out of Warmisham House, and into the night's quiet darkness.

She wore faded overalls and a men's tunic, and her long dark curls were carefully tucked under a cap. On her back she carried a heavy canvas pack, and the gold coins she'd managed to acquire were hidden close against her skin, under the large swath of fabric binding her chest.

She was ready.

It had been weeks of secret, silent preparations, painstakingly concealed from Warmisham House's ever-present, ever-vigilant servants. She'd re-assembled her hidden stash of supplies, rigorously planned her route, surreptitiously researched the best available travelling options. She'd even made multiple deeply upsetting visits to her bank and a variety of reputable lawyers, all of whom had confirmed the worst.

Her inheritance was gone. And without her husband's direct intervention, it would never again return to her hands.

And with the truth of that still fresh and bitter in her thoughts, Maria had resolutely turned her attention to the main thrust of her revenge. To gaining her husband's thorough, devastating defeat, in as public a way as possible.

And it wasn't enough, she'd soon realized, to be merely kidnapped by orcs. Not when such an event might only prompt her immediate pursuit and rescue, or be swiftly covered up again. Not when it would surely offer her husband spectacular grounds for his sought-after war.

No, it had to be more lasting than that. More insidious. More... permanent.

So after much deliberation, Maria had turned to letters. Such small, simple things, letters—but not, perhaps, when they contained such sordid, scandalous revelations as these. Not when they were then sealed and left with the lawyers Maria most trusted, with explicit instructions for their delivery in precisely one month's time. And surely not when the letters' intended recipients included typesetters, columnists, rabble-rousers, and known enemies of her husband—as well as a select list of the well-placed busybodies who'd so carelessly helped destroy Maria's own public reputation.

And tonight, on her lady-in-waiting's weekly night off, Maria left her bed rumpled, her window latched, her few distinctive pieces of jewelry—including her wedding-ring—entirely untouched at her dressing-table. Offering no immediately obvious reasons for her abrupt disappearance—and thus also gaining enough time, she hoped, to reach her destination without disruption. Enough time, even, to perhaps make her letters truth.

A lord, in the prime of his life, cuckolded by an orc.

Maria cast one final glance up at Warmisham House behind her, at its symmetrical square elegance, its deep, deceptive whispers of safety and family and home. And then she resolutely turned her back, hoisted her pack on her shoulders, and fixed her gaze due west.

Toward Orc Mountain.

Her plans for the evening's travels were fully set, and thankfully, they all unfolded exactly as expected. She walked undisturbed on foot for several hours, hired three separate carriages on a circuitous route, and then spent the night in a reputable working-class inn. The accommodations were sparse but clean, and after an admittedly fitful night's sleep, Maria climbed aboard the morning coach, and continued making her way west.

The days and nights began blurring together after that, marked only by one new inn after another, by night after night of uneven, uncertain sleep. Waiting, constantly, for the sudden raised alarm, the storm of her husband's soldiers. *The Duchess of Warmisham's on the run, we've found her, apprehend her at once—*

But the alarm never came, and neither did the men. And Maria's only true surprise, as the days plodded past, was just how easy it was to slip back into this role as an unremarkable, unimportant commoner. As though her father had never inherited the wealth that had marked his later years. As though the memories were close enough to touch, after so many years spent thrusting away their painful promises of happiness, of home.

Let's ride to the sea today, her father would say with his contagious grin, dragging both Maria and her mother tight into his big barrel chest. *Let's go cheer on that jousting-match. I wish you could come away on campaign with me too, my sweet Maria. Someday we'll all travel the realm together, won't we?*

But even after the money, that day had never arrived. Foiled first by the accumulated injuries that had left her father bedridden, and then by the fever that had forever destroyed everything. And now, here was Maria, finally on a journey, alone and brittle and empty, and growing steadily wearier with every endless, wretched day that passed.

"You canna be wantin' to go to that mountain, boy," said the fourth wagon-driver she flagged down, on that miserable seventh morning. "There's where the orcs live. *Thousands* of 'em."

Maria hoisted up her pack—now far lighter than it had once been—and met the man's gaze with a flinty glare of her own. "Yes, I'm aware, thanks," she said curtly, using her father's old accent, dropping her voice as low as it would go. "The orcs have hired me on as a trading manager. Trying to improve their routes, on account of the treaty and all."

The man's lip curled, his eyes flicking doubtfully up and down Maria's grimy form. "You got coin?"

Maria silently held up her last gold coin, and after a long, suspicious look toward it, the man sighed. "I'll take you as far as the woods," he said, jerking his head at his hay-filled wagon. "An' after that, you're on your own."

Maria nodded gratefully and clambered up behind him, sinking down into the wagon's sweet-smelling hay. Gods, it felt good to rest, and she dropped her head onto her knees, and finally let her eyes flutter closed.

She was doing this. Granting her husband all his worst fears on a silver platter, while the entire realm pointed and laughed.

And as for what came next—or after that—Maria had found, to her vague surprise, that she didn't particularly care. Even the threat of what she was likely to face at Orc Mountain—and what horrors were sure to be inflicted upon her person there—had oddly dwindled during her journey, sinking into a numb, distant detachment.

Perhaps she would somehow survive this. Perhaps she would somehow emerge with an income, and her freedom intact. Or perhaps, more likely, she was walking straight into her death. Either at the barbaric orcs' swords, or birthing their huge, violent sons, or once they'd used her up and cast her out for good...

But it was still better than life at Warmisham House. It still gained Maria her revenge, and her husband's public shame. And that, at this point, was all that mattered. Nothing else.

"So 'ave you ever *met* an orc, boy?" cut in the driver's voice, and when Maria glanced up, he was keenly watching her over his shoulder, ignoring his steadily plodding horse. "Are you sure you know what you're gettin' into?"

Maria tried for a shrug, and wiped a shaky hand at her sweaty forehead. "Sure I've met orcs before," she replied, still in her accented deep voice. "Would have to, to get this deal, wouldn't I?"

The man looked unconvinced, but Maria didn't drop her gaze, and finally he shrugged and turned back to the road. "I'm just sayin'. Those orcs are ugly, an' I'm not just talkin' about their faces. Word is, they love baby-faced fellas like you. Get you trapped in that mountain, treat you just like a woman, until..."

Maria's stomach heaved, but thankfully the man didn't finish, and she squeezed her eyes shut, hauled in a hoarse breath. Yes, she still believed the orcs were a mistake, a waste, a glut of sheer stupidity upon the realm—but that didn't mean all the stories weren't true, either. Orcs *were* brutal, coarse, uncivilized beasts. They were cruel and hideous and deadly. And the few orcs she'd seen in her lifetime— though usually at a distance, and usually in the midst of some gruesome public punishment—had all been huge and scarred and vicious,

flailing and growling in their crude black-tongue, threatening immi-
nent danger to all who came too close.

"An' with the *actual* women, they're even worse," continued the
driver, clearly undaunted by Maria's silence. "Trapping 'em deep
underground, biting and swiving upon 'em like beasts. Whelping as
many of their spawn as the women can bear, until they're used up an'
eaten. Jus' like *hens.*"

A sudden, inexplicable giddiness was bubbling in Maria's gut—
here she was, the Duchess of Warmisham, volunteering to be used up
and eaten like a *hen*—but after a few more breaths, the panic slowly
flattened again, sinking into the familiar empty resignation. She would
have her revenge. Nothing else mattered.

"Well, here you go, then," the driver said, after what felt like far too
short a time. "Follow the road from here, you canna miss it."

Maria's bleary eyes blinked up, following the man's pointing
finger—and she felt her body snap to stillness, her heart lurching
toward her throat. She was here. Already.

Orc Mountain.

It was huge and grey and craggy, its snow-capped peak soaring up
over the surrounding forest, streaming multiple plumes of thick black
smoke. Orc Mountain, *here*, at the end of this very *road*, and for an
instant Maria could only stare, and fight to find her breath. She'd
come this far. She would do this. She *would*.

She somehow managed to shove her shaky body off the wagon,
and paid the man his promised coin. And all too soon he'd rattled
away, leaving her standing alone and impoverished at the edge of a
forest, and blinking up at Orc Mountain. At her revenge.

The panic was bubbling again, clawing deep inside, but Maria
clamped it down, and held her eyes on the mountain's looming bulk.
She could do this. She would.

So she began walking, ignoring the aches in her sore body, the pain
in her weary legs. Plodding on and on and on, step after endless step,
until her feet were fully numb, and sweat streamed off her brow. And
finally there were no thoughts left, no fears, only the distant darkening
resignation, blunting all else under its weight. She would keep going.
She would do this. She would...

The wall flashed to life without warning, rising huge and powerful before her—and Maria's unseeing, exhausted body crashed straight into it. Into heat, strength, solid and rugged and *alive*, and wait, wait, *wait*—

She reeled back, badly staggering, blinking wild-eyed up at the wall before her—and oh gods, oh gods, it wasn't a wall at all, it was, it was...

It was an *orc*.

3

The orc was *massive*.

He towered over Maria like a violent, vengeful god, his broad chest bare and battle-scarred, his deep grey torso wrapped in heavy, deadly muscle. And at his side hung a gigantic orc scimitar, a vicious curve of sharp shining steel, eager to disembowel, to devour, to *destroy*.

Maria gaped at that sword, her breath clutched in her throat—and somehow she forced her eyes to slide up, and up, and up, until they found the orc's face.

And it was—*horrifying*. It was the stuff of nightmares, with its heavy-cut jaw, deeply scarred cheeks, and badly bent nose. With its swollen, ruined ears, one still tapering to a tall pointed tip, the other looking as though it had been bitten off halfway.

But most terrifying of all were the orc's *eyes*. Deep, glittering, pure black eyes, piercing into Maria, *through* Maria, like sharpened deadly daggers. Like they could see everything, *everything*, and Maria swayed on her shaky feet, her limbs seized, her whole body shivering. While the panic began rattling again, clanging deep inside, raging, revenge, *run*—

But she couldn't move, nothing moved, the world suspended in place around her. And then it began tilting, ever so slowly, and Maria *had* to do this, she would, revenge, it didn't matter, it was just an orc, oh gods oh *please...*

"If you're going to kill me," someone said, *she* said, her voice very far away, "could you please just—do so now? Quickly?"

The orc's eyes blinked, once—and in that instant, it was like his deadly command had broken, spattering to the earth. Releasing the last of whatever had still been holding Maria upright, the ground abruptly sagging and swaying beneath her numb, staggering feet.

And as she slowly pitched sideways, there was the certainty, flat and resigned, that this would hurt. And why did everything have to hurt so much, why wouldn't it all just *stop*—

Until suddenly, the orc *moved*. His huge body shifting, flashing toward her—and then his powerful bare arms curved close around her trembling form, his big hands spreading wide against her back.

The orc had—*caught* her.

And he kept holding her, cradling her in place with exquisite, stunning gentleness. At full odds with the raw power of his massive body, with the glinting, undeniable *meaning* in his bottomless black eyes.

"Peace, woman," he said, his deep, heavily accented voice rumbling into Maria's chest, into her heart. "I no harm you."

Oh. *Oh.* And even as a distant part of Maria was wildly, desperately protesting—how had he known she was a woman through her disguise, why hadn't he let her fall, why couldn't he have just used that scimitar and finished it all for good—she felt her exhausted body sagging, sinking deeper into the impossible strength of his warm arms.

Into—*safety.*

The orc still hadn't moved, hadn't stopped looking at her, searching her with those glinting, piercing eyes. And as Maria stared back, she felt her own shaky hand somehow moving on its own, rising up into the space between them...

Until her trembling fingers found the orc's huge, hot bare *chest.* And then slowly flattened against it, feeling the deep, steady thud of his rapidly pulsing heart.

And good gods, Maria was touching an orc, *voluntarily*—but in this taut, hanging instant, there seemed no reason to move, to resist. Only the hazy, urgent need to stay, to accept, to *be.* To drink up the sheer power of him, the strange unaccountable *reassurance* of him, the fierce galloping thunder of that heartbeat under her fingers.

The orc's eyes had widened, his nostrils flaring, almost as though he were *smelling* her—and as Maria stared, blunted and dazed, a long, sinuous black tongue slipped from his mouth, and curled against his lips. Baring a set of vicious white teeth, complete with sharp deadly fangs, clearly meant to bite and tear and *kill*—

But instead of the disgust or the terror Maria surely should have felt, her jolting thoughts were trapped, suddenly, on the surprising sensual fullness of the orc's lips against those sharp teeth, on the smooth, shameless slide of that supple black tongue. On the rich, rugged scent that had somehow begun twining into her nostrils, heavy and sweet, stirring something deep inside that had almost been forgotten...

And for a skittering, blissful breath, there was—*peace*. This orc's powerful eyes and hands, his full focus, all so intent upon her, holding her safe, while her own hand held his roaring heart. And what would it feel like to fully vanish into his strength, to lose herself in his eyes and his mouth, to forget everything, forever...

But wait. No. *No*. She was here for a reason. For her plan. Her *revenge*.

"Then please, good sir," she said, taut, riveted, choked, to those watching black eyes. "Take me as your own, and allow me to bear you a son."

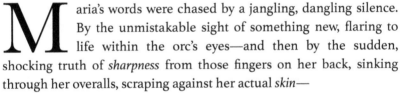

4

Maria's words were chased by a jangling, dangling silence. By the unmistakable sight of something new, flaring to life within the orc's eyes—and then by the sudden, shocking truth of *sharpness* from those fingers on her back, sinking through her overalls, scraping against her actual *skin*—

And in a swift scuffle of movement, everything changed. The orc's powerful hands abruptly thrusting Maria away, settling her onto her badly shaking feet, while his hulking grey form lurched backwards, well out of her reach.

One of his huge hands had gripped his thick steel sword-hilt, the other snapped to a fist at his side—and somehow both hands now bore black *claws*, long and curved and deadly. And the tension in his massive body felt almost palpable, every muscle clenched and rippling, his skin covered in a shimmering sheen of sweat.

But most telling of all were his eyes. The eyes that had pierced Maria, *known* her, given her that blissful, priceless instant of *forgetting*—they were suddenly narrow and chilly and distant, glinting with something that might have been *hatred.*

"You ken this is good game, woman?" the orc hissed, his voice far harsher than before, heavy with menace and danger. "Seek to defeat Enforcer with false pledge? With false *son*?"

Maria felt herself staggering backwards, her thoughts clambering and churning all at once. Defeat Enforcer? False son? A *game*?!

"It's—it's not a game," she stammered, fighting to raise her eyes to his. "I've come here to—to meet an orc. To meet *you*."

The orc's lip instantly curled, his hand flexing on his sword-hilt. "Women no wish to meet orcs," he growled. "You *lie*."

Maria's brain kept scrambling, shouting, and gods, why did it matter, she'd chosen this, he was just an orc, she didn't care, *revenge*...

"I'm not lying," she countered, though her voice still wavered, her gaze dropped back to the orc's massive booted feet. "I'm *finished* with human men. And I have no income, and all my blood relations are dead, and several physicians have confirmed that I'm in excellent physical health, and likely to handle child-bearing very well. And I've heard again and again how desperate orcs are for sons, so I thought—"

She couldn't seem to finish, even though it was exactly what she'd rehearsed. Even though there was no whiff of falsehood about it, because apart from that one single vital point—her husband being the Duke of Warmisham—Maria had no intention of lying to these orcs. Not when the truth would do just as well.

But there was no answer from the huge orc, and when Maria finally mustered the courage to meet his eyes again, he was still glowering down toward her, his scarred face cruel, furious, uncompromising. And gods, how had she ever found his face even *slightly* intriguing, clearly she was even more exhausted than she'd thought—

"I hoped we could reach an—agreement," she made herself continue, the words thick in her mouth. "I'll give you a son, but in exchange I want room and board, and your protection throughout my pregnancy. And then, if the birth is successful"—she swallowed hard—"I'll hand our son over to your care, permanently. But as compensation, I also want fair payment from you. Enough to secure me a small annual income afterwards."

Maria couldn't quite hide her wince as she spoke, because she knew it was far more likely that the orcs would simply take her, and do with her as they pleased. But they were bound to be suspicious of her motives in coming here, and a mercenary explanation surely would be the easiest for them to swallow.

And, Maria could admit, a distant, foolish part of her still carried some hope—however small and pathetic—that she might still survive this. And that one day, maybe, she could be free again. Make a real family. A real *home*.

But this orc's reaction wasn't encouraging, his heavy black brows furrowing, his mouth thinning into a fierce, bitter grimace. "You wish to *sell*?" he spat, the distaste all too clear in his deep voice. "Sell womb, sell own *son*, for *coin*?!"

Maria felt herself flinch, but she kept her eyes steady on the orc's furious face, even as his narrow, flinty gaze flicked up and down her filthy body. And though she held no delusions about her attractiveness in her current state, her stomach still twisted at the visible scorn, the *contempt*, in those assessing, all-seeing black eyes.

"Why sell to orcs," he growled at her. "You are tall woman. Strong. Ripe. *Easy* to sell to men. *Easy* to bear tiny man-sons."

There was a strange, laughing hiccough, lurching deep in Maria's throat. "I told you, I'm *done* with human men," she shot back. "And they're done with me. My husband, he—"

Shit, *shit*, she was not supposed to be bringing that swine into this—but it was too late, and the orc's harsh face had somehow, impossibly, become even more contemptuous. More disapproving. More—*disgusted*.

"Ach, your *husband*," he sneered at her. "Now I ken this game, woman. You use orc—you use *son*—for *vengeance*. You strike shame at husband when you bounce upon fat orc-prick, and suck foul orc-seed into empty womb. Ach?"

For a jolting, hanging breath, Maria truly couldn't speak, and instead only stared at this crude shocking orc. How had he known. How had he seen through her so easily. All her plans, all her revenge, what else could he see...

She couldn't fail now. She couldn't be defeated by a single, horribly astute orc. It was too late. She'd already come too far, done too much. She *couldn't*.

"Yes," she shot back at him, spitting the word out, hearing it ring with biting truth. "I *hate* my husband. I will do whatever it takes to escape him, and heap shame upon his head. And therefore, yes, I will happily bounce upon you, and bear you a son, and allow you to do whatever you *wish* with me!"

But it wasn't working, oh gods it wasn't working, the scorn and the revulsion and the sheer visceral *hatred* flashing across the orc's eyes. And for an instant, there was the fear, raw and choking, that maybe he would just draw that sword after all, and fell her where she stood—

"You claim wrong orc for *game*, woman," he snarled, every word a deafening thud in Maria's belly. "I am Enforcer of Orc Mountain, and thus I abide no *trap*. No *buy*. No weak human *vengeance!*"

Maria's breath was heaving, her eyes inexplicably prickling—what did he mean he was Enforcer, and he truly didn't *want* her?—but no, no, it didn't matter, it was just an orc, nothing mattered, but revenge...

"Very well," she whispered, raising her head, meeting the force of the bare *loathing* in those black orc eyes. "If you will not have me, sir, then please, take me to another orc who will."

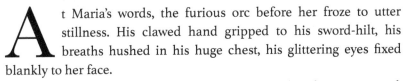

5

At Maria's words, the furious orc before her froze to utter stillness. His clawed hand gripped to his sword-hilt, his breaths hushed in his huge chest, his glittering eyes fixed blankly to her face.

A strange, unfamiliar noise was rising from his throat—a *growl*, Maria realized, as she gaped slack-jawed at his taut, immobile body. This orc was *growling* at her, this orc hated her, maybe this orc truly would still kill her, after all...

But then, in a stiff jerk of movement, he spun away from her, muttering something under his breath. And then he strode off, his steps long and graceful, his huge black boots surprisingly silent on the loose rock and dirt under his feet.

Maria blankly blinked after him, her gaze catching upon the gleaming braid that hung down his broad bare back, brushing against more scars, more powerful rippling muscles. The braid was wrapped with thick strips of leather, studded with what looked like bone, or perhaps *teeth*—and was that actually a *dagger*, embedded deep into the base of it?

And the sight of that dagger, glinting so innocuous and yet so brazen in this orc's actual *hair*, seemed to snap the awareness back to

Maria's blunted thoughts. This was an *orc*, and he was walking toward *Orc Mountain*, still huge and craggy and streaming smoke above them—and wait, wait, was the orc actually *taking* her there? Like she'd asked?

But yes, he was darting a dark, baleful glance over his shoulder, clearly expecting Maria to follow. And somehow her aching body lurched into motion again, staggering after him, straight toward what appeared to be a solid stone cliff at the base of the massive, smoking mountain.

She only distantly noted what looked to be a few outbuildings around them, perhaps sheds, or stables—because the orc had angled his huge form sideways, slipping with unnerving ease through a narrow crack in the stone. A crack which, upon closer inspection, turned out to be a cleverly engineered *opening*, leading into the mountain's gaping darkness.

Maria felt herself hesitating at the edge of it, her gaze darting longingly behind her to the sky, the open air, the sun—but then she squeezed her eyes shut, shook her head. It didn't matter. Nothing mattered, but revenge.

She silently repeated that truth as she stepped over the threshold, following the massive orc inside. Into *Orc Mountain*, quiet and close and cool, and illuminated with a faint flickering glow.

Maria's body stilled again, her eyes searching, blinking, adjusting to the dimmer light. And then finding, to her genuine surprise, that she was standing in an actual *corridor*, carved smooth and square out of the mountain's solid stone. It was just as wide and tall as any of the hallways in Warmisham House, and the light came from a series of intricate wrought-iron *lamps*, embedded at regular intervals into the seamless stone walls.

Maria couldn't stop staring, first at the lamps, and then at the perfectly smooth walls, and then at what looked like a *door* up to the right, carved tall and square into the stone wall. And good gods, Orc Mountain wasn't supposed to look like a *house*, it was supposed to be a vermin-infested *hovel*, a black hole of violence and disease and *death*—

She shot an uncertain glance toward the huge orc, who was now looming in the corridor up ahead, and glowering back toward her.

Waiting for her, Maria's scrambled thoughts noted, and she jerked a nod, and hurried to catch up again.

The orc grunted, a sound that might have almost been approving, if not for the still-furious scowl on his harsh face. But this time, to Maria's vague surprise, he wasn't aiming his scowl at her, but instead at—*another orc*. Yes, another orc, jogging straight down the corridor toward them, his full attention clearly fixed upon—*her*.

And without at all meaning to, Maria felt herself edging backwards, behind the massive bulk of her orc. Or rather, the *first* orc, and that was *all*—but even so, it somehow seemed as though he'd angled his huge body before her too, almost entirely hiding her from this new orc's view.

"Simon!" the new orc exclaimed, skidding to a halt before them. "You've brought home a *woman!*"

Maria could see her orc—*Simon?*—further stiffening, but he didn't make to move away from her, or indeed offer any kind of introduction. A blatant discourtesy that the new orc seemed wholly undaunted by, as he peered around Simon's shoulder to flash Maria a wide, sharp-toothed smile.

"Greetings, new Skai woman," the orc said, with a fluid little bow. "Welcome to our mountain. I am Baldr of Clan Grisk, Left Hand to our captain."

Maria blinked back at this—*Baldr* orc, who unlike her orc was fully dressed in a proper tunic and trousers, with no obvious adornments in his own long black braid. And while still massive, he was noticeably smaller than her orc—than *Simon*—and he looked younger, too, his grey-green face smooth and symmetrical, his visible scars far less severe.

Baldr kept smiling as Maria inspected him, his dark eyes eager and expectant in the lamplight. As though he was waiting for her to *speak*, and good gods, orcs weren't supposed to be polite, or friendly, and why couldn't she *think*—

"Um, hello, Baldr," Maria finally croaked, around Simon's huge shoulder. "I'm Maria. From Preia. Very happy to meet you."

She was still speaking with her father's accent, and she was counting on the fact that no one but her parents had ever called her

Maria. And indeed, there wasn't even a trace of suspicion from this Baldr, but only another genial smile, another flourishing little bow.

"I am happy to meet you also, Maria," Baldr said, and she belatedly noticed that his own voice was also faintly accented, with a distinctive melodious lilt. "It has been many moons since a Skai has brought a mate to our mountain."

Wait, a *mate*? Simon's hulking shoulders seemed to hunch higher, and he glowered down at Baldr, his clawed hand fidgeting at his sword-hilt. "*No* mate," he growled. "Woman who *wishes* for mate."

Baldr's glance at Simon's face was surprisingly warm, perhaps almost teasing. "Ach, I can smell," he said lightly. "You must needs finish fulfilling her wish, ach, brother? Mayhap you shall take her to the Skai wing now, and I shall send for food, and oil, and a hot bath?"

He shot another encouraging smile at Maria as he spoke, and then, if she wasn't mistaken, he actually *winked* up at Simon. A gesture that Simon instantly returned with a ghastly frown, as one clawed hand rattled the sword at his side, and the other snapped up to rub at his visibly grinding jaw.

"I said, *no mate*," he hissed at Baldr, his voice deep, bitter. "Woman seek to *sell*. To *trick*. To play *game*."

Baldr's smile faltered, his brows furrowing as he glanced back at Maria—and for a choked, stilted instant, she felt almost—*guilty*. Ashamed. Regretful, somehow, for falsely raising this cheerful orc's hopes on his bad-tempered brother's behalf. And truly, this was all *ridiculous*, orcs were *not* supposed to be kind, they were *not* supposed to *live in houses*, and most importantly, this Simon orc *loathed* her. Didn't he?

"But your scent is strong upon her, brother," Baldr said to Simon, and his dark eyes looked troubled now, perhaps even pained. "And hers upon you. And I can smell your—"

He didn't finish, darting another furtive glance at Maria—and suddenly Maria found she couldn't even meet his eyes, her own gaze dropping to the floor. It didn't matter. Nothing mattered, but *revenge*.

"Need meeting," Simon's deep voice rumbled. "Now. With Captain. Drafli. Nattfarr. Silfast and Olarr. John-Ka. Mayhap mates also."

If Baldr gave a reply, Maria didn't hear it—and when she looked up again, he was already jogging away, while Simon glared after him, his clawed hand still rubbing at his sharp jaw. Which, Maria distantly noted, was shadowed with thick black *stubble*. And for an instant, there was a compulsive, *completely* irrational urge to reach up, to trace her finger against it—

But thankfully Simon stalked off again, striding with long, silent steps down the corridor, and Maria belatedly followed, dragging in deep breaths, and forcing herself to actually take note of the mountain around her. This area seemed to be a main thoroughfare, with regular square-cut openings in the walls, and occasionally it broke into yet more corridors, twisting away into darkness. None of the adjoining rooms or corridors were illuminated, but she could sometimes hear deep murmurs from within, speaking in what must have been the orcs' foreign, unintelligible black-tongue.

"Here," Simon's gravelly voice snapped, and when Maria blinked toward him, he'd stopped outside one of the doors in the wall, jerking his dark head toward it. "In."

Maria hesitated, and shot a wary glance at the room beyond him. This one was lined with more of the wrought-iron lamps, and in their flickering light, she could see what appeared to be a proper *meeting-room*. With a large low table occupying the bulk of it, a shelf of neatly organized books and papers off to the left, and a small fire merrily crackling in a grate on the opposite wall.

It was again surprisingly welcoming, not at all the sort of place one would expect to find in *Orc Mountain*—and when Maria shot a helpless, searching glance up toward Simon's watching eyes, it was almost as though he could again see *into* her, reading her thoughts as they passed.

"You ken you find *dump* here, ach?" he hissed, his lip curling. "Orcs are no *beasts*. Go. Sit."

Maria winced, but jerked a nod, and made to step inside—but that meant she had to pass very close by Simon's hulking form, still looming in the doorway. And as she did so—curse *all* the gods above— her hand somehow, unaccountably, brushed against Simon's *thigh*. His hot, solid, muscle-wrapped thigh, straining against the fabric of his trousers...

She yanked her hand away, far too late—but suddenly, something *caught* it. Clamping tight around her wrist, holding her there, tense, close.

Simon's *hand*.

Maria's body froze in place, her dazed eyes blinking down at the feel of that hand, the heat of it, the barely restrained strength coiling behind those massive fingers. And gods, the *sight* of it, those vicious black claws gently caressing the delicate skin on the inside of her wrist, while that rich, rugged scent slowly unfurled through the air...

Maria's body had leaned in toward him, almost as if instinctively seeking more of that scent, this heady solid strength—and finding it, here, so close. In the intensity beneath those still-gripping fingers, the rich sweetness now filling her breath, the harsh heat of his exhale against her cheek. In the restless nearness of his huge brawny body, almost close enough to touch—

And then—something *did* touch. Something unfamiliar, and entirely new, nudging with power and purpose against Maria's belly. Something that was swelling fuller behind the front of Simon's *trousers*, something long and thick and hot, and deeply, thoroughly shocking...

But more shocking still was how Maria reacted to it. How she didn't even *attempt* to yank herself away, or defend her dignity, as any proper duchess should. How instead, she blinked down at the sight, drew in a shaky, desperate breath—and then watched as her very own appalling, audacious hand slipped down, and *stroked* him.

It had only been a light touch, soft and careful—but the hard bulk behind those trousers leapt with immediate, astonishing force, shuddering deep into her fingers. Almost as if it *wanted* to be held, wanted her full attention, wanted *her*...

Maria's fingers curled closer, curving against its thick pulsing heft—and discovering, oh *hell*, that she'd barely gripped halfway around it. That this orc had truly grown a *monster* in his trousers, one that had already begun streaking actual *dampness* against the tight fabric, against Maria's actual *skin*. And suddenly, there was the unreal, *unspeakable* urge to reach inside, to draw him out, to see what such a thing might *look* like in the light...

Maria choked out a low gasp, her lips parting, her eyes finally darting up toward his face—and her fingers instantly stilled, her whole body bolted in place. Because Simon was *growling* at her, his lips curling up to show all those sharp white teeth, his black eyes flashing bright and intent with something that surely had to be rage.

Oh, *hell.* Maria leapt backwards, away, *far* too late—but then reeled toward him again, because her wrist was still gripped tight in his huge clawed fingers. And he seemed to realize it at the same time she had, because he swiftly released her, freeing her to stagger back into the lamplit room, her hands rubbing desperately against her face.

But that smell was here again, *everywhere*, musky and rich, emanating from Maria's very own *fingers*—and wait, *wait*, did that mean the smell was from... *that*?! And as she thrust her treacherous, trembling hands back down again, she realized that she'd just groped an orc in a public *corridor*, in *Orc Mountain*, and he *loathed* her, and surely he hadn't even slightly *wanted* that—

"G-good *gods*, I'm so *sorry*," Maria stammered at him, scarcely able to meet his eyes. "I—I haven't touched anyone in *years*, clearly I'm far more deprived than I thought, I'll just—"

She jabbed her finger at the opposite end of the table, and then immediately spun and propelled herself toward it. As far away as possible from this appalling orc, his appalling eyes, his appalling—

There was the distinct sound of a snort behind her, and when Maria whirled back around to stare, she found that the appalling orc was now—*smirking* at her. And worse, *far* worse, was how his huge clawed hand had dropped down to slowly, casually adjust himself in his trousers, his fingers' easy grip clearly showing the length and width of the monstrosity lurking beneath...

"Still wish to play game *now*, woman?" he purred, his voice low, taunting, dragging deep in Maria's belly. "Or now go back to piddling little *husband*?"

It was pure derision, of course, it was his clear statement that surely now Maria would run away screaming—but instead, she only kept staring, her cheeks burning, her heart threatening to charge out of her chest. While Simon's brazen hand purposefully gripped tighter, and then slowly, deliberately *slid up.*

Maria's groan was audible, indefensible, her eyes shamefully locked to the sight—and good gods in *heaven*, he dropped his hand, and did it *again.* Even slower this time, firmer, smoothing all the way up his truly massive length. Almost as if displaying himself, *flaunting* himself, showing off for her greedy, starving eyes...

It felt nearly impossible to stop staring, but Maria desperately needed to see his face, see what the hell this was—and when she somehow found his eyes, they were still fixed to hers, still *knowing* her. And still speaking, surely, of something that *had* to be rage...

Or was it? And if Maria were to stride back across this rapidly warming room, and cup her hand close over his, would he mock her? Push her away? Or would he keep looking at her like this, let her lean into his solid strength, into that beautiful *forgetting*...

But then his big hand abruptly dropped from his trousers, clenching into a tight, flexing fist at his side. As if somehow, again, he *knew*. Knew that his ill-thought attempt at intimidation hadn't worked in the slightest, because, clearly, he'd fully failed to consider the depth of Maria's sheer, shameful desperation.

And it *was* shameful, it bore the familiar rotten reek of *hysteria*, and Maria hurled herself down to sit beside the table, yanking off her cap, dragging her shaky hands through her tangled curls. It *had* to be the exhaustion. The shock of this damned unexpected mountain, and this horrible confounding orc. It couldn't truly be hysteria, it *couldn't*...

She was thankfully spared further conjecture by a rising clatter of noise, of rapidly approaching voices—and suddenly there were more people, spilling into the room. More huge, intimidating orcs, with their harsh faces and bare chests and ubiquitous black braids, and with their—wait—their *women*?

But yes, *impossibly*, there were *women*. Multiple women, of varying ages and appearances, striding easy and undaunted alongside these orcs, and even casually *touching* them. All while sporting a variety of entirely inappropriate attire, from tight men's trousers to a flimsy, fully transparent *shawl* that showed *everything* underneath.

Maria's mouth had fallen open, her beleaguered brain frantically grappling with these brand-new shocks to the senses—but then, more shocking still, was the realization that these women were almost all *pregnant*. Their bellies heavy, visibly rounded, with what *had* to be the orcs' sons.

And as staggering as this truth was, the next one was worse—*far* worse. Because one of the women—the only one who *didn't* look pregnant, in this moment—was *cradling* something. Something she was cooing and smiling at, while the scarred orc beside her affectionately watched. Something small, squirming, with deep greyish-green skin...

It was a *baby*. A baby—*orc*.

And while Maria of course knew, intellectually, that producing a baby orc was a primary part of her purpose here, she suddenly couldn't move, couldn't breathe. Couldn't even look away from this shocking woman, and the shocking creature in her arms. At how the woman was cuddling it like it was something *real*, something she actually *cared* about, something she'd truly *wanted*. Just like how Maria had been wanting it for years and years and *years*, oh gods oh gods oh *gods*—

The woman had smiled down toward Maria, saying something Maria couldn't hear over the roaring in her ears, the panic screaming in her chest. And she needed to pull herself together, she needed to convince all these unnerving, completely horrifying people that she was genuine, she was here to give these orcs one of these—*babies*, and then *leave* it again—but she couldn't look away she couldn't move she was ruining *everything*—

"Maria," cut in his voice, *Simon's* voice, rumbling deep—and Maria jerked to look at him again, almost as if compelled. Realizing, first, that her fingernails were digging into the wooden table, and second, that cold sweat was trickling down her back. And third, that Simon was still standing over by the door with his arms crossed, and he hadn't even been speaking to her. Instead, he was talking to the tall, narrow-eyed, rangy-looking orc beside him, who was frowning at her with equally visceral dislike.

"She say she is Maria," Simon continued, his voice flat. "She seek to claim me. To bear me son. For *coin*. For *vengeance*."

Maria's head was pounding, her stomach twisting, the cold sweat still uncomfortably prickling—but Simon was looking back at her, holding her in those steady, all-seeing eyes. And even if they were glinting with contempt, with that familiar furious *disapproval*, they were still solid and sure on hers, all hers, here, *safe*...

And somehow, it was enough. Enough that Maria could breathe again, *think* again. Enough to make her square her shoulders, clear her throat, and face the mass of suddenly silent orcs—and *women*—before her.

"He's right," she made herself say, her quiet voice still somehow piercing into the room's taut stillness. "My name is Maria, and I've come here to bear Simon a son."

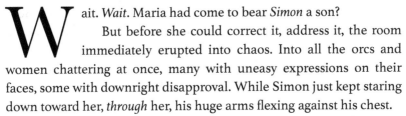

6

Wait. *Wait.* Maria had come to bear *Simon* a son?

But before she could correct it, address it, the room immediately erupted into chaos. Into all the orcs and women chattering at once, many with uneasy expressions on their faces, some with downright disapproval. While Simon just kept staring down toward her, *through* her, his huge arms flexing against his chest.

Gods, what the *hell.* One thoughtless grope in the corridor—one monstrosity grown in his trousers—and now she'd come here to bear *Simon* a son? Really? *Really?*

"*Silence*," cut in a deep, menacing voice—the big, heavily scarred orc, who had raised both his clawed hands, his eyes intent on Maria's. "We welcome you to our mountain, Maria of Preia. I am Grimarr of Clan Ash-Kai, Captain of Five Clans. And this"—he reached for the woman before him, the one cradling the *orc baby*—"is my mate Jule. The mother of my son."

Jule. That sounded vaguely familiar, and Maria's thoughts churned as the woman again smiled warmly toward her, bowing her dark head. "I was once Lady Norr, of Yarwood," she said, "if that might ring any bells?"

Good *gods*. Maria's gasp of shock was fully audible, echoing through the room—this was *Lady Norr*, and she was truly *here*, alive in

Orc Mountain, wearing men's trousers, and lugging about an *orc baby*?! But thankfully Lady Norr didn't seem offended, and only gave a wry laugh, a tolerant roll of her eyes at the scarred orc beside her.

"You know, I seem to be getting this a lot lately, Grimarr," she said. "You really need to stop telling people you *ate* me."

The huge orc actually smirked back down at her, his thick brows rising, his black tongue flicking out to curl against his lips—but Maria scarcely noticed through the continued pounding in her skull, her wildly racing heartbeat. It was only random, sheer luck of the gods that she and Lady Norr had never been properly introduced, that she'd caught a nasty cold before that ball at Norr Manor two years ago, and that Lady Norr wasn't at this very moment saying, *Wait, I know you, it's the runaway Duchess of Warmisham*—

"Should you truly wish to make this pact with us, Maria of Preia," continued the orc captain's deep voice, "you shall now yield to our hearing, and our terms. Do you yet wish for this?"

The panic and the relief were still clanging through Maria's chest, but she somehow jerked a nod toward him. "Um, yes," she croaked. "I do."

"Good," replied the orc captain. "Then our brother Nattfarr shall next Speak with you, and seek your truth. After this, Simon shall judge your fate."

Wait, *Simon* would judge? Maria's eyes darted back up to where he was still standing with the rangy orc beside the door, his black eyes still glaring down at her, *into* her. "She hold orcling also," Simon snapped, jerking his head toward the—the *orc baby*, still curled in Lady Norr's arms. "*Then* I judge."

Oh gods, now Maria had to *hold the orc baby*?! And how did Simon know, how in the gods' names had he *seen* that—but no one argued this plan, and Lady Norr even shot Maria another encouraging smile, and then strode over to sit beside her. After which the rest of the orcs and women settled down too, thankfully turning their attention not toward Maria, but instead toward one of the orcs, now seated straight across the table from her.

This orc sported an astonishing amount of jewelry, including a bright gold nipple-ring, multiple rings on his clawed fingers, and a thick gold band around his huge bicep. And tucked under his bare arm was one of the pregnant women, a very pretty reddish-blonde one, who was also wearing an extensive array of jewels, several of them brazenly glinting beneath her highly revealing *cape*.

"I am Nattfarr of Clan Grisk, Speaker of Orc Mountain," said the orc, his low voice carrying, his eyes glittering. "Shall you speak your truth to me, Maria?"

Even across the distance of the table, there was something unnerving about this orc's eyes, and Maria's panicked gaze had again, inexplicably, darted up toward Simon—but his scowl back toward her remained rigid, forbidding, unrepentant. Wanting Maria to agree to this, whatever the hell it was. Expecting her to *yield*, for his *judgement*.

So Maria again nodded, quick and frantic, and soon found herself caught in the strangest, most surreal interrogation of her life. With this disconcerting orc asking her an astonishing number of prying questions across the table, his eyes not once leaving hers, while Maria spouted off an assortment of deeply personal answers, despite the room full of highly alarming strangers listening to every word.

Yes, I truly wish to bear an orc a son. Yes, I wish for a financial settlement in exchange. Yes, I know it may risk my life. Yes, I have a husband. No, I hate my husband. I never wish to return to him or touch him again.

Thankfully the orc didn't ask after her husband's name, or details of her home in Preia—though he did ask, with damnable coolness, about *Simon*. Would Maria truly take Simon as her mate, for up to a full year, or perhaps even longer, while she carried his son? Would she truly mate with him, even if the mating act might cause distress or pain, or build a lasting and powerful bond between them? Would she vow to obey and honour him before all his kin, and follow the ways of his clan?

Much to Maria's rising humiliation, she freely agreed to all the orc's audacious questions, without the slightest hesitation. And it was only once the orc had finally seemed to finish, his dark eyes angling toward the captain again, that Maria managed to gather her wits, and blurt out what she surely should have said, prior to even beginning all this.

"L-look, I know I said I wanted to bear *Simon* a son," she stammered, darting another furtive glance up toward his still-scowling face. "But in truth, he's already made it very clear that he's quite unimpressed with me. So I'd be happy to take any of you, if that might help matters along?"

The stillness snapped again across the room, almost as though Maria had hurled out some kind of grave, deadly insult—and she didn't miss the sudden frown on the pierced orc's face, or the wince from the woman under his arm. And from behind them, Maria could actually hear Simon's *growl*, deep and vicious—and when she forced her gaze back up, he seemed to be almost vibrating in place, his dark eyes fierce and furious on hers.

"Your scent is already strong upon Simon, woman," cut in the captain orc, a tangible warning in his deep voice. "And his upon you. Thus, no other orc in this room shall touch you without his leave."

Oh. But surely Simon would give his leave, surely he *hated* her—but before Maria could argue that perfectly valid point, the captain raised his hand, and gave a purposeful gesture toward Lady Norr. Toward—the *baby*.

And this was a test, Maria knew it was a test, and if she wanted her revenge, she had to face whatever fresh hell this awful exhausting day wanted to throw at her. But even so, it felt almost impossible to follow the captain's eyes, to turn her head toward it. Toward—*him*.

"His name is Tengil," said Lady Norr, her mouth curving up into another encouraging smile. "He's three months old, and he likes to be held. Watch the claws, though."

And then Lady Norr held the baby toward Maria, offered it, waiting—and somehow, as if by utter desperate instinct, Maria reached out, and took it. Took this final, frightening death-knell of her future into her arms.

And. In a blinking, broken instant, everything just—vanished. The humiliation, the confusion, the exhaustion, all swept away, and leaving only—this.

He was an orc, yes—but he was *wonderful*. A tiny, wriggling, grey-skinned little *marvel*, with delicate pointed ears, a snub nose, and huge, shining black eyes. And he was gazing up at Maria with open, trusting curiosity, his long lashes fluttering, his tiny nose eagerly twitching and sniffing—until he scrunched up his little face, and *sneezed* at her.

The sound rang through the room, into the heavy watching

silence. Into the strange, foreign feeling of Maria's mouth tugging up, while a fraught, unfamiliar noise choked from her closed-off throat.

"Oh, I *know*," she crooned to him, to those blinking, innocent eyes. "I'm so filthy! And I *reek*. I won't be surprised at *all* if you've become instantly allergic to me, and begin peppering me with your tiny baby sneezes every time we meet one another. You adorable little *scamp*."

The wee orc promptly gurgled back at her, as if in wholehearted agreement, and Maria felt another choked sound lurch from her throat. A laugh, or a sob, or maybe both—and she felt herself belatedly blinking up, and meeting Lady Norr's smiling, knowing eyes.

"He's *lovely*," Maria croaked at her, as she reluctantly handed his tiny wriggling form back again. "You must be so proud."

And Maria meant it, she meant every single damned word, even if it was an orc baby, even if it was supposed to be a travesty. And none of this was how it was supposed to be, not the mountain, not this room, not these unnerving orcs and women, nothing was right, none of this made sense...

And worst of all, still, was Simon. The way Simon was looking at her, *into* her, still with that rage and contempt and maybe even *regret* in his glittering black eyes.

"Ach, Simon?" asked the captain, into the still-silent room. "What is your judgement? Shall you take this woman, and gain the Skai a son? Or shall you send her away?"

Shall *you*. Again, as if there had never been any question whatsoever of another orc's involvement—and as Maria stared up at Simon's forbidding face, there was the bizarre, inexplicable realization that she hadn't truly wanted another orc, either. Not since that first moment, when he'd caught her so gently in his arms, and she'd held his heart in the palm of her hand. And even if he taunted her, mocked her, *hated* her, it didn't matter, nothing mattered, but revenge...

"I shall take her," Simon said, wooden, flat, a monotone. "But she shall honour me, and *obey*, and follow all the ways of the Skai. And if she betray me, or fail me"—his eyes darkened even further—"she shall be cast away. With no coin, no son, no *vengeance*."

Maria swallowed hard, blinking wide-eyed at his harsh face—he was truly going to *accept*?—but no, no, surely it was only about the son, and he would *cast her away* if she failed. And did that mean—if she failed to obey? Or if she failed to—to deliver his son alive?

The panic was finally trickling back in again, rattling raw and rickety in Maria's chest, and for some reason she kept frantically searching Simon's face, searching for reassurance, for even a hint of that quiet, powerful safety. But this time there was no comfort, no kindness, nothing but danger in those flat, furious black eyes.

"And I warn you this only once, woman," he snarled, a threat, a bitter mockery of a vow. "When people play game with Enforcer of Orc Mountain, they *die*."

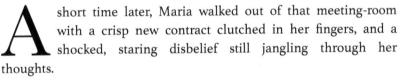

7

A short time later, Maria walked out of that meeting-room with a crisp new contract clutched in her fingers, and a shocked, staring disbelief still jangling through her thoughts.

The orcs had—*agreed*.

They'd agreed to feed and house her for a full year, while she attempted to bear Simon a son. They'd offered a surprisingly in-depth plan for her care throughout her pregnancy, along with reassurances that her survival was not only likely, but in fact highly probable, thanks to their steadily increasing knowledge and expertise.

And after the deed was done, they'd even promised to *pay*. An amount that was more than Maria could have possibly hoped for. Enough to start a new life. A new family. *Freedom.*

The thought still felt too tenuous to be real, like some kind of bizarre, upside-down dream that would surely soon disappear—but as Maria blinked down at the contract, it was still there, still real, still written in vivid black ink under her fingers.

And all she had to do—her eyes darted back toward Simon's massive bulk silently striding down the corridor before her—was honour and obey an orc who hated her, and give him a *son*.

One of those wriggling, wide-eyed, sneezy little orcs. *Alive.*

The panic had begun bubbling again, simmering deep in her chest, but Maria shoved it down, and gripped tighter at that contract. That impossible promise of freedom. Revenge. *Hope.*

"*Now* bring bath," Simon snapped at someone he'd passed in the corridor—Baldr again, leaning against the wall outside the meeting-room. Almost as if he'd been standing there waiting for them, and he indeed shot Maria an eager, expectant smile.

"Ach, I shall, brother," Baldr said, pushing off the wall, and falling into step with—Maria startled as she glanced back—the tall, rangy-looking, angry-eyed orc, who'd apparently been walking very close behind her, his footfalls completely silent on the hard stone floor.

"It is good that you shall stay for a spell, Maria," Baldr said, his cheerful voice slicing through the silence. "Tell us, what do you know of orcs? Has Simon yet spoken to you of the clans?"

There was an irrational urge to laugh, to point out that Simon had scarcely spoken three full sentences to her, most of them mocking her in some way or another—but Maria could almost see his huge body tensing ahead of her, could feel the discomfort rolling from him in waves. She was supposed to be *honouring* him. *Obeying* him. *Revenge.*

"Not yet," she managed, glancing back toward Baldr. "Um, but Grimarr just said he was the captain of your clans, right? Five of them?"

"Ach, five," Baldr replied, flashing Maria another smile, even as his fingers made some kind of incomprehensible hand signal toward the tall orc beside him. "All orcs come from one of these clans: Ash-Kai, Bautul, Skai, Ka-esh, and Grisk. All these clans bear their own ways, and live in their own part of the mountain."

Maria mentally filed these points away, and darted another uneasy glance toward Simon's stiff form ahead of her. "And you told me you were from Clan Grisk, when we first met, right?" she asked Baldr. "And Simon is from Clan Skai?"

Baldr's smile widened even further, genuine approval flaring across his face in the flickering lamplight. "Ach, Simon is Skai, and Drafli is also," he said, jerking his head toward the rangy orc beside him. "The Skai are oft the scouts and hunters and fighters among us. They sacrifice much to keep our kin aware, and fed, and safe."

Right. That wasn't surprising, Maria supposed, as her eyes dropped to the gleaming scimitar at Simon's side, to the way his booted steps were, like this Drafli's, fully silent on the stone floor. Almost as though he prowled, rather than walked.

"The Skai also serve as the captain's Right Hand," Baldr continued from behind her. "Since Grimarr took the place of captain, almost two years past, Drafli has filled this place, whilst I serve as the captain's Left Hand alongside him."

Baldr's bright gaze had again angled toward the Drafli orc, and there was obvious pride in his voice as he spoke, warmth in his sparkling eyes. Sentiments that this Drafli didn't at all seem to share, and Maria belatedly noticed that Drafli was also excessively armed, his clawed hand caressing almost hungrily at the hilt of the huge scimitar hanging at his side.

"Um, how lovely for you both," Maria stammered at Drafli's flat black eyes, before glancing back to the relative safety of Baldr again. "So what does a captain's Right Hand do? And a Left?"

"I am the captain's nose, and oft his ears," Baldr replied promptly. "And Drafli is his sight, and his sword. His link to the Skai's Enforcer."

Huh. Maria risked another glance at this intimidating Drafli orc, who this time wasn't looking back toward her, but instead up at—Simon. Simon, who had indeed called himself the *Enforcer*, hadn't he?

"And Simon is your Enforcer?" Maria asked, carefully now. "Of just the Skai clan, you said?"

Baldr glanced at Simon too, and shook his head. "Of late, our captain has honoured Simon's service, and granted him this title on behalf of all our mountain. This was the way of Enforcers in ages past, but that truth was lost, until Simon worked with our Grisk and Ka-esh brothers to regain this."

So Simon had recently gotten himself a promotion, then, for whatever the hell his job was. "And what *is* an Enforcer, exactly?" Maria ventured. "What does he do?"

"The Enforcer seeks darkness," Baldr replied, quieter than before. "And then he brings it to the light, where he cleanses it, or quells it."

Quells it. That sounded ominous, and Maria's attention turned toward Simon again, toward the hard, tense set of his huge shoulders. And for a completely absurd instant, there was the temptation to slip up beside him, to stroke her hand against his scarred back, to say, *It's all right, I understand...*

But no, no, *hell* no. Apart from that first moment outside the mountain, Simon had been nothing but rude, and coarse, and mocking, and cruel. He had, in fact, all but threatened to *kill* Maria, if she displeased him, or failed him. And now she'd sworn to honour him, and obey him, and bear him a son, and that meant that next, she would need to...

"*Bath*," Simon barked at Baldr, over his shoulder—and after a furtive wave goodbye toward Maria, Baldr scurried off down a passage to the left. Leaving Maria trapped walking between these two silent orcs, both of whom were clearly only tolerating her for her reproductive capabilities. For her *son*.

Which she'd promised to—*leave* with Simon. Forever. While she ran away with the orcs' coin, never to be seen again.

Maria's shaking hands were rubbing at her face, the panic whispering and simmering—until Simon's huge form turned sideways, into one of the dark openings along the lamplit corridor. And when Maria followed, she found herself in another corridor, dimmer and narrower and twistier, with multiple doors studded along both walls.

Simon kept striding past them, down another even darker hallway, until he halted next to one of the doors in the wall. And in the very distant light from down the corridor, Maria could just make out the huge shadow of his form waiting beside the door, the glint of his gaze locking to hers.

And somehow, again, it was like Maria had been caught. Trapped. Skewered in place upon this orc's pointed judgement, and somehow found badly wanting.

"In," Simon hissed, voice hard, so Maria ducked her head, and obeyed. Taking great pains to keep herself well away from his bulk this time, and holding her breath for good measure.

The new room was pitch-black inside, but she could feel Simon's huge form silently moving behind her. And suddenly there was light again, from a single tall candlestick, flickering to life in his clawed hand.

And in the light, Maria saw what might have been a *bedroom*. Not large, and not structurally different from the rest of the mountain she'd seen so far, with its smooth grey floor, and perfectly square stone walls. However—she swallowed hard, and blinked all around—it was also a jumbled, chaotic *mess*.

There were sharp, deadly weapons *everywhere*, hanging on the walls, standing in the corners, even scattered across the floor. Random papers and stones of varying sizes were dotted on the floor between them, along with an assortment of what might have been rags, or perhaps clothing. And the room's few pieces of wooden furniture—a bench, and a set of stacked shelves—were covered with yet more papers and stones, including a pile of carved, person-shaped figures. And upon closer inspection, even the *walls* were marred with a meaningless mess of dark-coloured markings, all different sizes and shapes.

Maria's increasingly frantic gaze couldn't seem to stop scanning around her, searching for perhaps a path through the deadly maze on the floor, or even a safe corner to take refuge in. But the only area free of the room's general mayhem appeared to be—she gulped—a huge, flat, knee-height pallet against the nearest wall, covered over with a mass of brown and grey furs.

His *bed*.

Maria's cheeks were suddenly smarting with heat, and she shot another swift, reflexive glance up toward Simon. He'd set the candlestick down on the shelf among the carved figures—thereby casting a multitude of sinister-looking shadows on the wall behind him—and he was staring at her again, his eyes narrow, his muscled arms folded over his bare chest. Almost as if he was waiting for Maria to speak. To expose herself, again, to his judgement.

"Um," she made herself say, her voice cracking, "*this* is where you live?"

It came out sounding shocked, perhaps even repulsed, and Maria grimaced at the immediate thinning of Simon's lips, the clench of his clawed hand on the hilt of his sword.

"Ach," he said flatly. "And now you also."

Right. Maria had to take several deep breaths, her eyes again darting around at the chaos. She could do this. She'd come this far, she'd committed to a vast number of alarming things, surely she couldn't be undone by a single frightful *room*. But perhaps it was the hysteria again, bringing with it this appalling, almost irresistible urge to laugh, to say...

"It holds no vermin, or lice, or fleas," Simon cut in, voice curt. "It is *no dump.*"

It was like he'd read the last straight from Maria's thoughts, and gods *curse* her, but the peal of laughter escaped before she could stop it, ringing far too loudly through this wreck of a room. Sparking a sudden flash of danger in Simon's already-angry eyes, and a sound from his throat that might have been a bark.

"You swore to honour, and obey," he hissed at her. "You no like, either you clean, or you *leave!*"

That was enough to instantly drain all the mirth from Maria's form, and she made a face, drew in a bracing breath. "I'm sorry," she made herself say, as steadily as she could. "I'm grateful for your hospitality. And I *am* reassured about the lice and fleas, at least."

She tried for a hopeful smile, which had no effect whatsoever on Simon's ever-deepening scowl—when suddenly, Baldr strode into the room. And before him, he was carrying a huge metal basin of steaming *hot water.*

Maria's breath caught at the sight—gods, she hadn't properly bathed since she'd left Warmisham House a whole *week* ago—and Baldr grinned at her as he kicked clear a spot on the floor, and set the massive basin down with surprising ease.

"For you, Maria," he said brightly, now producing what appeared to be a bar of actual *soap* from his trouser pocket, and dropping it into the water with a *plunk.* "Is there aught else you might need?"

His glanced at Simon as he spoke, his eyebrows rising, and in return Simon replied with a sudden, startling stream of the orcs' blacktongue. The words deep and harsh and oddly eloquent-sounding, rolling gracefully from his full lips, and for some reason Maria found herself staring at him, and swallowing against the dryness in her throat. Of course he would speak his own language fluently, this wasn't remarkable in the least, and in truth it sounded just like the noises a snuffling *pig* would make...

Baldr was answering in kind, the foreign words sounding somehow far flatter in his mouth, and then he sketched another little bow toward Maria before striding from the room. Leaving

Maria and Simon alone again, but now with a steaming hot bath between them.

Maria blinked at the bath, and then down at the contract in her hand—and then at Simon. Simon, who had briefly turned away from her, hanging his scimitar on the wall—and who then dropped his huge form onto the wooden bench. Sprawling there spread-legged and alarmingly casual, his brawny bare arms folding back behind his head.

He was waiting for her. *Watching.*

Maria swallowed again, while the ever-lurking panic reared up, shouting and rattling against her ribs. Simon wanted her to *undress.* To bathe in this basin, right here before him. To perhaps give him some kind of *show...*

And it had been *years* since anyone but her servants had seen Maria undressed—and even before that, her husband had never shown much interest in looking, or in extending matters beyond the bare minimum. It had always left her feeling so unseen, so unsatisfied, so *unknown*, and now she had to—to—

"Bathe," Simon's deep voice snapped from the bench. "You smell of filth. Of *husband.* I no touch until clean."

Maria's face flooded with shock, with *shame*, and her trembly hand immediately fumbled for the now-empty pack still on her back, and dropped it to the floor behind her. Next she grasped for the straps of her baggy overalls, and managed to shove one down, off her shoulder—but she couldn't seem to even clutch at the other one, prickling ice pooling in her fingers, her lungs, her breath—

"You wish for help?" taunted Simon's horrible voice from across the room. "Or *now* you turn and run?"

Maria's chagrined gaze again darted down to the contract still in her other hand, now visibly fluttering in her shaking fingers. Of course she couldn't run now. Not after she'd made such surprising headway on her freedom, her revenge. She'd gone to bed with Duke Warmisham, *surely* she could do it with an orc, she could bear him a sneezy little son and then leave it forever, she could, she would, she *had* to—

Her trembling hand had almost dropped the contract in the bath—*shit*—and she belatedly flung her shivering body toward the mess of papers on the nearby shelf, and carefully set the contract on top. Smoothing it out with her unsteady fingers, while sucking back one breath, another.

She'd come this far. It was just a bath. He was just an orc. It didn't matter. *Revenge.*

"Maria," came Simon's voice, quieter than before, instantly snapping her eyes to his ever-frowning face. "You... wish for this. Ach?"

Maria badly flinched, and jolted away from the shelf. "Um," she heard herself say. "Yes. Absolutely. Most definitely."

But it came out sounding abominably weak, pathetic, and of course Simon caught that, his eyes narrowing, his huge body leaning forward on the bench. "Then why you *tremble*," he said, jabbing a single clawed finger toward her. "Why you smell of such *fear*. You *lie* to me of this?"

Maria had to haul in breaths, force her gaze to stay on his, make her shoulders sharp and square. "I wasn't lying, and I'm not afraid," she shot back. "I already told you, it's just been a while, and surely you can understand I might be a little nervous!"

"To have *bath*?" Simon countered, his deep voice flat, bitter. "When you have sworn in ink to *fuck* me?!"

Maria's hands had snapped up to her face, dragging against her hot cheeks, the mess of her hair. "Well, you're just sitting there *watching* me! And frowning at me like that, with all your clothes still on, like you're just waiting to judge me, and *mock* me. Just like you have ever since the first moment we *spoke*!"

The words rang through the too-small room, pulsing painfully in Maria's skull, and she braced for Simon's snarl, for the mocking retort that would surely come—but there was only an odd, stiff stillness. And as Maria stood there, dangerously and inexplicably on the verge of tears, Simon's hulking body seemed to jerk on the bench, his hands dropping to his waist, yanking at his thick leather belt—

And then he rose up to his feet, the movement surprisingly graceful—and shucked his trousers full to the floor. Revealing muscled grey calves, huge, powerful, hair-dusted thighs, and—Maria's breath lurched in her throat—everything at his groin.

Everything.

Maria couldn't stop staring, blinking, drinking up the sight. The mass of thick, soft-looking black hair. The twin weights of his hanging bollocks, nestled against those powerful thighs. And most imposing of all, that thick, veined, dangling length of him, alarmingly large even at rest, perhaps on a level with the sword-hilt on the wall behind him...

The shock had sucked away all Maria's breath, all possible protests, and she only vaguely noticed him smoothly kicking off his boots, hurling them—and the trousers—off into the room's distant chaos. Because gods, he was *magnificent*, his massive muscles shifting and rippling with every movement, that thick grey length swaying to match. And as he gracefully dropped to sit on the bench again, his huge thighs sprawling wide and shameless apart, Maria nearly choked on the vision of it, the power of it, the gods-damned illogical *longing*.

"Better?" his low voice purred, dark, taunting. "Now that I too wear naught but my skin?"

And in this hazy, surreal instant, Maria didn't care in the least if he was mocking her, judging her, challenging her. Even the contract, the revenge, had seemed to fade off into a vague, powerless distance. Leaving only the wild, almost irresistible urge to step closer, to smell, to *touch*. And then...

"Bath," he ordered, and this time Maria faintly registered *amusement* in his voice, in the glint of his watching eyes. "Clean."

Right, *right*, and Maria's hand scrabbled for her other overall-strap, and somehow yanked it off her shoulder. And then she shoved the overalls downwards, all the way to her ankles—and after a moment's awkward fumbling, she'd untied her boots too, tugged off her socks, and kicked the whole lot off into the surrounding mess.

It left her standing there barefoot in an orc's bedroom, wearing only a men's tunic and knee-length drawers, while a fully naked orc dispassionately watched from his bench. But he wasn't speaking this time, wasn't mocking her—at least, until one of his heavy black brows ticked up, and his huge hand gave an insolent, impatient wave toward her tunic.

Keep going, it clearly meant. *Bath.*

Maria's teeth were gritting together, but the panic had simmered down to a manageable murmur again, and her fingers only slightly shook as they began unbuttoning her tunic. Working from the top downward, and slowly revealing the wide swath of fabric that tightly bound her breasts beneath.

Simon actually snorted at the sight, but thankfully still didn't speak, and Maria somehow found the courage to keep going. Tugging out the tucked-in end of the binding, and then unlooping it around her once, again, again—until it, too, fell to the floor at her feet. Leaving her torso completely bare, her heavy breasts fully exposed to the room's cool air. To Simon's eyes, and his judgement.

And she could *feel* his gaze prickling upon her, hot and close and surely critical. But curse it, she was doing this now, she was getting it the hell over with—so she rapidly untied the drawers too, and shoved them off onto the floor. Which left her standing stark naked before an orc, every secret and flaw shamefully bared for his watching, mocking eyes.

But for a hanging, shivering instant, there was only—silence. Thick, charged silence, tickling up Maria's back, skittering across her bare skin. And when she finally dared to glance up, to find Simon's watching face, he was just—*looking* at her. His dark, glinting eyes slowly sliding down her naked form, lingering on the fullness of her breasts, the curve of her waist, the patch of hair between her thighs...

His big body had slightly shifted on the bench, his hand easing with deceptive casualness toward his own groin. And wait, that was because—something clenched low in Maria's belly—the thick grey length of him was... *moving*. No longer dangling innocuously toward the floor, like it had been previously, but instead thickening, lengthening. *Rising*.

And perhaps he'd meant to hide it with his hand, but there was no possible hiding such a thing. Not with it visibly *vibrating* like that, jutting up and out toward her, dark and heavily veined, and rapidly swelling to a length and width that rivalled Maria's entire *forearm*. And as she stared, her breath locked in her lungs, the smooth skin at the head of him slowly peeled down, revealing a dark, glossy cleft, a deep slit, and a thick bead of slick, viscous white, oozing from the tip...

Maria truly couldn't move, couldn't drag her eyes away. Couldn't stop her hoarse, betraying moan as that growing bead of white at the head grew, and grew, and grew—until it *burst*. Running down the veined length of him in shiny, hungry rivulets, pooling and glistening in the black mass of hair below.

Oh, *hell*. Another unwilling moan had escaped Maria's mouth, and she only distantly noted that Simon had groaned too, low and dusky in his throat. But it was enough, somehow, to drag her gaze away from that mesmerizing, thrilling sight between his legs, and up to his watching, judging eyes.

And they *were* still judging. Still roving over her naked body, lingering on her flushed face, her parted lips, her large, damnably peaked brown nipples. And most intently of all, on her own groin, which suddenly felt uncomfortably hot, swollen, hungry...

Simon's other hand had jerked up toward her, making a motion with his clawed finger that clearly meant, *turn around*. And Maria should have protested, refused, launched into hysterics, *something*— but instead, she silently nodded, and *obeyed*. Spinning her body slow and careful, her heart thundering, her skin tingling at the silent touch of his eyes upon her back, her thighs, the bare swell of her arse...

And when she came around again, there was something new, something entirely unfamiliar, in those watching, glittering eyes. Something almost like *approval*. Like... *awe*.

"Come," his low voice rumbled, his fingers beckoning, his eyes lazy, half-lidded. "Closer."

Closer. Maria's breath shuddered in her throat, but she somehow again nodded, and took a slow, tentative step toward him. And when his fingers beckoned again, she stepped again, and again. Until she found herself standing naked and shivering between his sprawled-wide knees, her breath dragging in that rich rising scent of him, her hardened nipples jutting straight toward his watching, greedy eyes.

"You hid your form from me," he said, his voice a deep, husky purr, his black tongue slipping out to brush against his lips. "You *lie*."

He was judging her again, *challenging* her again—but he was also still looking at her like that, like she was a goddess who had materialized here before him. And through the wild, hurtling beat of her pulse, Maria somehow managed a snort, and even a respectable roll of her eyes.

"What, so rather than making you a rational, civilized *offer*," she replied, her voice hoarse, "I should have just yanked these out, and shoved them in your face instead?"

Simon scoffed, loud and derisive, but it didn't quite reach his eyes. Or his huge clawed hand, which had been palming that monster at his groin, and now—Maria twitched all over—circled cool and deliberate around the base of it.

"Ach," he said finally, the word a low grunt. "These please me."

Gods, he was so crude and vulgar and utterly *appalling*—and yet, Maria couldn't stop staring as his fisted hand slowly, smoothly begun *sliding up*. Milking out more of that thick, slippery white, spurting from that slit, streaking down to pool on his fingers...

"Touch them," he breathed, so soft Maria scarcely heard him. "Show me."

The outrage sparked and surged, somewhere deep inside—but then submerged again, drowning in the sight of his black tongue, now trailing slow, insolent, *hungry*, against his full, parted lips. While that brazen hand slid up again, perhaps gripping tighter, and the resulting white actually spurted *up*, landing in a long wet streak against his muscled bare torso...

"Show me," he repeated, deeper this time, an edge of command creeping into his voice. "Obey me, woman."

And yes, yes, Maria had sworn to that, she *had*—and again her shaky body somehow, impossibly, obeyed. Her fingers snapping up to her aching, swollen nipples, stroking soft and shameless against the too-sensitive skin.

The moan wrung out before she could stop it, burning through the room—and at the sound, Simon actually *laughed*. His broad shoulders shaking, his mouth curving up, showing a glimpse of sharp fangs against his full bottom lip. And it distantly occurred to Maria that she hadn't yet seen him smile, and the sight was—it was—

Another moan wrenched from her throat, even louder this time, and Simon's smile slowly slipped, shifted, into another sinuous curl of that tongue against his lips. Into his hand blatantly pumping himself again, faster now, spurting more of that slick white onto his own fingers, his own belly, and if he kept going, he would...

Maria moaned again, her betraying fingers now squeezing and caressing at the full weight of her breasts, plucking at her firm nipples. Sinking far too easily into her own familiar touch, the only touch she'd had in *years*, and again, it was almost as though Simon *approved*. His eyes dark and fluttering on the sight, his breath heaving through his huge chest, his hand moving with such filthy, flagrant ease...

"Ask me," he breathed, his voice hitching, heated, hoarse. "To cleanse these."

To cleanse them. And Maria had no sweet conception what he could possibly mean—or did she, because those words of Baldr's were flashing through her thoughts, the *Enforcer*, who *cleansed*. And as Simon kept gazing up at her under thick black lashes, she caught something almost... *longing* in those eyes. Something that craved relief beyond just the physical, needed to seek the darkness, find the darkness, and...

So Maria nodded, *nodded*, and her unthinking, trembling hands even thrust herself out, closer toward his dazed, blinking eyes.

"Then please, Simon," she whispered. "Enforce me."

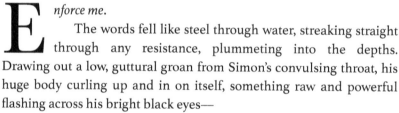

8

nforce me.

The words fell like steel through water, streaking straight through any resistance, plummeting into the depths. Drawing out a low, guttural groan from Simon's convulsing throat, his huge body curling up and in on itself, something raw and powerful flashing across his bright black eyes—

And then the beast in his hand *exploded*. Firing out stream after stream of thick hot white, spattering and spewing all over Maria's breasts, her belly, her groin. Painting her with it, flooding her with it, until it was running in slick streaks down her heated skin, coating her with its rugged scent, with the enthralling power of its bared, broken *hunger*.

And as Maria stood there, stunned and blinking, drenched with an orc's actual *leavings*, her first thought wasn't disgust, or shock, or even, surprisingly, shame. No, instead it was the undeniable, unequivocal *truth* of this, here, smelling of heat and hunger, dripping off her skin.

He'd *wanted* her.

And gods, it had been so *long*. Years, without a single look like that, or words like that, let alone a... *response* like that. And even if it was an orc, even if it was *this* orc, it was still... true. Real. *Here*.

Maria still hadn't moved—hadn't found any space in her brain beyond standing here, and breathing—but before her, Simon's huge form had sagged back against the wall behind him. His throat visibly swallowing, his sharp jaw flexing, his eyes fluttering closed. While his streaked-white hand purposely slipped away from his rapidly diminishing length, and clenched into a tight fist on his thigh instead.

Oh. *Oh.* He was—what? Upset? Disappointed? *Regretful?*

And where the strength of his eyes had been, there was suddenly only shame, surging through Maria in a flood, flattening her beneath its ruthless, devastating weight. She'd stripped naked before an *orc.* She'd fondled herself while he'd watched. She'd moaned and gasped and *obeyed*, and then she'd begged him to—to—

She was still dripping, her whole front coated in sticky slick white, and when she darted a panicked glance downward, it almost felt like it was crawling on her skin. Like something foreign, something wrong, something that was invading her very *soul*, the smell was everywhere *everywhere* oh *gods*—

She staggered backwards, away, *away*—and then nearly tripped over the damned wash-basin, still sitting there steaming behind her. But yes, please gods, *anything*, and she immediately leapt in, dropped herself neck-deep into the scalding-hot water, and buried her face in her hands.

What had she just done. *Gods*, what had she done. It was just like *hysteria*, and it couldn't be, not now, *please*—

"Maria," came Simon's low voice, an instant clarion call in the chaos, and even as Maria cursed herself for it—hated herself for it— her head snapped up, her eyes searching for his. And finding them, far closer than she'd expected, his big body now leaning forward on the bench, his elbows resting on his knees, his clawed hands gripped tight together.

And those eyes were steady again, unapologetic, unashamed. Holding her in their strength, seeing her, knowing her, *safe*...

"You wish for this," he said, his voice very even. "For *me*."

The words were perhaps again a taunt, a challenge, cutting straight to Maria's deepest shame—but his face, oddly, wasn't. And as she stared at his watching eyes, she caught a glimpse of surprising... uncertainty.

"You are *sure* you wish for this," he repeated, quieter now. "You chose this freely. Ach?"

And yes, that was *doubt* in his voice, his eyes—and somehow it almost felt worse than the mocking. Like he'd stripped away any semblance of cover he'd given her, like he'd dragged her bodily back up out from the water and exposed *everything*.

"Yes," Maria snapped at him, pulling her knees close in the basin, wrapping her arms tight around them in the safe liquid heat. "Yes, yes I did, as I keep telling you! Though I *am* beginning to wonder if all this is just an elaborate *joke* at my expense, because you've barely stopped mocking me since the moment we met, and this"—she desperately fumbled for the soap, and began frantically scrubbing at her front, at where it *still* felt sticky on her skin—"was clearly some kind of degrading *statement* on your part, to show me just how little respect you have for me!"

Simon's brow had furrowed, his eyes narrowing—but rather than immediately replying, he reached up behind his head, and smoothly drew out—a *dagger*. The dagger that had been hidden in his *hair*, oh *gods*, and maybe Maria had finally offended him beyond repair, maybe he was finally going to use it, he was finally going to *kill* her—

She gasped and flinched all over, cringing back in the basin, bracing for impact—but the look Simon shot her was dark, disapproving, perhaps even *exasperated*. And his other hand was groping down toward the floor, clutching at a large flat *stone* that had been lying near his huge bare foot—and as Maria stared, entirely bewildered once again, he began scraping the stone against the dagger's edge, the sound a loud shirr in the choked silence.

"When an orc grants his scent to another," he said finally, slowly, not looking up from his methodically sliding stone, "this no *degrade*. This shows—favour. This shows I claim you. This lifts you above the shame you bring me."

The shame. Wait, the shame she brought *him*? Maria's skull was distantly throbbing, caught somewhere between relief and frustration, and she rubbed at her temples, exhaled a juddery breath. "And how, exactly," she gritted out, "have I brought you shame? By tolerating your mockery? By doing everything you've asked of me so far? Or maybe by risking my *life* to offer you a *son*?!"

"No," Simon growled back, his eyes flicking brief and narrow to hers. "You no offer. You *sell*. For *vengeance*, against *husband*. Man you swore vow to *honour*."

Maria winced, and immediately opened her mouth to counter that—but no. No. She could *not* risk speaking more of Duke Warmisham with this too-astute orc, never again, what if he guessed, what if she ruined *everything*...

Simon's snort was bitter, deep, and he scraped the stone harder against his blade. "Skai orcs never *buy* mate or son," he said, glowering down toward it. "We *never* trade or sell for this. We track. We *hunt*. We seek worthy mate, one who is ripe and lusty and strong. When we gain her"—he raised his hand with the stone, jabbing a sharp finger toward her—"we claim her before all our kin, and *then* keep her. *Then* spark son upon her."

Something churned in Maria's belly, thick and nauseating, and she gave a wild shake of her head, clutched her knees closer in the hot water. "And you think that's somehow *better* than this?!" her mouth spat at him, before she could clamp the words away. "You pick out a woman like a piece of meat, and then *hunt* her? And after that, what, you *make* her have your son? That's—barbaric. It's *disgusting*."

Simon blinked at her, once—and then he huffed a harsh laugh, scraping just as loud as the stone on his dagger. "But it is no *disgusting*," he said, his voice heavy on the word, "to break own vow to *husband*? To claim orc, and birth orc *son*, only because you ken this shall *disgust* husband, and thus gain you greater vengeance against him?"

Maria's stomach churned again, and she had to bite her lip, search for words that were safe, true. "This isn't just about vengeance," she countered. "It's about gaining my own *life* back. My *freedom*."

"Ach, your *freedom*," Simon sneered at her. "And for this, you grow and birth son, and next *sell* him? You run away with *freedom*, with *coin*, and forever forget own *son*? You leave father to raise him *alone*? This"—his stone scraped louder, sharper—"no *disgust* you, woman, but *I* do?"

The words clanged against Maria's ears, ringing deep into her throbbing skull, and it was only the sheer *unfairness* of it all that kept her head up, her eyes pinned to his. "I made you an *offer*," she hissed back. "I was honest and upfront with you about what I wanted, and what I was able to give you. And if my offer was that damned loath-some to you, you should have behaved like a rational human being, and just said *no!*"

Simon's growl was almost a bark, his eyes blazing, his huge claws audibly scraping on the stone clutched in his hand. "I am no *human being*," he snarled. "I am *orc*. And in this *offer*, you swear to *honour* me. You swear to *obey* me. You swear you *wish* for me. You swear you wish for my claim, and my scent, and my *fuck*."

Shit. *Shit.* The panic had begun simmering again, bubbling up with the hammer of Maria's heartbeat—but Simon was still speaking, forceful and inexorable and dreadful. "And yet, you *scorn* me," he hissed, his lip curling. "You tremble and hide, as if you are *afraid.* As if you *lie.* You claim *shame* when I seek to honour you, and make you my own. You say I am *appalling.* I am *disgusting.* I live in *dump.*"

There were no words, no possible answers to this—and with a swift, furious jerk of movement, he yanked back his arm, and hurled the stone in his hand straight across toward the opposite wall. Where it smashed with a vicious, deafening *crack*, and then shattered into dust.

Maria cringed into the water, her eyes wide and suddenly terrified, her wet hands pressed tight against her ears—but Simon's huge, threatening form had risen from the bench, his hand gripping his newly sharpened dagger, his eyes on fire, his rage a living, breathing *beast.*

"I warn you, woman," he growled, his voice ringing through Maria's fingers, reverberating deep inside. "I play no human *game* with you. You wish to stay, you *obey.* You *learn.* When I honour you, you *thank.* You bear no more fear, no more shame. You *never* cower when I speak. I am Enforcer of Orc Mountain, and you are *mine* to use and judge and fuck as I *wish!*"

He was looming over her, bellowing at her, *condemning* her—and Maria *was* cowering beneath him, fighting for air, the panic shudder-ing, flailing, finally breaking its way out. Becoming the chaos, the hysteria, her wet fingers scrubbing and clawing at her face, he was only an orc she wasn't supposed to care this was revenge her freedom *everything—*

"I-I'm s-sorry," she gasped, though the gulping breaths. "I'm sorry. Please. I-I'll try harder. I just—"

But the gasps were swallowing her voice, swallowing everything. Ruining everything, because this enraged orc didn't want her to cower or be afraid and she was still doing it, all of it, couldn't stop, couldn't find words air *anything*—

She could feel him looming silent and still above her, watching, mocking, *judging*—and without warning, his huge body *lunged*. Sinking down before her, close and horrifying and deadly, and Maria choked out a yelp, whipped her head harder, dragged her fingers deeper against the burning skin of her cheeks. She couldn't *breathe*, this couldn't be happening, not here, not before an orc, revenge, breathe, *hysteria*. He was going to condemn her, *quell* her, send her away, everything was *ruined*—

Until two warm, powerful hands snapped around her wrists, and drew them away from her face. The movement careful, restrained, maybe even... gentle.

"Maria," came his deep voice, and somehow her wide, terrified eyes blinked up—and found his face. And when had he come so close, he was kneeling directly beside the wash-basin, his hands now submerged in the water with hers. And his forehead was creased, his mouth thin, and Maria couldn't at all read that look in his eyes, perhaps mockery or derision or revulsion, and next he would laugh, send for a snide physician, call her unstable or hysterical or...

"Peace, woman," he said, still so painfully quiet, and Maria's spiralling, spattering thoughts somehow registered the sudden... weariness in his eyes. The regret. The... *defeat*.

"Ach, this was ill thought, no?" he said, his voice a worn, heavy exhale. "I no wish for lies and games, and you no wish for wrathful orc who lives in *dump*. Even promise of son—even *freedom*—shall no alter this, for us."

Oh. Maria kept blinking at him, not following, not thinking. And that twist on his lips might have been a smile, if not for the bitter darkness in his eyes, the slight clench of those solid fingers against her wrist.

"So we shall now wash away this vow in ink," he said, "and you shall run, as you truly wish. Go further west, mayhap. Seek other way. Find other *vengeance*. Ach?"

He abruptly stood up, releasing her wrists, but not before Maria again caught that—that *defeat* in his eyes, the telltale grimace on that damning word *vengeance*. And he was striding toward his shelf, so smoothly, and his huge wet hand had plucked up the contract from the top of the pile, the ink already streaking under his touch—

"I shall ask my brothers for new ink," he continued as he turned to stride back toward her, his voice wooden. "They shall grant safety as you run, and fair terms."

He thrust the contract down toward her, his hand very steady, his eyes dark, distant, *defeated*. Waiting, waiting for her to take it, to finish it, to end this before it had even truly begun. And flashing in Maria's thoughts was a sudden, incongruous vision of her husband, sitting smug and seething in his bed. *Shall I set you out upon a plain, wife, and wait for an orc to come and ravage you...*

But this confounding orc wasn't ravaging anymore. He wasn't even moving, or blinking. He was offering Maria safety, escape, *fair terms*. He was abandoning his son, the son he must have wanted very much, and instead conceding defeat. For her freedom.

He kept holding out the contract, kept waiting, looking at her like that—and something was swelling in Maria's chest, knocking against her ribs. And without thinking, without at all knowing why, she lurched to her feet, naked and streaming water—and put her hand to his heart.

His big body froze against the touch, but his heart thundered back against her fingers, beating fast and loud and sure. And somehow Maria was breathing again, gulping air heavy and deep, and this was all that mattered, so steady, so safe...

"I don't want to go," she said, holding his eyes, her every word a ringing, terrifying truth. "I want to stay. And"—she tried to smile at him, courage, *courage*—"I want you to kiss me."

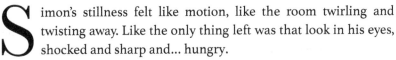

9

Simon's stillness felt like motion, like the room twirling and twisting away. Like the only thing left was that look in his eyes, shocked and sharp and... hungry.

And yes, yes, *hungry*. His throat visibly bobbing, his huge chest hollowing, his black tongue flicking brief and sinuous against his full lips...

But then his eyes snapped shut, and that was surely a grimace on his mouth, grinding in his jaw. And his hand was gripping tighter at Maria's contract, crumpling it slightly in his claws, and he was going to refuse, he was going to say no, he was going to *send her away*—

The panic was rising, the *hysteria*, Maria's fingers pressing hard against his hammering heart. And her other hand had found his chest too, feeling it, drinking up its steady strength—and then sliding, somehow, upwards. Wet fingers slipping up over smooth skin, hard muscle, the broad ridge of his collarbone. Until she'd found his neck, thick and corded and scratchy with stubble, his pulse throbbing tight beneath it...

And in a jolt, a breath, Maria tilted her face up, drew his head down—and *kissed* him.

It was only a brief brush, wet lips meeting warm skin—but in its wake, something seemed to shatter between them, streaking white and wild up Maria's back. Swarming her with heat, with that rough, rugged scent of him, sparking upon her tongue...

Simon still hadn't moved—hadn't reciprocated, hadn't *breathed*—but Maria could still *feel* him, taste him, drink up the increasingly erratic flare of his heartbeat beneath her fingers. He liked this, he wanted this, wanted *her*, and gods he tasted like earth, like hunger, like *heaven*...

So she drew him down closer, stood on tiptoes in the basin—and kissed him again. Harder this time, deeper, her traitorous tongue slipping against the line of his warm full mouth. Silently pleading with him, begging him to open, to let her in...

He relented with a groan, thick and guttural from his throat, vibrating against Maria's still-clinging fingers—and suddenly, there was *chaos*. His huge hard body melting fluid and fierce against hers, his powerful hands gripping at her waist, yanking her fully out of the basin—and his mouth was here, his strong lips and tongue caressing, taking, *invading*, filling her with his scent his breath his *truth*—

And Maria was dragging it up, drinking deep, because she'd never been kissed like this before, never known hunger or power like this—and her only thought, bright and blaring, was to drink more. Clutch him closer. Grind her starving, pulsing groin against the rapidly swelling beast digging into her belly, already streaking slick against her wet skin...

Her arms had both circled around his neck, somehow, her leg hitching up behind his thigh—and in another fluid flash of movement, he lifted her off the floor entirely. Freeing both her legs to circle around his powerful waist, spreading her wide apart against him—and *fuck*, she was naked, he was naked, and that meant he was—*there*. That huge monster pressed tight and raging and *alive*, shuddering and swelling against the full exposed length of Maria's parted crease.

And rather than complaining, protesting, Maria could feel her body gripping at him, slipping against him, greedy and depraved. While his slick powerful tongue delved deep against her actual *throat*, perhaps hinting at what he would like to do below, oh *gods*—

But then the trampling pleasure yanked back, away. Simon's mouth yanked away, even as he'd been smoothly striding toward the bed—

and suddenly Maria was standing on a cold floor, naked and hot and trembling all over.

"Maria," Simon's voice breathed, a low hissing heat, and when she blinked at him, he was leaning backwards, slightly away from her. Even as his tongue kept stroking his lips, as his hands stayed gripped on her waist, that slick swollen beast still grinding close against her belly...

"You are—*sure* of this," he whispered, his eyes glittering so bright, so *hungry*, on hers. "You wish for this."

The sound barking from Maria's throat was half-laugh, half-growl—and she felt her sparking, shivering body hurl itself back toward him, her starving fingers spreading wide against his chest, revelling in the smooth heated skin, the pebbled grey nipples, the ever-constant thunder of his heart...

"Yes," she gasped at him, as one of her audacious hands slipped around his back, stroking against the hard curve of it, the warm rippling muscle beneath his skin. "Gods, I keep telling you, yes. I groped you in a *hallway*. I begged you to *spray* yourself on me."

And in this moment, in the screaming haze of this hunger, the memory of him doing that was suddenly a deep, raw, primally powerful thrill. Claiming her, he'd said, marking her, covering her with his scent...

Gods, she needed it, needed more—but when she lunged for his mouth again, he yanked back with astonishing speed, his claws pressing brief and dangerous against her skin.

"And after this, you cowered, and shouted, and *wept*," he countered. "I yet taste your *fear*, woman."

"Yes, because you *raged* at me!" Maria replied, though the words came out heated, breathless. "You smashed a *rock* against your wall, when I innocently insinuated that maybe your room could use a little *tidying*!"

Simon's brows instantly furrowed, the low growl rumbling in his throat—but it somehow seemed far less terrifying than before, even when those claws flexed sharper, threatening, against her skin.

"Maria," he said again, harder this time. "It was no only this. And should you stay, it no be only"—he hesitated, his fingers spreading on her waist, claws digging deeper—"*this*."

Maria gasped and shivered before him, her lips parted and panting, her hungry hand again creeping toward his chest. "Then what will it be."

That chest heaved against her touch, his breath harsh enough to flutter her damp hair. "You obey me, and yield to me," he replied, his voice so low, so smooth. "You no fear this, or bear shame. You *welcome* this. You *honour* me in this."

And it was hysteria, surely, finally consuming her whole—but Maria's arms only grasped for him, yanked him, felt the hazy thrill of that huge body moving so easy toward her—

"And this isn't honouring you?" she breathed, as she shoved him—*shoved him!*—down toward the fur-covered bed behind his knees. "This isn't what you want?"

And it *was*, he'd settled there with his legs sprawled wide apart, his hands still gripping at her waist, his length jutting up hard and veined and dripping. And like this, his face was almost on a level with hers, his black eyes glinting—and it was easy, so damned easy, to step closer between those legs, to reach for that huge shuddering heat—

"Maria," he hissed again, as one of his hands snapped up, catching both her wrists in its powerful grip. "It is more than this. I shall bare you. *Flaunt* you."

He spoke it like a threat, hoarse and hot in his throat—but he'd also shifted his grip on Maria's wrists, turning her palms inward. And then—her breath twisted into a groan—he placed one of her own hands firmly upon her breast, and pressed the other to her groin.

"I shall bring you to the light," he whispered, grinding her hands close against her skin, making his silent command all too clear. "Show you to all who wish to see."

Maria whimpered, her body prickling and shivering all over—and abruptly Simon released her hands, and leaned back slightly on his bed. Raising a heavy eyebrow at her, that familiar bitter mockery playing on his lips.

It was a challenge, *again*, but suddenly, lost in the chaos, Maria didn't care. Didn't care if her own shocking fingers were again caressing her own breast, flicking and pinching her own nipple. Or if her other hand, even more depraved than the first, slipped down over her coarse dark hair, brushing against her swollen, throbbing heat.

Simon was watching it, his eyes intense and unmoving, his claws rubbing at the shadow of stubble on his jaw. "More," he breathed. "I show them more than this."

Them. The alarm flared brief and bright, skittering past Maria's thoughts—and in its wake, there was more mockery on Simon's mouth, more grim satisfaction. As if he knew, as if he'd defeated her, and he wasn't, he *couldn't, no*—

So in a gust of wild, breathless courage, Maria jerked forward, closer, grasping for his huge smooth shoulders—and then clambered up, and knelt on his *lap*. Or rather, perched precariously on his spread thighs, her own thighs thrust wide, her groin open and blatantly exposed between them...

Simon's black eyelashes fluttered, once, but he didn't move, didn't speak, didn't make any attempt to touch her. Only sat back and watched her like that, waiting, challenging, *judging.*

And Maria would earn his approval, she *would*—so she braced one hand on the strength of his shoulder, took a gulping breath. And then, while an orc sat there and watched, she slipped her other hand back down between her own spread-open legs, and sank a single finger slow and smooth inside.

It felt hot, swollen, abominably slick, and Maria moaned at the feel of it, the faint hint of relief in the touch—but far louder was Simon's growl, husky and deep. And his hands, his hands were sliding up her thighs, so warm, so easy—and then tugging her a little closer, tilting her toward him, providing a better view for his judgement...

"No enough," he murmured, though his gaze was intent on the sight, on Maria's long, audacious, wet-slicked finger now slipping in and out of her swollen folds. "More than this."

Oh, hell, and Maria gulped more air, shifted her weight, and—*nodded.* And then brought down her other hand, only slightly trembling, to open herself wider, further apart. And then, slow, deliberate, *unthinkable*, she took two fingers this time, and sank them up deep inside.

Fuck. It felt better, more like relief, but it most assuredly wasn't. Not with this orc's glinting eyes watching like that, not with one of his huge hands slipping up her thigh, and palming at her bare arse.

Tilting her hips out even further, showing him more, and oh gods what did he see, what was he *thinking*—

"Better," he breathed, "but no yet enough. You have"—his mouth twisted into a smirk—"seen my prick, ach?"

And damn him, but of course the words snapped Maria's eyes downwards, to where that waiting beast had somehow come abominably, breathtakingly close. Swollen to a truly shocking length and width, ridged and bulging with veins, the deep slit oozing a steady stream of white down into the mass of black hair below...

And as Maria stared, struck still at the sight, it actually bobbed out toward her. Almost as if reaching for her, longing for her, wanting to seek its way inside. And it was quite possibly the most arousing vision of Maria's *life*, an orc's massive twitching monster, brazenly threatening to find her, to fill her, to conquer her for its own...

But Simon himself still wasn't moving, was still watching her, still with that mocking curve on his lips. Still waiting, wanting, judging. *No yet enough*, he'd said...

So Maria shuddered, nodded, breathed—and then opened herself wider, swirled all four fingers against her slick, dripping heat. And then— oh *hell*—she slowly sank them up inside, careful, tight, hot, *delicious*.

Her moan was reflexive, far too loud in the taut silence, and as she pressed deeper, she could feel the tightness slipping into pain—but Simon was watching, his throat swallowing, hard enough that she could hear it. And there was no mockery in his eyes now, not even judgement, and Maria pushed deeper, breathing through the resistance, he had to see, he *had* to approve...

"Pretty," he murmured, the single word a hard, flashing thrill up her shivering spine. "It pleases you to be filled, ach?"

Maria nodded, the shame rapidly bubbling and churning, while distant memories swarmed of the loneliness, the craving, and her own ever-more-drastic measures to abate it. Leaving her alone and gasping in bed, brutally and painfully sated for the time being, until the next empty night, and...

"Good," Simon purred, the word another sharp flare of pleasure, of wild hitching relief. And his eyes were pleasure too, suddenly, warm and approving, enough to chase away the memories, the shame...

"But," he continued, husky, "I yet fill you more than this. Ach?"

His hand had slipped down to brush against Maria's knuckles, nudging her fingers deeper inside, choking an instant, broken moan from her throat—but she was nodding again, shameful, shivering. "I know," she whispered. "I—I'll try. To please you."

But the hardness flicked back through his eyes, his head shaking, slow. "You need learn," he breathed. "This is no *try*. It is no *game*. I speak, you listen, and *obey*. You open for me. You face pain and fear. You *worship* at my altar. You learn this, *do* this, and earn my good cleansing."

Good gods. Something was rattling and writhing deep inside, but those hard steady eyes kept holding hers, speaking his truth, his safety. "When I wish to fuck," he continued, his voice rising, "you *do* this. In your womb. In your throat. In your *rump*. You obey me, and honour me. You seek to cover the shame you bring me!"

Oh. *Oh.* And in this shocking moment, sitting so deeply exposed upon her own fingers, with these shocking words spilling deep and harsh from this watching orc's mouth—Maria should have indeed been shocked. Subdued. Ashamed. *Defeated.* He'd just threatened her with fear and pain, she would take him in her throat and her *rump*, she would *worship* him...

"You follow now, wilful woman?" he asked, his mouth a thin line. "*Now* you run, ach?"

He'd even waved her away, his claws flicking cold and casual toward the door. As though all this had meant nothing to him, her showing him such shameful secret things, him judging, approving, *good*...

But his eyes. So hard, so bitter, so... *broken.* As if this had broken him, and maybe not only this, maybe this was just one of many breakings. And Maria followed that, she'd *lived* that, she *understood*...

And it was hysteria, surely, *surely*—but in this moment, maybe Maria didn't want more secrets, more defeat. Maybe she wanted to be bared, and flaunted, and brought to the light. Maybe she *wanted* to worship, and obey, and be... *cleansed.*

So she slowly drew her fingers free, lifted her chin, and held those bitter, defeated eyes. And as Simon blinked at her, his head tilting, his brow furrowing, she shifted forward upon him. Moved up, closer, there, oh gods *there*...

There. That huge, dripping hardness finally, *finally* nudging at her, swelling its slick head against her wide-open, desperately clenching heat. And Simon's eyes suddenly looked just as exposed as she felt, blown-out and snapped wide, locked on the screeching truth of this moment—

"Maria," he croaked. "You shall—"

"Do this," Maria gasped, around her dragging breaths, because fucking *hell*, he felt good. That hot, slick, slippery-smooth head of him, shuddering and vibrating hard against her hungry open warmth...

"Honour you," she managed, her eyelids fluttering. "Cleanse you. Cleanse *me*."

Simon's eyes widened again, his throat audibly convulsing, and his inhale was jagged, hoarse. "Maria," he whispered, and this time it sounded almost pleading, almost... a prayer. As if this was her altar too, it was something to be revered, to be wanted. To be *worshipped*.

That huge heft was still shuddering, swelling even fuller and hotter against her. Just beginning to seek deeper, to spread her swollen lips open around it—and already Maria was gasping, groaning, choking. Fuck, it was big, it was bigger than anything she had ever put *near* there—but it was also silken, smooth, coated all over with that slick spurting white. And when she took a breath, settled herself a little deeper, she could feel it pumping up within her, soaking her even more, easing its way...

And it kept easing, ever so gently, breath by breath. Spreading her wider and wider apart around that smooth seeking head, slowly betraying the true strength of its huge, ever-growing heft, opening, stretching, breaching—

Maria's body was wildly clamping and clenching, fighting it even as she sought to welcome it, and she had to pause, suck back air, fight to relax, breathe, *open*. But there was somehow no panic, not even a taste of it, not even with an orc's massive cockhead jutted up just inside her, steadily soaking her with its juices. Only the bright disbelief in Simon's still-blinking eyes, and the desperate, streaming need for more...

And yes, she could take more, she wanted more, she would honour him—so she sank down a little deeper. Gasping at the full width of him now, stretching her fully taut and open around its hot invading strength. Just beginning to tease at danger, at pain, and she gulped in air, sought more calm, more ease. Breathing into it, into him, and she distantly realized he was breathing too, deep and shuddering, his eyes now locked on the sight, on his body locking into hers...

"Good," his voice bit out, the word a single rumble of heat. "More."

Fuck. Maria choked, nodded, and somehow thrust down further, wrenching him deeper. Hurling out the first real sparks of pain, her breath sucking in between her teeth—but she was honouring him. Fucking him. Cleansing.

And gods, his eyes, the scent of him, the impossible agonizing onslaught of his still-sinking cock, filling her, drilling against her core. Plunging into the breach he was making, pumping her emptiness with slick and heat and longing, so full and so forceful and she was straining, shouting, she was going to split in two—

The ecstasy flashed and screamed, clutching and clamping at the beast inside her, bolting it fast, breaking it—and with a hard, juddering flare, it *ruptured*. Pouring into her with molten liquid pleasure, spurting and spewing deep within, flooding the last of her empty spaces with his heat, his power, his *cleansing*.

The relief burned from Simon's throat in a howl, his head thrown back, his scarred cheeks flushed with sweat. His hands clamping tight on Maria's hips, holding her there upon him, while that beast inside her kept pumping, filling, emptying. Until she could feel it straining one last time, shuddering deep—and then settling again, slightly softening, finally spent.

And suddenly Maria felt spent too, her whole body sagging down against him—but her eyes couldn't seem to stop looking, searching. Sweeping over Simon's sweat-drenched chest and shoulders, his convulsing throat, the deepening hint of a beard on the flexing joint of his jaw...

And then, finally, his eyes. His eyes, slowly blinking at her, looking dazed, heated, *warm*. Glinting with something almost like indulgence, or amusement, or perhaps even... *approval*.

"Wilful woman," he murmured, his voice so slow, so smooth. "Soon, you shall learn to take all of me, ach?"

Soon. And the single, exquisite thrill of that promise soared above all the rest, beyond even that nagging hint of Maria's failure to do so this time, or the increasing soreness between her legs. Or the way a thick, slippery white heat had begun seeping from between their still-locked bodies, streaking down her trembling thighs.

But Simon's eyes had flicked downwards, a trace of an actual *smile* playing on his full lips, and his clawed hand on her hip slipped around, spreading wide against her belly. Which somehow looked fuller than before, almost as if engorged with his strength, and his seed. And soon...

The thought of that was finally enough to set the panic rattling again, distant and blunted inside—until a gentle hand brushed against Maria's chin, tilting it up. Making her meet his eyes again, locking her safe within them, just as his strength still locked her safe below...

"Peace, woman," he said, low, soothing. "You are weary. Rest now."

Maria's hand had somehow fluttered toward him, finding that sweat-slicked chest, the familiar thud of that powerful heartbeat. Enfolding her in its comfort, its safety, even as big capable hands drew her closer, downwards, onto soft whispering furs, into *peace*.

"Rest now," the voice repeated, just as soft as the furs. "Sleep. Seek to grow me a son."

And with a deep, contented breath, Maria nodded, closed her eyes... and *obeyed*.

10

When Maria blinked awake the next morning, she found herself lying sprawled on a soft bed, covered in warm, cozy furs. Someone had lit a candle, a low shirring sound curled through the air, and she felt languid, relaxed, and...

Wet. Very, very wet.

Her eyes snapped open, her hand jerking downward—and good gods, she was *naked* under these furs, and her thighs were *coated* in thick stickiness, and that was because—

She squeezed her eyes shut, and dragged in one heavy breath, and another. Yes, she had come to Orc Mountain. Yes, she had signed a contract. And yes, she had fucked an orc—*that* orc. And now...

Her hands reflexively slipped to her belly under the fur, feeling, searching—*did* it feel rounder than yesterday?—and when she pressed down against it, she felt a sudden, shocking surge of wet heat gushing from between her legs. Good gods, she'd truly fucked an orc, he'd drenched her with his—his *personal effluents*, and, and—

She forcibly halted that line of thought, breathing in thick through her nose. No. She'd done exactly what had needed to be done. It hadn't been hysteria. It *hadn't*.

No, it was *revenge*, and it was unfolding even better than she could have planned. Even if the orcs and their mountain hadn't been at all what she'd expected, she'd still managed to keep it together, and gain her main objectives. She had a contract. She had an orc. She was attempting to bear said orc a son, and thereby heaping shame upon her husband's head, and seeking her damned freedom.

And surely, even when—*if*—it reached that particular final point, surely it would be manageable. Surely any son of Simon's wouldn't be innocent or wide-eyed or sneezy in the least. He'd be hulking and deadly and aggressive, lashing about his claws like a feral little beast, and surely there would be no further need for Maria's involvement whatsoever.

The thought was surprisingly reassuring, enough that Maria blinked her eyes back open, and turned over. Seeing first the single flickering candle, still sitting atop the shelf, and then the already-familiar mess of a room, only lacking the wash-basin from the night before.

And there on the bench, again, was Simon. Still fully naked, but this time he was balancing a large, smooth rock upon his knee, and methodically scraping what appeared to be a carving-knife against it.

His gaze hadn't lifted from his work, but somehow Maria could feel his awareness, his knowledge that she was awake and watching. Almost as though he were waiting for her to speak, or...

"Good morning!" cut in a cheerful voice. A *new* voice. Prompting Maria's body to skitter upright in the bed, her head whipping around, her hands yanking the fur up to her chin.

It was—a woman. One of the pregnant women from the meeting the day before, in fact. She was small and blonde and pert-looking, she was clutching a stack of papers against her far-too-short loose tunic, and she grinned at Maria as she picked her way across the mess of the room.

"Hi, I'm Rosa," she said brightly. "And you're Maria, right? It's so *lovely* to have you here. I think having a woman around will benefit Simon *enormously*, don't you? He's a *notorious* grump, if you haven't already noticed."

She accompanied these astonishing words with a teasing wink at Simon, and Maria couldn't help noticing that Simon's frown back toward this pretty, delicate Rosa wasn't quite genuine—and also, that he was *still naked*. A fact which didn't seem to disturb either of them in the least, and as Maria blinked at Simon—and particularly at that beast at his groin, dangling thick and shameless toward the floor—something flared in her gut that felt dangerously close to *jealousy*.

"Simon's cleverer than he looks, though," Rosa continued, with another teasing smile. "You should have heard his common-tongue even six months ago, Maria, it was truly *atrocious. Ach, Simon?*"

Simon actually replied this time, but it was in the deep tangled black-tongue, rumbling low from his throat—and whatever it was, it prompted a peal of laughter from Rosa, and another inexplicable, unpleasant flare in Maria's belly. It didn't matter, surely it didn't, he was just an orc, and...

"I imagine you're still getting settled in, Maria," Rosa continued blithely, "but I wanted to introduce myself, and bring you some reading material. A welcome package, of sorts."

She'd halted beside the bed, and with an excited little flourish, she thrust out the stack of papers she'd been holding. Leaving Maria to hurriedly wipe off her still-sticky hand, and then awkwardly reach out from behind her fur to take them.

"Um, thank you," she said, glancing down at the clump of papers now clutched in her fingers. On which the topmost sheet boasted a vivid, block-printed image of an orc, and above it, a title printed in large, neat gothic letters.

An Alternate Account of the Orc-Human War, it read. *From the League of Informed Inferiors.*

Oh. This was—the orcs' *propaganda*?

Maria's thoughts abruptly twisted backwards, catching on the vision of her husband, sitting in his silk sheets. Complaining about the orcs' propaganda, and claiming it had targeted his advisors, and even his own son. Claiming they'd been... *compromised.*

And as Maria stared down at the vivid printed orc clutched in her fingers, it distantly occurred to her that she hadn't actually *believed* that claim. That she hadn't, perhaps, thought the orcs capable of campaigns, or cleverness, or even communication. *A feral passel of monkeys beneath the fucking sea...*

She felt herself wince, her eyes darting reflexively at Simon—and he was frowning back at her, his heavy brows pulled close together. Almost as if, once again, he'd seen straight into Maria's soul, and found it deserving only of his contempt, and his mockery, and his *judgement*.

And suddenly, there was the inexplicable, almost overwhelming urge to prove him wrong. To show this temperamental, judgemental orc that she could keep her damned word, and honour him, and whatever the hell else this was.

"Um, this indeed looks highly informative," Maria made herself say, forcing her gaze back to Rosa's expectant, eager face. "I, uh, look forward to reading it. Did you, um, produce these pamphlets? Here?"

It was the right question to ask, thankfully, because Rosa instantly launched into an extensive monologue about how accurate, readily available public information about orcs was critically lacking, and about how she and the Ka-esh clan had worked with some *very* helpful contacts in Dusbury to arrange for printing and distribution throughout Sakkin Province, and how they were currently looking for distribution channels in Preia. And how soon, they would celebrate their one hundred thousandth copy by hand-dropping it at the door of the realm's ruling Citadel.

"Of course, it will only infuriate those horrid lords, who can't bear the thought of losing a *whit* of their *entirely* unearned power and influence," Rosa continued, without seeming to have once paused for breath. "But it's the common people we need to reach with this information campaign. The people who are suffering under that Council's completely incompetent administration. The people struggling with poverty, and disease, and *injustice*."

She finally paused there, her expression deeply disgruntled—and blinking back toward her, Maria couldn't seem to collect her thoughts, or find a single coherent word to say in return. And there were so *many*, things like, *I couldn't agree more, I wish you all success, and by the way, my husband is in charge of that Council, I hate him just as much as you do, I should dearly love to see his face when you drop this upon his doorstep...*

"Rosa-Ka," interrupted another new voice, this one low and smooth, and again coming from the door. Making Maria startle in place, her head whipping around to find—another *orc*. Another orc she vaguely recognized from the meeting the day before, in fact, and he was surprisingly handsome, his face strong and symmetrical and unmarked by scars.

And in another world, one with less befuddlement clogging her brain, Maria might have almost been gratified by the way this orc was standing stiffly in the doorway, his arms folded over his grey tunic, while his dark eyes glanced about at the room's chaos with unmistakable distaste. Perhaps, even, with *judgement*.

"John-Ka!" Rosa crowed, and she instantly trotted over toward him, slipping her delicate form easily under his arm. "I was just saying hello to Maria, and bringing her something to read. Maria, this is my mate John, of Clan Ka-esh. He's the Priest of Orc Mountain, which means he manages all *sorts* of intriguing projects, especially down in the Ka-esh wing. You ought to come over, we'll happily give you a tour, won't we, John?"

This John twitched a silent nod toward Maria, and she managed a faint smile in return—at least, until Simon gave a deep, heavy grunt from across the room. "No Ka-esh wing," he said, voice flat. "No *tour*. Maria shall stay here, with Skai, until she earns this right."

Wait. That was new, wasn't it? And wait, did Simon mean—did he mean he was keeping Maria prisoner? *Here*? In this disaster of a room?

But Simon was glaring down at his knife again, scraping it against the stone with renewed intensity, and Maria's searching glance toward Rosa and John found them looking just as confused as she felt. "You're *confining* Maria here?" Rosa asked, her delicate brows furrowing. "Why? For how long? I thought you Skai didn't approve of—"

She was interrupted by Simon's bark of a growl, and another loud, grating scrape of his knife. "This woman stays here, in Skai wing," he said, slow, deliberate, "until she gains our trust. Until she learns to obey me, and honour all our Skai ways."

Oh. So at least she wasn't just trapped in this one room, then—but it still felt like a slap, a curse, an *insult*. Because Maria *had* honoured Simon last night, hadn't she? Or at least, she'd thought she had. He'd seemed pleased with her... hadn't he?

Or had he, and now it was only uncertainty swarming Maria's thoughts, coiling cold inside her chest. Had she already failed, somehow, without knowing why? Had she perhaps again insulted Simon, in some way? Dishonoured him?

"Well, we'll try to come by for visits, then," Rosa said, with a rather forced-sounding cheerfulness, though her eyes were glancing apprehensively toward John beside her. "Although, I hate to say, we're going west tomorrow for a passage dig we've been planning, so... after next week, then?"

Maria managed a nod in return, and another halfhearted smile— and after a stilted goodbye, she and Simon were left alone again. With Maria still huddled under the fur, now gripping a stack of orc propaganda in her clammy-feeling hands, while her thoughts unpleasantly twisted and churned. She was trapped here. She was Simon's *prisoner.* Until she earned his trust, and honoured all his *ways,* whatever the hell that meant.

And Simon still wasn't even looking at her, though he'd finally stopped carving, tracing his blunt fingers over the inscrutable hollows he'd made in his stone. And then nodding, almost as if satisfied, before setting his carving aside—and then, with a purposeful flick of his hand, he beckoned Maria over toward him.

Maria twitched, but accordingly put down the stack of pamphlets, and shifted to the edge of the bed—and then discovered, to her chagrin, that the mess still between her legs was now rapidly worsening, bringing with it a rising, throbbing soreness. Not only that, but her clothes from the day before didn't appear to be anywhere within reach... and in fact, they didn't appear to be anywhere in the surrounding clutter at *all.*

"Um," Maria ventured, tugging the protective fur a little higher. "Might you have my clothes nearby?"

Simon's eyes on her narrowed, and his sharp claws seemed to visibly *lengthen* from the ends of his previously blunt-tipped fingers. "No," he said flatly. "I have sent these for cleaning. Now come."

His now-clawed fingers beckoned again, more impatient this time—and Maria cast an uncertain, uneasy glance down at the fur still gripped in her hands. It was far too large to drag off the bed and use as a covering, and surely he couldn't mean, or could he—

"*Come,*" Simon barked at her, and Maria lurched her stark-naked body up out of the bed, her skull ringing, her heart pounding. She'd sworn to do this, and he'd seen it all last night anyway, and perhaps he had other clothes stashed around him somewhere—

But even standing up felt like a challenge, suddenly, Maria's legs gone weak and wobbly, the soreness between them throbbing deeper with every breath. And the mess, oh gods it was *everywhere*, pooling behind her on the bed, running down her thighs, exposing her with thick sticky shame.

Her hands were fluttering down toward it, trying in vain to cover it, to wipe it away—but a sharp growl across the room made her abruptly abandon the attempt, her feet shuffling through the room's chaos. Toward where Simon just sat there gazing at her, his eyes flat and dispassionate on the mess still streaming between her thighs.

Maria jolted to a halt before him, her cheeks burning, her hands gripped to fists at her sides. And for a long, jangling moment, Simon didn't say anything, but just kept gazing between her legs, and then, up to her waist. His eyes lingering, almost as though he were searching for something, and that *couldn't* be possible, not yet...

Good gods, Maria couldn't *think*, and she scrubbed at her face with her clammy, twitchy fingers. "Do you have something else I can wear for now, then?" she asked, her voice wavering. "Or even just something to clean up with?"

And to her vague surprise, Simon accordingly nodded, and grasped something on the bench beside him. Something surely fabric-like, thank the *gods*, and the relief shuddered up Maria's back as he held it out toward her. "Here," he said. "I wish you to wear this."

This. Maria's hands had eagerly clutched for it, shaking it out—but wait. *Wait.* It was only a slim leather belt, with two pieces of soft brown leather hanging from it. Almost as though it were... it couldn't be...

"Um," she heard herself say, hoarse. "What is this?"

Simon's expression was wholly unreadable, and his hands reached for hers, and guided the belt up against her waist. So that one of the leather bits covered her groin in front, and if she were actually wearing the belt, the other piece would cover the back, and...

Simon wanted her to wear... a *loincloth*?!

"Y-you expect me to wear *this*?" Maria said, her voice rising. "By *itself*?!"

Simon's face still hadn't changed, but he jerked a sharp, decisive nod. "Ach," he said flatly. "This is the garb of a Skai woman. It shall help flaunt my gain, and prove my claim upon you. It shall show my favour before my kin."

Wait. Maria's body skittered to stillness, the implication of those words somehow resonating far louder than the rest of the deluge currently flooding her brain. Simon wanted to show his favour with this... among *other people*?!

"You can't possibly mean," she heard herself say, slow, incredulous, "you want me to wear this not just for you—but in *public*?"

"Ach," he said again, cold and clipped. "From henceforth, you shall wear only this amongst my kin."

His hand gave a vague, fluid wave, surely encompassing a world far beyond just this room. The Skai wing he'd mentioned, perhaps. And Maria couldn't stop staring at his set face, her mouth dropping open, her heartbeat driving frantically against her ribs.

"I *must* be misunderstanding you," her distant voice said. "You can't truly mean for me to wear a *loincloth* here—*all the time*?"

Simon kept gazing at her, and she could see his eyes darkening, his jaw grinding in his cheek. "Ach, I do," he replied. "You no honour me, in this?"

And shit, *shit*, Maria's promise to honour him surely hadn't meant *this*—had it? A *duchess*, walking around Orc Mountain on display and dripping an orc's leavings, like a—a debauched, depraved, vulgar *trollop*? No, *no*, surely this had been a mistake, a miscommunication...

"I *asked* this of you," Simon continued, deep, inexorable, horrible. "I said I wish to bare you. Cleanse you. Flaunt you before my kin. You ken what you said to this?"

And as Maria kept gaping at him, she heard—*more footsteps* behind them. And when she whirled around, her blood roaring in her ears, this time it was—*Baldr*. Strolling casual and smiling into the room, and carrying what seemed to be a large wooden *chest*.

"Here you are," he said lightly, beaming toward Maria as he strode straight over to the bench, cleared off a spot beside Simon, and set down the chest. "How are you settling in, Maria?"

Good *gods*. Maria belatedly lurched into motion, her hands frantically, awkwardly jerking on the loincloth, and yanking it tight around her waist. Providing some small modicum of concealment, for her lower half at least, and Baldr's swift glance down toward it might have been approving, or perhaps almost even... *envious.*

"Ach, Skai like to flaunt their m—, er, their women," he said, his voice catching. "Very pretty. Is there aught else you need, brother?"

Simon had kept sitting there through all this, rigid and dispassionate, still without a stitch of clothing on, with his legs sprawled wide. With that—*beast*—still dangling toward the floor, thick and heavy and languid, as if he truly didn't care in the slightest what anyone saw, as if almost *taunting* Baldr to look his fill—

"No," Simon replied, voice curt. "I thank you, brother."

Baldr flashed them both another quick smile, and spun on his heel toward the door—but then hesitated, and turned back again. "Will you be long, Simon? The captain waits to speak about that new—"

He broke off there, his eyes darting sidelong toward Maria, and she belatedly flailed to cross her arms over her breasts, to hide herself from his gaze. But Baldr was already glancing back toward Simon, and if possible, Simon looked even more disapproving, more forbidding, than before.

"Ach, I soon come," Simon said flatly. "I must first show this woman to the Skai."

Show this woman?! The words sparked another stunning, staggering blaze of panic in Maria's chest, so overwhelming she scarcely noticed Baldr's reply or retreat. And all that was left was Simon, still sitting there sprawled and shameless, with that insolent cold *disapproval* in his watching orc eyes.

"Y-you truly *mean* this?" Maria choked out, as evenly as she could. "You're going to *show* me to other orcs, like *this*? Are you—are you playing some kind of *game* with me?!"

But Simon slowly shook his head, grim, bitter, *judging.* "I told you, woman, I play no game. You swore to bare. To *honour.* And thus, should you wish to stay, or gain your freedom here, you *shall.*"

Maria's breath was lurching in her throat, the panic clattering and jangling, the numbness tingling in her hands and feet. "You did *not* specify," she somehow managed, "that this would include me not being *permitted*"—she gulped in air—"to *dress!*"

"Ach, I did," came Simon's voice, now betraying an unmistakable thread of anger. "And you swore you wished for this, again and again and *again*. I bear no more *lies* upon this from you, woman!"

Good gods, Maria could no longer speak, or think, or move, but Simon seemed entirely undeterred, his clawed hand reaching for the chest Baldr had brought. "Now, woman," he continued, flat, ruthless, as he snapped up the lid. "This shall be yours, whilst you stay. Here I shall put your things, and your food and drink for each day."

The disbelief was tilting toward unreality, toward a strange twirling distance, but Simon only kept gazing at her, now waving at the contents of the chest. "You shall also find oil," he continued, "and tools for each day, to help ready yourself for my taking."

Wait, what? Maria's dazed, blinking eyes had finally dragged themselves away from his forbidding face, and down toward the chest. Registering vaguely the basket of food, the bottle of milk, a vial that must have been oil, and—these *tools*. Two long, thick, smoothly polished items, with tapering, rounded heads, carved out of what looked like *stone*...

"What," she croaked, "are *these*?"

But her distant screaming brain knew very well what they were, oh *gods*—and Simon actually snorted, and then reached inside to pluck one out. Gripping it with astonishing familiarity between his clawed fingers, and holding it out toward Maria as though it were something—*normal*. Something everyday and ordinary, not—not—

"Last eve, you took not half of my prick," he said coolly. "These shall help you learn."

Maria was fully beyond all words now, still gaping down at the—the *implement* in his hand. Fighting not to think of all the times she had used such shocking things, hiding away furtive and ashamed, desperately wishing they had been real, with flesh and blood beneath...

"I shall find your fresh scent upon these each day," Simon continued, steady, brittle. "You shall use them each time I am away from you. And when I return, I shall find you stretched and open and ready for me. Any part I might wish to take. Ach?"

There was no comprehending this, no accepting or answering this—but Simon was *waiting* for her, his eyebrows raised. "Ach?" he asked, the challenge dark and deadly in his voice. "Shall you obey me in this, woman?"

The panic was wailing and raging, and Maria could finally feel her eyes darting around, desperate, searching—and yes, *yes*, there was the contract, sitting rumpled on top of his shelf. The sight of it so compulsively powerful, speaking so loudly of her freedom, her *revenge*. And it had all been going so well, unfolding better than planned, and now...

"Or, mayhap you run *now*?" Simon's voice continued, cold and relentless, as though he'd again peered into her very thoughts. "After you swore to me, again and again, how deeply you wish for this? How you wish to *honour* me?"

Good gods, *fuck* this utter bastard—and somehow, somewhere in the mayhem, Maria's rage had finally flared to life. Surging high above the worst of the panic, the fear, the shame.

"I *can't* run now," she hissed at him, her voice breaking. "And you know it. After last night, I'm likely—we likely—I—"

But it wouldn't finish, the words wouldn't keep coming out, and something cruel and dangerous shot through Simon's black orc eyes. "That no need stop you," he hissed. "You ken my brothers shall no fix this for you? You ken they must no oft wreak this, for fickle women such as you? Women who speak such *lies* to us?!"

A vicious, devastating chill streaked up Maria's back, but she somehow managed to hold herself steady, to return the fury in his glare. "I *didn't* lie to you," she gritted out. "And I have every intention of keeping my word to you. But I certainly do *not* wish to be used as a vulgar plaything, or paraded around before your friends as a cheap crude *joke*, or targeted as the shameful butt of your *mockery*!"

But Simon scoffed at her, loud and obnoxious, his mouth leering, his eyes fierce. "Should you no wish for *shameful butt of mockery*," he sneered, "you stretch it open as I command, and learn to suck my prick deep inside it!"

Gods *curse* this brute, this odious revolting *lech*, and Maria rubbed her hands against her burning cheeks, and fought down the rising, almost unbearable urge to start shouting, to punch and kick at him, to run over and rip that contract to shreds—

But no. No. She *wouldn't*. Her freedom. Her *revenge*. And she was committed to this now, she'd done the deed with this vile vulgar *beast...*

"I made you *offer*," Simon's deep voice said, the words thudding into Maria's belly, into her hands somehow now clutching tight against it. "I spoke truth to you again and again. Should you no truly wish for this, you ought to show yourself *rational human being*, and speak *no!*"

A rational human being. Maria badly flinched, because those were her own words, being thrown back in her face by a hateful sneering orc. And surely she *had* been irrational when she'd agreed to this, hysterical, and what was she supposed to do now, what was left, beyond this almost overwhelming urge to scream, to rage, to fall to her knees, to beg and plead for his mercy—

"You choose," continued Simon's voice, dark, inexorable. "You wish to run, we still send you away safe. You wish to stay, you *honour* me. You come, and show yourself to my kin, and thus keep our ways, and earn my trust. As you *swore* to do!"

And in the chaos, the cracking deep inside Maria's chest, there was finally only... defeat.

No. *No.* She would not care what this horrible orc said, or what he did next. He could mock her, and flaunt her, and humiliate her, and do whatever the hell he wished. And Maria sure as hell wasn't giving him the satisfaction of giving up. She was *not* going to run, because she did. Not. Care.

She was getting her revenge, and her freedom. There was no other path. No other way.

Nothing else mattered.

So she made her head lift, made herself face those glittering orc eyes. Made herself face the humiliation, the shame, the *defeat.*

For now.

"Very well," she said, her voice a whisper. "I'll come."

11

Simon marched Maria down the corridor in silence, the single candle clutched in his clawed hand. His eyes were fixed straight ahead, his steps soundless on the stone floor, and his hulking body was still entirely bared, his massive muscles rolling and rippling with every smooth step.

And only a few moments ago, Maria might have been tempted to let her gaze wander, to see what this movement did to that still-dangling beast at his groin. But instead, she could only seem to glare down at the floor, desperately fighting to ignore the painful heat in her cheeks, the sweat prickling down her bare back, the furious gallop of her heartbeat.

She would do this, for revenge. He was just an orc. She didn't care what he did. She *didn't.*

"You are sure of this," came Simon's voice, quiet and unexpected. "You are *sure* you no rather run."

Good gods, not this again, and the rebellion flared in Maria's chest with raging, vehement force. "Yes, I'm sure!" she hissed toward the floor. "I told you I would do it, and I *will!*"

There was a harsh huff of breath beside her, a movement that might have been his hand rubbing at his face. "Then I take you now to our Skai common-room," he said, voice flatter than before. "This is where my kin most oft meet. It is where we rest, and speak together, and fuck."

Maria didn't lift her head, or make any acknowledgement of this, but somewhere, distant and blunted in her brain, there was the wild, nonsensical urge to laugh. To say, *Of course you have a whole room dedicated to fucking, of course your kin would be the ones to fulfill every horrible tale about this horrible mountain—*

"We Skai no oft dress here," Simon's flat voice continued. "To dress is to hide. To show weakness. To make shame of joy, and betray those who grant this joy to you."

It was an explanation, Maria's distant thoughts realized, or perhaps a warning—but before she could fully prepare for what that might mean, Simon's huge hand gripped at her bare shoulder, and steered her toward one of the openings in the stone wall. One that seemed to have a mass of noise emanating from it, noise that suggested...

This. Dissipation. Depravity. *Debauchery.*

And while Maria should have been far beyond shock at this point, she still felt suddenly struck to the floor, her eyes seized on the sight before them. On the room full of huge, naked, sweaty orcs, thrusting and writhing against one another. Slapping and touching, groaning and grunting, using hands and mouths and—*and*—

"Ach, my kin," cut in Simon's voice, deep and powerful—and in an instant, it was like the room had hollowed, snapping into silence. Into every fornicating orc's head turning at once, and staring toward them. Toward—*Maria.*

Her knees wavered beneath her, her body staggering sideways—but Simon had somehow edged behind her, circling his arm around her waist, holding her steady. *Displaying* her, for this room full of strange, staring, deeply debauched orcs.

It didn't matter, Maria's brain silently shouted, it *didn't,* she'd agreed to this, she'd *wanted* this—but the shame still kept flooding her from the inside out, threatening to escape in wails or curses or wild ugly weeping. While Simon's immovable arm kept her firmly upright, her cheeks flaming, her body trembling, as these equally awful orcs looked their fill, and *judged.*

And they *were* judging, Maria realized, as another staggering surge of shame crashed against her. Their dark eyes lingering on her face, her full breasts, the still-sticky mess on her thighs. Many of them were openly leering, licking their lips, while others frowned or sneered or smirked. The only orc whose face showed no expression at all was—*Drafli*, who'd shoved away the unfamiliar orc kneeling before him, in favour of leaning against the nearest wall, arms folded, his eyes narrow on Simon's face.

And while Maria's scattered, screaming brain should have been disgusted by Drafli's nakedness, or the fact that the kneeling orc was now coughing, spitting white liquid onto the floor—instead she seemed strangely, bizarrely caught in the way Drafli was looking at Simon behind her. His face harsh, blank, devoid of expression, except for... the *pity*.

"Ach, my kin," Simon said again, his voice even and slow. As though he'd been giving them *time* to stare and leer, as though he'd *wanted* them to make their horrid judgements. "This is Maria. I have bought her to bear me a son."

Bought her. Maria winced all over, the shame flaming higher, hotter—and then worse, so much worse, at the sudden burst of orc voices, and with them, *laughter*. Yes, *laughter*, these watching judging orcs were openly laughing at her, mocking her, dragging her in her shame—

"*Silence*," hissed Simon's voice, deep and menacing. "I have taken this woman, and marked her, and filled her. Thus, she shall bear us a Skai son. You *will* honour this."

Some of the mockery had faded from the watching orcs' faces, but several were still blatantly jeering, their black eyes alight. One in particular—a huge, barrel-chested orc nearly as big as Simon—had actually stepped forward, slow and swaggering, fully ignoring the smaller orc still clinging to his naked form.

"You seek to *claim* her?" the orc asked, his voice rough and deep. "A woman you did not hunt, nor lead a rut upon?"

A *what*? Maria's shivers had returned in force, and even through the terrified mortified *misery*, she could feel Simon's already-tense body stiffening behind her. "Ach," he replied. "She wished to sell to me alone, and swore in ink to honour and obey me until this is done. There shall thus be *no rut*."

There were several actual *groans of disappointment*, scattered across the room, and this time another orc stepped forward, tall and ugly and leering. "No even upon her throat?" he asked, his hoarse voice heavily accented, his eyes lingering on Maria's lips. "She bear good mouth for this."

The awareness of what they meant was slowly dawning, sparking more sickening fear in Maria's gut—but Simon's arm around her waist had clamped harder, closer. "No," he hissed. "Until my son is birthed, and she is free of her vow to me, no other shall touch her without my leave. Lest you wish to taste your Enforcer's *fists*."

The first big orc loudly scoffed, his huge clawed hands opening and closing at his sides. "This is not the way of the Skai," he growled. "Even the Enforcer has no grounds to alter this upon us."

"I alter *naught*, Ulfarr," Simon snarled back. "This is no *mate*. She is only woman I *buy*. Woman who births *son*. This is *all*."

This is all. It felt like a slap, straight across Maria's already-stinging face, and she would have again staggered sideways, if not for Simon's iron clasp still around her waist. Clutching her even tighter as her breaths came shallower, her exposed skin burning and prickling hotter, oh gods...

"Then shall you now take her before your kin, as our fathers have taught us?" continued the big orc, his brows rising, his eyes lingering with purpose on Maria's heavy bare breasts. "We should like to see her spurt and squeal upon a strong Skai prick, ach?"

Maria's gulping breaths cracked in her throat, her body snapped to brittle ice, waiting for Simon's reply—but there was only silence, fraught, simmering. And behind her she could feel his chest filling, and hollowing, and then—*that*. That thick, dangling beast, which had been pressed unnervingly but innocuously against Maria's bare back, was—swelling. Rising. *Wanting.*

The terror flashed through Maria's form, bright and horrifying, and the urge to run was trampling her flat, swallowing her whole. But surely there was no escape, Simon was going to make her do this, he would make her leak and scream upon him, expose all her most secret shameful longings for their judgement, and they would *laugh*, and she didn't care, she didn't she didn't she DIDN'T—

"Ach, brothers," interrupted a voice, a familiar voice, just behind them—and when Maria jerked to look, it was again—*Baldr*. Baldr, standing there fully clothed and oddly menacing in the doorway, his previously genial eyes gone narrow and chilly as they swept across the room. As they held first on Simon, and then this Ulfarr, and then—Baldr's mouth visibly tightened—on Drafli. And on the orc still kneeling at Drafli's feet, licking his wet lips with gusto, and eyeing Baldr with something that might have been *triumph*.

"The captain awaits our Skai brothers, and loses his patience," Baldr snapped at the kneeling orc, at Drafli, at *Simon*. "Can this not wait?"

No one spoke or moved, though Maria could feel the orcs' alertness, their anticipation of what would come next. Their eyes darting keen and watchful between Simon and Ulfarr, and for an instant, it felt like the tension was about to explode, and flash into something dangerous, *deadly*—

Until across the room, Drafli shoved off the wall and strode toward the door, swiping something from the floor on the way by. Something that proved to be a kilt, with a huge, gleaming scimitar attached, and by the time Drafli reached the door he was dressed and armed, his sharp shoulder knocking against Baldr's as he passed him in the doorway.

"Simon?" Baldr asked, his narrow eyes finally flicking away from Drafli, and settling on Simon's face. "Are you done?"

Simon's body behind Maria twitched, and somewhere beneath the still-screeching mortified terror, she realized that he'd been just as tense as she'd felt. And at the feel of him relaxing against her—the feel of that prodding beast slightly softening—she could somehow breathe again, her lungs dragging in air, the blood slowly returning to her hands and feet.

"Ach, we are done," came Simon's reply, and it might have been relief in his voice, in the harsh exhale of his breath against her hair. "Come, woman."

Maria obeyed without hesitation, lurching toward the door on her staggering, sparking feet. Away from those horrible, hostile orcs, from the mockery, the leering eyes, the judgement. *Shall you now take her before your kin. She has good mouth. We should like to see her spurt and squeal...*

Simon's heavy hand had settled on Maria's shivering shoulder, and she reflexively flinched away from him, her arms clamping over her chest. Her breath was still coming in thick, draining gulps, and her vision of Baldr's stiffly striding form ahead of her seemed to be blurring, worse and worse, no matter how frantically she blinked her eyes—

"In, woman," came Simon's low voice, his hand nudging against her back, and though Maria flinched again, she once more obeyed. Finding herself back in his mess of a room, but it had the bed, with those *furs*, and her shivering body sprinted straight toward them, toward protection, toward *safety*. Almost hurling herself under the soft whispering warmth, fully concealing her humiliation beneath.

There was the sound of a slow sigh somewhere behind her, and then a distant, prickling awareness of Simon moving. Coming nearer, hesitating over her at the edge of the bed.

"I would no yet take you before them," said his voice, quiet. "No when you are so fearful of this."

No *yet*?! A hard shudder wracked through Maria's body, and she curled herself tighter, clutching the fur up to her chin. "I'm not—*fearful*," she countered, though her teeth were chattering, her voice badly cracking. "I'm—*horrified*. At you, and your awful clan. I c-can't believe you d-id that. Y-you truly made me into a—a *joke*. A trinket to be *shared* and *laughed* at. A—a—"

She couldn't say it, couldn't even bear to remember him saying those words. *This is no mate. She is only woman I buy. This is all...*

"I said, I no share you," came Simon's reply, flatter now. "And you were no *joke*. Skai all long for tall, ripe, buxom woman like you. Woman with strength and will to bear strong ploughing, and grow hale, hearty Skai sons."

If that was supposed to be comforting, it achieved the exact opposite, because Maria's badly trembling hands had skittered down to her waist, searching desperately against it. It couldn't be fuller already, that *couldn't* have happened from one time, in a single day, please gods please...

"You... swore you wished for this," Simon's voice continued, quiet again. "Ach?"

And was it an accusation, or was it mockery, or was it... uncertainty. Yes, yes, it was fucking *uncertainty*, still, after Maria had done that, proven that to him, gone through this sheer *hell* to please him. She hadn't shouted, she hadn't wept or begged, she'd held her head high and kept the hysteria at bay and fucking *honoured* him like he'd wanted, and now *this*? *Again*?!

The rage felt like a battering eruption, like *relief*. Powerful enough to snap Maria's gaze up, to where this hideous brute was standing far too close, separated only by the safety of the fur, still clutched in her trembling, sparking fingers.

"*Yes*, you great *prick*," she croaked at him. "I've told you again and again, I am committed to this, and I will do it! I gave you my word, I swore to honour you, and I *have*! Even when you marched me straight into a sickening den of *debauchery* for the sole purpose of publicly *mocking* me as a cheap vulgar *tramp!*"

Shut up, shut up, her distant brain was shouting, but it was too late, her own rage catching and kindling in Simon's hard black eyes. In the straining fists clutched at his sides, in the deep, sneering laugh from his cruel mouth.

"If you truly wish to *honour*," he growled back, "you no falter and fuss at each command from my mouth. You no whine and wail when I only seek to claim you and keep you safe. You no *reek* of fury and fear when I flaunt you before my kin, as I again and again swore to you I would!"

What? The rage was a screaming white light, obliterating all else in its strength, and Maria's bark of a laugh was loud, brittle, painful. "Oh, so now you're not only judging my actions," she spat at him, "but you're condemning my *feelings*, too?"

Simon's eyes were glinting with black bitterness, his lips peeling back from his sharp teeth, a low growl scraping from his throat. "Silence, woman," he hissed. "I no play *aught* more of your games. You swore to honour me!"

"Because I thought you would be *reasonable!*" Maria's voice shouted, on its own, before she could possibly halt its escape. "I was beginning to think I was *wrong* about you orcs, and perhaps you weren't the vulgar barbarians you're made out to be! Come to discover"—she hauled in air—"I've bound myself to a coarse, hideous, dim-witted *tyrant* who only wants to use and mock and *humiliate* me!"

Shit, *shit*, what the *hell* was she saying—but the words were out, they were truth, reverberating through this suddenly small-feeling room. And the way Simon was looking at her, it might have been the rage, or disbelief, or—*hurt*.

He shoved away from the bed, the movement unusually jerky, and lurched toward the mess of clothes in the corner. Grasping for something—a pair of trousers—and yanking them on with forceful hands. Keeping his back to her as he then snatched for what looked like a leather sword-belt, and wrapped it around his waist.

Maria briefly squeezed her eyes shut, opened her mouth to speak—but Simon had whirled around with astonishing speed, and somehow there was a scimitar in his hand. *That* scimitar. Huge, curved, gleaming, made to disembowel, to destroy...

"No more," he snarled, his eyes snapping, his hand flexing on the sword's hilt. "You honour me, or you go. *Today*. I play no games, woman."

Maria's throat badly convulsed, her cursed mouth opening again on its own. "Look, I didn't—"

But his bark was far louder, his body lunging closer, that sword glinting so deadly in his fingers. "*No*," he growled again. "I shall hear no more of this, woman. From henceforth, all I shall bear from your mouth is its tight, eager suckling upon my prick!"

And with those appalling words still ringing through the room, Simon spun and strode for the door. Leaving Maria, with that—that *threat* hanging so brutal and heavy behind him. That utter—*disregard*, a cold cruel slap in the face, when she truly *had* sought to please him, to honour him. And why had she ever imagined that he'd wanted her, he didn't want her to speak, to feel, to even *be*—

"You utter *bastard*," she hissed at his broad back, her eyes blinking hard. "I *hate* you."

Simon's big body lurched to stillness in the doorway, his shoulders square and stiff. "This matters naught," he said, his voice harsh and final. "You honour me, woman. Or you go. *Today*."

12

After Simon left, the hysteria finally came.

It took Maria's breath, leaving only strangled gasps and sobs. It took her heart, whipping it into a frenzy, thundering against her ribs. And it pooled to her limbs, quivering and trembling uncontrollably under the fur, shuddering and seizing against the bed.

And throughout, as always, it crept deep into her head. Screaming and mocking, pounding and aching, blurring and flickering white. Frigid. Barren. Difficult. *It's not my fault you don't arouse me, I have no need of more children, I have no interest in bedding a madwoman. This is no mate, she is only woman I buy. All I shall bear from your mouth is its tight, eager suckling upon my prick...*

It felt like hours of it, consuming Maria with suffocating power, flaying her raw in its wake. And when it finally, finally faded away, she found herself shivering, curled up, drenched in cold sweat. Her arms were scraped from her clutching fingernails, her head felt swollen and sore, and her eyes were scratchy, her mouth bone-dry.

"Gods damn it," she croaked to the stone ceiling, as she forced her still-shivery body onto her back, scrubbing at her eyes. "*Damn* it."

But at least she'd been alone. At least no one had been there to point, or mock, or judge. And now that it had passed, and Maria could somewhat feel herself again, there was also a chilly, detached emptiness. Resignation. *Melancholia,* her husband's horrid physicians had called it.

But within the melancholia, Maria could still feel that same, settled certainty. The clarity. The choice.

She'd come to Orc Mountain. She'd signed a contract. She'd found an orc, and fucked him. She'd set all her plans into place, achieved all that she'd meant to do. And next...

Maria groaned and scrubbed at her face again, dragging in deep breaths. It didn't matter what happened next. What Simon did next. She was here for her revenge, and her freedom, and that was all she cared about.

It had to be.

So she wiped at her wet eyes, and shoved herself up to sit on the side of the bed. She would do this. She would be silent, and stay where Simon had put her, and do all that he commanded. She would even keep wearing this blasted *loincloth.* In public.

Even so, she awkwardly tugged it down as she stood, and picked her way through the mess of the room. Toward the wooden chest Baldr had brought, still sitting on the bench, its lid propped open.

And yes, there was still food inside, and drink, all that Simon had wanted her to eat. So Maria numbly took it all out, taking great care not to touch at those—*implements,* and then sagged her loincloth-clad arse down onto the bench, and slowly, methodically ate. Scarcely even registering what the food was, some kind of dried meat, bread, an apple, because it all tasted the same, all blank bleakness on her tongue.

Next she drank down the small bottle of milk, and abruptly realized that she hadn't used a latrine in what felt like *days*—and after a few moments' frantic glancing around the room, she came to the grim, miserable understanding that nothing here would suffice. And even considering the current state of the room, there was no way she was adding that kind of mess here, surely it would be disobedience of the highest order, surely Simon wouldn't hesitate to send her away after *that*—

Her eyes were squeezing shut, her hands clutching painfully at the bench beneath her—but the need was becoming rapidly more pressing, and gods knew when Simon would return. No doubt he would stay away as long as possible just to spite her, and she had to do this, she would gain her freedom, her *revenge*—

So she lunged for the still-burning candle on the shelf, grasping it tight in her trembling fingers. And before the fear could start shouting, she hurled her loincloth-dressed body toward the open door, and out into the darkness beyond.

The curving corridor felt far larger and darker without Simon's bulk, its smooth walls leading ominously into black shadow. Providing no helpful hint as to where a latrine might be located, but surely one had to exist *somewhere*. There had been no sign so far of the orcs despoiling their own home, no conspicuous smells or stains, which therefore stood to reason—

But as Maria crept down the shadowy corridor, her candle flickering unnerving shapes against the grey walls, she felt the fear skittering higher, closer. There seemed to be no one here, no more voices or telltale noises. And when she carefully peered into the dark doors she passed, they were all entirely empty, with no latrines to be seen—and also no furnishings, no personal effects, no signs of life.

It was odd, Maria's distant thoughts pointed out, that Simon's room was so separated from the rest of his clan—but wait, that den of debauchery had surely been nearby, hadn't it? Surely in this direction, but there seemed to be no sign of it, and had they truly walked this far—

"Ach, woman," came a rumbling voice behind her, and Maria whipped around, her heart leaping—and then plummeting again. No, it wasn't Simon, of course it wasn't, and she *surely* wouldn't care if it was—but all the same, this orc was quite possibly the last orc she would ever wish to find, when standing alone and dressed only in a loincloth in a strange dark corridor.

It was *Ulfarr*. The big, burly, barrel-chested orc, who'd so openly challenged Simon in that awful room, and mocked Maria while all those orcs had watched and leered. This was the orc who'd wanted Simon to *show her off* to them, to make her spurt and squeal...

He was at least wearing trousers this time, but his top half was still fully bare, displaying his broad scarred chest, his massive arms, the ripples of muscle bulging beneath his grey skin. And his lips were curling up, showing sharp white teeth, and Maria realized, with an unpleasant jolt, that he was *smiling.*

"Um, hello," she made herself say, fighting to ignore the slow, unsettling slide of those black eyes down her form. "I'm just searching for a latrine. Or perhaps a chamber-pot?"

But those eyes were still looking, slipping with deliberate slowness over her breasts, her belly, the leather hiding her groin. "Ach, you have needs, woman," Ulfarr said, his voice just as deep and unhurried as his eyes. "And my stubborn brother has not well met these, has he?"

Something cold was prickling up Maria's spine, but she held her chin high, gripped tighter to her candle. "Simon was called away," she managed, "as you know. Could you please direct me to the nearest latrine?"

Ulfarr didn't make to move, or direct her anywhere, and he kept smiling, smooth, easy, unnerving. "Ach, I ken what you seek, woman. But first, mayhap, we shall speak, for a spell? Learn more of one another?"

His eyes had again drifted to Maria's breasts, lingering with distressing intensity, and finally she crossed her arms over them, narrowly missing her own hair with the candle's flickering flame. "I'd rather not, at the moment," she said, "as I'm in quite urgent need of a latrine. Please."

Ulfarr's eyes wandered back to her face, and good gods, he looked... *amused.* Like he was enjoying this, standing here, blocking her, *mocking* her. "Ach, I ken you would forget this latrine," he purred, "if you come with me, and better meet your new brother."

Maria stared at him, because this orc was truly saying this—wasn't he? Saying he—he *wanted* her, but no, no, surely he didn't. Couldn't. Surely it was—

"I wish to better know you, Maria," he said, his voice smooth, soothing, like soft music on her name. "I am sure you must wish for this also. Ach, even my brother Simon should wish for this."

Simon. It scraped down Maria's back, shuddering against the rising chill, and she swallowed hard, glanced beyond Ulfarr down the corridor. "You know, I'm not sure he would," she said, as clearly as she could. "If you'll excuse me—"

She lunged to rush around his huge form, to slip past him, to escape—but in a swift, fluid flick of Ulfarr's hand, her *candle* blinked out. Leaving her standing there in utter blackness, alone with this highly alarming orc, and the panic was steadily rising, clanging, not this, not now, please—

"Come, woman," Ulfarr's deep voice said, and that—oh *hell*—was the feel of a big hand, warm upon her arm. "I shall grant you what you seek."

No, no, this couldn't be happening, Maria's breaths heaving against her hammering heart—and in a fierce jolt, she wrenched herself away, out of his grip. Into the pure darkness of the corridor, she couldn't *see*, where was the wall, this was a wall, if she could just—

But there was a huff of laughter just before her—*he* was before her, how had he moved so silently?!—and her groping hand had brushed against something smooth, hot, powerful. His bare *chest*.

"You shall find great joy with me, woman," his voice murmured. "Skai know pleasure better than any others in this mountain."

The panic shouted louder, deeper, and Maria could feel Ulfarr's warm weight settling closer. His scent swirling into her lungs, heated, sweet, *not Simon*—

"I'm pledged only to *Simon*," Maria's shaky voice pleaded. "I have no interest in finding *anything* with you except a latrine. *Please*."

But Ulfarr only chuckled, low and indulgent, and she could feel him coming yet closer, now backing her flat against the wall, his arms blocking her in, *not Simon*, she'd signed a *contract*—

Maria flailed hard against Ulfarr's bulk, but he was solid, heavy, immovable. And he was easing closer, closer, and this couldn't be happening and why couldn't she speak, scream, *something*, where was the fucking hysteria when she needed it—

"Maria!" roared a voice, Simon's voice, bellowing through the darkness, bristling the hairs all over Maria's skin. "Halt this. *Now!*"

13

Halt this. Now.

The words sounded like ice on Simon's voice, like shards of fury and accusation, and Maria cringed back against the wall, the terror and relief blaring through her skull. Simon was here. Furious, clearly, but *here*.

She could feel him coming closer, could hear the hard rush of his breath streaming through the corridor. And then movement, swift and forceful, as Ulfarr jerked away, leaving Maria blessedly untouched, shivering in the darkness.

"Your new *purchase* was lost," said Ulfarr, and Maria didn't miss the smirk in his voice, the *mockery*. "She sought my... *help*. Ach, woman?"

Maria wanted to spit at him, kick him, thrust something sharp between his ribs—but she couldn't even see the swine's face in the dark, couldn't find a way through the heavy silence from Simon at her side. "I wanted a *latrine*," she said, her voice badly wavering. "That's *all*."

But no one answered, no one came to her defense, or acknowledged that she'd even spoken. And Maria felt the bitter rage rising, lurching in her throat—and she clapped her hand against her mouth before she could start wailing or shouting. And she wasn't supposed to care, she *wasn't*, but why didn't Simon say something, why didn't he move, was he going to send her away, would they just keep standing here until she—

"Come, woman," hissed Simon's voice, slicing through the taut darkness. While hard fingers grasped at her arm, dragging her after him, and Maria staggered to keep up, stumbling through the pitch-black corridor. And when Simon turned her again, off to the left, she nearly lost her footing altogether—until those powerful hands gripped at her waist, and half-carried, half-dragged her over to something, and thrust her down to sit upon it.

Cool air hit Maria's bare arse, and comprehension flooded her brain in bright relief—and before she could stop it, her bladder was releasing its long-held contents, while humiliation burned her cheeks. While Simon just kept standing there, looming close in the blackness, no doubt leering, mocking, *judging*.

Maria's humiliation kept scalding hotter, and with it the bleak, abject certainty that once again, she'd surely somehow displeased him. He hadn't defended her, hadn't called out Ulfarr on his obvious rubbish, hadn't spoken a single word of kindness or comfort. And good gods, Maria needed to stop caring, why was she even expecting such things from a vicious vulgar orc, she hated him, and he obviously hated her, and he only wanted an empty, silent shell for his use. *Only woman I buy. Your purchase. This is all...*

When Maria's ongoing mortification had finally ceased, Simon grasped her arm again, drawing her back to walking. Turning left, and then right, as Maria's distant thoughts realized she must have missed a corridor somewhere—and then the movement abruptly halted, and a flare of light burned across her eyes.

They were back in Simon's room, and he'd lit another candle, glowing with shocking brightness in the dark. And in its light, Maria's squinting eyes instantly locked to Simon, standing massive and menacing beside her. His body taut, his hand clamped on his sword-hilt, his eyes crackling with... rage?

But yes, surely, *rage*. Curling his mouth, drawing his already-harsh face hard and cruel, burning from his throat in a low growl. His muscles flexing and heavily corded, his shoulders hunched, his furious gaze glinting on Maria's face.

Oh gods, oh *hell*, and Maria fought the desperate, swelling urge to wring her hands, to hurl out curses and accusations. Because she'd sworn to this, she would see this through, and he couldn't send her away, please, not *now*, not today. *You shall honour me*, he'd said, *all I shall bear from your mouth is its tight, eager suckling upon my prick...*

Maria's knees buckled beneath her, sudden and painful, but she didn't fight it. Didn't stop her trembling, frantic hands from clutching at that immobile body before her—and yes, finding that powerful hardness, swelling behind his trousers. And he still wanted it, oh please, that had to be a good sign, *had* to be—

Her fingers fumbled, yanked, pulled—and in a rush of musky-smelling warmth, he was out. That thick, veined, vicious beast bulging before her eyes in the candlelight, like an obscene vulgar gift from the gods, its deep slit already oozing white...

"Maria," Simon's flat voice said, and she flinched all over, her gaze snapping up to his face. To where he was watching, of course he was, but the anger somehow seemed to have faded from those eyes, in favour of something almost like... confusion.

"You wish for this," he said, frowning at her—and suddenly there was the urge to scream again, to rage, to clutch the hysteria close and never, ever let it go, *I told you, I want this, I need this, why do you keep doing this to me*—

But somehow—*somehow*—she choked it back, bit her lip, stayed silent. Nodded. Waited. Honoured him.

Simon's head tilted, his heavy brow furrowing, even as his hand smoothly, casually slipped down before Maria's blinking eyes. And in an easy, fluid movement, he reached inside his trousers, and drew out his huge, swollen bollocks, too. Truly displaying himself, flaunting this without shame, simmering something deep within Maria's belly...

But no, *hell* no, she hated him, she was only a woman he'd bought, he wanted her silent and sucking. And she could do this, she wanted this, he would see—

So Maria gulped in more air, courage, her *freedom*. And then leaned closer, parted her dry lips, and—*kissed* him.

It was only a small kiss, brushing gentle against the surprisingly smooth skin of that veined shaft—but the beast instantly leapt against her mouth, hard, hot, eager. As if wanting more of this, wanting *her*, and Maria fought that awareness even as it burrowed, slithering deep.

No. *No.* He only wanted an empty shell. A sucking mouth. That was all.

So she did it again, kissing harder this time, feeling him again leap against her lips. Feeling the hot, silken-smooth skin, shuddering out its pleasure...

Skai know pleasure, Ulfarr had said, and surely Simon knew far better than this—but he still kept swelling, pulsing, vibrating against Maria's carefully searching tongue. And the scent had begun rising from him, rough and rugged, and *that* was because—she drew back slightly, blinking her hazy eyes—he was still oozing from the head, slick, thick, dangling in a string of viscous white.

And if Maria were to lean closer, to just lightly brush her tongue there, she would find—*fire*?! Yes, sweet, hot, liquid fire, burning and shimmering like a thousand molten sparks, and what the hell and what was this and *why*—

She lunged for more, sweeping her tongue closer this time, feeling her eyes flutter at the taste, the heat, the ecstasy. And surely this was pure hysteria, rearing its horrible head, dragging a harsh gasp from her lips as they greedily searched for more...

And from above her, from within the otherwise unmoving bulk of his judgement, Simon—laughed. *Laughed*, mocking her, surely—but when Maria's chagrined, fleeting gaze darted upwards, she found his eyes almost... warm. Indulgent. Approving.

But then they darkened again, as though angry at the very *sight* of her, and Maria felt the panic wash through her again, her throat painfully convulsing. Right. He wanted a shell. A sucking mouth. Not her wants or her voice or her feelings, not *herself*—

So instead of tasting, learning, enjoying, as some awful whispering part of her might have wished to do, she shifted her position, winced at the hardness beneath her bare knees. And then she reached up, took that beast firmly in hand, and thrust it deep between her parted lips.

It fit, but only barely. Filling up the whole of her mouth so tightly that she could scarcely suck or move, and though the fiery taste was still there, it was blunted now, pooling toward the back of her throat. And swallowing felt impossible, suddenly, beyond the mass of pulsing flesh swelling inside her mouth, and oh hell, how was she supposed to *do* this—

She drew off slightly, gulping for breath, granting herself the briefest true taste of fiery sweetness—and then sank deep again, plunging him into her throat. Fighting to ignore the rising tightness in her jaw, the wild heave of her pinched-off breaths, the saliva already pooling shamefully from her stretched-open lips...

But she was doing this, pleasing him, honouring him. And it was fine, she'd chosen this, she'd accepted this, she would *not care*. Even if her husband had always wanted an empty shell too, or even if this was beginning to feel just like *that* had, because this had been one of the few things he'd deigned to give her before he'd stopped coming to her bedroom altogether. Use her throat hard and brief and painful, finish the job and leave again—

Maria's breaths were choking louder, but she kept going, jamming Simon's hardness deep with every endless thrust. Her jaw aching, her head pounding, her knees radiating with pain from the cold stone beneath them. Her eyes prickling, her face smarting and hot, it couldn't last forever, he had to finish at some point, please gods *please*—

"Maria," came his voice, the word a single sharp flare through her whirling thoughts. "Stop."

Stop. Oh gods, he didn't like it, it wasn't good enough—so Maria's frenzied mouth sucked him deeper, gouging him into her gagging throat. Until Simon actually *growled*, deep and hoarse and surely not pleasure, his hand clutching against her hair.

"Stop," he repeated, deeper, an order. "Obey me, woman."

Obey. Right, *that*, and oh gods she was failing, she was losing it, what if he sent her away, he couldn't, not now, he *couldn't*—

Maria had somehow jolted to utter stillness, her mouth still half-full of him, her eyes blinking up at his watching face—and seeing, with a flash of furious misery, that look in his eyes. Distaste. *Disapproval.* She'd honoured him, she was sitting here kneeling naked before an orc, with his—*appendage*—still fully clogging her mouth, and he still *disapproved*—

Something hot slipped down Maria's cheek, not for the first time in this—and that was another flash of misery, plummeting fierce and deep. She was *weeping*, oh gods, she was sucking him off and *weeping*, and no wonder he disapproved, she was *ruining everything*—

He drew himself out, slow, deliberate, devastating. Drowning out any remaining hope Maria might have had of salvaging this, and as the last of him slipped out from her still-sucking mouth, she felt a sob bubble in its wake, escaping between her swollen, stretched lips. How could he take this away too, what happened now, what else would come in this endless hell—

She couldn't seem to stop the weeping, the hysteria finally breaking free for the second time in one damned day, escaping this time in choked, gasping sobs. And Simon just stood there watching, still judging, why couldn't she stop, this was her revenge, her *freedom*—

His voice said something, rumbling past Maria's ears, but she couldn't hear it through the gasping, breaking sobs. Could scarcely even feel it as two strong hands grasped her waist, lifting her up, carrying her bodily across the room.

Her arse sank onto something soft—the furs of his bed—and when she somehow blinked up from where she was sitting, Simon was still standing there, so close, looking back down toward her. With something in his eyes Maria couldn't at all read, and what would he do now, would he finally say it, was this the end—

His hand reached out, slow and intent, his claws carding through Maria's haphazard curls, and she instinctively shivered at the touch, her wet eyes snapped wide. Because he was using the leverage to tilt her head up, while his other hand slipped down, warm, quiet, to stroke against her lips.

"I no wish you to choke," he said, the words carrying no meaning in the mess of Maria's brain. "You only taste. *Suckle.*"

Maria kept blinking, not thinking, as that hand drew her mouth open—and then his huge body eased forward, slow. And that beast was here again, still here, so *close*—and it was brushing its velvet-soft tip to her lips, gently, smearing sweet liquid fire against them.

He pulled it back again, out of her reach, holding her head still—and Maria's only recourse in the chaos was to lick her swollen lips, taste that hot sweetness sparking on her tongue. And Simon nodded, once, *approving*, and leaned in again, smearing more this time, lingering...

This time her lips met it, tasted it, and that was surely a grunt of approval from above, a caress of claws against her scalp. And then again, and again, soft gentle kisses from an orc's smooth oozing prick, shuddering and swelling against her parted lips...

And the taste of him, oh *hell*. Swarming, spluttering, unspooling on her tongue. Such sweet, hot heat, rich and rugged, the full embodiment of his still-unfurling scent. Tempting her, enticing her, to open further, to kiss it deeper, to welcome it inside...

There was another low grunt from above—he *liked* it?—and he drew slightly away again, holding her head still. Giving her just the tip of him again, just that kissing slick slit—and then back to more, seeking into her mouth, pooling its heavy sweetness fuller onto her tongue.

Gods, it was good, and Maria's body had somehow seemed to reorient itself around this, easing away from the misery, the panic, the shame. Instead sinking into the strange, surreal truth of a deadly, menacing orc, standing vicious and powerful before her, and feeding his huge, demanding heft so gently between her eager lips.

And when he sank a little deeper, it felt easier this time. Easier to breathe, to swallow, to *accept*. And better, too, with him shuddering and swelling like that, smooth skin and raised veins dragging so slowly against her lips, the walls of her mouth, just brushing the back of her throat...

He drew out again before she could choke, but the effort to breathe set her teeth reflexively clamping against him, oh *shit*—but a frantic, furtive look up at his eyes sent the fear scattering away again. Because that was still approval, surely, and maybe even—*amusement*.

"I no fear your flat little teeth, woman," he purred, smooth and easy. "Bite me as you wish."

Maria's throat groaned around him, her eyes wildly fluttering, and she felt her teeth clamp again, as if actually *testing* that audacious claim. But there wasn't even a flinch from the heft in her mouth, not a whisper of pain or disapproval in those warm watching eyes.

"Ach, thus," he murmured. "Now suckle me deeper."

It should have been appalling, the way Maria groaned again at that order—but there didn't seem to be space for it. Only the need to ease him further inside, learning this, kissing, tasting, suckling. Revelling in the rising steady growl from his mouth, low and husky and smooth, he liked this, he *wanted* this—

And yes, yes, he *had* to, his hand now dropping to find hers, guiding it up to where his exposed bollocks were still bulging out over his trousers. And Maria obeyed the silent order all too eagerly, stroking tentatively at first, curling her fingers around those soft, heavy weights. And then gripping harder at the audible catch in his groan, the immediate, fundamental shudder of his heft filling her mouth...

Maria's other hand had still been at her side, but now it somehow snapped up too, circling tentative around the massive base of him. Earning an even deeper hiss from his throat, those claws brushing against her scalp, approving, liking it, *wanting* it...

And surely this was even worse than before, with both Maria's hands frantically fondling an orc, while his rock-hard monster kept sliding its way in and out of her stretched, swollen mouth. Picking up strength and speed, invading her, plundering her, saliva streaking and dripping, the noises loud and shameful over the low steady heat of his growl—

But in it, this time, there was also... ease. Relief. Because again, despite everything, he truly did want this. He wanted *her*. He had to, it was here in his approving eyes, in that deep rumble from his chest. In his shuddering heft hesitating as it drew out, lingering to kiss and spurt softly at her suckling lips, before plunging back deep between them—

"When I fill you," he breathed, grinding that slick smooth head into her throat, "you shall swallow all. You shall welcome my cleansing."

Maria nodded, reckless, desperate, while a distant recognition danced, just out of her reach. His cleansing, Enforcer of Orc Mountain, *only woman I buy*...

But surely he wouldn't cleanse one he didn't mean to keep, surely he wouldn't have told her to stop, so he could take such care with her mouth. So he could kiss her and consume her like this, fill her throat with his thrumming ecstasy, cleanse her fresh and new—

"And after," he gasped, his low voice fraying, his heft plunging, ploughing, *owning*, "your clean mouth shall speak with care. You shall seek to watch, and listen, and learn. You shall seek to become a true Skai, fit to bear a strong Skai son. Ach?"

And despite that deeply alarming mention of his offspring, something rippled from Maria's chest, thrilling to her head and her toes. Simon *wanted* her to speak. He would cleanse her mouth. And she needed it, suddenly, craved it with wheeling desperation, sucking him deeper, embracing his powerful onslaught. Learning to accept, to *be*, he was relief he was *peace*, fuck, *please*—

One last gouge into her throat, a hard, juddering jerk against her tongue—and the molten, liquid sweetness surged, and *flooded* her. Pumping out again and again, spurting thick and fast into her throat, and she couldn't possibly swallow all this, oh gods—

But there was nowhere else for it to go, his massive girth holding still, stretching her lips tight, blocking off all escape. And that was surely a challenge, sparking in those watching eyes—and somehow Maria swallowed down one mouthful, and another, and another. Again and again, until the blooming surge finally faded to a slow trickle, oozing warm and sweet onto her tongue.

She kept sucking until he drew away, slipping his spent heft out through her lips with surprising care. And his black eyes on hers had changed again, flicking to something else. Not challenging. Not judging. Just... watching.

And Maria was watching back, blinking hard, her brain slowly beginning to whirl again. Darting back to what had come before this, what came next...

"Peace, woman," Simon said, his voice heavy. "This pleased me."

Maria felt herself nod, silent and jerky, but the unease kept welling, the uncertainty rising. She surely *had* displeased him before this, he *had* been angry, he hadn't defended her against Ulfarr, he'd done *nothing*—

"Peace, Maria," Simon continued, with a sigh. "I no wish you to always taste of such anger and fear."

The urge to laugh was suddenly almost overpowering, but Maria somehow kept her mouth clamped shut, her eyes fixed to the coarse fabric of his grey trousers, still stretched tight over his powerful thighs. And she made herself nod, jerking her head up and down, she didn't care, he was just an orc, whatever he wished...

"Maria," he said again, and she could feel his hand still on her face tilting it up, wanting her to look at him. "I shall no harm you. You have naught to fear from me."

The disbelief crashed over Maria with astonishing force, and she couldn't stop the sound from her throat this time, thick and incredulous. "Naught to fear?!" she echoed, her voice shrill. "There is *everything* to fear from you, Simon! Just today, you refused to allow me to properly dress, you mocked me to a room full of strangers, you made me your *prisoner*, you threatened to send me *away*! And when I *tried* to obey you today, I nearly had your horrible friend *attack* me in a *corridor*!"

Shit, *shit*, and she forcibly bit her lip, squeezed her eyes shut, clamped her fingers tight on her bare knees. "And I keep *saying* this shit to you," she heard herself say, her voice cracking. "*Feeling* this shit. I know you don't want it, and I sure as hell don't want it, I just want to stop caring, and do what I agreed to do! I have to, I *need* to, but—"

The silence rang out after her voice, watching, *judging*, and she shook her head, even as the rest of the words kept spewing free. "But what if you send me away, to deal with our son alone?" she choked. "I would never want to—to *prevent* him, so what happens to me then? To *him*? Or—or what if you really *are* trying to advertise me, or compromise me, so you can wash your hands of me, and hand me off to another orc? To maybe sell me to the highest bidder? To—*Ulfarr*?"

She winced as she spoke his name, the fear and revulsion surging in her belly, and she could feel her breaths coming shorter, sharper. Because yes, this fear had been lingering, whispering, ever since Ulfarr had said with such certainty, *My brother Simon should wish for this*—

There was a strange sound from above her, rasping, convulsive— and in a swift heave of movement, Simon sank onto the bed beside her. Not touching her, not looking at her, but instead with his bare upper body leaning forward, his elbows on his trousered knees, his clawed hand rubbing against his stubbled sharp jaw.

"No, woman," he said, sounding oddly... worn. *Tired.* "I ought no have spoken thus to you today, in my rage. I shall no allow any of these. I shall *never* send you away to birth or raise my son alone. And Ulfarr shall *never* touch you or frighten you thus *again*."

The fury had crept back into his voice at the end, and Maria blinked sideways at him, frowning. "But you didn't," she gulped, "*care*."

It came out sounding like an accusation, a curse, and she saw him twitch beside her, his hand clenching against his mouth. "Ach, I care," he said, his voice flat. "I ken all that Ulfarr sought. He saw this chance to steal you away from me. For a *play* against me. A *game*."

There was sheer hatred in his voice again, the tension shuddering back into his shoulders. "I marked you and sought to claim you before my kin, as our ways demand," he continued, his jaw jumping in his cheek. "I even *dress* you as Skai mate. This is to prove you are mine, and thus keep you safe. I no *fathomed* that Ulfarr would take his game against me thus far."

Maria's whirling brain fought to digest this, to match it to the sudden, visceral *rage* in Simon's voice, in his clamped-tight form. So maybe—maybe his anger hadn't been directed toward her, after all. It had been toward... *Ulfarr?*

"But why would anyone do such a thing, for a *game*?" Maria heard herself ask, her voice plaintive. "What does Ulfarr have against you?"

Besides your many obvious and grievous faults, she could have said— but she didn't. Just sat, watched, waited. Seeing Simon's big chest rise and fall, his unblinking eyes fixed to the opposite wall.

"I am Enforcer of Orc Mountain," he said finally. "Before me, Ulfarr's father held this place among the Skai for many, many summers. Ulfarr has thus wished for this place for all his days, and yet sees it as his rightful due."

Oh. "So now Ulfarr's trying to undermine you... by *stealing* me?" Maria asked, hoarse. "And that's just *fine* around here?!"

Simon huffed a heavy sigh, his hands clenching against his thighs. "When I *buy* you thus," he said slowly, "I test the ways of the Skai. Should I have wished you for a true mate"—he exhaled, his jaw again grinding—"I should have hunted you. Failing this, I should have led a rut upon you, as Ulfarr said. These are the ways of the Skai. It is only this *contract* that escaped this for you. You are *no* my true mate. You are only woman I *pay*."

Right. Maria swallowed hard, not quite able to speak, and she watched blankly as Simon's hand snapped up behind his head—and then flipped out that *dagger*. The dagger he'd somehow still been wearing in his *hair*, and he twirled it in his clawed fingers, frowning down at its flashing steel blade.

"When Skai orcs break our ways," he said, deliberate, as though weighing each word, "the Enforcer seeks truth, and then chooses their fate, as he sees fit. His justice holds great power, and stands above all claims. Thus"—he exhaled, slow—"when Ulfarr seeks to steal you after I claimed you thus, he plays Enforcer with *me*. He takes my own mantle upon himself, and thus mocks me and judges me before my kin."

So Ulfarr's horrid behaviour in the corridor had been an attempt at *punishment*, then. A public challenge against Simon, for presuming to enforce his people's adherence to their ways, while also apparently testing those ways himself. By accepting Maria's proposal as he had, without the hunt required by his clan. Without the... *rut*.

"And do I want to know," Maria whispered, "what a rut is?"

Simon's shoulder jerked a shrug, and she watched his finger test the sharp tip of his blade, hard enough to draw a bead of blood. "I would choose a band," he said, "and we would each have you. Me first, and last. When you swell with son, the orc who has fathered it keeps you as his own."

Maria's stomach roiled and churned, her eyes gaping at Simon's harsh profile. "You wouldn't," she gasped. "Would you? Truly *do* that to a woman? That's—that's—and how would any woman *ever* want you again after that, and how would you even *know* whose son it was, I—"

She belatedly clamped her mouth shut, whipping her head back and forth, as though to thrust the vision out—but thankfully Simon didn't seem to take offense, and shrugged again as he flipped his dagger from hand to hand. "We smell this, oft soon after it is done," he said. "And ruts are no oft held now, for most Skai would rather hunt a mate, and thus be sure to keep her. But"—his chest hollowed—"this is yet the way of our clan fathers, from many ages past."

Good *gods*. Maria could only gape at him, shock clashing against sheer disbelief—but as she stared, it occurred to her that this was *reluctance* in Simon's form, his face. That he hadn't *wanted* to do that. That he was testing his own clan's ways, to avoid doing that. Risking his own place of power among his people. Giving his long-time rival a chance to publicly move against him.

And while Maria surely shouldn't care about Simon's horrible-sounding job, or the fact that he was risking it by flaunting his people's horrible-sounding rules—she also, perhaps, *understood*. More than she'd understood yet in this exhausting, utterly bewildering day.

"So why can't you just... enforce *Ulfarr*, then?" she asked. "Denounce him, or fight him off, or whatever you do, and put him in his place? Surely, this whole situation today would give you valid grounds to do so?"

And maybe that was pure presumption on her part, wildly inflating her own importance in this—but Simon gave a sharp nod, his hands spinning the dagger so fast it was a silvery blur. "Ach, it shall now soon come to this," he said toward it. "But I no dare risk this battle yet. There is work I first need finish. Work I must no leave undone."

Maria felt her head tilting, her brow furrowing. "What does that have to do with anything?" she asked. "Can't you just finish your work *after* you deal with Ulfarr?"

Simon shook his head, his gaze fixed to his still-spinning dagger. "With this battle," he said, "comes another way of my clan. Should I fail to win this fight for my place as Enforcer, I shall lose all."

Lose all. There was something about the way he'd said that, the finality biting on his tongue, and Maria studied his harsh profile, the blankness in his eyes. "Lose all?"

"Ach," he replied, clipped now. "All. My blades. My goods. My mate, should I have one. My son. My *life*."

What?! Maria's mouth had fallen open, her body snapped to utter, chilly stillness under the fur. "You mean—you would fight Ulfarr to the *death*?!" she demanded, her voice shrill. "And if he won, he would then take *everything* that's yours? Even your *mate*, and your *children*?! And your clan would *approve* of this?!"

Simon's nod was slow, deliberate, and Maria had to haul in air, breathe over the renewed churning in her gut. "That's *barbaric*," she choked, before she could stop it. "Your clan sounds *horrible*. Appalling. *Disgusting*."

Simon's eyes had suddenly narrowed, angling sharp toward her, and he abruptly jerked to his feet, up, away. And it was as though the barrier had slammed back down between them, thick and impenetrable, reeking of angry, bitter judgement.

"Ach, and what of *your* people?" Simon sneered over his shoulder. "*They* no freely kill, and steal, and swear their cruel ways in ink? They no crush those beneath them with their laws and their lies? They no fight war against my kin that goes back beyond *memory*?!"

Maria winced, and Simon whirled to face her again, his shining dagger now gripped tight in his flexing fingers. "My clan is *dying*," he hissed at her. "At the hand of *yours*. You no see why we cling to our ways, in the face of this? You no see why we cling to what power we find, when we must *mate* with humans who *destroy* us?"

Oh. *Oh.* And while Maria might well have argued, perhaps, that one cruelty didn't merit another, that women surely weren't out there actively murdering orcs, that orcs had done plenty of murdering themselves—instead she only sat there, struck still and silent. And thinking, oddly, of—her *husband.*

Her husband, with his ceaseless vendetta against these orcs. Her husband, who indeed created and enforced cruel laws, based on little more than his fear. Her husband, who so desperately wanted to start another *war.*

And for her husband's sins, Maria was actively seeking vengeance upon him. Spitting in the face of his weakness. Clinging to what power she could find.

And sitting here, blinking up at Simon's stony eyes, it occurred to Maria that *he* was doing it, too. He'd already risked his job—and perhaps his *life?!*—by agreeing to do this with her, and now he was clinging to what power he could find in it. *Obey me. Come. Suckle. Honour me before my kin.*

And Maria had sworn that to him, written it in ink, in the way of her people, her *husband*—and then she'd turned and openly condemned him. Said all those furious things. *Vulgar. Crude. Awful. A coarse, hideous, dim-witted tyrant.*

I hate you.

And it was *true*, and he was just an orc, she wasn't supposed to care—but Maria's loincloth-clad form had somehow lurched up off the bed, straight toward Simon's rigid, watching body. Not knowing what the hell she was doing, what she was thinking—at least, until she hurled herself full against his solid chest, one hand clinging around his stiff back, the other slipping up to find the safety of his rapidly thundering heart.

"Thank you for explaining all this to me," she heard herself whisper, into the warm skin under her mouth. "I—understand, more than I did before."

She could feel his chest rising and falling against her, the race of his heartbeat slowing beneath her fingers. "Ach, I ken," he said finally, his voice rough. "You know not me or my ways. I must better speak of these. I must learn how to better teach you, amidst all your *feeling*."

There was a beat of silence between them, while something almost like astonishment flashed through Maria's thoughts. He—wanted to speak to her. He wanted to teach her. He wanted to help her... understand? Amidst her *feeling*?

"Ach, you are weary, woman," he said, his voice back to clipped again, even as she felt his hand settle, big and warm, against the small of her back. "You shall further rest now."

There was the distant urge to protest, to point out that she surely hadn't been awake for even half a day—but then, far stronger, came the understanding that this was still an order. That Simon still expected her to obey. To do whatever the hell he wanted. To honour him.

But as he looked down toward her, his black brows raised over watching eyes, it suddenly felt—different. Not mocking anymore. But instead... waiting. Assessing.

So Maria swallowed, and then slipped away from his touch, and strode toward the bed. Feeling his steady gaze upon her as she went, close, prickling, intent.

It wasn't until she was tucked under the warm fur again that she risked a glance back up toward him. Finding, still, that heavy, silent watching, almost as if he was deciding something—and then a curt, quick little nod. He *approved*.

"I shall stay, whilst you rest," he said. "There is naught more to fear, whilst I am with you."

Maria nodded back, while an inexplicable relief seemed to settle upon her, sinking deep into the softness of the bed. She'd pleased him, and now he would stay, now she was safe...

But wait. No. *No*. In the few hours since Maria had awoken today, Simon had subjected her to exposure, humiliation, and shame unlike any she'd ever known. He'd imprisoned her, he'd left her alone in a deeply precarious position, he'd thrown at her all these rules, those *implements*, he hadn't even offered a damned chamber-pot, and she was still wearing an actual *loincloth*...

But in this moment, as Maria watched him silently stalk over to sprawl in his usual place on the bench, his free hand grasping for one of his scattered stones, she almost... somehow... *accepted* it. Yes, he was still horrible, his clan was still deeply appalling, and she probably still hated him, and she still wasn't supposed to even *care*, and...

And. "It pleased me, when you honoured me as you did today, even in the face of your fear," his low voice rumbled, beneath the loud shirr of his rock against the blade. "After this, I shall take more care with you. I shall no place you in such danger again. I shall keep you safe."

Oh. And somehow, there was more quiet, more relief. More warmth settling low in Maria's belly, soothing the last of her tension, slowing the pulse of her heart.

She'd *pleased* him. He'd *liked* it. She was *safe*.

And with that strange, tenuous certainty rocking against her ribs, Maria closed her eyes, and slipped off into sleep.

14

Maria's awareness returned with a low shirring sound, pooling into her ears. Smooth, steady, rock against stone, hissing again and again into the silence.

She yawned and rolled over, and let her bleary eyes linger on the sight. On this orc, sitting upon that same bench, sliding a stone against the gleaming scimitar in his lap. He was wearing trousers again, but nothing else—and without looking up, he gave a telltale jerk of his head toward Maria. Saying, again, *come.*

And this time, Maria didn't protest. Didn't delay, or hide behind the fur. Instead, she slipped to her feet, straightened her loincloth, and then strode across the room toward him.

The approval was there, flashing brief through Simon's lingering eyes, and for an instant, Maria thought—*hoped?*—that he might reach for her, draw her close. But instead, he reached for something nearby—perhaps one of his tunics, rumpled and massive—and held it up before her.

"This day past, you pleased me," he said, slow, deliberate. "You showed yourself eager, and quick to learn for me. And thus, as your reward"—he tossed the tunic toward her—"you may wear this today, should you wish."

Wait, she could *wear* something?! Maria blinked down at the tunic, thoroughly astonished—and before Simon could change his mind, she swiftly shook it out, and yanked it on. It fit rather like an oversized sack, reaching nearly to her knees—but she wasn't complaining, because it was still clothes, and it still covered *everything*. And after an instant's silent frowning at her, Simon even grasped for a long strip of leather that had been strewn nearby, and tossed that over, too.

Maria willingly tied the leather around her waist, and then rolled up the huge sleeves, all of which improved the ensemble significantly. And for an instant, there was the rising, highly irrational urge to grin at him, or to reach and stroke his muscled shoulder, or even to find his lips with hers. To *thank* him, good gods, for granting her the basic decency of *dressing*, and not even in her own *clothes*.

"Um, so does this mean," Maria managed instead, "you'll allow me to dress from now on, then?"

Simon's eyes studied her for a moment too long, his black brows rising. "I no say that," he replied, voice cool. "I say you please me, this day past, so I reward you. You please me more, I reward you more."

Wait. Maria stared at him for a blank, blinking instant, while the disbelief crept through her thoughts. Simon was going to—*bribe* her, with *clothes*? This damned orc, who last night had been so intent, so sympathetic, almost even vulnerable—had now decided to play a *game* with her?

And for an orc who supposedly hated games so much, this was surely a brutally effective one. Because Maria was already clinging reflexively to her new tunic, while also fighting the sudden, helpless compulsion to beg, or shout, or spit straight at his smug, insolent, arrogant face.

"Look, I already signed that damned contract," her voice snapped at him, before she could bite back the words. "And as I showed you yesterday—*again*—I'm committed to this, and I've honoured you in multiple *extremely* explicit ways. There is no need whatsoever for you to start playing some kind of twisted new *game* with me!"

But the challenge was still there in Simon's eyes, his lip curling. "This is no *game*, woman," he said, calm, infuriating. "I spoke of this to you before you slept, and since then, I have dwelt long upon this. There is much you must yet learn, if you are to earn my trust, and become a true Skai. But"—he leaned forward, and jabbed his clawed finger toward her—"you yet fear our ways, ach? You fear my kin. You fear *me*."

Maria swallowed, and opened her mouth to make some very well-justified statements about his horrible clan, and their horrible *ways*—but Simon hissed a low growl, and jabbed his claw again. "I no blame you for your *feeling*, woman," he continued flatly, "but I yet no wish for your fear. I wish to have you again hungry, and willing, and eager to learn for me—but *without* this fear, ach? Thus"—his lip curled into something that might have been intended as a smile—"we seek new way. You seek to honour me, I seek to reward you."

With that, he leaned back against the wall, as though supremely satisfied with this new pronouncement. Leaving Maria to gape open-mouthed toward him, while her thoughts clanged and clambered through her skull. "You're truly proposing that you—*train* me?" she said, the incredulity far too clear in her voice. "Like I'm some kind of disobedient *lap dog*? And I don't get any kind of say in this?!"

Simon's eyes narrowed, but he didn't move, beyond folding his arms over his muscled chest. "I no make you *pet*, I make you *Skai*," he said, as if this were a crucial distinction. "And you have already sworn to honour me in ink, ach? You are yet bound to obey me, whether I grant you reward or no. You wish me to take my reward back?"

And in an impossibly swift flash of movement, his huge hand was gripping at the neck of her new tunic, threatening to take it, to *tear* it—and Maria yanked away from him, her eyes wide, her fingers clutching it close. "No," she choked out. "No. *Please*."

And gods, it was humiliating, pathetic, and Simon leaned back again, smiling and complacent. "Ach, I thought thus," he said, his voice enragingly smooth. "You shall learn, woman."

Maria glared down toward him, her arms still crossed tightly over her tunic, and Simon kept smirking as he rose to his feet, looming huge and deadly over her. "And we shall start now," he said, striding over to his shelf, and grasping for a lantern Maria hadn't noticed before. "Come."

Come. Complete with a sharp little jab toward the floor beside him, as though Maria really were a wayward puppy he'd decided to whip into shape. And between the still-curdling outrage and disbelief, there was something even more infuriating—the fact that there was no actual reason to refuse. Because he was still *right*, curse him.

She'd signed that contract. She'd sworn to obey him. And if he'd decided to start giving her rewards in the bargain, she should damn well just accept it, and humour him, and take whatever the hell she could get. He was just an orc. For her freedom.

But even so, Maria couldn't seem to stop glaring at him as she stiffly strode across the room, and halted in the spot he'd indicated. Earning for her efforts another smug smirk, and then the abrupt sight of his broad bare back as he stalked toward the corridor.

Maria silently followed, her hands in fists, her eyes darting uneasily at all the smooth stone around her. It was far easier to see it all in the bright light of Simon's lamp, and she couldn't deny a spark of surprise as he led her through a nearby empty room, and then into a smaller, twistier corridor that had been tucked into a crevice in the back wall.

"I take you to the Skai shrine," Simon said over his shoulder, as he turned into another hidden, tucked-away corridor. "Here, you shall learn to worship with me and my kin."

She would? Maria shot him a blank, startled look—she'd never been a particularly pious person, especially after the gods had so cruelly betrayed her with her marriage—but of course Simon entirely ignored it, and ushered her into a warm, sweet-scented room.

And despite Maria's still-curdling irritation at all this—at him— she couldn't help glancing around with genuine interest. The room appeared to be carved in a circle, with multiple doors in the rounded wall, and a variety of fur-covered benches scattered about. And in the room's very middle, there stood a cluster of life-sized figures, carved out of yet more stone.

And as Simon stepped closer, raising the lamp, Maria realized that the stone figures were all orcs, and that they were unnervingly lifelike. And, perhaps more unnerving still, none of them wore *clothes*— instead, they all proudly displayed bared chests, muscled limbs, and distinctive, swollen *monsters* at their groins.

"You shall worship Skai-kesh, the father of the Skai," Simon announced, with a purposeful wave toward the largest figure, who was also, predictably, the most impressively endowed. "I shall now show

Skai-kesh the rite of my favour, whilst you offer him your prayer. He seeks three new truths each day: a fear, a longing, and a blessing. Ach?"

Maria's uneasy eyes were flicking up and down the figure—*Skai-kesh*—who along with his shocking genitalia also boasted a mess of cropped black hair, and a pair of oddly unnerving, black-painted eyes. They were unsettling enough that she had to glance away, and she found Simon staring down at her with equally unnerving intensity.

"Ach?" he repeated, his voice hard, his hand waving toward the nearest bench. "Kneel, and honour me."

The rebellion flared brief and powerful in Maria's gut—Simon had truly decided to dictate who and how she *worshipped*, as part of his damned *game*?!—but she forcibly shoved it down again, and drew in a deep breath. She'd sworn to honour him. She would take what she could get, and gain her damned freedom. And truly, of all the things Simon could be demanding right now, a prayer was surely manageable. *Surely.*

So Maria made herself nod, and lurched stiffly toward the bench. It was higher and wider than she'd first supposed, almost more like a table—and as she clambered onto it, there was the sudden, startling feel of Simon's big hand on her waist, helping her up. And then that hand *lingered* there, holding her bottom half in place, fingers spreading wide against her hip...

Maria twitched all over, and whipped her head around to look at him—and wait, wait, *wait*. That was surely another challenge in his eyes, brazen, *taunting*—and he'd moved to stand closer behind her, enough that she could feel his warmth radiating through her tunic. And then—she gulped aloud—his clawed hand slowly, deliberately reached down inside his trousers, and brought out—

That. Yes, good gods, *that*. Huge, veined, swelling and filling, jutting out toward her. Looking far too similar to the stone depiction at this Skai-kesh's groin, and wait, surely this wasn't that, *surely*—

"S-Simon," Maria gasped, and oh *hell*, he was already drawing up her baggy tunic, exposing her loincloth beneath it. "What the *fuck* are you doing?"

Simon's eyes narrowed on hers, stubborn and scornful. "I show Skai-kesh my favour toward you," he repeated, with exaggerated patience. "Thus, I must fill you and cleanse you whilst you pray, this first time. It is a rite of the Skai. Should you wish to gain my next reward"—his brows rose, cool and imperious—"you shall seek to please me, and welcome this."

His next reward. Gods, this infuriating *prick* and his infuriating damned game, he could not truly mean this, he couldn't—

But his warm hand was already skating up Maria's exposed hip, catching on her loincloth—and then he flipped that up, too. Fully exposing her bare, bent-over arse to the room's cool air, and suddenly it was like she was spinning, twirling into an inconceivable abyss, as she felt Simon spreading her legs apart, shifting forward, closer, until—

She yelped aloud, because wait, *shit*, this was indeed truly *that*— and Simon was truly *there*, nudging hard and smooth and slick against her exposed, spread-apart heat. And this was clearly a public room, surely other orcs could walk in at any moment and see *everything*, and Maria was a *duchess* and this was truly *appalling*—

But for some ridiculous reason, she couldn't even seem to speak. Because all the world had somehow again coiled into this, an orc standing massive and menacing behind her, his big warm hands gripped easy and proprietary to her bare hips. While his huge, hot, shuddering heft kept prodding her, its rounded head sinking slightly deeper, just beginning to spread her open upon it...

"S-Simon," Maria finally gasped, even as her eyes rolled back, her shocking heat clutching close and convulsive against the strength seeking to invade it. "Th-this is a *p-public room*."

"Ach," came his reply, shameless, *mocking*. "You no wish many others to see, you open wide for me in a hurry, and you *pray*."

Oh, good *gods*. A full-body shiver swept down Maria's back, and there was the awareness, brief but desperately powerful, that she surely needed to refuse this, yank herself safely away from this, tell him just how completely and thoroughly *outrageous* he was—

But instead, a low moan had escaped her mouth, and she again felt herself spasm against that hot, seeking truth. And flashing across her thoughts, inexplicably, was a vision of the night before, of the sheer power of their joined hunger, followed by the quiet weight of his words. *You no see why we cling to what power we can find in this. You shall welcome my cleansing. You shall become a true Skai...*

And no, no, surely Maria was not imagining she *understood* this orc again—let alone wanting to become one of his clan. Not when the Skai were obviously so completely horrid, when they didn't *dress*, and had whole *rooms* devoted to debauchery, and had rules that required thefts of other living *beings*, and *ruts*, and fights to the *death*. And even their worship couldn't be straightforward, when one apparently needed to be publicly *filled* while doing so...

"Open, woman," insisted Simon's hard voice behind her. "You wish to honour me, and earn my reward. You wish for *me*. Ach?"

And gods curse him, because it was still this enraging orc... *asking*. Making sure Maria wanted this, still, even in the face of his damned *training*. And swirling between the sensation and the rebellion there was something else, something stronger, almost like... *determination*?

And it had to be the hysteria, surely. *Surely*. But Maria somehow felt herself gritting her teeth, sucking in a bracing, shuddery breath—and then... *agreeing*. Shifting her knees a little wider, arching her back, tilting her arse up toward him. Willing herself to relax, to open for him, even if this was public, even if someone else walked in. Saying... yes. *Yes*.

Simon didn't even acknowledge it, the bastard, but Maria could feel the huff of his breath on her bare arse, his sharp claws nudging against her hips as he pushed a little deeper. Parting her tight heat wider around him, drilling into her with his throbbing rounded smoothness, piercing her upon him...

Maria's breaths were already dragging, high-pitched, because even after the first time, gods, this was still so *much*. Too much, stretching her, punching ever stronger into her, pulsing its slick liquid thick and powerful inside. And she couldn't even think beyond the fullness, the power, he felt so good, gods he had *no right* to feel so fucking *good*—

"More, woman," hissed Simon's voice behind her. "*Pray*."

Pray. And oh gods, what the hell had she been supposed to pray, and she somehow raised her fluttering eyes to Skai-kesh—or rather, to the heft at his groin, to the heft that was still sinking into her, breath by breath...

And suddenly, Maria felt horribly, wildly exposed. Bared and kneeling in a public room, ogling an indecent god, while the real-life orc behind her drove his own huge ramrod strength deep between her spread-wide legs. And he still couldn't even be halfway yet, this wasn't even close to over yet, and—

"Pray," he ordered again, huskier this time, as he sank a little deeper, spreading her wider, pushing against her resistance. "A fear. A longing. A blessing."

Maria couldn't think, couldn't take it, couldn't do anything but gasp and choke and stare. Feeling the truth of this, the raw power of this, pierced and exposed in a shrine, a rite, the craving. A true Skai. A fear. A longing. A blessing...

"Y-you," she gasped, without at all meaning to, as she felt herself clamp even closer against him, trapping him there, sealing tight. "You, Simon. For all three. Fear. Longing. *Blessing.*"

Hysteria, her distant swirling brain chanted, surely she didn't long for this, surely this obnoxious orc wasn't a blessing in the slightest— but she'd said it, and the words felt real, just as real as he was, splitting her open and exposed upon him—

There was a near-silent groan behind her, the almost-painful clench of sharp claws against her hips. As the beast invading her swelled, caught, flared deep inside—and then released. Surging Maria full of his hot, liquid heat, in pulse after shuddering, powerful pulse, flooding her with his truth, his approval, his *cleansing*.

And in the shocked unreality of this moment, with Maria still impaled upon a spurting, gasping orc, and blinking up at the obscene god—Skai-kesh—before her, there was almost... *relief*. Relief in the god's glinting black eyes, in the still-shuddering heft jutted halfway up inside her.

"I ask your blessing, father, upon this woman," came Simon's voice behind her, hoarse, breathless, *sincere*. "I beg you to sate her fear. Grant her longing. And pour out deeper blessing upon her."

The words flashed an odd, visceral thrill up Maria's back—Simon was begging the god to give her more of *himself*? Almost as though he truly did want this, as though he *approved*...

And when he drew away from Maria, leaving what felt like an unholy mess in his wake, his warm hands on her lingered. Slipping soft against heated skin, caressing with something that felt almost like reverence...

And again, almost like *approval*. Like relief... or like *peace*. Like a slowly spreading quiet, deep in Maria's soul...

"Good, Simon?" cut in a low, heavily accented voice. "You like?"

The *hell*?! Maria's body froze in place, her head whipping around, her eyes frantically searching in the dim light—

And there, shit, *there*. Leaning casually against the wall beside them, arms crossed, his eyes glinting with an unnerving, impossible awareness.

It was... another orc. And he'd seen *everything*.

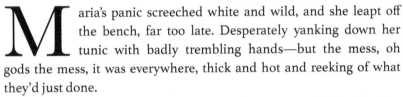

15

Maria's panic screeched white and wild, and she leapt off the bench, far too late. Desperately yanking down her tunic with badly trembling hands—but the mess, oh gods the mess, it was everywhere, thick and hot and reeking of what they'd just done.

And the watching orc knew, he saw it, he was *amused*. His glittering eyes flicking down below the hem of Maria's baggy tunic, and back up to her face. And she could see the challenge in his eyes, the waiting curiosity, the anticipation. As if he fully expected her to panic, to run, to collapse into hysterics, for his gods-damned *entertainment*.

And oddly enough, that awareness somehow seemed to catch the panic, holding it still, while Maria's narrow eyes darted up to Simon, searching his face. His harsh, set face, written all over with stubbornness, and with... *guilt*. Because curse the bastard, he'd *known*. He'd *known* this strange orc was watching. Had perhaps *wanted* him to watch.

"Ach," Simon said, pulling up his still-hanging trousers with unhurried ease—and Maria realized, aghast, that he was answering the orc's previous question, about whether he'd *liked* her. "She is sweet. Ripe. Eager."

Wait, she was? But the watching orc was already jerking a curt, complacent nod, almost as though he'd expected no less—and then he *winked* at Simon, pushed off the wall, and strode past them out of the room. Giving Maria a better look at his tall, wiry form, his wild cropped-short hair, the clear satisfaction in his glinting black eyes.

And standing there, glaring up at Simon's stubborn, set face, there were surely a dozen well-justified things Maria might have said. *How dare you hide something like that from me, you could have at least said something to me, you wanted to expose me and shame me, you've been wanting to do so ever since I came here...*

But then, already, she could hear Simon's answers, curt and angry. *You swore to this. I spoke to you of this. I wish to flaunt you before my kin. You no wish for this? You wish me to take back my reward? Now you run?*

So Maria forcibly bit her lip, and swallowed hard, and crossed her arms tight over her chest. Waiting, stiff and still, while Simon finished tying up his trousers, his eyes on hers almost intent enough to be a touch. And perhaps he was waiting too, for the inevitable argument or hysterics, for another opportunity to wield his damned *judgement*.

But Maria only stood there in silence, staring at the floor, the tension jangling in her ears—until finally she felt Simon's hand on her chin, tilting it up, making her look at him.

"It pleases me, that you welcomed this rite from me," he said, quiet. "It pleases Skai-kesh also. I am glad I brought you before him."

Oh. Well. Maria jerked a shrug, her eyes darting reflexively, darkly, toward this Skai-kesh, and then toward where that strange orc had been *watching* them—and again Simon lifted her chin, snapping her gaze back to his.

"This orc was Joarr, the Chief Scout of this mountain," Simon explained, to Maria's vague surprise. "When Joarr no wish to be seen, he shall no be seen, ach? But he is mayhap the nearest I have to blood kin, and he has granted me a great kindness of late. It was right that he, of all orcs, should first witness this."

First witness this. Suggesting, all too clearly, that there would be more in the future—but before Maria could fully digest this thoroughly alarming thought, Simon had slid a broad hand down to spread against her back. "Now come," he said firmly. "For this, you have earned your next reward."

Her next reward. The rebellion again flared through Maria's belly, thick and powerful, but she somehow choked back her waiting retort, and walked through the twisty corridor beside him. He was just an orc. She would take what she could get. Gain her damned freedom. And that was *all*.

Simon seemed to be leading her back the way they'd come, and Maria recognized the door to his bedroom—but instead of stopping there, he led her into another room just beyond it. This one again appeared empty, at first sight, but in the back there turned out to be another hidden crevice, which housed a little... *latrine*?

"Your reward, woman," Simon announced, with a grand flourish of his hand. "You may now come here, and use this, when you need."

Maria once again felt struck to stillness, gaping around at the little room in the lamplight. It was small and stark, but seemed mercifully clean—and there was even a little stack of rags, and what looked like proper drainage, to gods knew where. But. But...

"You're really giving me *potty privileges*," Maria heard her incredulous voice say, "as a reward for *converting* to your *religion*?!"

And curse her, but something new was lurching in her throat. Something that surely should have been outrage at the sheer audacity of this orc... but which instead felt like a rising, almost irrepressible urge to *laugh*.

"Ach, I am," came Simon's reply, his eyebrow raised, his voice impossibly cool. "You no wish for this reward? You wish to instead have little pail to piddle in, mayhap?"

And in spite of all Maria's most heroic efforts, the bubbling laugh finally escaped her mouth, far too loud in this cramped room. "You *prick*," she managed. "If you make me use a pail, I *will* dump it on you while you sleep, I swear to the gods."

Something moved in Simon's eyes, and Maria belatedly braced herself for his retaliation, his certain deadly anger—but wait, his mouth had actually twitched up too, sparking something quick and hot in her belly.

"I should like to see you try this, woman," he purred. "Now use your new latrine for me, before I choose to instead fuck you raw upon it."

Maria's face swarmed with heat, and she couldn't seem to muster a coherent retort, or even demand he leave the room. And once she'd

finished, that was surely again approval in his eyes, in the easy brush
of his hand against her back as he led her out into the corridor
again.

"And for your next reward," Simon continued, his voice sounding
almost chipper, "I have gained you Baldr. He has agreed to stay beside
us for a time, to help guard you whilst I am away."

There was only more bewilderment at this, swarming Maria's flustered brain—where was Simon going, and she needed *guarding*?—but
he had already halted at the door to the room just beside his, waving
Maria toward it. And when she tentatively stepped inside, there,
indeed, was Baldr. Kneeling next to a big wooden box, and unloading
its contents—furs, clothing, more weapons—into a neat set of piles
around him.

"Greetings, Maria," he said with a grin, as he rose to his feet. "We
shall now be neighbours, ach?"

Maria couldn't deny an inexplicable relief at this announcement,
but she also felt her forehead furrowing, her eyes glancing around at
the otherwise empty room. "Um, that sounds lovely," she said. "But
you're from the Grisk clan, right? Surely you don't wish to be parted
from them, in order to be stuck alone in here?"

Baldr's dismissive shrug was accompanied by a somewhat
reddened face, and behind Maria Simon huffed a loud snort. "It shall
be no hardship for Baldr to stay here," he replied, his voice more
tolerant than Maria might have expected. "And he shall no oft be
alone here either, I ken. No with my brother Drafli so close, ach?"

The red in Baldr's face deepened as he bent to snatch up what
looked like a tunic, and carefully re-folded it into a perfect square.
"You do not know that. There are plenty of other... options. Especially
around *here*."

There was a distinct note of bitterness in his voice, and Maria was
vaguely surprised by the sight of Simon stepping around her, and clapping a heavy hand on Baldr's shoulder. "Ach, and now your sweet
scent shall taint them all," he said firmly, "and tempt my brother
astray, even stronger than before."

But Baldr's head jerked back and forth, his hands crumpling the
neatly folded tunic. "But Drafli does not *want* to be tempted astray
from your precious Skai *ways*," he said, his voice unsettlingly plaintive.

"And if he thinks I have moved in here just to get closer to him, he will—"

He broke off there, biting his lip with a sharp tooth, and Simon squeezed his shoulder, gave it a hard little shake. "He shall no," he said, voice flat. "He knows I shall no risk another Skai in this now. No when this shall only draw Ulfarr's eye. Ach?"

Oh. Wait. So this thing with Baldr moving in—this *wasn't* really a reward, after all. No, it was about—*Ulfarr*, and this whole heightened rivalry between him and Simon. Because of... Maria. Because she wasn't... *safe*? Enough that she needed constant *guarding*?

Her thoughts had flashed back to that instant in the corridor, to the way Ulfarr had blocked her in, trapping her, *mocking* her. Not because he'd truly desired her, but because he wanted to punish Simon. He wanted to... *kill* Simon, and steal everything he owned. He wanted to steal *her*.

An unpleasant chill trickled up Maria's back, hardening into a full-on shudder—to which both Simon and Baldr snapped around to look at her. Simon's eyes with a mulish wariness, Baldr's with visible concern.

"You need not fear this, Maria," Baldr said, after an instant's stillness. "We shall keep you safe. This is why Simon asked me to come. Your welfare is now his most pressing priority, ach?"

For an instant, Simon glared at Baldr, as though he hadn't approved this little disclosure in the least—but then he exhaled, his jaw tightening in his cheek. "There is naught better orc than Baldr to help in this," he said. "He learnt to fight with the Skai, and is thus a match for any of my kin. He also has the ear of the captain and his mate each day, and this is of great worth to us. Now"—he gave Baldr's shoulder another shake—"come with us for a spell, ach, brother?"

Baldr willingly obliged, and soon they were all striding down the corridor together, Baldr in front, Maria and Simon behind. And as Maria walked, she couldn't seem to stop glancing at Simon's sharp, ever-frowning profile in the lantern-light, while her thoughts twisted and churned.

He was really—*protecting* her, against Ulfarr. As his most *pressing priority*. And thus, bringing in an orc he trusted, to live in a room directly *beside* her. While also comforting said orc about his personal problems, and apparently even playing his hand at *matchmaker*? Being... *kind*?

And for an instant, there was the abrupt, almost overwhelming urge to touch him. To lean into him, to stroke her hand against his stiff back. Perhaps even to say, *Thank you, this was a lovely reward, even if I know it wasn't really a reward at all...*

But no. No. Maria did not—*could* not—understand this orc in the slightest. Gods, in the short time since she'd awoken, he'd treated her like a dog, he'd exposed her before his friend, he'd given her latrine access in exchange for converting to his fucked-up religion...

And when Simon finally glanced down toward her, it was almost as though she saw her own misgivings reflected in his eyes. As though that wall had again snapped down between them, hiding him away, leaving only a taunting, mocking sneer behind.

"Now, woman," he said coldly, "I take you to the Skai arena. Where again, you shall seek to please me, and earn your next reward."

That was surely the challenge back in his voice, perhaps even a threat. And Maria shouldn't rise to it, she shouldn't—but the retort was somehow already there, escaping out her mouth. "Oh, and what might this thrilling reward be?" she demanded. "Maybe you'll feed me? Give me a drink of water?"

But Simon's curling lip was all distant, insolent amusement, reeking of provocation, of danger. As though—an unpleasant chill rippled down Maria's back—he was surely about to enjoy this, whatever fresh hell it might be.

"No, woman," he said firmly. "It is where you shall learn"—his grin sharpened—"to fight like a true Skai."

16

Maria would learn to *fight*?!

She must have squeaked some kind of inappropriate response, because the challenge in Simon's eyes only flared brighter as he guided her after Baldr through yet another hole in the wall.

"The Skai arena," he announced, with a broad wave of his hand. "The best in Orc Mountain. It is an honour to spar with us here."

And once again, Maria seemed struck in place, her eyes blinking blankly at this huge, echoing room of—*chaos*. Teeming with multiple massive, half-dressed orcs, lunging and swinging at one another, growling and grunting, making impact with fists and feet and an astonishing variety of blunt wooden *weapons*.

The room's ceiling was higher than any Maria had seen so far, and stone steps angled up the edges of it all around, providing vantage points from which spectators could sit and watch. And in the very middle of the room was a circular, flat stone dais, perhaps as tall as Maria herself—and upon it, two orcs were furiously brawling, fighting to hurl one another off the sheer edge to the hard floor below.

Their battle was surrounded by yet more brawling orcs on the floor, and while several of the orcs had glanced over to look at the door—at *Maria*—none of them actually stopped their fighting, or made any attempt to approach. And as she stared at them, one of the orcs who'd been staring back was promptly tackled face-first into the floor by his opponent, who then leapt off, kicked him in the ribs, and *laughed*.

And even if Maria could admit, in some distant part of her brain, that the idea of learning to fight wasn't an entirely unpleasant one, did Simon really expect her to do so *here*? Like *this*? Like that vicious-looking orc, over there, who—she winced—had just grabbed his opponent's groin with his claws, and *yanked*?!

"Come, woman," Simon cut in, voice brisk, before striding off toward the nearest empty area. "You shall obey me in this, and seek to learn our ways, and earn my reward."

Maria glowered at his back, and briefly considered arguing, protesting, making a scene—but then again, a room full of brawling orcs and deadly weapons seemed perhaps an unwise place to risk such a thing. And beside Simon, Baldr had actually grinned at her over his shoulder, his eyes sparkling with clear anticipation.

So Maria gritted her teeth and followed, vaguely noting that at least this particular area was empty, and its hard floor was covered with an assortment of soft-looking furs. However, this brief reassurance was instantly ruined by Simon, who'd waved Baldr away, and then whirled around to glare down at her, his arms crossed over his chest.

"Have you ever known aught of work, woman?" he demanded. "Or of sweat, or struggle?"

He'd cast a disdainful glance down at Maria's hands—at their smooth, uncallused skin, no doubt, speaking of a life of comfort and leisure—and she felt her face flushing, her hands tightening to fists. "I'm not a total weakling, if that's what you're asking," she replied flatly. "I did *plenty* of work growing up, and I've always preferred being busy. But after my marriage, I—"

She bit the words off, far too late, because an all-too-predictable shadow had passed across Simon's eyes. "Ach, to this *husband*," he sneered at her. "Show me your strength, then. Seek to strike me."

To *strike* him?! Maria gaped at him, again utterly dumbfounded—gods, she'd never truly struck anyone in her *life*—and Simon gazed straight back at her, cold, implacable. "In aught way you wish. *Now*, woman."

Now. The rebellion flared again, choking at Maria's throat—but she dragged in breath, stamped it down again. He was just an orc. She would humour him. Gain her freedom. That was *all*.

So she clenched her fists, braced herself, scowled at his obnoxious face—and then *punched* him. Driving her fist straight into his exposed neck, since surely it would be softer than the rest of him—

But even so, the sudden impact of her pristine knuckles against hardened orc sent her staggering sideways, pain spearing down her outstretched arm. Good gods, it had been like punching a *rock*, and surely that was enough, now? Surely?

But Simon, who hadn't even moved or flinched at the impact, was already frowning, giving a curt, predictable shake of his head. "*Ach*, no," he said flatly. "Come closer. Feet wide, held hard to the floor. And you no use arm to push. Use here."

His hand dropped down to the rippled muscle at his own bare waist, gripping it with careless nonchalance—and somehow, against all fathoming, Maria's eyes followed to linger on the sight, while something dipped low in her own belly. Recalling, too clearly, those other times, when that hand had gripped even lower, easy and familiar, and...

"Again, woman," Simon's voice broke in. "Obey me."

Right, right, and when Maria glanced up, that was without question a smirk, curling cool and mocking across his lips. As if he'd known *exactly* what she'd been thinking, the prick, and truly, if he was giving her a chance to punch him in the neck, she should be taking full advantage of the opportunity.

So she stepped closer, and widened her stance, just as he'd instructed. Feeling for the floor, for the strength in her own torso—and then drew back her fist, and pummelled him straight in the throat.

The impact still felt like a hammer-blow, reeling down her outstretched arm, but she'd actually managed to hold herself in place this time. And the punch had felt stronger, too, and though Simon still hadn't moved, something else had flicked across his watching eyes. Something almost like... approval?

"Better," he said. "Again."

Again. Maria didn't hesitate this time, just shot out for his throat—and as she made impact, Simon actually *blinked*. Blinked, from *her punch*. And for some inexplicable reason, she felt herself half-smiling at him, her brows rising, as if waiting for his comment, his *favour*...

"Good," he said, sparking an undeniable swirl of warmth in her chest. "Again."

Maria obeyed, willingly this time, earning another grunt of approval as her reward. And when Simon ordered her to aim for his belly next, and then to switch and use her other arm, she obeyed that too. Again and again and again, punching against this solid, infuriating orc with as much strength and speed as she could muster, until her brain was inexplicably, blissfully empty, and the rest of her was sore and hot and gasping, and dripping sweat all over.

"Enough, woman," Simon said, easily catching her fist before her last punch made impact—and his eyes held to hers, brief, *approving*, before dropping down to her reddened, stinging knuckles. And then, to Maria's astonishment, he raised her hand to his mouth... and *licked* it. Trailing his slick black tongue over her raw, pulsing skin, lingering, *tasting*.

Maria stood very still and watched it, *felt* it, her chest still heaving from the exertion—and when Simon lowered the hand, and gestured for the other one, she immediately lifted it, her lashes fluttering at the feel of his hot tongue, seeking against hot skin with strange, heart-swarming purpose...

"Is this reward enough, woman?" he murmured, his breath skating over her knuckles. "Has the pain yet passed?"

Maria blinked at his eyes, at his slowly smirking mouth—and there was the distant, astonishing realization that her hands actually *didn't* hurt anymore, and that they even looked less raw than they had just moments before. And that the rest of her now felt very sore indeed, and what if this audacious orc were to use that tongue on *all* those hungry places, and...

"We shall return to this," Simon murmured, his lips still curling up—and in this dangling instant, Maria had no idea if he meant the punching, or the licking, or both. "Now rest. Regain your breath, and watch us. And drink the water we fetched you, ach?"

Her *water*? He'd jerked his head toward the nearest raised steps, where Baldr was currently sitting next to a bulging waterskin. And Maria didn't know whether to be pleased, or highly insulted—had Simon truly intended the water to be her *reward*?—as Baldr leapt down, and grinned at her with palpable approval.

"Nice mettle, Maria," he said with a wink, as he walked past her, rolling out his shoulders. "Skai like that."

Maria's face flushed even hotter, and she rushed for the safety of the steps, where she grabbed for the waterskin, and yanked the stopper out. She did not care, she told herself, as she gulped the cool, refreshing liquid down her parched throat. She didn't care about Simon's stupid games, or his stupid rewards, and she surely didn't care what he thought of her *mettle*. Did she?

But as she lowered the waterskin, her eyes settled almost instinctively back on Simon, who was now circling around Baldr with slow, prowling steps. He moved so lightly, so gracefully, his massive body loose and relaxed, his clawed hands hanging easy at his sides...

Baldr lunged for him with astonishing speed, his fist striking straight for Simon's face—but somehow, impossibly, he *missed*. Because Simon had slid only a half-step backwards, just out of Baldr's reach—forcing Baldr to catch himself, shift his stance, before lunging in again. Aiming for Simon's gut this time, surely too fast for *anyone* to avoid—

But Simon somehow caught the punch with his hand, his leg kicking out behind Baldr's—and in a flurry of movement, they crashed to the floor. Baldr slamming his elbows into Simon's belly, and aiming sharp kicks toward Simon's groin, while Simon grunted and shifted, grasped Baldr's arm, his grip snapping tight—

"*Mercy*," Baldr croaked, kicking at Simon with his leg—and instantly Simon was off, away, on his feet. But also reaching down a hand, and drawing up Baldr after him.

"Again," Simon said, as he stepped back, his body loose, his eyes warm. "And watch my legs, ach?"

Baldr nodded, breathing deep—and then once again lunged, driving hard and fierce for Simon's form. And again, Simon avoided, evaded, waiting—until he tackled Baldr in a shocking display of brutal force, trapping him in a painful-looking headlock this time, while Baldr pounded out his defeat onto the floor.

"Better," Simon said with a grunt, as he released Baldr's neck, and rose back to his feet. "Again."

It was the same way he'd spoken to Maria, the same pattern—and as she watched Baldr lunge back in, she realized it was the same restraint, too. The same... generosity. Simon was... *teaching*?

But yes, surely, he was *teaching*. Because while Baldr was clearly a quick and powerful fighter, he was still visibly, vastly outmatched by Simon—a fact that Simon didn't seem to care about in the slightest. Instead using his superior size and skill to test Baldr, to show Baldr his errors, to give him room to experiment and play and learn.

And in watching them, Maria found she was learning, too. Noticing how Baldr exclusively aimed for Simon's face, throat, or groin. How Baldr kept his hands in fists, because the one time he didn't, Simon took him down with a single yank on his fingers. How Baldr was far better off prolonging things on his feet, using his smaller size to weave in and out, because once they were on the ground, it was always only a matter of breaths before Simon was victorious.

It was truly engrossing, fixing Maria's full attention to every attack and counter-attack, while the rest of the room melted away. And when something moved beside her, she actually yelped, and flinched sideways—only to discover that it was *Drafli*. Lounging silent and unnerving on the step beside her, arms crossed, as though he'd been sitting there this entire time.

He was dressed today, at least, but his eyes were just as disdainful as every other time they'd met, narrowing dangerously on Maria's face. And then he leapt up without a word, striding over toward where Simon had, once again, pinned Baldr to the floor beneath him.

Drafli didn't speak as he approached them, but instead kicked his bare foot at Simon's side, and reached down to drag Baldr up. An action that Baldr willingly accepted, though his flushed-red face didn't quite look at Drafli, not even when Drafli flicked a clawed finger against his sweaty cheek.

"Still better each day," Simon said to Baldr, with a heavy clap of his hand to his back. "Some day, I shall be the one calling for *your* mercy."

"Ach, when we are both *elders*," Baldr countered, but Maria could see the flush deepening in his cheeks. "Thank you, brother."

Simon returned this with a nod, and then slid his gaze to Drafli, brows raised—to which Drafli smirked back, and then nudged Baldr away. His hand lingering rather longer than necessary against Baldr's arse, and Baldr's stride back toward Maria was jerky, his eyes bright. Looking unmistakably pleased, though when he reached the step he sagged hard onto it, his hands rubbing at his red face.

"Are you all right?" Maria asked him uncertainly, eyeing what looked like an assortment of purple bruises blooming over his greenish skin. "That was awfully... intense."

"Ach, it always is," Baldr said with a shrug, a wry glance toward her. "But orcs heal more quickly than humans, ach? And this shall help."

He twitched his head toward where Drafli and Simon had now begun circling each other, their movements watchful, deliberate. "Drafli is one of the best unarmed fighters in this mountain," Baldr continued. "Along with Simon, and the captain, and Ulfarr. But Simon cannot fight Ulfarr or the captain, so this"—his eyes sparked with genuine eagerness—"is mayhap the best equal match you shall see here."

Maria felt her own eagerness sparking too, but it was also tainted, tangled, by that mention of the horrid Ulfarr's name. "Simon *can't* fight them?" she asked carefully. "Or he won't?"

Her thoughts flicked back to the night before, to all those awful, hushed truths Simon had told her—and Baldr winced. "Both, perhaps," he said, quiet. "This would be a clear challenge. A test of standing and power. One of them would not walk away from this."

Right. Maria swallowed, opened her mouth to ask her next question—but then Baldr crowed aloud, leaning forward, his weariness instantly vanished. Because Drafli had lunged in toward Simon, moving with impossible speed—and somehow, he actually landed a tight, vicious kick straight into Simon's gut.

Simon grunted, hinting that it might have actually *hurt*—and Baldr whooped again as Drafli shot out another kick, toward Simon's groin this time. An attack that Simon avoided, but narrowly, while Drafli dove in again, claws slashing, aiming for Simon's face.

Simon reared back, but not before Drafli's claws dragged against his cheek, drawing actual *blood*—and Maria only distantly noticed the room's other orcs gradually abandoning their own altercations, in favour of coming over to watch this one. Because Simon was clearly putting in an effort now, his eyes sharp and intent on Drafli, his jaw grinding in his bloody cheek.

He met Drafli's next lunge with a lunge of his own, a visible attempt at tackling him to the floor—but Drafli was too fast, and Maria heard herself groan alongside a few of the other orcs, despite Baldr's loud cheer beside her. Drafli *was* good at this, his movements so swift they blurred together, and he was just as tall as Simon, his reach perhaps even longer. And his strategy was clearly to keep Simon up and unsettled and moving, using his heavier weight against him, seeking to tire him out. And Maria could see how it was working, Drafli's foot slamming straight into Simon's groin—

Simon bent double this time, his howl echoing through the room, and Maria again heard her own shout rising, joining the chorus of watching orcs. But Simon had already raised his head, his eyes narrow and focused—and in a whirl of motion, he charged. Crashing into Drafli with alarming strength, wielding his far larger size to topple them both to the ground.

But Drafli was good at the grappling too, slithering out of the holds that had incapacitated Baldr, while also landing brutal, repeated blows to Simon's groin and face. And Maria was truly hollering now, not even caring who saw or heard, because Simon could *not* lose to this snide sneering orc, he could *not*, it was there in his stubborn watching eyes, until—

Now. His huge body snapping tight against Drafli's, yanking him close—and in a wild twisting jerk, he had Drafli's arm bent precariously backwards, just the way he'd done to Baldr. And finally, *finally*, Drafli was the one banging out his defeat, sparking a chorus of groans and shouts through the room, while Simon leapt to his feet again, wiping at his still-bleeding cheek with a clawed hand, shaking the blood onto the floor.

He'd *won*.

Maria was somehow shouting with the rest of the room, loud enough that she drowned out Baldr beside her. And when Simon's eyes inexplicably flicked through the chaos to meet hers, she found she was actually *grinning* at him, her body warm all over, her eyes alight.

Simon's gaze held to hers, brief—but then angled away toward Drafli, who had also risen to his feet, his face blank. And in another flash of movement, Simon yanked Drafli close, his huge hand slapping against his back.

"A worthy match, brother," he said, his deep voice easily carrying through the hubbub. "You near had me, ach?"

And Maria was still grinning, the warmth scattering wide, because even in this, Simon was being... *kind*. Because based on that last bit, there was no way he truly would have lost that match. None.

Drafli had clapped at Simon too, but then shrugged out of his grip, and stalked toward the corridor. Clearly done with this, and beside Maria Baldr visibly twitched, and then darted off out the door after him.

Which left Maria somehow still alone with Simon, in a room crowded with noisy orcs, because he was looking straight at her again, brows lifted, his mouth twitching up. And when he strode toward her, intent and purposeful, Maria found herself meeting him in the middle, her hand finding his hot heaving chest, her eyes roving over his battered, bloody face.

"That was," she managed, around her thoroughly uncooperative tongue, "*appalling*."

Something shifted in Simon's eyes, but his lips were still quirking up, his shoulder shrugging. "And yet, this pleased you," he replied, low. "Even without my reward. Ach, wilful woman?"

And Maria was nodding, *nodding*, still grinning so broadly her face hurt—and Simon slowly smiled back at her, a little crooked, showing all his sharp white teeth. And the sight was somehow swallowing Maria's breath, her hand slipping round to catch against his broad sweaty back, and if he could just come closer, just like that, fill her senses with his ease and his strength, his heart shuddering under her fingers—

"Brothers!" called a voice, a new voice, freezing both Maria and Simon to stillness—and it was a new orc, another huge orc, dashing through the door. His face craggy and hard, his clawed hand gripping tight at his gleaming sword-hilt.

"Our captain calls you to arms," he said, his deep voice burning through the suddenly silent room. "The first band of men has come."

17

The new orc's proclamation sparked a single beat of silence, thudding through the room. Sharpening the assembled orcs' eyes, snapping their bodies taut, while Simon's heart skipped a beat beneath Maria's spread-wide fingers.

And then everything moved at once. Orcs dropping any weapons they'd still been holding, streaking for the door, their voices rising in their wake. And abruptly Maria was moving too, Simon half-guiding, half-dragging her out into the corridor, the lantern clutched in his other hand.

"W-what does that mean?" Maria asked, as she belatedly began jogging along beside him. "Why are there *men* here? You're not truly going to *fight* them, are you?"

Because surely that was against the rules, the peace-treaty, *something*—but Simon didn't immediately answer, hauling Maria sideways into his room, and then angling toward the wall. Toward his scimitar, which he strapped to his hip, pulling the belt tight.

"I no ken we fight today," he said curtly, as he next went for his huge boots, yanking them onto his feet. "The captain makes a show, in this. Scare these men away, before others come."

These men. "*Others* are coming?" Maria echoed, her voice shrill. "From *where*?"

Simon jerked a shrug, ducking to grasp an assortment of gleaming weapons from among the mess on the floor. "Same as always, I ken," he said, as he thrust a smaller scimitar into his belt on the other side, and then began shoving knives into his boots. "From the human lords of the north."

The human lords of the north.

Maria's body froze all over, though her heart had kicked, pummelling with distant, alarming force against her ribs. That meant... her husband. His allies. His *Council*. Didn't it?

Her *husband* had sent more men here? *Now*?

"You wait here, woman," Simon continued, without looking at her, as he shoved another dagger into his belt. "Ulfarr shall come out with us, so you shall be safe here. If Baldr scents aught amiss, I shall come for you. Whilst you wait, you shall eat, and read, and seek to honour me."

With that, he turned and strode for the door, his steps long and purposeful—and without at all meaning to, Maria lunged after him, and clutched at his huge arm. Wanting him to wait, *needing* it, perhaps—and to her distant relief, Simon instantly halted, his muscles flexing under her fingers, his eyes frowning over his shoulder.

"You'll be—" Maria began, her voice thick, and she had to swallow hard, clear her throat. "Safe. Right?"

Simon's bark of laughter was sudden, deep, surprisingly warm. "Ach, woman," he said, with palpable amusement. "I could defeat this whole band alone, should I wish."

And with that arrogant but no doubt accurate statement still ringing through the room, he strode out the door, without looking back. And for some foolish reason, Maria lurched after him into the corridor, watching him go, his weapons glinting in the last of the dim lamplight.

"Stay, woman," his voice called back, echoing against the stone. "Obey me. *Honour* me."

Honour him. With no mention of a reward this time, but even so, Maria gave a nod he couldn't see, and ducked back into the disaster of a room. And then stood there, breathing hard, her heartbeat roaring in her ears.

Her husband was sending men. Attacking the orcs. With the aim of... what? Of *her*?

But no, no, *surely* not. She'd left no actual hint of orcs when she'd run. Her incriminating letters wouldn't be sent for nearly another month—and even then, she'd been sure to avoid any obvious grounds for war within them. She'd planned her escape so thoroughly. She'd been so, *so* careful.

This shouldn't have anything to do with her. It *couldn't*.

But the discomfort kept prickling, her heart pummelling, something much like *fear* grasping at her chest with cold, slippery fingers. What if she'd been found out. What if she'd somehow destroyed an entire peace-treaty. What if this meant death, for innocent orcs, or innocent men.

And what if the orcs discovered who she was. What if *Simon* discovered it. What happened then, would he send her back, would it ruin *everything*...

The panic had begun bubbling in earnest, for what felt like the first time since that Skai common-room. And how absurd that it should return now, instead of during any other point in this thoroughly ridiculous day so far—and it felt even worse after its unfamiliar absence, like a grinding wheel churning through her belly. And she couldn't sink into this again, not now, please gods please—

Her eyes were darting through the room, skittering over the mess, seeking, searching, *something*—and then catching, suddenly, on that wooden chest Simon had given her. *Whilst you wait, you shall eat, and read, and honour me.*

And that was something, it was, and Maria stumbled toward the chest, and yanked it open. And inside, on top, there was indeed a basket full of meat and cheese and fruit. Along with another bulging waterskin, a bottle of milk, and that stack of treatises Rosa had brought. The uppermost one still reading, *An Alternate Account of the Orc-Human War.*

And yes, Maria would do this, so she grasped for the basket and the treatise, and hurled her shaky body down to the bench. And then started stuffing her face with food, while rapidly scanning her eyes over the treatise's first page.

It began with... a tale. A tale of an ancient elf named Edom, who had been cast out by his own kin, and sought refuge under a great mountain across the sea. And there, he met a human woman named Akva, who he loved with his whole heart—and together, they birthed five sons, who became the five clans of orcs.

The tale then delved into the clans' lives and losses, their constant struggles to survive in this foreign, forbidding land that treated them with mistrust and fear. It spoke of the gods' cruel curse upon them, birthing them only sons, and never daughters. It spoke of the sons' ceaseless quest for kin and companionship, their deep longing for women and sons of their own. It spoke of the drastic measures some orcs took to gain this—and then the drastic retaliations, the blood and battlefields, the bounties and fires, the poison and disease.

It spoke of an entire realm caught in a bitter, brutal war for years, lifetimes, generations. All because of... *loneliness*. Because of a constant, ever-spiralling *revenge*.

Maria didn't quite notice when she'd stopped reading, the treatise fallen slack in her hand, the basket of food entirely empty at her side. Her eyes gazing blankly at the opposite wall, at the mess of marks upon it.

And had it only been last night, when Simon had told her all those quiet, powerful things? *My clan is dying,* he'd said, *at the hand of yours. You no see why we cling to our ways, in the face of this?*

The discomfort kept growing, churning and curdling in Maria's belly, and she leapt to her feet, desperately needing to move, to pace, to *do* something—until her foot painfully caught on yet another rock, just sitting in the middle of the floor in the mess. And good gods, she could barely *move* in this room, it truly beggared belief that an orc twice her size would ever want to *live* like this...

She glared down at the rock, and then at the disaster of this room all around her. Suddenly loathing it, loathing *everything*, her horrible husband, this horrible orc, this stupid horrible *war*, and...

She lunged for the rock, grasping at it with both hands, and then dropped it back down beside the bench with a loud *thunk*. And then the next rock, and the next one, building what was beginning to look like a crude, tilting pyre. But still propped up close to the bench, directly beside where Simon seemed to like to sit, so he could continue his incessant sharpening as he pleased.

There must have been twenty or thirty rocks scattered about, and by the time Maria moved them all, she was once again hot and gasping, sweat trickling down her back—but this was something, *something*, and next she fixed her attention to the mess of clothes and rags. Gathering them, too, into a single large pile, this time near the wooden shelf. Where she next launched into a steady stream of sorting and folding, stacking the ridiculously oversized garments in neat piles of trousers and tunics. While also clearing off the shelf's haphazard papers and carved figures, creating more piles as she went.

She was making considerable progress, but there was still no sign of Simon's return, or of any distant orc voices. So Maria just kept going, finishing her folding, and next turning her attention to the papers. Stacking them without really looking, her thoughts still distantly whirling, until her attention caught on a line of text, written in what looked like a child's uneven hand.

I am Simon of Clan Skai, it said, the charcoal letters slightly smeared across the page. *I am Enforcer of Orc Mountain.*

The sentences were repeated down the page, again and again, and Maria's scattered brain vaguely noted that it looked like... practice. A worksheet, perhaps. The kind of thing she'd done in school as a girl.

Simon was learning to *write*?

But flipping through the other loose pages, Maria realized that surely, that was what this was. This was Simon, sitting here alone in his mess of a room, sharpening his weapons, and writing out words in common-tongue, over and over again.

And perhaps it was that damned treatise she'd just read, or the very pointed memory of herself hurling out that awful word *dim-witted*, but there was an odd lump rising in Maria's throat, battling against the still-swirling mess in her head. Strong enough that she had to thrust the papers aside, her hands instead finding... yes. Fine. These. The carved stone figures, scattered in a jumble across the shelf.

But as she began to set them carefully upright on the top of the shelf, here was the equally disconcerting realization that they were carvings of... people. Of orcs, and *humans*. And while they were roughly hewn, they were also surprisingly vivid, unnervingly expressive. One slim, sharp-looking orc was furious, with brows pulled low over his eyes. Another bigger orc with a barrel chest was smiling, his hands clutched in huge fists. And a tall, voluptuous woman was haughty and severe, regarding the world through half-lidded eyes of stone.

There were a few smaller steel knives scattered around them, not unlike the knife Maria had seen Simon carving with the day before. And blinking at the knives, at the carvings, she realized that these had to be Simon's, too. He'd... *made* them.

Maria carefully placed the carved woman on the shelf with the rest, and then sat back on her heels, and looked at them. And looked, and looked, while that tightness kept growing and catching in her throat.

Gods, this place. These orcs. Her horrid husband, out there spending her inheritance, possibly even starting more war based on anger and revenge. And Simon was still mostly awful too, with his horrid games and his horrid *rewards*, and he was just an orc, this was exactly what Maria had wanted, and she wasn't supposed to care...

She dragged her hands down her face, groaning aloud—and then jumped again to her feet, and stalked back toward the chest. Gritting her teeth and glaring down inside it, as though certain unnerving implements might disintegrate through the sheer ferocity of her gaze—but they were still there, so innocuous, so blatant, so gods-damned *alarming*.

I shall find your fresh scent upon these each day, Simon had said. *Obey me. Honour me.*

And fine, yes, Maria would do this, something, *anything*—and she grasped for both of them, and lunged for the bed. And before she could think better of it, she yanked off her tunic, dove beneath the fur, and snatched its hot weight up over her face.

She lay there breathing for a long moment, hidden safe in the stuffy pitch-blackness. Where no one could see her, no one could mock her or judge. And Simon had wanted this, and Maria would gain her freedom, and that was *all*...

So she fumbled for the implements under the fur, feeling at the smooth carved shapes of them. One was almost a perfect cylinder, long and thick, with two rounded-off ends. And the other—her face flushed hotter under the already-hot fur—was softly pointed at one end, and gradually widened before narrowing and flaring out again.

Two implements, for two... *places*. Just as Simon had said.

And Maria *had* done this many times before, in the depths of her loneliness. Surely she could do it here. Surely there was no actual harm in taking the less intimidating of the two in both hands, stroking its softness, its heft, its weight. Smaller around than Simon had been, surely, but perhaps almost just as long...

Soon, you shall learn to take all of me, he'd told her, and here in the sweaty quiet darkness, Maria could feel her belly clench at the memory of it, the heated promise in those words. At how it had felt both times so far, when he'd opened her wide, impaled her so tight upon him, pumping her full of slick hot ecstasy...

And how each time, he'd surely wanted it. He'd wanted *her*. He'd *approved*.

So Maria swallowed hard, and slipped a hand down between her parted legs. Down to where it already felt hot, swollen, pulsing against her touch. Craving more than a memory, more than just her own fingers...

The first brush of the hard stone was gentle, surprisingly cool against Maria's convulsing heat, but it quickly warmed as it nudged closer, deeper. As Maria began to feel the true heft of it, spreading her wide and forceful apart.

But it felt good—gods, *so* good—and she drew in a deep lungful of breath, huffed it out. Made herself relax for the stone's invasion, widened her thighs further for it. Let it slide out a bit, easing the pressure—and then sinking back in, a little deeper, a little harder. And then again, again, again.

And when she reached for the second stone, slicking it all over in more of Simon's slippery scent, it almost felt... easy. Easy to slide it inside too, her body heating, her hunger catching, twitching into something again almost like determination. She would do this, prove this. She would shove back against the war, her husband, the mess in her head that kept fighting to drown the rising, sparkling pleasure.

But in this moment, Maria had the upper hand. She was impaling herself in both places, with both stones, she was gasping hard and throwing off the hot fur and arching up. Revelling in the pressure, the power, the triumph, as her hand pressed flat to her trembling seizing heat, holding them both fully inside, glorying in the truth of her victory—

And at that perfect, horrible instant, someone strode into the room. It was *Simon*.

18

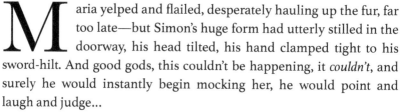

Maria yelped and flailed, desperately hauling up the fur, far too late—but Simon's huge form had utterly stilled in the doorway, his head tilted, his hand clamped tight to his sword-hilt. And good gods, this couldn't be happening, it *couldn't*, and surely he would instantly begin mocking her, he would point and laugh and judge...

And no, *no*, he was already striding over, closing the space between them in three large steps, his gaze darting around at the floor with something that might have been surprise. And in one sharp movement, he reached toward Maria's fur—and then yanked it off her entirely. Revealing her cold and quivering form beneath, clad only in that damned loincloth, her betraying hand still clamped tight and shameful between her spread thighs...

Maria squeezed her eyes shut, bracing for his laughter, his certain mockery—but beyond a soft, unexpected thump, nothing came. And when she risked opening one eye again, it was to the disconcerting, thoroughly unnerving sight of Simon—*kneeling*. Yes, kneeling beside the bed, so close, his eyes glittering in the candlelight.

Those eyes didn't leave hers as his big hands slowly reached up, grasping for her legs—and then he yanked her bodily sideways, dragging her arse almost to the edge of the bed. And dragging her loincloth up with it, so that the sight between her legs was fully bared, directly before his eyes. And good gods, what was this, what was he doing, what would he *say*...

"Show me," he murmured, and Maria felt herself shiver all over, her shaky hand pressing tighter against the shame between her legs. Her fear sparking up bright and powerful, he was going to laugh, he would...

"Peace, woman," he breathed, his hand spreading her thigh a little wider, his fingers nudging warm against the goose-pimpled skin. "I wish to see. Honour me."

Honour him. And yes, yes, that had been the whole point of this utter *absurdity*, and Maria was doing this, she didn't care, she *didn't*...

So she yanked her trembling hand away, digging her fingernails into the fur beneath her—and then she lay there, mortified, legs spread wide, exposing the depth of her shame. Of her most secret place, fully invaded and owned, the flared stone locked firmly inside—while the other stone, previously hidden within her dripping clutching heat, slowly, brutally revealed itself. Nudging out smooth and obscene, breaching her from the inside out—

And it kept slipping out, bit by bit, surely coated all over in her slick. While Maria felt herself clenching desperately against it, uselessly fighting to keep it there—but only birthing it out faster, straight toward Simon's watching eyes. Until its solid heft finally escaped her altogether, falling heavy into Simon's waiting fingers.

Maria jolted at the loss of it, the sheer licking shame of it, her hands snapping up to her hot face—until she felt those warm fingers on her thigh carefully stroking, guiding her open wider. And then— she gasped—the slick rounded stone nudged her again, soft, gentle, seeking its way back inside.

Maria couldn't look, couldn't bear to—but there was something in the way it breached her this time, something in the warm huff of air on her skin as the stone sank steadily deeper. Breath by inevitable breath, pressure coiling and rising, emptiness filling with strength—until she could feel her traitorous lips closing around the stone's rounded end, once again seating it fully within.

"Pretty," Simon's voice breathed, unexpected enough that Maria's eyes flew open—and found, with a jolt of surprise, that he wasn't even looking at her. That his eyes had fluttered shut, black lashes thick on his cheek, as he leaned in close, and *inhaled*.

"Again," he whispered, the word a soft broken caress—and a wild, raging part of Maria nodded, and *obeyed*. Pushing against the stone with purpose this time, feeling it emerge hard and slick from inside her. A bare, humiliating proof of her depravity, prodding out into Simon's waiting hand, while his hooded eyes watched with an almost feral intensity.

He slid the stone back inside without hesitation, harder and faster, thrusting her full—and she pushed it out faster too, meeting him, matching him. Seeing the answering quirk in his mouth, the faint flash of warmth in his watching eyes.

"Wilful woman," he murmured, driving it in even harder—and this time he held it there, blocking its escape, making Maria feel it. Her ever-warming body clenching and gasping, convulsing against the callused skin of his hand, pooling steady slickness onto his huge palm...

At some point his eyes had found hers again, glinting fierce and dark, and she choked aloud as he slowly, gently drew out both stones, tossing them aside. And then he rose up over her, revealing that muscled bare chest, the rippled hardness of his abdomen, and then... *that*. The monster at his groin, jutting out thick and dangerous from above his pulled-down trousers.

"You shall take me now," he breathed, hot, a promise. "All of me."

Maria nodded, gasped, dragged in air—and she felt him exhale his approval, his eyes roving over her skin. Lingering on her face, her neck, her bared breasts, his clawed thumb rising to brush against a peaked nipple, his fingers skittering against her ribs.

And when a new hardness pressed against her swollen hungry heat, Maria was ready. Ready to relax, open, feel the slick delving head of him, soft and smooth and *alive*. Flexing and throbbing as it nudged its way deeper, parting her around it, piercing her upon it.

Simon's black eyes had dropped to the sight, his hands shifting to grip at both Maria's thighs, and he spread her wider, exposing her, laying her bare for his rapt, unblinking gaze. For the truth of this grey, veined, pulsing beast sinking into her, driving through her resistance with exquisite, powerful intent...

Maria quivered and gasped beneath him, her invaded, stretched-open heat convulsing even tighter—but he didn't slow, didn't relent. Just kept plunging deeper, feeding her fuller and fuller of him, he was already halfway in, oh gods, oh...

Maria's gasps had sharpened toward cries, her eyes fluttering, sweeping over the impossible, unimaginable sight. A massive, scarred, muscle-bound orc leaning down over her, his grey skin glimmering with sweat, his black claws digging into her thighs. His eyes blinking thick lashes against his cheek, his half-lidded gaze burning into her, as the jutting, juddering heft at his groin kept jamming into her, packing her full of hot orc-flesh and oozing wet slick. Splitting and stretching and squeezing, pressure and pain and unreal pleasure, all whirling and thronging in its wake—

And in one final blaring jolt, a deep grunt from his chest—he was in. His groin thrust up hard and flush against Maria's, his heavy bollocks pulsing tight against her crease. And his monster fully vanished, vanquished, locked deep inside her frantically convulsing heat.

The sounds from Maria's mouth were shocking, breaking through the room, and the rest of her was breaking too, writhing and clamping, stretched to her utter limit. Impaled full of massive bulging orc, an orc had truly rammed *that* all the way into her, and the look on his watching face was suddenly jubilant, proud, *approving.*

"Ach, my pretty one," he purred, as he slightly tilted his hips, moving Maria's entire lower half with him. "It is good, ach?"

It is good. Good, to be punched full of orc-prick. To feel it shuddering within her very skin, pumping out its hot, wicked seed. To feel its slick head kissing at her, deep inside, finding the home for its leavings, its base swelling, sealing tight—

Simon howled as the seed sprayed, spurting out of him again and again, flooding Maria, consuming her. Pouring itself out so deep within her, deeper than anything she'd ever known, so deep it felt like he was seeping into her very soul—

And then she was the one shuddering, screaming her relief, her back arching, her peaked breasts aiming at the ceiling. While Simon groaned his steady approval, his big hands gripping her hips closer while she clutched and kissed against him, brazen, wanton, *whole.*

The ecstasy soared longer than it ever had before, as though needing to wring out every last pulse and clench and gasp. Needing this orc to keep looking at her like that, his eyes shining black and deep, his lashes still fluttering, his sharp white tooth biting hard against his lip...

"Ach," he breathed, tilting his head back, his stubbled throat visibly convulsing. "This was good, ach?"

And in the still-shivering chaos, the sheer unreality of this moment, Maria was—nodding. *Nodding*, agreeing with him, lost in him—and Simon caught that, his eyes flaring on hers, his chest heaving out a slow, thick exhale.

His hands abruptly gripped her hips tighter, drawing her up against him—and in an easy, powerful shift of movement, Maria was lying fully on the bed again, with an orc lying long atop her. Off to the side, slightly, so he wasn't crushing her with his full weight—but that invading heft between her legs was still firmly there, thrust and trapped deep, even if it felt somewhat softer than before.

Maria's breath was heaving in gulps, and her hands settled on Simon's hard back, fingers spreading against sweat-slicked skin. While he buried his face in her neck, his breath hot and oddly reassuring, and she felt her own breaths slowing, settling into the rugged, rich scent of him. Drinking up the truth of this orc's vital, powerful, untamed body, still hidden and cradled close inside her.

Warm. Safe. At *peace*.

"How did your battle go?" she heard herself whisper, hoarse. "Did you end up fighting the men?"

Simon didn't move, though she thought she could feel him slightly stiffening, his claws flexing against her belly. "It was naught," his husky voice replied. "Only a show, as I said."

Oh. The relief skittered through Maria's chest, but she could still feel her own tension rising, the chaos beginning to swirl again in her thoughts. "But that orc said," she whispered, "that this was the *first* band of men. Like there could be—more *war*."

More war from my husband, she wanted to add, the words so close, so deadly. *More war on my account. What if I've destroyed your entire peace-treaty by coming here.*

But Simon scoffed into Maria's neck, deep and dismissive. "We no fear these foolish men," he said flatly. "They only come here to rattle their swords and bows, and piddle away the last of their lords' waning riches. They only play their fool *games*."

His voice sounded truly derisive—he truly didn't *care*?—and Maria shifted to look at him, searching his lazy, half-lidded eyes. "But—you told me your clan was *dying*," she countered. "And you wanted me to read that treatise today, and it"—she swallowed—"it made an admittedly convincing argument that this war has been *terrible* for you orcs. And that if you're going to survive, it needs to end."

"Ach," Simon replied, without a trace of hesitation. "And this is why the Ka-esh write these words. This is why we spread them across the land. Without this, these men shall always find new cause to come here and rage against us. This war"—his breath exhaled, heavy, against Maria's neck—"shall only be won with words. With whispers. No with swords."

It was a completely bizarre statement, from someone who probably had thirty deadly weapons currently scattered around his room, and—Maria's audacious hands flitted up, feeling at his head—a *dagger* still hidden in his hair. His hair, which she was now touching for the very first time, and it felt surprisingly smooth, like soft silk under her fingers...

"You really believe that," she said, the incredulity ringing through her voice. "*You*. The Enforcer of Orc Mountain."

"Ach," came his reply, his head tilting into the touch of Maria's still-lingering fingers. "I no always think this, but our captain has proven its truth. You no find peace in war. You find peace"—his hand slid up, his claws tapping at Maria's head—"in *here*."

Oh. Maria blinked at him, again and again, her thoughts whirring, her heartbeat jangling. *You find peace in here.* With beliefs. Words. *Whispers.*

And surging up, suddenly, was the realization that this was—*familiar*. Because wasn't this was *exactly* what Maria had done, in coming here? Her husband was far too wealthy, too powerful, to be defeated by force—so she had instead resorted to those letters. Words. Whispers. Perceptions.

A lord, in the prime of his life, cuckolded by an orc.

And said orc was smirking lazily toward her, as though he *knew* all that was currently crashing through her thoughts—and Maria grasped for words, for some crumb of coherent truth. "Well, that's a lovely sentiment, orc," she heard her shaky voice say, "until we remember how you apparently need to fight to the *death* to keep your place within your clan."

But if she'd hoped for a concession, she was disappointed, because Simon only shrugged, his claws lightly tapping against her head. "You ken I no think of this, when I Enforce my kin?" he said coolly. "Or when I buy ripe, yielding woman to bear me a son, with no hunt, and no rut? When I keep her safe in my home, whilst she seeks to please and honour me, and earn my rewards?"

Wait. *Wait.* Did he mean—he couldn't mean—he had some kind of master *plan* with all this? He'd done it all on *purpose*?!

"You bastard," Maria gasped, stiffening all over, gaping at his smug face. "Do you mean—you're playing another *game* with this? Not just with your ridiculous *rewards*, but with—me? Us?! Against your *clan*?!"

Simon's forehead instantly furrowed, his mouth sinking into a scowl. "I told you, I play no games, woman," he replied. "I only seek to be true Skai. Seek to watch. Listen. *Learn.* Seek to find new ways. Find new *future*. Find *peace*."

And once again, it was almost as if this unnerving, alarming orc had somehow slipped inside Maria's very thoughts, and begun speaking them back into her soul. New ways. New future. *Peace.*

"I wish this for you also, Maria," he said, quiet. "I wish you to forget these old ways, and seek new ways with me. Ach?"

Oh. And for some entirely inexplicable reason, Maria found herself—softening. *Relaxing.* Her body sinking against the warm furs beneath her, into the raw, reassuring force of those bottomless, glittering eyes.

"You want me in thrall to you and your horrid rewards, you mean," she said, but there was no heat in it, and good gods, she might have even been *smiling* at him. "When you haven't even *granted* me one yet, after I obeyed you so thoroughly today."

And there was the familiar smirk, curling slow across Simon's mouth—but, perhaps, without the mockery this time. "Oh, you shall have your reward, wilful woman," he purred. "In the shape of two new tools, to further open your pretty holes for me. These ones today were too easy for you, ach?"

Gods, he was such a crude and infuriating *lech*, and Maria glared at his sparkling eyes, and elbowed at the massive weight of his body over her. "That was *not* easy," she archly informed him. "I worked *hard* for you today."

And damn him, smiling down at her like that. Slow, crooked, true, almost like he meant it. Like he was pleased. *Approving.*

"Ach, I ken," he murmured, his face ducking back against her neck, breathing in deep. "Now show me more proof of this, ach? Fuck again?"

And surely it was the hysteria, swallowing her alive—but Maria's eyes had fluttered, her legs slipping up to catch behind his. Her arms curling again around his muscled bulk, her fingers twining deeper in his hair. Stroking, careful, *careful*, against the dagger still hidden within it.

New ways. A new future. *Peace.*

"Oh, *fine*," she whispered, as she drew him down, and touched a kiss to his warm, waiting mouth. "Again."

19

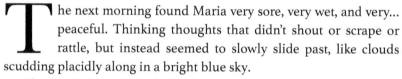

The next morning found Maria very sore, very wet, and very... peaceful. Thinking thoughts that didn't shout or scrape or rattle, but instead seemed to slowly slide past, like clouds scudding placidly along in a bright blue sky.

She was in Simon's bed. She'd spent the night curled into Simon's arms, hearing him snore softly into her ear. The beast at his groin had stayed hidden inside her while they'd slept, whispering quiet and close. And when she'd blinked awake into pure blackness, and felt him swelling within her, she'd gasped, and ground her hips against him, and moaned his name as she came.

She'd fallen asleep again after that, and she could remember Simon getting up at some point in the night, his warm heavy body easing out of the bed. But now she could hear him again, from the direction of his bench, the already-familiar shirring sounds slicing through the stillness.

She yawned and rubbed her eyes, and then rolled over to look at him in the lamplight. He was sharpening what looked to be a smaller knife, with a smaller stone—and as she watched, bemused, he carefully placed the stone on top of the haphazard pyre she'd made, and then raised the little knife to scrape hard against his throat.

Maria gasped, and jerked up to sitting—to which Simon shot her a look that was surely amused, as he scraped the knife again, curving it up over his heavily stubbled jaw. He was—*shaving*?

Maria's mouth made a hoarse, reflexive sound—a *laugh*—and in this easy, quiet moment, there seemed no reason not to sit here and watch him. His hand so deft and capable, the knife stroking quick and efficient against his skin.

"You shave?" she heard her voice ask, with an unfamiliar low lilt. "Every day?"

In return Simon shrugged, and beckoned her toward him with a lazy flick of his fingers. "Most days, ach," he said, once Maria had slipped out of the bed—valiantly fighting to ignore the resulting mess—and strode over to stand before him. "No so oft when I am away."

Away. "Are you away often?" Maria asked, belatedly realizing, first, that the floor had still been relatively clear, from her frantic cleaning spree the day before—and second, that her loincloth must have come off at some point in the night, and that Simon was still naked too. And third, that he was half-smiling at her, his eyes warm and approving as they flicked up and down her fully bared form, lingering on the sticky mess between her thighs.

"Ach, oft," he said, as his big hand reached to grasp her hip, drawing her closer between his sprawled-apart knees. "Today, I must go see some brothers to the west. You shall wait here whilst I work, ach?"

Oh. Waiting again. Maria's thoughts had been dwelling, absurdly, on the arena, or perhaps even on the idea of asking Simon to show her more of the Skai wing—and she felt her eyes drop, her stomach sinking in her belly.

"I don't suppose," she heard herself say, "I could go on your trip with you?"

And even as the hope was foolishly rising—gods, it felt like an *age* since she'd seen the sky—Simon's low, disapproving growl instantly dashed it again. "*Ach*, no," he said, his voice hard. "I spoke to you of this, woman. You are to stay here in the Skai wing, and honour me. Whilst I am away today, you shall eat, and pray here to Skai-kesh, and read these words the Ka-esh have written. I have also granted you these new tools I spoke of, and you shall make good use of these for me."

With that, he gave Maria's hip a firm pat, and then smoothly rose to his feet, and strode around her toward the shelf she'd organized the day before. His hand briefly settling on one of the carved figures—the smiling orc with the barrel chest—and he carefully moved it to the front of his neatened little collection, before reaching below to tug out something from the pile of clothes. A pair of trousers, Maria realized, and he swiftly drew them on, and then stalked over to strap on his usual scimitar.

"When you have done all this," he continued, "you shall go to Baldr"—he jerked his head toward the next room—"and obey what he tells you. And if you again please me in all this, tonight I shall again grant you my reward. Ach?"

Oh. So he really was planning to be away for some time, then. And last night—perhaps last night still hadn't changed anything between them, after all. Not if he was truly still playing this damned rewards game with her. And gods, Maria wasn't even supposed to care, this was only about her freedom, and that was *all*.

So she fought to hold herself still, to ignore the lurching dip in her gut as Simon strode for the door. He was just an orc. She would take what she could get. It didn't matter, it didn't...

But then, abruptly, Simon hesitated. Turned back. His big hand settling warm and powerful against Maria's cheek, tilting her head up, making her meet his intent black eyes.

"I no wish to leave you thus today," he said, his voice low. "But when I come back, my reward shall surely please you, ach? You shall scream even louder than last eve, whilst I plough you with good seed."

The warmth studded and swirled, escaping in a low, reflexive gasp from Maria's throat, and Simon's mouth pulled into a crooked little smile, his teeth glinting sharp against his lip. "Think upon this, my pretty one," he purred, "whilst you use your new tools for me."

With that, he turned and stalked out the door, leaving Maria standing there naked behind him. Feeling oddly hot and shivery, and again, almost... content. Peaceful. Perhaps even... *eager.*

And suddenly it felt easy, somehow, to obey the orders he'd given her. To speak a short, fervent prayer to Skai-kesh, with today's fear, and longing, and blessing. To go for the chest, pull out the waiting basket of food, and eat until it was empty. To read another of the orc treatises—this one a highly reassuring, if also unnerving, discussion of processes to ensure safe orcling birth. And then, finally, to turn her attention to those new... tools. Almost indistinguishable from the previous two, but for their slightly larger size.

At least the increase wasn't too terrifying, so Maria gamely took them in hand, and once again made for the bed. Where she indeed thought of Simon, of his huge powerful body trapped deep within, as she coated the smooth stones in the heavy, scented slickness still oozing from her crease. And then she eased them inside, one and then the other, feeling herself gasp and writhe at the heat, the burn, the invading uncompromising fullness. Until there were no thoughts left but this, the power and the pleasure, her whole body wracking with her breaths.

She finally stopped once the relief had soared and settled, leaving a heated soreness behind—but also, again, the strange, inexplicable contentment. And once she'd wobbled back to the chest, and safely hidden the tools away again, she dressed in another of Simon's tunics, combed through her tangled curls with her fingers, and straightened out the messy bed. And with all that accomplished, she almost felt a little jaunty as she picked up the lamp, and went for Baldr's new room next door.

"Baldr?" she asked, as she reached the dark doorway. "Simon wanted me to—"

But the words broke in her throat, her stomach flopping—because Baldr wasn't alone. He was with—*Drafli*. And Drafli currently had him pinned face-first to the wall, trousers yanked down to his knees, his hips snapping hard against Baldr's bared arse.

Good *gods*. Maria had, of course, already seen far worse sights in this mountain—but even so, for an instant she seemed frozen in place, her eyes fixed wide to the sight. To the almost predatory intensity in Drafli's fluid driving form, the unmistakable pain and pleasure in Baldr's half-lidded eyes. To the way Drafli's head bent to Baldr's neck, while Baldr arched and moaned, his claws dragging down the wall—

When Drafli's face drew away again, there was *blood* pooling down Baldr's neck, staining his grey tunic. And without breaking his rhythm,

Drafli slowly, deliberately turned his head toward... *Maria*. Showing her the blood smeared all over his mouth, his lips drawing back to bare all his sharp teeth, his eyes narrow and glittering and *furious*—

Shit. Maria jerked away from the door, far too late, and dodged back for the safety of Simon's room. Wishing, irrationally, that there was a door to slam behind her, to help block out the shocking reality happening just next door. Drafli had... *bitten* Baldr. And Baldr had... *liked* it.

And now, of course, swarming through Maria's thoughts, were visions of Simon. Did *Simon* want such things? Expect such things? Would he command her to bear it, and expect her to obey, or bribe her with yet another *reward*?

A sharp shiver rippled down Maria's back, one that didn't feel entirely like fear, and she groaned aloud as she thrust down the lamp, her eyes wildly flitting about the room. Catching, abruptly, on the haphazard array of armour and weapons scattered about, which she'd scarcely *touched* in her cleaning spree...

She lunged toward the nearest stack with a gulp of relief, her hands frantically digging through the mess. Separating it by type— knives, swords, scabbards, belts and baldrics—and stacking it all into neat piles on the floor around her. And then frowning as she searched the room, because there was in truth nowhere to put *any* of this...

"Maria?" came a tentative voice from behind her—and when Maria whirled around to look, it was Baldr. Fully dressed in trousers and a fresh tunic, and standing a bit stiffly in the doorway. His grey-green face was suffused with pink, his gaze not quite meeting hers, and his neck looked truly *ravaged* with raw, reddened, deadly-looking teeth-marks.

"Are you all right?" Maria asked, breathless, her eyes locked on his neck—and in return Baldr nodded, silent, his cheeks flushing even redder. Clearly not wanting to talk about it, and Maria swallowed hard, and forced her attention back to the piles of steel around her.

"I don't suppose you know the best way to store these things?" she asked, her voice unnaturally loud. "There are so *many* of them, and it can't be good for them to just be scattered everywhere on the floor, right? There are hooks in the walls for some of them, but the rest are—"

She flapped her hands helplessly at the mess, and she could hear Baldr's exhale as he strode over to stand beside her. "Ach, it is a lot," he replied, still rather stiff. "I ken Simon should wish to keep them close at hand, so hanging ought to be best. Should you wish, I could speak to the Ka-esh upon this, as they are the ones who direct such work."

Maria shot him a grateful smile, and in return Baldr gave an uneasy smile back. "Simon wished me to take you to our Chief Healer," he said. "His clinic is just at the edge of the Skai wing, if you should come with me?"

By this point, Maria was all too enthusiastic to go somewhere, *anywhere*, and soon she was walking down the corridor with Baldr, eagerly glancing around in the lamplight. However, Baldr hadn't again spoken, and the silence seemed to scrape louder between them as they walked. Enough that Maria had opened her mouth to ask about something as inane as possible, perhaps these weapon-hanging processes—

"I hope I did not," Baldr blurted out, sudden and loud, "frighten you, Maria. I did not intend—"

He broke off there, grimacing, and Maria attempted a shrug, a lightness in her voice she didn't at all feel. "You didn't frighten me in the least, Baldr. Though I will admit that your Drafli is a *little* terrifying, don't you think? And he surely loathes me, though I'm not sure I understand why?"

Beside her Baldr's shoulders had sagged, though the grimace kept twisting at his mouth. "Drafli is not *mine*," he said, his voice thin. "Skai orcs do not claim other orcs, or offer them fidelity, like they do with women. *Ever*. And Drafli does not hate *you*, he only"—he jerked a shrug—"struggles with women, ach?"

Oh. Maria couldn't help a searching look toward Baldr, her head tilting. "Struggles with women how?"

Baldr sighed and ran a clawed hand against his braid, surely about to speak—but then something changed on his face, his form. His eyes narrowing, his steps slowing, his breath inhaling sharp. His body swiftly easing in front of Maria, smooth and powerful, and he suddenly seemed unnervingly large, angry, deadly.

"Little brother Baldr!" boomed a voice from up the corridor, deep and horribly familiar—and Maria flinched all over as *Ulfarr* strode out of the darkness ahead. He was flanked by two big, unfamiliar orcs with scarred, rugged faces, and he was *smiling* at Baldr. Smiling at *her*.

"And our fair Maria," Ulfarr continued, as he swaggered to a halt before Baldr, his gaze intent on Maria behind him. "What brings you away from your stubborn keeper this morn?"

Maria truly could not speak, her voice locked in her throat, and thank the gods Baldr hovered close before her, his arms crossing over his chest, his eyes narrow and unafraid. "Simon works today, to serve us all," he said flatly. "As you well know, Ulfarr."

But Ulfarr scoffed a laugh, his eyes still unnervingly intent on Maria. "Ach, he moves against brothers who only follow their true natures," he said, "and leaves alone those who break the deep ways of our clan."

Maria could feel Baldr bristling, a low hiss burning from his throat. "And the *deep ways* of your clan demand you honour your Enforcer and his judgement," he shot back. "As well as the claims your brothers make upon their mates."

Ulfarr's smile only broadened, his eyes mocking as they flicked to Baldr's face. "Ach, but our pretty Maria is not a truly won Skai mate, is she?" he purred. "Just as you are not either, my pretty Grisk. No matter how oft or how easy you bend over for our Right Hand—or how scent-bound you keep yourself for him. Ach?"

Baldr didn't immediately reply, and Ulfarr laughed again, lower this time. "There is naught binding you to us," he said, his eyes sliding lazily from Baldr, to Maria, and back again. "Beyond the Skai's deep need to spill our seed into the tightest hole, and despoil all that is fresh and pretty, until it is broken and begging at our feet. Mayhap"—his eyes settled on Maria, heavy—"our Maria, at least, shall soon learn more of this, and taste the ways of a true Skai mate. Ach?"

A hard chill ripped down Maria's back, and she was deeply, distantly grateful for the sound of Baldr's loud scoff, breaking into the tension around them. "Keep dreaming, Ulfarr," he snapped. "Simon is *not* about to let her go that easily, most of all to the likes of you. Now fuck off, we have places to be."

With that, he shoved his way past Ulfarr, dragging Maria after him by the wrist. Her feet stumbling, her heart racing, her eyes still trapped on Ulfarr, on the smug superior *mockery* on his face.

"Farewell, my pretty Maria," he crooned, low, taunting. "We meet again soon, ach?"

Baldr made a sound much like a bark over his shoulder, and pulled Maria along faster. Around a corner, down a black corridor with no doors, around another corner, up a twisty little ascent. Straight past multiple groups of new, unfamiliar orcs, some of them looking at her with curiosity, others with suspicion, others with a startling, visceral *dislike*.

"Woman Enforcer *paid*," one of their voices growled, as Baldr dragged her past. "*Cheated* Skai on rut. Not even on *mouth*."

Baldr thoroughly ignored this alarming statement, but the next group was even louder, openly pointing and muttering as they passed. "She is Enforcer false mate," one of them hissed to the orc beside him. "He no yet fuck her before us. No even scent of *son* yet, ach?"

Baldr snapped something back at these orcs, but Maria couldn't seem to hear it over the sickening, curdling echoes in her brain. *Paid. Cheated Skai. No yet fuck her before us. Not even scent of son. Need to despoil all that is fresh and pretty...*

We meet again soon, ach?

The shivers were racing down Maria's body, wracking against skin and bone, and Baldr had sped up to nearly a run, dodging past any orcs they met in the corridor. Until finally they burst into a room, a new room, one with multiple beds in it—but Maria could scarcely see them through the blurring in her eyes, the worsening tremors in her limbs, the shudders stealing her breath. The panic rising, rising, familiar, horrible...

Not here. Not now. This couldn't be happening here, not again, *please*—

Baldr was saying something else Maria couldn't hear, urgent and low. And another huge, unfamiliar, terrifying orc was lurching forward, his clawed hand outstretched, reaching straight for her face—

But before he could touch her, the terror caught, flashed, exploded—and the world screamed, and screamed, and finally went black.

20

Maria awoke to the sight of... orcs. Three huge, looming orcs, leaning over her in the bed. One of them familiar—Baldr, her sluggish brain supplied—and two of them new. Mostly new. Except...

"Hello again, Skai," said one of them—the scarred, ugly one—and Maria twitched at the sudden memory of him lunging for her, before the encroaching darkness. "I'm Efterar of Clan Ash-Kai, this mountain's Chief Healer. And this"—he tilted his head toward the slimmer, loose-haired, bare-chested orc beside him—"is my mate Kesst. Are you well, woman?"

Maria blinked dully toward him, and reflexively wriggled her arms and legs—and found, to her genuine surprise, that she *did* feel well, with no hint of pain. And odder still, no chaos, no panic, no terror screaming through her thoughts. *Nothing?*

"You were about to be caught in a panic spell," the scarred Efterar orc continued, his voice surprisingly calm and soothing. "So I put you under for a moment, to clear some of the stress from your system. I apologize if I've alarmed you, Skai."

Panic spell. Stress. *Skai.* Maria's brain still wasn't following all this, though she somehow felt, quite strongly, that she ought to be alarmed, ashamed, afraid—but there was no judgement in these orcs' watching eyes. No mockery.

"Um," she said, stupidly, as she shoved uncertainly out of the bed, and up to her thankfully steady feet. "What's a—a *panic spell?*"

The two new orcs exchanged glances, and the Kesst one flashed her a quick, halfhearted smile. "It's what happens to some of us, after we've had to deal with too much in one go," he said. "Did something in particular set this one off, sweetheart? Or is it just the combined effect of being stuck in that mess of a Skai wing for days on end?"

Maria blinked blankly toward him again—surely these orcs didn't think her hysteria was *normal?*—and thankfully Baldr shifted beside her, and cleared his throat.

"Ulfarr has been out there causing strife again," he said, voice hard. "Stirring up the Skai. Pushing them to take sides on this, and make their opinions known."

He waved a vague hand toward Maria, meaning *her*, and a grim comprehension flared across Efterar's eyes, while Kesst gave a loud snort. "Typical," he said. "Leave it to the Skai to try to run off their first woman brave enough to come here in a decade. Don't take it person-ally, Maria, they've always been a disaster. Someday our captain will sort them out, when he's in the mood to risk a complete mutiny. But until that happy day comes"—he shrugged a sharp-looking bare shoulder—"we're stuck with them."

Maria kept blinking at him, digesting that, while her memories flipped through images of the other orcs—the non-Skai orcs—she'd met so far in this mountain. The cheerful, considerate Baldr. The quiet, handsome John. The other orcs she'd met that first day here, who'd universally seemed to support her contract with Simon. And even these new orcs, now standing a respectful distance away from her, without even the faintest trace of leering or mockery in their eyes. Because they weren't...*Skai?*

"Skai aren't *all* like that," Baldr interjected, and his eyes darting between Maria and Kesst were troubled. "Many of them seek to right their clan's darker ways. Simon most of all."

There was an instant's stillness, in which Kesst raised his black brows at Baldr. "And Drafli?"

Baldr shrugged, though a distinctive redness was creeping up his cheeks. "Drafli is not supposed to take sides in any of this," he replied stiffly. "As the captain's Right Hand, he is expected to stand for the Skai alone."

Maria's brain was still fighting to catch up, piecing this together with the rest of the bits and pieces she'd learned so far. "And why would the captain's Right Hand stand *only* for the Skai?" she asked, without quite meaning to. "I thought your captain commands all five of your clans?"

If the orcs felt the question was impertinent, they didn't show it, and Baldr easily nodded. "Ach, this is so," he said. "But the place of the captain's Right Hand has always been held by a Skai, as far back as memory goes. Without this, the Skai would not keep their allegiance to the captain, or this mountain, or even their own Enforcer. And then—"

There was another beat of silence, and Kesst snorted again. "They're off running ruts, raising hell with other orcs, and trying to steal each other's women and sons. Not to mention starting fresh wars with the humans willy-nilly in their wake."

Oh. A powerful chill flashed down Maria's back, and she wrapped her arms around her waist, squeezing tight. "Ulfarr wants," she heard herself whisper, "to steal *me*. From Simon."

And gods, why had she betrayed such a thing, to these strange orcs she'd only just met—but perhaps this was why, the grimness tightening in Efterar's mouth, the contemptuous roll of Kesst's dark eyes.

"Of course he does," Kesst snapped, voice brisk. "That prick wants everything Simon touches, and always has. Keep your distance, Maria, Ulfarr's a *complete* ass. And a total rubbish fuck compared to Simon, too."

Maria had already begun silently nodding, agreeing—until the truth of those words settled, burrowing deep into her churning gut. *A total rubbish fuck, compared to Simon.* Which meant—which *had* to mean—

Maria's head had instantly swarmed with painful visions of her husband, sprawled in silk sheets—and blinking at this Kesst orc, she belatedly realized that he was actually rather good-looking, with his long lean form, silken dark hair, and wry, speaking eyes. And curse her, but now she was envisioning it, Simon freely being a *good fuck* for this confident, handsome, laughing orc, and what that would have looked like, *felt* like. Without a contract, without secrets and games and rewards. *She is only woman I buy...*

Maria swallowed hard, her eyes now intently studying the stone floor, and she heard Kesst clear his throat. "That was *ages* ago, by the way," he said, a little stilted. "And Simon's not the kind of orc to go sneaking around on a mate."

Maria felt herself twitch all over, the twist tightening in her gut. "But I'm *not* Simon's mate," her wooden voice said. "I'm just a woman he's bought to bear him a son. He doesn't even really *like* me."

There was more silence, thick and tense, until finally Efterar loudly coughed. "Was there something I was supposed to be looking at here, Grisk?" he asked, clipped, and when Maria glanced up, he was frowning irritably toward Baldr. "Your neck, maybe?"

Baldr grimaced and shook his head, his face flushing bright red. "No, thank you. But, er, Simon wished you to check over Maria. About, er—"

He didn't say it, but he didn't have to, his chagrined eyes briefly flicking toward Maria's waist. And now Maria was the one flushing, her cheeks burning with heat, her eyes foolishly prickling, she wasn't supposed to care, not about any of this, her *freedom*—

"I see," Efterar replied, voice still crisp. "Are you comfortable with me examining you for signs of pregnancy, Maria?"

Right. They were saying this out loud, then. And yes, Maria had been intimate with Simon multiple times now, with that single goal in mind—and suddenly she found she urgently, desperately needed to know. If they had—if she had—

"Yes," she said, her voice cracking. "Yes, please, whatever you can do."

Efterar nodded and stepped a little closer, his eyes fixed on Maria's belly. "I'll need to touch you, if that's all right?"

Maria waved him forward, her body snapped taut, and in return Efterar reached out his clawless hands with deliberate slowness. Until they settled flat against Maria's waist over her tunic, his eyes gone distant and thoughtful.

"This is good," he said, to Maria's vague surprise. "You're whole and hale inside, with no tearing or bruising. Simon has clearly been careful with you, to his credit. Do you have any pain, from anywhere he's taken you? Or anywhere else?"

The heat kept burning Maria's cheeks, but she somehow shook her head, and in return Efterar gave a firm nod. "Good," he said again. "Though I see you haven't released your own seed in a while—due to stress, most likely. But I can already feel it warming, and if you're just patient a little longer, it will soon come. Simon's seed will surely help too, if he keeps filling you like this."

Efterar seemed very certain of all this, his voice and eyes betraying only a clear satisfaction—but Maria's shock was still swarming, rattling close and precarious against her ribs. "How," she managed, "can you possibly *know* such things?"

"Well, with ripe women, even those with reproductive challenges, orc-seed often prompts various—" Efterar began, glancing up at her face—and then he grimaced, and shook his head. "Right. I am a healer in the ways of orcs, you see, rather than humans. And thus, I use my scent, and the gift of my fathers' sight, to see what is hidden."

It took Maria's still-whirling brain far too long to truly understand the truth of this, of what this orc was actually saying. Because he *was* saying that. Wasn't he? And wait, all those rumours about orcs and their evil black magic had been *true*?!

"Truly?" her strangled voice gasped. "You're using... *dark magic*? To see *inside* me?!"

Something much like wariness, or perhaps distance, passed across Efterar's eyes, and Kesst immediately stepped closer to him, slipping a long arm around his waist. "Indeed, he is," Kesst said coolly. "Efterar is quite possibly the greatest healer in the realm. It's a rare gift for a human, to have one such as this caring for you."

Shit, shit, she'd *insulted* them, and Maria rubbed at her suddenly pounding temples as Kesst kept talking, his voice even colder than before. "But if you'd rather a healer who works more in your primitive human ways, perhaps Salvi will better help you?"

His eyes had flicked beyond Maria as he spoke, and when she belatedly spun around to look, there were two more strange new orcs, striding into the room. Both fully clothed, with relatively smooth faces and long black braids, and Maria was forcefully reminded of the John orc, with his equally unmarked skin and almost elf-like appearance.

"What am I helping w—" began the taller of the two new orcs, but his voice caught as his dark eyes settled on Maria, flicking up and down. "Wait. *This* is Simon's new mate?"

Maria's throat felt too choked to speak, but the new orc didn't seem to notice. Instead, he was darting an increasingly amused glance down at the smaller orc beside him—an orc who had hesitated in place, blinking at Maria, his sharp white tooth biting at his lip.

The first orc's mouth had twitched into a delighted smile, his eyes gleaming as he strode over toward Maria, tugging the second orc along after him. "Ach, it is *great* joy to meet you, woman," he said, his voice sounding almost gleeful. "I am Salvi, of Clan Ka-esh. And this is Tristan, my mate."

Another orc with an orc mate. Maria's ever-whirling thoughts darted toward Baldr, and what he'd said about Skai and orc mates—but then she dragged her attention back to these new orcs, and attempted a smile toward them. "Hi, I'm Maria," she replied. "It's lovely to meet you both."

The first orc kept grinning at her, his gaze darting between her and his mate Tristan. Almost as if he were expecting something from them, or perhaps *comparing* them, and Maria didn't miss the sudden stain of pink, creeping up this Tristan's neck.

"*Elskan,*" the Tristan orc said, a low note of warning in his soft voice—but Salvi had burst out laughing, his shoulders shaking, his eyes still flicking gleefully between Tristan and Maria.

"F-forgive me," he said, fighting with visible effort to swallow his guffaws. "But it really is uncanny, ach? Even the *scent.*"

He was glancing at the other three orcs—all of whom seemed to be following his meaning without effort. Baldr giving a faint grimace, Efterar a twitching tightening of his mouth, and Kesst looking nearly as amused as Salvi did, his gaze also darting from Tristan to Maria.

It was some kind of joke Maria wasn't getting, presumably at her expense, and she glanced again at this Tristan orc, whose face looked just as red as hers felt. And it was in that moment, blinking at him, that she finally caught their meaning. This orc—*looked* like her. Or rather, she looked like *him*?!

And yes, yes, the resemblance was unmistakably there, despite this orc's pointed ears and grey skin. He was taller, but not by much, and his size wasn't far off from Maria's either, his build slim for an orc, hers strong for a human. But the similarities were clearest by far around the face, with the large dark eyes, the nose, the line of the jaw. Even the same curve and fullness to their mouths, though Maria's was obviously lacking the sharp teeth, which were still biting at this orc's lip.

Kesst had murmured under his breath toward Efterar, speaking in the orcs' black-tongue, but Maria was sure she caught the word *Simon* in it. And something else, too, the exact same note she'd so often heard in her life as a duchess. When people around her would whisper, and she would furtively look away, and pretend as though she hadn't noticed.

And perhaps it was the hysteria again, or the still-swirling mess in her brain, or just being sick to death of secrets and hiding and lies. But Maria felt her chin lifting, her eyes settling on this Tristan, her arms tightening over her tunic.

"Oh, so *you* were intimate with Simon too, I take it?" she said, as smoothly as she could, over the thunder rising in her chest. "And you're saying that maybe now"—she swallowed hard—"maybe Simon's hired me as some kind of *replacement* for you? Or for *him*?"

She jerked her head toward Kesst, noting again, this time with a horrible sickening feeling, that he was also slim for an orc, with softer features, and large dark eyes. And the reality of this was slowly settling in, had Simon truly only hired her because she reminded him of *them*? Of *orcs*? Because *that* was what he truly wanted?

The amusement had slipped at once from Kesst's face, and before her Tristan visibly blanched, his eyes gone very wide. "Ach, no," he said hurriedly. "Simon and I—I would *never*—"

He shot a helpless glance toward the Salvi orc, who had begun to look as though he regretted starting this, his gaze uneasy on Maria's face. "Ach, Tristan has always been mine," Salvi said firmly. "He should *never* choose to touch a Skai, ach, *sæti*?"

But that only made it worse, the misery pounding in Maria's ribs, at the back of her skull. So Simon *had* perhaps wanted Tristan, then, and been rejected. Maybe the same with Kesst, as well. And since, apparently, even these other *orcs* didn't want to be associated with the Skai, maybe it made perfect sense why Simon had agreed to buy her. Because she reminded him of *them*. Of an *orc*.

And while Maria had once thought herself an adequately attractive woman, or at least a handsome one—a duke had married her, after all—six years of marriage had already badly diminished her confidence. And now it felt like these orcs were stomping upon it, mocking, jeering at her orc-like face. *She is only woman I buy.*

Maria suddenly felt dangerously close to weeping, and she lunged away from these orcs, before they could see it, before they could laugh. Hurling herself unseeing toward the door, ignoring the instant rising swell of voices behind her. It didn't matter. It *didn't*. She was only here for her freedom. For revenge.

She was multiple steps down the rapidly darkening corridor before she realized there were no lamps here, and she had no light, and there was surely no hope of navigating this damned mountain in the dark. So she just stood there in the blackness, her breath heaving, her hands over her face, twitching at the sound of footsteps, jogging closer.

"Maria," said Baldr's voice, hoarse and breathless. "We did not mean to hurt you, or insult you. We all wish you to stay, and make Simon a good mate. I swear this. Ach?"

Maria twitched again, her hands jerking away from her face, and when her eyes caught Baldr's they were wide and dark, flickering in the light of the lamp he was carrying. "I *swear* this," he said again. "And Tristan and Kesst are oft named as the fairest orcs in this mountain, ach? Skai *like* fair, pretty, unmarked things, and they crave this in their mates most of all. You are *blessed*, to look as they do."

He'd waved a clawed hand at his own faintly scarred face, his voice tilting toward something like desperation. Saying, clearly, that *he* didn't look like that, that he wished he looked like *her*—and Maria again rubbed at her eyes, and dragged deep for breath.

"I'm just," she made herself say, "quite tired, I think. If you could please take me to my room—Simon's room, I mean—that would—"

Baldr nodded without delay, striding rapidly down the corridor, his face turned intently away from her. And gods, now she'd insulted him too, the one orc who'd been so consistently kind to her. An orc who'd clearly been rejected by the Skai, too. *There is naught binding you to us...*

"You ought not to compare yourself to others, Baldr," Maria made her wavering voice say. "You are a very handsome orc, and I am sure anyone who properly knows you would adore you, just as you are."

She could hear Baldr's swallow, catching in his throat, and his glance toward her was equal parts bright and bitter, his mouth a thin line. "You are very kind, Maria. But—"

His voice halted there, his eyes abruptly darting away from her, narrowing on something down the corridor. "Ach," he said, under his breath, almost more to himself than to her. "Simon has returned."

Simon has returned. And despite the chaos still chattering through Maria's thoughts—she reminded Simon of an *orc*—she still felt something leap, sudden and eager, in her chest. "He has?"

"Ach," Baldr replied, though his eyes were still narrow, and she could see him inhaling, slow and purposeful. "But mayhap—"

His body had hesitated, his gaze darting uncertainly around them, and Maria again felt the unease rising, scraping deep inside. "Could you take me to him? Please?"

Baldr kept hesitating, clearly reluctant now, as if he was *hiding* something, again. And Maria was so gods-damned *tired* of secrets and lies, and she turned to fully face him, her teeth gritted tight. "*Please,* Baldr," she said. "If you really want me to stay, you will take me to him."

It was probably manipulation, or even hysteria, but Maria truly didn't care anymore, and instead stood there, and waited. Until Baldr looked away, nodding, and lurched back to a walk again.

And as they weaved through the twisty Skai corridors, passing yet more frowning, leering orcs, Maria began to hear noise, up ahead. Noise that sounded like raised voices, like shouting, with one orc's distinctive deep voice booming louder than the rest...

"You *knew,*" it bellowed, rumbling through the air, plunging into Maria's belly. "You hid this from me. You *lie.*"

Baldr's eyes had closed, a pained expression flitting across his face, but he kept walking, not even looking where he was going. While another voice echoed around them, speaking in black-tongue, hard and clipped and mocking.

"No," Simon's voice growled back. "I *asked* this of you. You spoke *false* to me. Your scent was there. Did *you* do this, also?!"

Baldr was visibly grimacing now, and as they turned into a familiar-looking corridor, his hand clenched against Maria's arm, holding her still. And Maria didn't need telling, at this point, and she stared at the sight up ahead, at the mass of orcs filling the corridor, at the one massive orc in the midst of it all.

Simon. Tense. Furious. With dark streaks and splatters all over his trousers, his bare chest, his face. And backed against the wall before him was another orc, one who looked vaguely familiar, because—Maria's breath caught—she'd already seen him today. It was one of the orcs who'd been with Ulfarr, while he'd spoken to her and Baldr in the corridor. While Ulfarr had mocked, and threatened, and *laughed.*

And this orc was laughing too, as though Simon's rage were a *joke*, and that—Maria twitched—was because Ulfarr was here too. Standing close beside this laughing orc, easing his huge form between him and Simon.

"You have no right to Enforce Skaap over this," cut in Ulfarr's voice, dragging thick and awful through the tension choking the corridor. "Not when you yourself have broken our clan's ways, and half our orcs no longer support you. Ach?"

The words spewing from Simon's mouth were all in black-tongue, deep and dark and choked with rage. And the orc he'd been accusing only kept laughing, *laughing*, while Ulfarr crossed his arms over his chest, his chin rising, the image of superior condescension, of victory—

Until Simon—*lunged.* Somehow snapping his huge form around and behind Ulfarr, dragging out the laughing orc by the neck, while the orc's guffaws choked into silence—

Simon's arms and fists shot out, almost too rapid to see—and suddenly the laughing orc was screeching, all mirth vanished from his face. Because Simon had the orc's *arm*, oh gods, it was the same hold he'd had on Baldr when they'd been sparring—but this time he kept going, kept pushing, the orc's face contorting with pain, his scream raising the hairs all up Maria's back—

The crack of breaking bone echoed through the corridor, sharp and vicious and horrifying. While the orc's awful howls rose to a horrible new shrillness—and Simon's form shifted, fluid, easy. Lunging for the screaming orc's leg this time, and while Maria distantly knew she should cover her eyes, she *should*, she could only seem to stare, shocked and terrified, as Simon swiftly wrapped the orc's trousered leg in his own powerful grip, and then—*kicked* it. *Broke* it.

The screams were truly deafening, shrieking and roaring, but no one came to the orc's aid, not even Ulfarr. And Simon had risen to his feet, huge and deadly and merciless, and *spat* straight down onto the orc's writhing, screaming form.

"Should I catch you in *one more falsehood*," Simon growled, his deep voice carrying over the orc's screams, his booted foot sinking a hard kick into the orc's undefended side, "I shall break *every bone* you own, and *paint* these walls in your blood!"

The orc didn't answer—couldn't, through his piercing wails—and Simon whirled away, his face heavy with disgust and loathing, and stalked up the corridor. Toward—toward *them*. Toward *Maria*.

But behind him, Ulfarr was stepping forward, his hands in fists, his eyes narrow and cold. "You forget yourself, Skai," he said, his voice booming against the walls, reeking of mockery, of malice. "You forget your clan's own ways."

Simon answered with a menacing snarl, a snap of his teeth over his shoulder. "I forget naught," he hissed back, his voice just as dangerous. "I am yet your rightful Enforcer. I ken what I do."

Ulfarr's bark of a laugh was chilly, lethal. "Then you know also," he called, "how you must pay, *Enforcer*. On the rise of the next moon, I challenge you for the place of Enforcer, before all our clan. And when you fail"—he smiled, wicked and deadly—"all you have shall be *mine*."

21

Maria felt struck to the stone floor, while Ulfarr's threat echoed against the walls, her ears, her heart. He was *challenging* Simon? By the rise of the next moon?

And surely that was a matter of weeks? *Days*?

And Ulfarr was still smiling, with that vicious, vile certainty in his eyes. Eyes that had flicked, steady and sure, toward *Maria*.

"Twelve nights, Enforcer," he said, with a wink, almost as though he'd read her thoughts. "Enjoy your woman while you can, and put your affairs in order, ach?"

The urge to run was suddenly all-consuming, swallowing everything—and thankfully Simon was here, his huge arm swiping for Maria's as he passed. Yanking her wholly away from Ulfarr, from Baldr, dragging her up the corridor after him. And oh gods, what was happening, what had she just *seen*, twelve *days*?

But Simon only kept striding, jerking Maria around one corner, and then another, and then a final-feeling sideways halt. And when light sparked before Maria's eyes, they were back in his familiar room, his candle burning on the shelf beside his carvings, casting their ghoulish shadows on the wall behind.

And as Maria blinked blankly at Simon's massive, taut form, his huge clawed hand snapped toward one of the figures—the smiling, barrel-chested orc at the front—and spun it around, away, so it was facing the wall behind it. And next Simon's hand jerked up for his hair, for his *dagger*, flipping it out with astonishing ease—and before Maria could move, speak, *breathe*, he'd dragged the dagger-blade straight down his spread-open palm, surging bubbling red *blood* in its wake.

Maria's throat choked back a scream, her hands clapping over her mouth, but Simon entirely ignored her. And instead, he strode for the wall behind her, and thrust his bleeding hand flat against it.

It was nonsensical, irrational, *absurd*—but Simon's body kept holding still, purposeful, waiting. His head bowing, his eyes clenched shut, his shoulders rising and settling with his heavy breaths.

And when he finally yanked his hand away, there was—another *mark* on the wall. One more messy dark line, dripping thick and red, beside all the rest. But this one bright and fresh and new, and Maria's eyes felt trapped on the rest of them, dozens of them, had Simon done all this, *why*—

And suddenly she was looking at him, really looking, frozen in the sight of the streaks and splatters all over his bare chest, his trousers, his hands. All dark reddish-black, not fresh, not like that new mark on his wall—

"W-what happened," she heard her shaky voice stammer. "D-did you—you didn't—"

And gods, she couldn't even say it, and Simon was glaring straight back at her, his black gaze cold, flinty, utterly unrepentant. As though daring Maria to continue that sentence, as though he were making a silent, but very real threat. As if he were saying, *Don't you dare call me out on this, human.*

Something kicked inside Maria's belly, harsh and disbelieving—after all she'd already borne to honour him, he was really going to do this? He was going to stand here and glare at her and refuse to tell her why he was covered with *blood*? Why he'd just broken an orc's bones in a public fucking *corridor*?!

"What *happened*," Maria repeated, steadier this time. "Why did Ulfarr challenge you. Why did you just *do* that!"

But Simon's lip had curled, his head shaking, his eyes dangerously flashing. "You no judge me, woman," he hissed at her. "I am yet Enforcer."

"Yes, I'm aware," Maria snapped back. "And I'm not judging you. I just want to know what the hell is going on!"

But it was like Simon's anger was a sparking flame, catching and rising upon hers, and he came a sharp, deadly step closer. "I am Enforcer," he said again, dragging out the words, as though Maria were far too foolish to comprehend. "I Enforce my kin."

Maria's frustration kept circling, rising, the anger jolting harder, stronger. "By maiming them?" she demanded. "By *killing* them?!"

And good gods, that look on his face, because yes, that was exactly what he'd done. He'd *killed* someone today, and there wasn't even a trace of regret in his eyes, only the ever-rising rage. "Ach," he snarled back. "You no judge me, woman. This is no your place. Your place is to honour me, and *obey!*"

He'd come another step closer as he spoke, looming over her, his eyes crackling, his hands in fists. Cold, bitter, mocking. *Paid. Naught binding you to us. Only woman I buy...*

And *surely* it was the hysteria, now. Rising like a devouring beast, swallowing Maria up, leaving only darkness and rage behind. A rage that somehow—impossibly—lurched her forward, the rest of the way, into this terrifying orc. Into his blood and violence and mockery, so she could grasp at his groin, and grip her hand around the beast waiting beneath.

And of course, he was already hard. Swollen vicious and hungry, the predictable lech, just as she'd somehow known he would be...

"Like this, you prick?" she hissed back at him, incredulous, *furious*. "This is what you want from me, after you *abandon* me here all day, while you go off and *murder* someone?!"

Something feral and malevolent blazed through Simon's black eyes, a deep growl rippling from his mouth—and then his forceful hands grabbed Maria, and the world juddered sideways. Shifting and swirling, rising and falling, thrusting her face-down onto the bed, on her hands and knees. While hard clawed fingers yanked her legs wide, thrust up her tunic and her loincloth, exposing her bare and open and quivering before his raging watching eyes.

"Ach," his voice gritted out behind her. "And you no judge me, woman, for *you* wish for this also!"

And fuck the utter bastard, because he was gripping tighter on her thighs, yanking her further apart. And that hot, slick, pulsating hardness had already settled there, finding its place against her, huge and brutally uncompromising, while Maria gasped and arched and moaned—

"Ach?" he snarled, holding it there, pulsing, swelling, seeping its warm liquid inside. "You wish for this?"

Maria's thoughts were wildly spiralling, her hungry heat clamping against him, fighting for more, *more*—and he *laughed*, cold and mocking and cruel. "Ach?" he repeated, nudging just a little deeper, and Maria felt herself groan, her hips angling up, her body desperately convulsing, pleading, oh gods, oh please, he *had* to still want her...

"Ach, woman?" he demanded. "You wish to be filled and used by orc you call *murderer*?!"

And Maria was nodding, *nodding*. Even as the vision of Ulfarr flashed again through her thoughts, together with the memories of Kesst, of Tristan. The lovers Simon had *really* wanted, she was only a woman he'd bought...

"Ach?" Simon barked at her, his voice sending a hard shudder down Maria's already-trembling back. "Speak, woman! You wish for this?"

There was no possible way to lie, to hide the shame, not now, not with the truth of him there, taunting her, *wanting* her. "Yes," she choked, desperate, craving. "*Gods*, yes."

For a single, hanging instant, all was still—and then Simon drove inside with shocking, breathtaking force. Slicing in straight and deep, slamming those swollen bollocks hard below. Wringing a shrill, helpless whimper from Maria's mouth, her body suddenly invaded and owned, at the utter mercy of a huge, punishing orc.

He ground inside for a breath, as though to make her feel it, to *mock* her with it—and then he yanked out again. Holding himself just at the trembling edge of her, perhaps watching this, savouring this—before slamming back inside again, brutal, merciless.

"Still?" he hissed at her, his hands yanking her hips back harder against him, pinioning her even deeper upon his strength. The sheer sensation scattering all conscious thought into emptiness, so pure and potent that it took Maria far too long to follow what his question meant. Still. Did she still wish for this now.

And she nodded, yes, *yes*, as her impaled body clutched tighter against the hot flesh jammed inside it. Quivering upon him, milking him, craving him, and it was impossible that she should still want this, appalling, *unthinkable*—

But she did. She did, even when Simon drew out again, and slammed in hard enough to make her teeth chatter. And then again, and again, setting up a ruthless, powerful rhythm, fierce and raw and punishing. Using Maria as he pleased, as an object, a *purchase*, and somewhere in the whirling senseless chaos there was Ulfarr again, his words sounding so sure, so *true*.

There is naught binding you to us. Beyond the Skai's deep need to spill our seed into the tightest hole...

And behind her Simon was grunting, hard and guttural, once again buried to the hilt—and Maria could feel the seed spraying, flooding her, drenching her deep inside. Done, he was done already, and beneath the inexplicable disappointment there was also relief, settling shaky into her chest. Maybe he would be calm again now, maybe he would be pleased with her, maybe he would explain, or even give her one of his damned rewards...

But there was no praise, no explanation, no hint of a reward—and not even a softening of those hard, powerful hands gripping Maria's hips. The beast inside her was still fully swollen too, still stretching her tight around it, giving no respite, no relief—

Until he yanked all the way out, sudden and harsh, leaving Maria shivering, exposed, empty. Except, of course, for the gush of thick liquid she could feel already surging, pouring from where he'd opened her, bought her, *used* her...

And then—Maria froze all over—she felt him *there*. Felt slick, hot strength prodding further up, at that shameful, hidden pucker of heat. In the place where she'd used his tools, yes—but she'd *never* actually done such a thing with another living person before. And most certainly not with something so intimidating as this, oh gods...

"Still?" Simon's rough voice demanded, almost taunting, and somewhere deep in the dregs of Maria's brain, she knew she should say no. Knew this was where the line should be, at least for today, judging by the way he'd just taken the rest of her...

But again, somehow, she nodded. Yes. Yes. *This.*

His grunt was deeper this time, surely hinting at his approval, his regard. And yes, that was exactly what Maria wanted, what she craved more than anything else in this utter disaster of a day. She needed Simon's approval, his taking, his *cleansing*, even if he was a *murderer*. And what did that mean, what did that make her, how hysterical had she truly become...

Because there was *relief* in this, in the way that hardness was lingering, feeling, seeking. Not punching in, like he had below, but perhaps knowing the danger in this. The risk. The trust.

But even so, the feel of his heft jutting against her was truly shocking, impossibly huge. Like an immutable barrier Maria somehow couldn't seem to scale, no matter how desperately she sought to breathe, to relax. To open for him, to welcome him, like she had below, she needed to please him, *needed* his cleansing...

The pressure increased, and she felt that slick roundness seeking deeper, widening her—but it was so much, too much, her muscles strained and tense, cold sweat trickling down her back.

"You swore to open this for me," came Simon's voice, dark and deadly behind her, as that invading heft nudged harder against her. "To use the tools I gave you. You *lie* to me, in this?"

Maria's body froze again, tightening its barrier against him, her breath shuddering out of her lungs. "I—I didn't lie," she gasped, her voice hoarse. "I tried, I did. I want this, want you. Want to *honour* you."

It was true, it *was*, and she fought to relax again, to open—but the tension wouldn't relent. And instead there was only more pressure, speaking of Simon's displeasure, his disapproval, her *failure*.

"Again you *lie*, woman," he hissed from behind her, the words skittering up her trembling back. "You no honour me. You say I *abandon* you, you say I am *murderer*! You ken this *honour* me?!"

The utter unfairness of that seemed to kick Maria in the stomach—he truly thought she wasn't *honouring* him?!—and finally, somehow, there was the strength to jerk her head around, to meet his glittering, furious eyes.

"But I'm *trying*, Simon!" she shot back, her voice nearly a wail. "I'm doing everything I can to trust you, and please you, and even gain your damned *rewards*! And of course I don't *want* to believe you're a murderer, but what do you expect me to think, when you won't even tell me why you *killed* someone?! Or why Ulfarr's now demanding *your* life over it?!"

And here was the understanding, sudden and bitter, that in the whole of this awful day, this was what hurt most of all. Not that Simon had wanted those other orcs, or even that he wanted this from her, or even, good gods, that he'd *killed* someone—but because Maria desperately wanted to know him, to *understand*. But clearly he still didn't trust her enough—didn't even *like* her enough, perhaps—to give her this one bit of truth.

And Simon's face was an utterly unreadable mask, his mouth not speaking a word, not denying this, not even trying. So Maria gritted her teeth, braced herself, and shoved herself back further upon his still-prodding heft. Made herself feel, for the first time in this, the true width of him, the distinct hint of smarting, streaking pain...

Her gasps had already begun to sound like wheezes, her eyes starting to water—but she craved this, *needed* this. Even as the rest of Ulfarr's words thudded through her thoughts, ringing deep and powerful and true...

... *need to despoil all that is fresh and pretty, until it is broken and begging at our feet.*

And was that truly what Skai did? What Simon did? With this murder, with this very moment? Was he taking... *satisfaction* from this, from Maria's failure, from the sounds from her throat that were sounding more and more like sobs? And he was supposed to be cleansing her, making her safe, making her forget, and she was supposed to be doing whatever it took, not caring, gaining her *freedom*—but suddenly the panic and the chaos were jostling and crowding, shouting wide and frantic, consuming her whole.

The blood on Baldr's mangled neck. The black magic no one had warned her about. The handsome orcs Simon had really wanted, the orcs she'd insulted, who'd then mocked her behind her back. *A total rubbish fuck, compared to Simon. Only woman I buy.* Because she reminded him of an *orc*.

And, louder still: *Cheated Skai on rut. He no yet fuck her before us. Skai like pretty, unmarked things. Maria shall soon taste the ways of a true Skai mate. It shall come within days, possibly sooner, all you have shall be mine, twelve days...*

And worst of all, the blood. Blood all over Simon's walls, his hands, his body touching hers, *inside* hers. Blood and broken bones and screams Maria could still hear, ringing louder and louder through her ears...

"I—I *can't*, Simon," she heard herself choke, her voice cracking. "You're right. I can't do this for you, not now. I"—she hauled in a shaky breath—"clearly I fail as a Skai. I fail at honouring you, and earning your trust. I'm not good enough. I *know*."

And gods, she was fully weeping now, the water dripping from her blinking eyes straight onto the fur below—and behind her there was a sudden stilted silence. A clench of sharp claws against her hips, digging deep into her skin.

"I know you didn't truly want me," she gasped. "I know I only reminded you of *them*. Who you really wanted. And there's nothing binding me to you, and I cheated the Skai, and I didn't try hard enough, and I'm not even *pregnant* yet—and that's why you're keeping me prisoner here. Why you can't even tell me why you *killed* someone."

There wasn't a sound behind her, not even his breath—but in a jerk of movement, he was gone. His heft and his heat and his hands vanished from Maria entirely, leaving her there on her hands and knees, empty and exposed and untouched. And that only seemed to make it worse, somehow, the sobs lurching out of her throat in hard, wracking gulps.

"I'm sorry," she gulped. "I've been trying, Simon, I have, but it's all so much, and so overwhelming, and there's so much I don't understand. And I know I'm already mostly broken, I *am*, but I thought you *knew*, I thought you were *safe*, I thought you were different from my husband. I thought you could give me a *future*."

And good gods, what was she saying, why was she babbling this rubbish, Simon was supposed to *pay* her for her future, enable her to achieve it herself—not *give* it to her, not here, not like that. He was just an orc. She wasn't supposed to care...

But Maria couldn't seem to take it back, either, and she somehow sunk down to sit on the bed, her knees pulled tight to her chin, both hands clutched to her still-empty belly.

She'd failed. Lost. Defeated.

Simon was still standing there before her, his huge body

unnaturally still, his previously swollen hardness hanging entirely flaccid again. Repulsed by her now, indeed just like her husband always had been, and Maria hugged her knees closer, and buried her wet cheeks against them.

"Maria," came Simon's voice, finally, low, hoarse. "I..."

Maria's dripping eyes darted up, finding his bloody, scarred face. Staring straight back down toward her, his black gaze unblinking, his skin unusually pale beneath the streaks of dried blood.

"Ach," he said, as his hand briefly rose to cover his eyes—and Maria realized his fingers were trembling, claws skittering against his skin. "I ought no—*never*—touched you, thus. Ought—send you away."

The misery surged again, clutching at the pit of Maria's stomach, and for an instant she thought she might be sick, right here on Simon's bed. But no, no, if he truly *didn't* want her, if he truly never would trust her, if this was truly her husband all over again—then she would rather go. She would. She had to.

So she choked back the sob in her throat, and forced herself to nod. And then made herself stand to her feet, staggering slightly as she lurched toward the shelf. Toward that contract, still sitting on top of all his careful, childish writing. *I am Simon. I am Enforcer of Orc Mountain.*

She pawed for the contract with shaky fingers, finally clutching it on her third try, and then turned back toward him. To where he hadn't moved, still standing there in the middle of the room, staring at her with those wide, unblinking eyes.

"Here," she made her strangled voice say, her wavering hand outstretched. "You win. I'll go."

22

For a long moment, Simon only stood before Maria, and stared at her. His eyes wide and dark, his face pale, and Maria thrust the contract toward him again, her hand badly shaking, fluttering the paper in her fingers.

"Here," she said again, her voice a croak. "Should I leave now? Or maybe tomorrow, is it day, or night, I don't even—"

And good gods, she was *sobbing* again, the tears streaking freely down her face. Absurdity, *hysteria*, an orc didn't want her and was sending her away and she wasn't supposed to care, it didn't matter, it *didn't*...

Simon's gaze had finally dropped to the contract in her shaking hand, and the look on his pale face was almost like... *revulsion*. Like the contract was something poisonous, odious, *alive*.

His huge body lurched abruptly back, away from the contract, as though he couldn't bear to touch it—and his eyes on Maria were wide again, stunned, unblinking.

"You wish," he said, his voice more uncertain than she'd ever heard it, "to *go?*"

And in those eyes, for the briefest of instants, there might have been... *fear*. And Maria wasn't at all following anymore, could scarcely stand upright at this point, and she watched her hand with the contract drop again, as though it was someone else's, somewhere far away.

"N-no," she began, and she gulped for more breath, for truth. "B-but you really don't w-*want* me. You only bought me to replace *them*, and you just want to keep me prisoner and use my holes and despoil me and leave me *b-broken*—"

She couldn't seem to finish it, her head shaking back and forth, her arms clutching over her shuddery chest. While Simon kept staring at her, his hands heavy at his sides, his head tilted, his brow creasing deep.

"Maria," he said, hoarse. "Who *spoke* all this to you?"

He sounded bewildered, almost pleading, and why was it so hard to breathe, to think. "Ulfarr," she whispered, "and the others. They didn't mean to, I know, they only thought it was a good joke, but I—"

Her eyes were on the floor now, on Simon's massive boots, which were streaked with mud, and perhaps blood, too. "I know I'm not really... *desirable*," she continued, wretched, with a sound that might have been a laugh. "Not like *them*. I know I'm only a body you bought, and I'm overwrought and hysterical and annoying to you, and we don't even *like* each other. But I thought, I was starting to think, maybe you... maybe we..."

And she couldn't even say it, gods why had she been about to, surely she hadn't even *thought* such a thing. Hadn't once thought about sneezy pointy-eared babies, about punching his neck in a room full of orcs, about a huge powerful body holding her close and safe while she slept. *My pretty one*, he'd called her, what now felt like an age long past. *I wish you to seek new ways with me.*

"Maria," Simon said, and suddenly there was a warm hand on her face, tilting it up, making her meet his eyes. His wide, wild eyes, reflecting the tension in his fingers on her skin, the heavy gust of his breath.

"You ken," he said, slow, rasping, "I wish for *who*?"

Maria blinked blankly toward him, her mouth opening, closing, opening. "Tristan," she choked, "and Kesst. You were apparently even *good* for Kesst, but with *me*—"

She was babbling, incoherent, her hand waving frantically toward the bed, toward what they'd just done. How he'd just taken her, vicious and brutal and foreboding with danger, with rage.

"And this—*Enforcing*," she continued, somehow, waving toward the door this time. "This killing. And I *want* to understand you, Simon, I *want* to give you the benefit of the doubt, and learn your ways—but you only growl at me, and order me to know my place, as if I have no right to even *ask*? As if I really am"—she gulped for more air—"just a purchase to you. Just your property. Just a tool to get you a son, and make a fucking *point* to your kin, and help you play your fucking *games*."

The words seemed to echo oddly through the too-small room, shifting through Simon's staring eyes—and she could see his throat convulse, once, and then again. His shoulders rising and falling, his breath shuddering and deep.

"I—killed a brother today," he said, the words quick, blank, a monotone. "I no wished for this, but his sins"—Simon's chest hollowed—"were too grave to stand, ach? I could no leave this. No with Ulfarr so ready to forgive this, should he take my place."

Oh. Maria's breath felt locked in her lungs, her eyes wide on Simon's face. On the... regret. The *grief*.

"And you couldn't," she heard her distant voice say, "have imprisoned this orc, instead? Or exiled him? Or"—she winced—"maimed him, like you just—"

She couldn't even finish the sentence, her stomach churning—but the sharp shake of Simon's head was immediate, vehement. "No," he said, heavy. "For a Skai, to be held in chains is worse than death. And if I maim him, or send him away, there is naught to keep him from this same darkness again, ach? Most of all if I am gone?"

His voice had tilted at the end, his eyes grim on Maria's, and she felt herself swallow over the lump in her throat. "But what," she said, almost pleading, "were his sins?"

Simon's eyes briefly closed, his breath exhaling harsh. "He has a son," he said, quiet, pained. "A sweet, pretty son, ach? Bjorn, of Clan Skai. Half-grown. Who was kept alone in this camp, far from our mountain, so we would no smell—"

He didn't finish, his lips pressing tight together, his jaw grinding in his cheek—but the comprehension had already swarmed Maria with sickening, horrifying force. Clapping her hands to her mouth, while the contract she'd been holding fell away, fluttering off somewhere else, forgotten.

"And Ulfarr is *fine* with such things?!" she demanded, incredulous. "He would just *forgive* such things, if he took your place?!"

"Mayhap," Simon said, and suddenly he looked and sounded worn, weary, his gaze dropping to the floor. "Our clan yet weakens and splinters with each passing day, and when I kill one of our own, I only draw nearer our doom, ach?"

Maria stared at Simon for a long instant, her heart lurching—and without at all meaning to, she threw herself back toward him. Squeezing her arms tight around his waist, burying her head in his chest.

"How *horrible* for you, Simon," she whispered. "What an awful decision for you to have to make. I'm so, *so* sorry."

Simon's body felt rock-hard against her, his heartbeat thundering in her ear—but then she could feel the tension slowly releasing, his bulk sagging into her touch. And then his arms slowly, carefully circled around her too, his head resting against the top of hers, his heavy breaths rustling her hair.

"You have naught to regret, woman," he said, his voice stilted. "It is I who should speak thus to you. I ought *never* touch you, when I am yet caught in battle-rage thus. This was wrong, ach? I beg your forgiveness for this. I only"—she could hear his swallow—"craved your sweetness. Your hunger for me. Your... peace."

Her peace. Hers. He'd wanted—*her*.

"I am sorry, woman," he continued, quieter. "I ought never have done this. Ought *never* stoke your fear and grief thus. Ach?"

And slicing through the sheer chaos swarming Maria's thoughts, there was only the compulsive, desperate need to squeeze him tighter. To embrace this huge deadly orc as close as she could, because in this moment, she truly didn't care what he'd done, or what he'd said. She didn't care that she wasn't supposed to care. She didn't care that this was still a contract, a deal, a *sale*.

He wanted her. He'd wanted her peace. *Hers*. And she wanted his, she'd wanted it the whole of this awful endless day, and finally it was here, within her reach, whispering in the still-rapid pulse of his heartbeat beneath her ear. And in, perhaps—Maria's hand slipped downwards, searching, caressing—the warm, swiftly swelling base of him, the pure, powerful proof of his hunger.

His big body had snapped to stillness again, his sharp claws clenching against her back—even as the beast in her fingers grew fuller, thicker, harder. Seeking her touch, pulsing eagerly against her, wanting her, surely speaking its truth...

And once again, the world jerked, and tilted sideways. Catching on the clutch of strong hands against Maria's waist, thrusting her fully down onto her back on the bed. And suddenly Simon was leaning over her, breathing hard, his eyes glittering with something Maria couldn't grasp, couldn't name.

"Still," he rasped, and it took Maria far too long to realize it was *that* question. The same question as always. Did she want this, still. Did she want him, even now.

And this time, there was no rebellion at it, no rage curdling in her belly. Only a stilted, slippery understanding, swirling for perhaps the first time. He wanted to know. Wanted to be sure she craved this, just as much as he did.

Maria's nod was jerky, fervent, true—and Simon nodded too, just as fervent. And then, in a rush of movement, he was gone—but not *gone*, only settling further down on the bed, kneeling between Maria's legs, spreading them apart.

Her thoughts were still skittering, uncomprehending, even as he yanked up her tunic and loincloth, baring her whole from the waist down. As he also drew her knees up, thrusting them wide, exposing everything in between to the room's cool air. To the feel of his own still-seeping wetness, the proof of his last brutal taking, slipping shameful and incriminating down the length of her raw, reddened, throbbing crease.

"Ach," he said, hoarse, and in that instant he looked almost haggard, or even ill. Making Maria freeze all over again, because wait, what did that mean, had she horribly misread this, was he still only making a point—

But even as the uncertainty kept ringing louder through her frantic thoughts, Simon's hands stroked her thighs with unexpected gentleness, settling them wider apart. And then he shifted his huge body further downwards, bent his dark head low...

And *kissed* her. *There.*

Maria choked and flailed up, the disbelief screaming, while the unfamiliar, *impossible* sensation kept whirling out in shivery stinging arcs. Because he was *still doing it.* This baffling, deadly orc was still *kissing* her, caressing her most secret places with warm full lips and a gentle hot tongue. Now slipping that tongue a little deeper, into where he'd already used her, opened her, filled her. And she could *feel* the liquid pooling fuller, faster, almost as if returning the touch of his lips, seeking for its own maker's filthy mouth...

"Simon," Maria finally gasped, through the shock, the still-whirling sparkling *wonder.* "Y-you—you c-can't—truly *want*—"

The sensation stopped, *stopped*—but wait, that was because Simon had raised his head to look at her. His lips parted, his teeth bared, his tongue blatantly curling and slithering against the mess on his face, slipping it shameless and hungry inside.

"Ach, I can," he said, his voice just as decisive as his watching black eyes. "I wish to eat my good seed from deep within my sweet woman, and hear her scream upon my strong cleansing tongue."

Oh, *fuck.* The moan escaped from Maria's lips without warning, without recourse, and Simon *smiled* at her, slow and crooked, and again bent his head low. And then kissed her *again*, full and deep, his tongue swirling against swollen skin. Licking, lapping, delving, caressing.

There was no possible protest, no possible response, only the shocking wheeling sensation, almost agonizing in its power. And perhaps just as powerful was the truth of it, the unshakeable certainty that Simon did want this, he wanted *her*, his tongue slipping deeper, drinking her from the inside out...

Gods, it felt good, and even better when his warm hand slipped up to the top of Maria's parted crease, his thumb circling gentle against the fiercely sensitive skin. Dragging it up, opening her up even more for him, his tongue swirling slick and hot and obscene. While his own seed kept pooling and dripping, the sounds wet and vulgar and wicked, as Maria writhed and moaned and choked upon his brutal, beautiful onslaught.

"Fuck," she gasped, without even realizing it. "*Fuck*, Simon."

He answered with a dark, satisfied laugh, an even deeper plunge of that slick, devastating tongue. Licking and slurping, drinking up his own seed with lewd, profane determination—and then, oh hell, slipping downwards. Back toward *there*, toward where Maria had tried and failed to take him, and this could not be happening, it could *not*—but it *was*, and she screamed with shock and sensation and euphoria as his slippery heat pierced her, soft and slow and sweet.

It was the utter opposite of what he'd done before, almost pure torment in its slow lilting gentleness, in the careful nudge of hot sinuous silk. In the way Maria could just see his closed eyes, the lashes fluttering against his bloody cheek, his inhale reverent and deep.

And it was, perhaps... an apology. It was this orc again saying, with his silently caressing tongue, that he did want her. That he truly hadn't meant to alarm her, or shout at her, or push her. That he still wanted her to stay.

The truth of that seemed to spin and fire with all the rest, dancing Maria further into chaos, into delirium. Into a wild, whirling place where the bare glance of his eyes set her body furiously pulsating around him, the pleasure sparking out in desperate white streams, every throb a jolt of pure, intoxicating bliss.

Simon kept kissing her as it faded, even gentler than before, his gaze still whispering of reverence and regret. And Maria was still lost in the frenzy, loose-limbed with hot skittering exhilaration, and she felt her tingling hands yank on his shoulders, drawing him up toward her.

He came, hovering close and silent above her, his eyes bright, his sweaty chest heaving. And Maria drank it up, drowned in it—and shoved him sideways. Wanting him on his back, and he willingly went, sprawling out beside her, though his black brows furrowed, hinting at confusion, or maybe even reluctance.

But his trousers were sagging down, exposing that still-swollen, rock-hard beast at his groin, jutting up toward Maria, twitching into the eager grip of her fingers. And it was so easy, so right, to slide herself up over him, to straddle his broad hips, to settle herself close. And then—she moaned, her body arching—to bring that dripping, pulsing hardness to where his tongue had just been, to the place he'd fought and failed to conquer.

But Maria had surely never felt so relaxed in her life, so full of calm, willing acceptance. And Simon wasn't pushing or prodding this time, only lying there perfectly still beneath her, his eyes watching with searing, piercing intent. With *awe*.

And Maria felt it, felt him, huge and deadly and aggressive, his body still streaked in blood—and welcomed him. Felt herself soft and open for him, craving him, needing his power filling her, bracing against her, holding her safe...

And it was. He was. Shockingly massive, impossibly so, as he slowly eased up inside her, splitting her apart upon him. But not pushing this time, instead finding her, meeting her, slipping into the space she was making for him...

The delirium was rising again, spinning and wheeling—and then skittered even higher when big warm fingers slipped between her legs, found where she was still empty, untouched. And then they began sinking inside too, gentle, inexorable, filling her in tandem with his dripping, driving strength.

It was so much, more than Maria had ever before sought or imagined, and the intensity was crawling against her, stripping her apart, consuming her in its raw, ferocious force. And when Simon's other hand jerked up, catching on her tunic's neckline, Maria only arched up, moaned, begged—

He tore it down the front with a single, devastating yank, freeing Maria's hungry breasts from within it, exposing them for his eyes. And then he yanked off the loincloth too, leaving her fully naked and writhing upon him, trapped, aching.

"Pretty," Simon gasped, his eyes fluttering, his free hand slipping up to pinch at a peaked nipple. "More."

More. *More*? And *gods*, this orc was such a greedy, shocking bastard—he was already fucking her on his fingers, as well as his merciless conquering monster—and somehow, in the chaos, Maria... *laughed*. The sound rich and smoky and approving, as she bore down and drank him ever deeper, impaled herself on his brutal invasion, thrust her breast into the grip of his warm waiting hand, drunk and feverish and lost—

The pleasure caught, sparked, kindled—and then, oh hell, it *detonated*. Hurling and howling from Maria's pierced, pulverized core, escaping in the clawed clutch of her fingers on his sweaty skin, in the base, broken wail from her throat. In the way the orc beneath her was gasping, his chest heavily hollowing, his eyes rolling back—and then he was arching up too, his jutting hardness shuddering and straining inside her, pumping her very innards full of his hot, wicked orc-seed.

And in this unreal, dreamlike moment, with Maria speared and screaming upon an orc—there was only... peace. Only the certainty, deep and sure, that he *had* wanted this. That Simon had wanted her, in the surreal, awful chaos of this day, just as she'd wanted him. And she'd taken him, she'd welcomed him, she'd been bared and whole and pure for him. For his... cleansing.

And surely it *was* cleansing, in the way his eyes were still sweeping over her. In the way his fingers so gently slipped out of her, stroking as they went, trailing soft up her bare belly. Seeking higher and higher, until they found her mouth, and then sank deep between her parted lips.

Maria's eyes fluttered as she suckled him, her tongue caressing against his callused skin. And as he watched, so quiet and intent, she could finally see the approval, flaring to life in his beautiful black eyes.

"Maria," he whispered, his voice rolling over the syllables, like it was magic, a song. "My Maria. My sweet, pretty, wilful woman."

A quiver of heat unfurled down Maria's back, and she smiled at him, slow, around his still-delving fingers. And kept smiling as he slipped the fingers out, and brushed them against her swollen lips.

"I thank you, for this," he whispered, so low, so reverent. "I no deserved this from you, my pretty one. No today."

There was truth in his eyes, in his voice, and Maria wasn't about to argue with it, not now. "No," she whispered back. "But if you'd just *told* me, Simon, from the start, I"—she exhaled, felt her smile fading—"I would have understood, you know?"

Something shifted in Simon's still-watching eyes, but he didn't speak, so Maria drew in breath, courage. "I thought you were going to teach me," she said, quieter. "I'm truly trying to learn. I'm trying to honour you. Aren't I?"

He still didn't speak, though his throat again convulsed, his fingers slack against Maria's lips—and she would say the rest of this, she would. "I want to know about your work. I want to know about your past, and if you really do still want Tristan, or Kesst, or whoever. And I want to know about your clan, even if"—she gave a reflexive grimace—"they surely don't want me here. Just like I'm still not entirely sure you do, either."

Simon's slowly heaving chest had stilled beneath her, silence skipping between them—and then warm hands gripped for Maria's shoulders, dragging her fully down upon him. Clutching her tight against him, his fingers spreading wide against her bare back.

"Ach, woman, I wish for you," he said, his voice rough. "More than I have ever wished for any other. You are so pretty, so sweet. So eager. So... *true.*"

Oh. The pleasure rippled down Maria's spine, brash and hot—but with it was more nagging unease, too. More awful, curdling whispers of what Simon had done today, and why. What Ulfarr had said.

"But is it true, though?" she asked, her voice a whisper. "About the Skai, only wanting pretty things, so you can... destroy them?"

She could feel the tension slipping into Simon's body beneath hers, and when she blinked back at his face, he was staring at the ceiling, his hand again rubbing at his mouth. Not wanting to say it, maybe, and Maria's own tension jerked higher, her heart thudding louder in her ears. What if that *was* only why he wanted her, after all...

"Ach," Simon said finally, on another sharp exhale. "This is truth, in part. I long for what is whole and sweet and true. This speaks to me. It—*calls* to me. It is, mayhap"—his throat convulsed—"what most Skai have never known, ach? So we envy this. We wish to gain this. We wish to make it our own."

Oh. Maria's shiver was sudden, involuntary, her eyes darting away from his face—until Simon's hand clutched at her hair, giving her head a gentle little shake. Wanting her to look at him. To listen. To follow his... *teaching.*

"And so oft," he continued, "it is humans who bear this wholeness. Humans like you, ach? With your fickle, carefree ways, and your unmarked skin, and fat bellies. Your kin have stolen our peace, and our lives, and mayhap even our whole *clan*—and yet, you walk easy and fearless and free, and flaunt this before us. You no even *see* the great wealth you bear, in this."

The discomfort flared in Maria's chest, and she opened her mouth to counter that. To point out her own struggles, her horrid husband, her dead parents, all she'd had to endure—but Simon's fingers had again come to her lips, pressing tight against them. Wanting her to listen.

"I ken many humans suffer also," he said, his voice deepening. "I no say this is no truth. But yet"—his eyes shifted, glinting—"you no live with only war, from your earliest days. You no learn to fight, before you learn to *speak*. You no learn to move in silence, to always hide, so you are no *killed*. You no feel the torment of blades and bolts and arrows in your skin, and then always bear these scars, these marks of your defeat. You no"—Maria heard him swallow—"watch your own father slain before you, after he make tiny fire to cook your *breakfast*. For you have loose tooth this day, and this pains when you chew raw meat."

Wait, what? It felt like those words had slapped Maria across the face, her eyes wide and shocked on Simon's—but he meant that, he did, his eyes dark and grave and clouded with... *grief*. And something was prickling behind Maria's own eyes, threatening to escape—and for some inexplicable reason, her head whipped around to look at his shelf. To find the carving of the smiling, barrel-chested orc, still standing with its back toward them, as if to look away from all this. Away from his... *son*?

But yes, *yes*, it was here in Simon's eyes, in their deep, hushed misery, their *truth*. "All Skai bear tales and truths such as this, ach?" he continued, so quiet. "And then, amidst all this, we must face you humans. We must mate with you, bring you into our homes, into our *beds*. You are so pretty, so light, so *free*. You think us crude, dim-witted, *disgusting*. You say you *hate* us. You say we no care, we *abandon* our own, we are *murderers*. And so, we then—"

He broke off there, his jaw grinding in his cheek, but this was familiar now, this was what he'd explained to her before. Except that those words—all of those awful, painful words—were *hers*.

Crude. Dim-witted. Disgusting. Murderer. I hate you.

"So then you cling harder to your ways," Maria finished, wincing, her voice cracking. "You cling to what power you can find. You maybe even show us"—she tried to smile, but horribly failed—"what we expect of you, because that might be safer, wouldn't it? Rather than showing us who you really are, and then being mocked or rejected for that instead?"

And Simon's eyes, it was as though they burned into her, seeing through her, boring into her very soul. And when he finally nodded, slow, minute, it felt like a thunder-clap of comprehension, of truth, ringing through Maria's skull.

"And yet," she said, searching those eyes, "you still seek a new way? You still want to change your Skai ways? You still want to—to treat women better, and try to change our minds about you?"

And abruptly it seemed impossible, unfathomable, that Simon could truly want to strive for such things—but he was again nodding. *Nodding*, though his mouth bore a bitter little twist, his hand dropping to cover his eyes.

"But this is no easy, ach?" he continued. "Many Skai yet cling to these old ways. For many of my kin, you are yet only our enemy. You make us weak. You bear what we shall never have. You flaunt our ways, you treat us with dishonour, you face us with shame and scorn and fear. You bear our sons, our only *hope*, and then"—his hand dropped from his eyes, his claw jabbing toward her—"you *run*."

Oh. Ohhhh. It felt like something had kicked Maria in the gut, suddenly, snapping her body rigid over his, her eyes wide and chagrined on his face. Because once again, he was talking about—*her*.

And good gods, he'd even told her, at the start of all this. Hadn't he? Maria had brought him shame before his kin, by cornering him with that contract, by breaking his clan's ways. And while Simon was trying to cling to his power in this, to use it to his advantage, to show his kin a new way—that contract was still there. With the selling, the running. The shame. The... *revenge*.

And wait, was Maria actually *hurting* his cause, in all this, rather than helping him? Because here he was, fighting for the future of his clan, fighting for her right to become a true Skai, without the hunt, or the rut—and here she was, still threatening to run away, and *leave* him? To abandon her own Skai son, *forever*? To fulfill every single horrible belief these Skai orcs held about humans?

Maria's heart was thundering erratically in her chest, her eyes blinking rapidly toward Simon's stiff, unreadable face. Because maybe he knew he'd called her out on this, just now. He'd cleansed her, and now he wanted to see her truth.

"Oh," Maria said, thick, bleak, exposed—and somehow, *somehow*, she'd jerked sideways on the bed. Grasping down for something, crumpling it as she snatched it up, here, before their eyes.

Their contract. Covered in its rows of clear black ink. Damning Maria as yet another fickle, careless human who only wanted to run.

"So," she said, her voice not quite hers, her eyes not quite able to lift to Simon's, "this contract is still useful, right? Since it's the new way you've claimed before your clan, and all. But"—she cleared her throat, blinked down at that incriminating line, the very last on the page— "we probably don't need to commit to that last bit, right? At least, not *now*."

And gods, it came out sounding so false, so foolishly casual—but Simon surely wasn't fooled. In fact, his gaze was sheer pointed intensity, boring into Maria, and then into that last line of the contract. The one that granted her the right to leave with his money, and never come back.

"And what, woman," Simon replied, his voice very even, "should you wish to write instead?"

The heat was prickling uncomfortably all over Maria's face, her back, her chest. "I—don't know," she whispered, wretched. "Can't we just—tear it off, or something, for now?"

Simon stared at her for another long instant, while blatant disbelief shimmered in his eyes—but then, without looking away from her, he slowly gripped the paper, and then dragged his claw across it, just above that line. Curling it off in a neat little strip, and unfurling something much like relief in Maria's belly.

And when he tossed the shortened contract aside, leaving only the little strip curled around his claw, there was more relief, almost inexplicable in its strength. And strength, too, in the intensity in Simon's eyes, as his hand briefly slid down behind Maria, lingering in the mess he'd made between her legs—and when the curl of paper came back, it was covered in his slick, dripping with thick white.

And as Maria watched, struck, breathless, Simon raised it to her *mouth*. Nudging her lips gentle but purposeful apart, and then slipping the soaked-wet slip of paper inside.

"Then eat this, woman," he ordered, so soft. "Honour me."

And somehow, caught in this frozen, unreal moment, Maria... *obeyed*. Understanding, somehow, as bizarre as it was, that perhaps he needed this. Needed to see her literally eat her own words, coated in his fresh seed. Needed to... cleanse her. *Enforce* her.

And once it was done, and Maria had gulped those incriminating words down her throat, there was... *peace*. In her eyes locked to Simon's, in the press of her fingers over his rapidly beating heart.

She would seek a better way. She would show him. She would... *help* him?

And surely, this was the hysteria again. Surely, the determination currently swarming her thoughts was disgraceful, appalling, *reprehensible*—but in this safe, whispering quiet, Maria couldn't seem to see why. Not with this orc now carding his claws through the mess of her hair, and bringing it to his face—and then inhaling it, deep. As though it actually *were* sweet. Whole. True.

"So, then, Simon," Maria heard her distant voice say, her mouth twitching into a small, genuine smile. "If you really *do* like nice pretty things, then what the hell was *this*?"

She flapped her hand toward his room, toward its somewhat tidied state—and Simon sighed, the breath heaving from his chest. "Ach, this," he said. "If it is pretty and clean, it only gains me more envy. More hunger from those who wish to take it from me."

Oh. Of course. From *Ulfarr*, he meant. Ulfarr, who would gain all Simon's possessions if he killed him. Ulfarr, who already wanted everything Simon touched. Ulfarr, who'd said that all Simon had would be his. Twelve days.

"Shit," Maria said, squeezing her eyes shut. "You said I should clean it if I wanted, so I thought—*shit*. I should have asked. I can— mess it up again, and—"

But Simon's hand had again slipped up to her mouth, his strong fingers pressing against her lips. "No," he said. "It pleases me, that you did this for me. And this battle now comes for me, with or without this, ach?"

Maria couldn't find a reply to that, and she studied him for another long, silent moment. Drinking up the darkness still in those eyes, the tension shifting in his jaw.

"You don't," she whispered, "truly think Ulfarr can *defeat* you, in twelve days. Do you?"

There was more silence, in which it occurred to Maria that until this very moment, she'd somehow been thinking of Simon as invincible. Untouchable. That he was obviously so strong, so powerful, that surely he would easily overcome any foe. Surely no one else would ever defeat him, and *surely* not Ulfarr. Right?

But beneath her, Simon's shoulder jerked a shrug. "Mayhap not with his fists," he said finally. "But defeat wears many faces, ach?"

Oh. Maria could only seem to blink at him, swallowing hard, her fingers widening over the bare, bloody skin of his chest. Over where she could feel his heart, hammering wild beneath it.

He was—*afraid*?

And in this moment, clutched close and naked atop this massive, thoroughly bewildering, blood-covered orc, Maria again—*understood*. Knew his thoughts, in perhaps the same way he sometimes seemed to know hers. Knew the fear, the regret, the many faces of defeat.

There were no words, suddenly, only Maria's fingers spreading wider against his still-pattering heart. And her face, her mouth, easing up to his cheek, and pressing a soft kiss to the stubbled, blood-crusted skin.

Simon's eyes fluttered closed, so Maria did it again, kissing down toward his jaw, his ear, his neck. Tasting the salt of his sweat, the copper of the blood, the deep richness of orc, of powerful male, of hunger.

He swelled inside her as she did it—he'd still been there that whole time, just like Maria had perhaps *wanted*—so she kissed harder, lingered longer, let her teeth scrape against his torn-off ear. Feeling his gasp now, the almost imperceptible tilt of his hips, his heart slowing to a smoother, steadier drumbeat beneath her spread-wide fingers.

"Good," she whispered, into the hot scent of his neck, into the drag of teeth on skin. "Now fuck again?"

And when she pulled back to see his face, her reward was there, waiting. In the sparkling heat of those black eyes, in the slow, crooked little smile. He *liked* it. He *approved*. She was *safe*. For now...

"Ach, my pretty one," he said, so soft, as he drew her down for a kiss. "Again."

23

Maria slept long and deep that night, tucked close into Simon's powerful form. Safe in the easy thud of his heart, the steady snores from his mouth, the awareness of his half-hard bulk, still hidden deep within her.

And when she finally awoke, blinking into the quiet darkness, there was once again a whispering, solid certainty, settling into her bones. Into her heart.

She was doing this. She would face this. And this time, it wasn't just for her freedom. It wasn't for revenge. It was... to seek a better way. To help Simon, in saving the Skai. To show him, and all his kin, that humans could be worth it. That they could be trusted.

So when Simon awoke, and rose to light the lamp, Maria got up too. Following him over to the shelf, where she carefully reached out, and turned around that carving to face them again. The big, smiling, barrel-chested orc. Simon's *father*.

"He looks very kind," she murmured, studying his carved stone face. "What was his name?"

"Sjovarr," Simon replied, just as quiet. "He was a good father to me."

Maria jerked a nod, and attempted a smile up at Simon's face. "Will you tell me about your other carvings? Please?"

And to her vague surprise, Simon actually obliged. Resting his hand carefully atop one carving, and then the next, as he spoke their names, and their importance to him. One bulky orc was a close child-hood friend, Arnthorr, who'd been killed in battle. The slim, angry-looking orc was Joarr's father, who'd apparently raised Simon after his own father's death. And the tall, haughty, voluptuous woman, staring at them with imperious, half-lidded eyes, was Simon's *mother*.

"I no met her, that I remember," Simon said, his voice very even. "She ran away after I was birthed. But my father said she looked thus. Tall, and proud, and lovely."

And looking at this woman's harsh, haughty face—this woman who'd abandoned her own *son*—Maria felt a horrible, visceral clutch in her gut. Gods, how had Simon borne this with her, when she'd sworn to do the same thing to his own son? No wonder he'd kept her his damned prisoner. No wonder he'd been angry with her. *Ashamed* of her.

"And how long have you been learning to read?" Maria asked, too quickly. "I noticed all your writing exercises?"

She waved helplessly toward the stack of papers she'd tidied, and Simon's gaze flicked there too, his shoulder shrugging. "A few moons now," he said. "Most Skai no learn this as orclings, but now we seek to mend this, with the help of our Ka-esh kin. This shall help us with these new ways we seek, ach?"

Right. Because Skai had only learned to fight as children. And without knowing how to read, how would they ever embrace this new future? These words, whispers, perceptions?

"That's very wise of you, Simon," Maria said, belatedly, with another attempt at a smile. "Very clever."

His glance down toward her was deeply suspicious, his brows knitted tight together. And perhaps Maria should have taken the hint, and stopped the questions there—but already there was another one, jostling even louder than the rest.

"Are you... all right?" she said, searching his eyes, and then angling a glance toward all those marks on his wall. "Doesn't it... bother you? This... Enforcing?"

Simon was quiet for an instant, his brows still furrowed, and though Maria braced for his retort, it didn't come. "Ach, some," he said finally. "But in this, I seek truth. I serve my kin. I serve Skai-kesh. I keep safe those who are weak. I honour the truth behind my fathers' ways."

Maria felt herself nod, caught in the conviction in his voice, his eyes—but then she blinked down at the carving of his father again. "And your own father?" she asked carefully. "Would he have wanted you to honour those ways too?"

That was unmistakably a wince, tightening Simon's mouth, and he jerked another shrug. "My father was peaceful orc," he said. "He *hate* killing. He no like to spar, even with me. There was naught that roused him to rage. My own ease with these ways"—his throat convulsed—"came surely no from him, ach?"

Oh. So Simon was suggesting—it was his *mother* who had given him such things. Yet more to bear, to face, from the human who'd birthed him, and then *abandoned* him.

"But mayhap," Simon continued, his eyes now fixed to the carving of his father, "I ought to seek new ways, beyond death. Seek beyond the Skai, mayhap. I only"—his shoulders sagged—"need more time. Ach?"

More time. Because he didn't have time, he meant, thanks to Ulfarr. Eleven days.

"But enough of this, woman," Simon abruptly said, as he ducked down, and yanked a pair of trousers from the shelf. "Now dress. I shall spend this day with you."

He would? A flare of warmth surged through Maria's chest, while that same determination—the certainty—seemed to twine deeper in her belly. She would support Simon. She would help him, in all this. She would show him humans could be trusted. He would see.

So she quickly dressed, and then accompanied him first to the latrine, and then to the Skai shrine. Where Simon again waved her toward the fur-covered bench—but this time, he knelt on it next to her, his head bowed toward Skai-kesh, his huge fist pressed tight against his heart.

And praying to Skai-kesh already felt easy, familiar, so Maria willingly offered today's fear, and longing, and blessing. Ulfarr, for her fear; Simon's success with his kin, as her longing; and for her blessing, this tenuous new certainty she'd found today. This... peace.

Beside her, Simon's prayer went on for some time, his big body utterly still, his elbow brushing against Maria's. But she felt no desire to disrupt him, so she quietly sat there and waited, caught on the sight of his harsh profile, on the solemn, quiet reverence that had seemed to settle all around him.

Simon's gaze lingered on Maria's face afterwards, but he didn't speak, and only guided her out the door. Taking her not toward the arena, as she might have perhaps hoped—but instead, further down the corridor, into what appeared to be a *forge*. A large, loud, fire-bright room, full of strange, sweaty, pounding orcs.

"Greetings, Argarr," Simon said, nodding at an older, heavily scarred orc with a silvery beard and hair. "I wish for a blade for my woman."

Maria couldn't hide her astonishment, blinking back and forth between Simon and this Argarr, but she didn't protest, or question it. And when Argarr waved her toward the rear of the forge, she accordingly went, with Simon striding silently behind her.

The forge's back corner led into another whole chamber, large and echoing, with rows of shiny, deadly-looking weapons hanging on the walls. And Maria soon found herself placed squarely in the middle of it all, while Simon and Argarr took turns thrusting a variety of swords and knives into her hands, and demanding that she grip them, and swing them about, and even hurl them across the room.

Maria hadn't wielded a sword since her father had been alive, and even then it had only been foolish playing around, never any kind of serious practice—and this entire experience soon felt completely surreal, especially once Simon and Argarr began arguing in black-tongue, clearly trying to choose between two particular weapons. A long, slim, razor-sharp rapier—Argarr's choice—and Simon's choice, a shorter, more powerful dagger, perhaps the length of Maria's forearm.

Unsurprisingly, Simon won the argument in the end, shooing Argarr and his rapier away. And after giving the new dagger one more satisfied spin, Simon stepped toward Maria, and yanked up her baggy tunic, so he could slide the dagger through a slit she hadn't previously noticed in her loincloth's leather belt.

"Here," he said firmly. "This is now yours, woman. Ach?"

And here, surely, was where Maria could have—*should* have—

protested. Pointing out, perhaps, that she had no real use for a dagger, or that she was very likely to injure herself with it, or that only orcs would remember to include weapons-bearing options in their women's clothing, while foregoing any actual *coverage...*

But no. She was doing this. She was honouring Simon. And Argarr was still watching, no doubt judging, from the door—and in truth, the dagger's heavy, sharpened weight *had* felt oddly reassuring in her hand. And perhaps even still felt so, brushing cool and quiet against the skin of her hip.

"Thank you, Simon," Maria heard herself say, and then her audacious body actually lurched toward him, leaning up to kiss his fragrant, stubbled neck. "I would be honoured to wear such a generous gift."

And gods, surely this was the hysteria, raised to heights never before seen—but there was an unmistakable glint of satisfaction in Simon's eyes as he led her back toward the door. And when Maria even managed to say a coherent thank-you to Argarr on the way past, Simon grunted his approval, and gave her arse a firm, heat-swarming little *slap.*

"This pleased me, woman," he said, as he nudged her through the twisty dark corridor. "And now, as your reward, you shall begin to better use your nose, as a true Skai should."

Her *nose?* Maria frowned up at him in the lamplight, once again thoroughly disconcerted—and that was surely another challenge in his eyes. One that only sharpened as he stepped away toward the wall, setting down the lamp he'd been carrying—and with a purposeful twitch of his fingers, the corridor blinked into utter darkness.

"*Simon,*" Maria's voice gasped, unnervingly plaintive, her hands frantically groping out into the black emptiness—but here he was, thank the gods. Still standing close before her, the skin of his bare chest warm and reassuring under her fingers.

"Ach, I am here," he said, low, almost soothing. "I shall no leave you. I only wish you to smell me."

To smell him. And very well, Maria could surely manage that—and she kept her clammy fingers gripped to his chest as she leaned closer, and inhaled. Indeed smelling that familiar scent of him, musky and rugged and deep.

"You ken my scent, ach?" Simon's voice asked, and at Maria's answering nod, she felt him step slightly backwards, out of her reach. "Now breathe again. You yet smell me?"

Maria obediently inhaled again, her brow furrowing—but yes, his scent was still there, fainter, but there. And when she nodded, she heard a low grunt of approval, felt warm hands heavy against her shoulders.

"Now turn," he said, guiding her around, so she was facing away from him. "You smell me now?"

Maria glanced uncertainly over her shoulder, but again nodded—to which she felt Simon's hands drop, his body moving behind her. "Now seek to find me. Seek where my scent is strongest. Ach?"

This, Maria soon discovered, proved to be remarkably difficult, and her first few careful attempts found only solid stone walls against her seeking hands. But Simon repeated it again and again, his orders consistently patient, his hands settling on her shoulders with reassuring frequency.

"It may help in this, I ken," he said, after yet another unsuccessful attempt, "if you seek no so much to smell, mayhap, or *think* so hard upon this—but instead *feel*. Seek for me in these strong *feelings* you so oft bear. Ach?"

Maria felt herself frowning—was he mocking her?—but his hands on her shoulders were again steady, soothing, patient. "Again. Feel me, woman."

Feel him. A little shiver snaked up Maria's back, but she drew in a bracing breath, and nodded. And then stood there in the pitch-blackness, breathing, feeling. Thinking, this time, not of sifting through the air for the strength of a smell, but instead lingering, perhaps incongruously, on the night before. Of how Simon had taken her, enfolding her in that rich scent, filling her with it, making her his own...

And this time, when she turned toward it—he was there. Here, breathing and alive under her seeking fingers, and she heard herself laugh out loud, the sound bright and joyous in the blackness. "I did it!" she said, foolishly, before she could catch the words. "I found you, Simon!"

And perhaps it was her imagination, but that might have been a huff of laughter from him too, his hands squeezing against her shoulders. "Ach, woman. Now show me again."

Again. Maria eagerly nodded, and again only *felt* for him in the darkness, inhaling deep. And this time she was sure of his presence before she even touched him, her fingers already spreading wide, finding the steady pulse of his heart.

"Good," he said, husky. "Again, woman."

So Maria did it again, and again, until Simon began moving further away, making the entire process that much more difficult. But still touching her, reassuring her, *teaching* her—and by the time he finally stopped, Maria was actually grinning up toward his familiar voice in the darkness, her eager hands clutching with willing ease at his chest, his heart, *hers*.

"This pleased me, woman," he said, as his hand widened on her arse, again guiding her down the corridor. "We shall work more upon this, ach?"

He hadn't lit the lamp again, but it felt almost easy to walk in the dark now, with that steady, reassuring touch against her. "Sounds good," Maria replied, her voice still warm with laughter. "It was fun. Thanks, Simon."

Simon's hand gave her another approving little slap, and then nudged her around another corner, toward what sounded like a wall of noise. "Ach," he said, his voice gruff. "Now mayhap you shall find joy in this for me, also?"

This, it turned out, once Simon re-lit the lamp, was once again the Skai arena. And once again, it was full of shouting, brawling orcs, who scarcely glanced toward them—and Maria realized that they'd actually been fighting in pitch-darkness. And that they'd been doing so last time she'd come here, too, and she felt a new, twitching appreciation for how truly impressive that feat was.

"Next," came Simon's voice over his shoulder, as he strode back toward the same fur-covered area as before, "you shall learn to wield your new blade. Ach?"

Maria had willingly followed him, though she felt her uncertainty rising, her fingers uneasily searching against the dagger-hilt through her tunic. "Um, I will?"

"Ach," Simon said firmly, spinning around to face her, brows raised. "Just as you have so far learnt to punch, and pray, and seek a scent in darkness. Just as you have learnt to take my prick in your throat, and your rump, and full to the root in your womb. Ach?"

Right. A furious blaze of heat burned up Maria's cheeks, and she seemed inexplicably caught on that look in Simon's eyes. The challenge. The assessing. The... *approval.*

"Ach?" he said again, softer this time. "Draw your blade, woman. Honour me."

And yes, yes, Maria could do this. She would. And her slightly trembling fingers were already seeking under her tunic, carefully pulling out her dagger by the hilt, while that approval again flared across Simon's eyes.

"Good," he said. "Now seek to strike me."

Maria couldn't help an unwilling flinch, blinking down at her shiny dagger-blade, and then back at Simon's face. "But," she protested, "it's *real*, Simon."

Simon's mouth tilted up, slow, *amused.* "Ach, I ken," he said, deadpan, as he came a step nearer. "Strike me, woman."

Maria made herself nod, moving closer, drawing in a deep breath. And then shifting, settling her stance, feeling the floor, just as he'd taught her last time—

And then she lunged forward, with as much power and speed as she could muster. Aiming the dagger straight for Simon's *groin,* good gods—but yes, yes, that was surely approval in his eyes again. Even as he smoothly eased out of the way, his hand snapping to catch the sharp, gleaming blade between his bared claws.

"For this strike, hold it thus," he said, as his other hand repositioned Maria's grip on the hilt. "And aim higher, so you no risk missing me, ach?"

With that, he demonstrated, actually guiding the blade's deadly edge up against where—Maria's breath choked—the monster in his trousers was fully visible, a thick, vertical ridge reaching nearly to his waist. And he was nudging Maria's dagger firmly against it, about halfway up its swollen length, his hands utterly nonchalant, his eyes not once leaving her flushed face.

"Ach?" he said, his voice almost a purr. "Again, woman."

And again, Maria soon found herself caught in one of the most surreal experiences of her life. Charging and swinging again and again toward an orc's bulging groin, while he easily avoided every one of her attacks, calmly corrected her stance and her hold, and smiled with wolfish, dangerous approval when one of her strikes finally nudged at the dangling drawstring holding up his trousers.

"Good," he said, once again catching Maria's blade in his bare fingers, and nudging it against that pulsing ridge at his groin. "A mite faster, and you should have caught me here, ach?"

And he was showing her, letting the dagger linger there, flaunting this appalling sight for her wide, hungry eyes. Taunting her, flashing her those sharp white teeth, while something flipped in her heaving chest, dipped deep in her belly...

"These devious distraction tactics of yours," Maria gasped, between her still-gulping breaths, "are *deeply* unfair, Simon. Unsportsmanlike, even."

But his crooked grin only broadened, and he smoothly plucked the dagger out of her fingers, and then pressed her bare *hand* to his groin instead. Wanting her to feel the ridged, swollen heft of him, leaping against her fingers. Wanting her. *Approving.*

"I no ken this is *unsportsmanlike*, my pretty one," he murmured, as her traitorous fingers circled around him. "For I am no man, ach? No man could ever wield a weapon so grand, you ken?"

Maria rolled her eyes at him, but felt herself grinning as she stepped closer, squeezed a little tighter. "Give me *my* weapon back, you grand prick," she breathed, "and maybe I'll cut you down to size."

Simon blinked at her, once—and then he actually laughed. *Laughed*, the sound deep and rolling, his shoulders shaking, his eyes on Maria so warm, so amused, so *approving.* Wanting her. Even, perhaps, *liking* her.

"Wilful woman," he murmured, flicking a gentle claw against her chin, as his other hand tucked her dagger back into her belt. "Should you truly wish to land me a felling blow, mayhap you shall grant me one more honour today?"

His mouth was still smiling, but his eyes were suddenly watchful on hers, perhaps even sober. As though he truly meant this, whatever it was. *One more honour today.*

Maria felt her own mirth settling, her head tilting, her eyes studying his. Her free hand reaching to find his bare chest, spreading against the truth of his rapidly beating heart.

"One more honour?" she repeated. "What is it?"

And this was important, it was something that meant something to him, and his eyes angled, brief, toward the other orcs still brawling in the room. Or, rather, toward the other orcs who had mostly stopped brawling to watch, their eyes held—Maria froze—to where her hand was still gripped tight around Simon's swollen, pulsing heft.

But Simon's claw flicked her chin again, gentle but purposeful, snapping her gaze back to his. And before he even spoke, she somehow knew, could feel it. Just the same as how she'd somehow felt him in the darkness, warm and close and powerful.

"I wish to take you," he said, very quiet, "before my kin. In the Skai common-room."

Maria swallowed, her heart picking up speed, her eyes searching his. To where he was... asking. Not ordering, this time. Not demanding she honour him. Not even offering a reward. Just... asking.

And looking at him, feeling him, her breaths still heaving in her lungs, it occurred to Maria that today had been... lovely. *Fun*, even. Better than any day she'd spent in *years*, without even a twinge of the ever-present panic or fear.

And behind Simon's constant stream of orders, he'd also been... kind. Patient. Teaching her his ways. Seeking to help her. Showing her how to belong. How to be a Skai.

But then—Maria swallowed hard—there'd been yesterday. Last night. The way Ulfarr—and those other orcs—had spoken to her. The threat Ulfarr had made to Simon. *By the rise of the next moon, all you have shall be mine.*

"Why do you want it?" she asked, her eyes searching his. "Why now?"

And it was a test, perhaps. A test of this new, precarious thing between them. Of whether Simon would keep teaching her. Keep telling her his truth.

And he knew that, Maria could see it in his eyes, in the slow rise and fall of his chest. "I wish to witness this," he said finally, his voice barely audible. "To claim you, and flaunt you, and know this joy. But also"—his head tilted, his mouth thinning—"this shall show my strength. It shall show me wise, rather than weak, in gaining you as I have. It shall mayhap grant me the fealty of Skai who know not which side to take, in what is yet to come."

What is yet to come. "And why," Maria whispered, "do they need to take sides? I thought this whole fight to the death thing"—she shivered—"was only between you and Ulfarr?"

But Simon shrugged, his eyes suddenly dark, distant. "If I am to keep my place as Enforcer," he said, "and seek these new ways, I need their trust, ach? If I defeat Ulfarr in battle, and my kin no welcome this, in truth I win naught, ach?"

Oh. So it wasn't only about winning against Ulfarr, then. It was about winning over his clan, too. Showing them this new way. Teaching them.

And in this moment, with one of her hands on Simon's hungry groin, and the other over his thundering heart, Maria again—*understood*.

And she had decided to do this. To honour him. To seek a new way. To *help* him.

And she would. She *would*.

"Very well," she whispered, the words caught on a breath, on *hope*. "Let's go."

24

Simon guided Maria back to the Skai common-room in stilted, wavering silence. He'd brought the lamp again, perhaps not wanting to add to her discomfort with darkness—but that meant Maria would see everything, all those dangerous watching orcs, all the potential mockery in their eyes.

Her heart was thumping erratically, her legs wobbly beneath her, but she squared her shoulders, drew in a deep breath. She could do this. She was gaining Simon's trust. She was helping him. She would.

"So," she heard herself say, unsteady, "is there anything I should know first? Anything I should expect?"

Simon's fingers widened against her back, his eyes flicking toward hers. "I shall wish to bare you," he said, his voice very even. "I shall wish to show myself a proud and strong Enforcer, and flaunt all you have learnt for me. With your mouth, and your womb."

Maria's panic leapt with alarming force, but she thrust it down again, drew in another dragging breath. "Right," she managed. "Um, multiple times, then?"

And gods, it felt like her skin was crawling, like her body wanted to leap clean out of it—and Simon's glance toward her held longer this time, perhaps seeing more than she might have wished. "Mayhap no," he said slowly. "Mayhap I shall only fill you once, this first time."

This *first* time. But it was a concession, surely, Simon's brow furrowing as he studied her, and Maria rapidly nodded, so hard her neck hurt. "Right," she said. "Right. Thanks."

He nodded too, still watchful, oddly intent. "You need no fear this," he said, quiet. "I shall be in this with you, ach? Even if I show myself as wilful Enforcer, I shall no allow any other to touch you, or speak ill of you. I shall keep you safe."

That did help, somewhat, and Maria felt her breaths coming deeper, her heartbeat slightly slowing—at least, until Simon guided her around one more corner, and through the door. That door. Into the room of wild, raging *debauchery*.

It seemed almost worse than last time, with perhaps twenty or thirty strange orcs inside. Caressing and grasping and writhing together, wielding swollen, hungry flesh against hands and mouths and bent-over arses. And across the room, Maria caught sight of a fully naked Drafli, sprawled on a fur-covered bench, while an unfamiliar orc worked over his groin—and there, not far away, was *Ulfarr*. Bending another orc double before him, driving in again and again, even as his lazy eyes flicked to Maria, and held there.

Shit. Maria's already-dragging feet had halted entirely, and now there were more heads turning, more eyes settling on her face. Some surprised, some curious, some disbelieving.

And Ulfarr, perhaps, looked the most disbelieving of all. His gaze flicking between Maria and Simon, his eyes rapidly narrowing, his mouth twisting with distaste.

He was—jealous. And, surely, *furious*.

And it was that, more than anything, that set Maria walking again, her own eyes darting for the safety of Simon's face. Simon's face, which abruptly looked different than it had before. Not so intent, not so watchful, but almost... cool. Relaxed. Indifferent.

He drew Maria to a stop in the middle of the room, encircled by a ring of cavorting, watching orcs. And close behind her was what appeared to be a table, covered with furs—but before she could quite follow that, she felt Simon's hand on her chin, tilting it up, making her look at him.

"You wish for me, ach, woman?" he asked, his voice just as cool as his eyes—but there, faint beneath, was that same glimmering intensity.

He meant this. He was truly asking, as he always did. And again, it was somehow enough to calm Maria's racing heart, to slow her breaths into something manageable again.

She'd sworn to do this. To honour him. To help him seek a new way, and prove that humans could be trusted. And she surely wouldn't back down now, not with all these orcs watching. Not with that truth in Simon's eyes.

"Yes," she whispered, the word somehow ringing through the rapidly quieting room. "You know I do, Simon."

He nodded, curt, relieved, *approving*. And then his hand reached to tug purposefully on Maria's baggy tunic, the silent order flaring across his eyes.

And yes, yes, she'd expected this—but even so, her hands still shook as she drew the tunic off, and let it drop to the floor. Exposing herself for a room full of watching orcs, feeling their eyes sweep close and proprietary over her bare breasts, her belly, her thighs. Making her suddenly, shockingly grateful for the still-present loincloth, which still covered her groin, at least, if nothing else.

Simon's eyes were sweeping over her, too, lingering on her peaked brown nipples, on her flushed-hot face. And as she watched, he smoothly shucked his own trousers, displaying everything beneath. Those powerful thighs, those heavy bollocks, the soft hanging heft above them...

And wait, he wasn't hard this time—he wasn't?—and Maria's uncertain glance up at his face found his brows raised, his eyes challenging, his mouth *smirking* at her.

"You truly wish for me, woman," he said, "you shall kneel, and make me ready for you."

Oh. *Oh.*

From somewhere far away, Maria heard laughter, loud and shrill— and then, even louder, Simon's bark of a reply, in deep growling black-tongue. Shutting the laughter back to silence, but his eyes were still on hers, waiting, taunting, *mocking*.

Kneel, and make me ready for you.

Maria's ears were ringing, a distant ache churning in her gut, while visions of her husband flashed across her thoughts—but she still somehow nodded, *nodded*, and dropped to her knees on the hard floor before Simon. Blinking blankly up toward him, toward *that*, dangling thick and soft before her, and gods what was she supposed to do, they hadn't done it like this before, what the hell did he want—

"Suckle," came Simon's order, low, his hand tilting her face up, his eyes glittering—and yes, yes, Maria could do that. And she somehow, *somehow* found the will to lean forward, to breathe in that familiar rich scent—and then, with one last little lurch, she kissed him.

He leapt against her mouth, powerful and immediate, and that was something, please—so Maria did it again, lips pressing light, her tongue tentatively seeking against the silken, heated skin. And again he pressed back, kissed back, rapidly swelling against her. Almost as if his smoothly rising head was searching for her lips, finding them with astonishing ease, slipping its way between...

And once he started sliding in, he didn't stop. Filling her slow, deliberate, breath by breath, opening her wide around him, until he was nestled hot and dripping against her throat. Holding himself there, while she desperately sought to swallow, fighting to ignore the sounds and foreign words from the watching orcs that surely meant approval.

Simon's hand flicked against her chin again—good gods, he wasn't otherwise even *touching* her—and when she blinked frantically up at him, he only raised his eyebrows, a silent order, a challenge. Saying, all too clearly, that he'd taught her what he liked. That he wanted to flaunt her.

And yes, Maria could do this, she *wanted* this—and she reflexively nodded, damn near choking herself upon his heft. And then she reached both her hands up, grasping and caressing him, giving herself the angle and leverage to drag her mouth back down the full length of him. Until she was licking and lavishing at his smooth seeping head, suckling his fiery sweetness straight from the source.

But Simon didn't grunt his approval this time, didn't even twitch. Just stared down at her, cool and insolent, as she again sank him inside, sucking hard, drinking deep. And when a nearby orc said something—good gods, when had one come so *close*—Simon actually chuckled, and replied in rolling black-tongue, his voice not even slightly faltering as Maria ground him into her throat.

Then another nearby orc spoke, earning another easy answer from

Simon—and he yanked out of Maria's mouth, swift and unexpected enough that it made a loud squelching sound, the saliva pooling down her chin. And when there was more laughter, *mocking* her, Simon indeed snapped back at it, his hand finally dropping to touch her, caressing at the mess on her face, streaking it wide.

"Ach, I ken you only envy this, Balgarr," he said, so even, so cool. "You only wish I share her with you, ach?"

There were more voices, more laughter, most of it clearly in Simon's favour, and he slowly slid himself in again, parting Maria's lips around him, settling deep against her throat.

"But you ken," he continued, without even a hitch in his voice, "this way, I no need to share, if I no wish. She reeks only of my scent, and leaks only my seed. And"—he grinned down at her, chilly and deadly—"since she has freely sworn her vow in ink, she seeks with great strength to please me, ach? She bears all that I should wish."

Maria's thoughts were wheeling, her heart thundering, her sucking mouth stuffed full of orc—and he again drew out, slow, all the way, popping from between her lips. And then—she shuddered all over—he slid down his hand, and gently circled it against her *neck*, holding her head still. While his other hand gripped his swollen, dripping heft, easy and casual—and then dragged it against Maria's *face*. Moving with unhurried, taunting care, streaking her with him, coating her with him, smearing himself on her lips and nose and cheeks—

"See?" he said smugly to the orc beside him, as he sank himself back deep between her parted lips, and drew all the way out again. "Now stand, woman. I wish to have you on your back."

He'd waved a nonchalant hand toward the fur-covered table behind Maria, and gods, her face felt so hot it hurt, her trembly hand wiping at her dripping-wet cheek—but she was in this now, she was proving this to him. And beneath the determination, there was something even darker, something surely so shameful she couldn't dare touch at it—

She jerked herself up to sit on the table, leaning back onto her unsteady elbows, as some distant silent part of her begged Simon to look, to approve. And he was looking, he was, but his eyes were still cool, challenging, utterly commanding.

"I can no fuck you thus, woman," he said, glancing down toward her tightly joined legs. "Open for me. Here."

Another wave of something dark and shameful flared in Maria's belly, swirling even higher as he jabbed his clawed finger against the very edge of the table. Clearly meaning for her to slide forward again, so he could—so he could stand there at the side of it, and take her that way, so all these watching orcs could see.

Gods, Maria could barely *think*—but her body was already obeying, her arse scooting closer to the table's edge. But then she couldn't seem to move any further, couldn't do anything but blink up at Simon's imperious eyes.

And as she stared, oh gods, something abruptly shifted in those eyes. Something uncertain and watchful. Something... *vulnerable.*

"You wish for me, ach?" he said, and though he surely meant it to sound flippant, the lightness rang false in Maria's ears. "You wish me to open you up, and pump you full of good Skai seed?"

There were grunts and hoots of affirmation from the orcs all around, but Maria scarcely heard them, because her eyes were fixed on Simon's face. On where that uncertainty had fully vanished again, leaving only that self-assured coolness behind.

But yes, he was still there, it was still *Simon* in the midst of all this—and suddenly it seemed to set the darkness loose, roaring free into Maria's chest, smashing against all her shame. The hysteria, surely, it had to be—but it didn't at all feel that way, not now. Not with the way her head was frantically nodding, her eyes fixed to this audacious orc, her body so hot it was burning alive...

And when Simon jabbed at the table again, black brows raised, Maria had to bite back a moan as she nodded again, and edged a little closer. And then, while a room full of jeering orcs watched, she held Simon's gaze, yanked up her loincloth with shockingly eager fingers, and spread her legs wide.

"Yes, Simon," she whispered, the words like dropping stones in the too-quiet room. "I want you to open me up, and flaunt me and claim me, and pump me full of your seed. Your *son.*"

And gods, how she was actually *saying* these things, her voice ringing through the taut silence, flashing something new across

Simon's watching eyes. Something that looked just as frenzied as she felt, something held together only by the merest threads...

"Ach, do you?" he breathed, a little too late, his corded throat convulsing, his gaze dropping to the sight between Maria's spread-wide legs. "Then you shall open as wide as you can for me, and show me all I have bought."

Of course he would go there, the utter bastard, and even as Maria twitched at that horrid word *bought*, she felt the challenge of it, the smoke of the tinder, the sheer thrumming craving. The darkness, the power, the *longing*.

So as a room of silent, vicious orcs watched, their collective gazes prickling all over Maria's bare skin, she reached her tingling hands down between her parted thighs, found her slick swollen lips—and then spread them wide apart, just as Simon had asked. Obeying him, honouring him, *flaunting* herself for him.

She could see his throat convulsing again, his eyes locked on the sight—and then flicking, brief, to her face. And then away again, and Maria was almost sure she caught a stain of red, creeping up his cheeks, the heat lighting, catching, flaring...

And then, in a sharp, deadly jolt of movement, he was there. That slick, pulsing head pressing into where Maria had opened herself for him, and driving slow and deep inside. Further, and further, without stopping, hurling away the last of her resistance, impaling her whole upon him in one merciless, primal, powerful stroke.

His eyes held to hers as he did it, blazing, flashing, shouting—and fuck, *fuck*, this was everything, this was all that could ever be. To be filled with an orc's shocking strength, to know beyond certainty that he was here with her, taking her, making her his own. And doing it while all the Skai watched in heavy silence, like it was another rite, a statement, a triumph. A *cleansing*.

And Simon knew it, holding himself like this, trapped deep inside, his bollocks pressing hard and full against Maria's parted crease. While she distantly, vaguely realized she was gasping, trembling all over, her back arching, her bare breasts jiggling and heaving with the weight of her frantic, streaming hunger.

Simon just kept standing there, perfectly still, but for the beast still buried deep within her. A beast that was twitching and shuddering, swelling and leaking, while her stretched-open heat clamped back against him. Needing more, needing him more than anything else alive, but he wasn't, he was waiting, until—

Maria's release flashed and screamed, shrieking through her pinned flailing body, milking the mass of this orc jammed up inside her. While his eyes unmistakably fluttered, once, catching bare and meaningful to hers—and then he slowly, surely drew out, taking himself away from her, but only for a moment, only—

His slam inside felt like a blow, chattering Maria's teeth, making her shiver and flail upon him—and then it came again, again, again. This massive orc pounding into her, meeting her writhing, shouting body with something almost like reverence, his eyes not once leaving hers, holding hers with a fierce, ferocious brightness. Needing this just as much as she did, this was beyond cleansing, beyond proving, it was—

And then, oh, *fuck*, it came. The sharp, furious blast of pleasure, spraying from the beast inside her, flooding her with its strength. Filling her with power and ecstasy and a wild screaming certainty, with a tilting whispering truth. Peace. *Freedom.*

And it kept ringing, shivering, even as Simon gently drew away. Showing these orcs what he'd done, what they'd done, made true in these streaming spurts of molten heat. And then even resting his hand there against her, as if to hold it in, as if wanting her to keep it, always.

"You please me, woman," Simon's voice rumbled, vibrating into Maria's very bones. "You show yourself worthy of a Skai. Ach?"

The last word was so quiet, so painfully tender, but it still seemed to echo through the otherwise silent room. Because it was a... declaration, Maria's whirling thoughts realized. A claim. A *promise.*

And when Simon stepped close, and gathered her up in his arms, that felt like a promise, too. In the way he curled her against his chest, his clawed hand stroking her hair, his mouth pressing to her forehead with something almost like *tenderness.*

He kept stroking her as he grasped for the lamp and stalked toward the door, not giving a single backwards glance. Though Maria's hazy eyes caught, somehow, on Drafli, still watching from the opposite wall, but now with his brow heavily furrowed, his gaze darting at—Ulfarr.

Ulfarr, who was glowering straight toward Maria, with sheer, visceral *rage* still crackling in his black eyes.

But if Simon noticed, he didn't seem concerned—and in fact, his face looked perhaps more content than Maria had ever seen it. And his glance down toward her was so gentle, so damned *affectionate*, that it stole away her breath.

"You have honoured me, woman," he said, his voice hoarse, as he strode through the corridor. "Greatly."

A sharp flare of warmth shivered down Maria's back, and she felt herself slowly smiling at him, the heat suffusing her cheeks. "Really?"

"Ach," he continued, oddly fervent. "With this, I have shown myself wise and powerful, and fulfilled all that is required of a Skai and his woman, but for the hunt or the rut. No other Skai shall *dare* touch you now, even if I am no with you. No even Ulfarr."

That was almost enough to cut through the hazy contentment in Maria's thoughts—Ulfarr still touching her had truly been a *possibility*, until now?—but Simon had already followed that, his eyes narrowing, his hands hoisting her closer.

"You ken I should *never* allow Ulfarr to touch you, ach?" he said firmly. "But now, my kin shall defend this also. Now that you have so bravely flaunted your hunger and your fealty toward me, with no even a *whiff* of fear."

Something much like pride filled his voice, and even as more warmth swelled all through Maria's being, there was suddenly something in that, something important. Something—Maria's tingly hand rubbed at her eyes—something *shameful*.

"But don't you think," she whispered, "that I—lost it, there, for a while? It was all a bit—*much*, right? Irrational? Hysterical?"

Simon's brows had pulled together, his head tilting, and oh gods, had she *insulted* him? "Not that doing such a thing necessarily equates to hysteria, of course," she continued, in a rush. "But truly, I've *never* done such a thing publicly before, let alone *begging* you for it, or not feeling *afraid* about it. And for a woman of my—my uh, *history*, that is, uh, of hysteria, you know, it's—I should have been—"

She couldn't even hear herself, her heart hammering furiously in her ears, and Simon kept studying her as he strode into his familiar room, and carefully set her down to her feet. And far too late, Maria

realized what she'd just confessed, just betrayed. A history of gods-
damned *hysteria*. And what would Simon say, oh gods, what would he
think—

But he only kept looking at her, and both his hands tilted her face
up, fingers spreading against her still-hot cheeks. Making sure she was
looking back at him, her eyes locked to his, to his truth seeking deep.

"Maria," he said, very steady. "Your hunger was a great gift to me.
There was naught amiss in this. Naught amiss with *you*."

But staring up at this bewildering, overwhelming, utterly
distracting orc, Maria heard herself bark a laugh, far too loud in the
sudden stillness. "But you're wrong, Simon," she choked out.
"According to three separate physicians, my husband, my entire
household in Preia, and *every single fucking acquaintance* I knew. Even
you, at first, you called me irrational, you condemned my foolish *feelings*, you *knew* I was broken, you—"

And what the hell was she saying, why was she bringing this up—
and Simon still only stared down at her, unblinking. And surely now
he would finally reject her, just like her husband, and gods she was not
going to weep in front of him, she was *not*—

Until Simon abruptly stepped toward her, and wrapped her tight
in his arms. Enfolding her deep against his chest, pressing her head
close against his loud pattering heart.

"Peace, Maria," he murmured into her hair. "I only no knew you
then, ach? I no knew the strength of your *feeling*. But this no mean you
are *broken*, ach? And"—his chest filled, hollowed—"even if aught *was*
amiss with you, this no yet bring shame. This only mean we next face
this. Seek to *help* this. Find new ways, and keep you *safe*."

Oh. The relief felt almost staggering in its power, and Maria
clutched at it, at his certainty, his solid form against her. At the feel of
his warm mouth, pressing against her hair.

"Also, you ken this husband is a fool, ach?" he continued, his voice
hardening. "You ought *never* heed his words as truth. For this man held
both your vow and your pure hunger thus, and yet *wasted* such a gift."

An odd, derisive laugh escaped Maria's throat—for all his faults,
Duke Warmisham was no fool, and she was surely no *gift*—but
Simon's hands had found her face again, tilting it up, making her look
at him.

"You were the envy of all my kin tonight, my pretty one," he continued, a low, vehement rumble. "You were all a true Skai should be. You watched me, and met me, and strove with all your strength. And when you said how you wished for me, and begged me for my son—"

His voice caught, and he again dragged her close, fingers spreading wide against her bare back. "This tasted," he whispered, "so *true.*"

So true. And standing here, cradled tight in a deadly orc's arms, Maria somehow felt herself—nodding. Saying—yes? Yes? It—*was*?

But she didn't take it back, couldn't take it back, not with the way Simon had exhaled against her, so heavy, so relieved. And surely it was hysteria, surely Maria was truly losing all rationality for good, and—and—

And Simon was easing her down onto the bed. Hovering close and gentle over her, spreading her legs apart. And as he once again pierced her, slow and beautiful and impossibly powerful, Maria somehow just—accepted it. Welcomed it. *Was.*

New ways. A gift. Cleansing. Whole.

"You shall be mine," he said into her ear, quiet. "You shall be Skai. Ach?"

And again, Maria... nodded. She would do this. She would prove this. She would become a Skai, for good.

"Ach," she whispered. "I will."

25

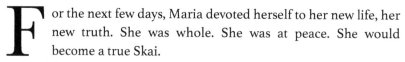

For the next few days, Maria devoted herself to her new life, her new truth. She was whole. She was at peace. She would become a true Skai.

And becoming a Skai, she soon discovered, was just... *fun*. Each day beginning with Simon's constant sharpening, easing her awake, drawing her naked body toward him on the bench. And then, while Maria curled on his lap, Simon would invariably begin some kind of lesson. The first day, it was how to clean and sharpen a blade; the second, what each of his weapons were best used for; and the third, even how to shave his beard, demonstrating by dragging Maria's gleaming new dagger against his stubbled throat.

"You must learn no only to harm with your blade," he told her, curling her fingers around the dagger-hilt. "But how to taunt, and tease, and do good. Ach?"

Maria laughed, and pointed out that her teasing was liable to result in Simon's being seriously injured—to which he only smirked at her, and sprawled his legs wide. And then, with infuriating coolness, he ordered her to practice by shaving him in certain other places, without missing a single spot.

It proved to be a singularly distracting endeavour, and one that Maria soon abandoned entirely, in favour of swallowing his too-tempting bounty down her throat. And afterwards, he kissed her with fierce, approving thoroughness, and promised to reward her when he came back from his work that evening—and even more if she once again sought to use her new tools, and honour him.

It did mean Maria was left alone in his room again, a pattern that had continued for multiple hours each day—but between Baldr, and her tools, and her prayers and treatise-reading, it proved to be mostly bearable. And when Simon returned that night, dusty and irritable and bearing strange new wounds, Maria dragged him close, and begged for her day's reward. And in return, he fervently drove into her, from both front and behind, plunging her full of his heat, his power, his safety.

He still wasn't always forthcoming about his daily activities, but Maria soon realized that it was after their shared pleasure, in the quiet warm contentment, that he was most likely to speak. To tell her, maybe, of the orcs he'd seen that day, or what he'd sought to accomplish. And despite the lack of detailed explanations, Maria rapidly began to understand that Simon's job as Enforcer wasn't only about punishment—but, perhaps even more importantly, about *awareness*. About Simon knowing his kin, and in that knowledge, keeping them *safe*.

And this information wasn't all gained by Simon personally, Maria soon learned, but by an entire network of Skai orcs. By what seemed like dozens of dedicated scouts, directed mostly by the spiky-haired, keen-eyed Joarr, but also sometimes by Drafli, and sometimes by Simon himself.

But the Enforcing still appeared to fall to Simon alone, as decreed by his clan's ways. And when he stalked in a few nights later, and again cut his hand, and streaked another bloody mark on the wall, Maria didn't rage, or shrink back, or demand explanations. Instead, she only clutched and clawed at his stiff, blood-streaked body, and met his angry mouth with hard lips and biting teeth. And then screamed with abandon as he pounded her into the bed, her hands pinned over her head, his fangs skating sharp and dangerous against the pulse thundering in her neck.

But he hadn't actually bitten her, it turned out, and afterwards he carefully licked her reddened skin, and drew her close. And it was then, stilted and hoarse, that he spoke. Telling Maria of the lone, faraway Skai who'd hunted multiple unsuspecting women, seeking to use his power to force, to harm, to *kill*.

"I wished to make him pay," Simon whispered, his voice thin. "I *wished* to hear him scream. Ach?"

And pinned beneath his still-rigid body, Maria swallowed the last traces of fear, and stroked her hands up and down his stiff back. And then dragged his head close, so she could press kisses to his cheek, his grinding jaw, his scratchy, fragrant neck.

"Thank you for keeping those women safe, Simon," she whispered back. "They needed you, and the justice of your fathers' ways."

Simon didn't reply, but Maria was sure she felt his body relaxing against her, his lashes blinking hard against her neck. And when she shoved him onto his back, and climbed on top, his eyes were oddly bright, his hands clutching powerfully at her hips as she rooted herself deep upon him, and rode him until he roared.

After they awoke the next morning, and Maria had shaved and then sucked him, Simon again spent the whole day with her. First taking her to the shrine, and then to an unfamiliar room he called the Skai bath. Which turned out not to be a bath at all, but a cool, airy, tucked-away alcove that had a genuine *waterfall* pouring out of the ceiling, pooling crystal-clear onto the stone floor below.

"Come, woman," Simon ordered her, as he kicked off his trousers, and then plucked off Maria's tunic, as well as her dagger. "Bathe with me."

With that, he dragged her loincloth-clad body into the pool—and she yelped aloud as the flood of water rushed over her head, drenching her in shocking wet coldness.

"Y-you *prick*," she spluttered. "This is f-freezing. And a *p-public r-room*."

But Simon only flashed her his teasing, crooked grin, and he yanked out his ever-present braid, shaking his long black hair around his head in a streaming wet arc. "Ach," he purred, low and husky, his damp hair adding a surprising softness to his rugged face. "Good for fucking, ach?"

And curse him, but Maria couldn't even argue, especially once she was fully plastered against his bare, powerful warmth, her legs clamped around his waist, his hands easily holding up her full weight. While that already-prodding beast at his groin sank slow and strong inside her, locking them together beneath the ice-cold spray.

"You wish for me to take you thus," he hissed into her ear, as he eased them into a rhythm, sliding Maria bodily up and down his invading heft. "You wish to be ploughed true and deep by your Skai, where any of his clan might see. Ach?"

Maria could only nod, and clutch tighter at his powerful shoulders, and bite back the rising urge to howl—and Simon flashed her that grin again, cool and mocking. "You wish to be bared," he informed her, thrusting harder, faster. "You wish to be flaunted. You wish for the reward of my good Skai seed. Ach?"

Maria nodded again, choked and frantic, the hunger flashing and swarming, skittering between the steady rush of ice over her, the furious heat impaling her again and again. "Yes," she moaned, her eyes wildly fluttering, her fingers scraping against his back. "Yes, Simon, gods, yes, *please!*"

Her voice had risen to a shriek, and Simon was gasping, still half-grinning, as he plunged her once more into him, grinding her deep— and then swarmed her with spurt after spurt of his blessed, glorious release. While she flailed and wailed and choked upon him, her own pleasure quavering out sharp and cold, filling her with icy shivery relief.

And once the shocks had faded, and Simon's eyes had angled surreptitiously toward the door, Maria wasn't even surprised to see multiple orcs standing there, and openly gawking toward them. And while she instinctively clutched Simon tight, burying her face in his warm neck, the shame somehow seemed to whisper away beneath the force of their joined truth. He'd wanted that. She'd wanted that. She was honouring him. Proving this.

And once Simon had drawn himself out again, and settled Maria down onto her wobbly feet, he rewarded her by drying her all over with a nearby cloth, and carefully braiding her hair. And then even dressing her again, tucking her dagger close against her side, and once he'd finished Maria smiled at him, and then leaned up to kiss his cheek.

"Thank you, Simon," she murmured. "I feel very refreshed."

He smiled back down toward her, slow and indulgent, and then actually proceeded to guide her over to the watching group of orcs, introducing them by name. Something he'd done more and more these past days, and Maria had begun to recognize, just from Simon's stance and his eyes, which orcs were on his side against Ulfarr, and which stood opposed.

And it was the latter orcs—including this shifty-eyed bunch—who were consistently the most obvious in their suspicion and dislike toward Maria, and humans in general. But she was still hellbent on honouring Simon, and she'd quickly learned that he was most pleased when she would smile sweetly at any new orcs he introduced, and then lean into him, or reach up and kiss his neck, or slide her hand over his firm rounded arse.

"*After* your lessons, greedy woman," Simon purred at her this time, once she'd gotten a good grip at his rear—and then he grasped for her other hand, and brazenly cupped it against the already-swelling bulge at the front of his trousers. "You must first earn your next reward from me, ach? Now, which lesson first, fighting or hunting?"

Maria shot him a grin that wasn't even slightly feigned—she'd begun to look forward to his daily lessons with genuine excitement—and eagerly pulled him past the watching orcs, and out into the corridor. "Fighting first," she said, "and then hunting? Please?"

Simon grinned back, wolfish and wicked, and obligingly escorted her to the arena. Where they proceeded to spend a thoroughly enjoyable afternoon together, with Simon teaching Maria with both blades and fists. Followed by another round of what had indeed proved to be hunting lessons—seeking to find him in the darkness, learning to identify and follow disparate scents, moving as quietly as possible, navigating the twisty Skai wing without light or assistance.

"Do you think I could practice hunting tomorrow, while you work?" Maria asked him, once they'd returned to his room, and were both lying sated and entwined on his bed. "By myself, I mean? Just in the corridors nearest here?"

She'd tried to keep her voice casual—she was truly trying not to ask for too much these days, doing her damnedest to honour and obey him. But after such a thoroughly delightful whirl of activity, the prospect of spending another day trapped alone in this room felt even more disheartening, more daunting, than before.

"Ach, no," Simon instantly replied, his head shaking. "No alone. Ask Baldr to take you, ach?"

But Baldr had actually been remarkably busy these past days, too. Either he was holed up in his room with the ever-vicious Drafli, as tell-tale gasps and moans emanated from the door, or he was off at important-sounding meetings. And in his absence, his room was regularly occupied by a rotation of Simon's scouts, Killik and Halthorr and Fulnir. None of whom were the talkative type, and all of whom seemed to spend nearly as much time sharpening their weapons as Simon did.

"Right," Maria belatedly said, angling her eyes away from Simon, fighting to ignore the heavy plunge in her gut. "Right. I'll ask Baldr if he's free."

But as usual, Simon missed very little, and his warm hand caught Maria's face, tilting it back toward him. "I ken this is no easy, ach?" he said, to her vague surprise. "No Skai wishes to be held thus. We wish to run and hunt free and easy under the sky. But—"

He broke off there, his brows knitting together, his mouth betraying an unmistakable grimace. As if he surely hadn't meant to say that, because—what? He still didn't trust Maria? Or he still didn't trust his kin? Or both?

"Rosa-Ka came back to the mountain, last eve," he said abruptly, his voice curt. "I shall ask her to come see you tomorrow whilst I work, ach?"

Maria attempted a smile, which Simon rewarded with a hungry nuzzle at her neck, a meaningful grip of his hand to her hip. And as he again drove her against the furs, it was almost easy to forget that little nagging darkness in her belly. Simon wanted her. She would prove this to him, and become a true Skai.

The next day's visit with Rosa helped too, especially when Rosa eagerly commiserated about over-working orcs, and told Maria a lively tale about how John had recently refused to sleep for four days, and had then fallen asleep while walking through the corridor. She also oohed and aahed over Maria's cleaning efforts, and said Baldr had put in an order for hooks, and she was quite sure it had been done, and perhaps she would go fetch Tristan and ask?

Maria grimaced at the thought, because she still held no desire whatsoever to see the handsome Tristan again, let alone his mocking mate—but Rosa had already bounded off, and soon returned with the pair of them in tow, as well as a bucket full of what indeed proved to be iron hooks.

"Thank you for having us, Maria," Tristan said softly, his face unmistakably flushed. "We should be honoured to help you today, ach? If you are sure you shall welcome this?"

He'd cast an uncertain glance toward his mate—Salvi—as he spoke, but this Salvi was smiling too, and looking distinctly apologetic. "I'll happily wait outside, if you like," he said, with a wry twitch toward the door. "But I assure you, decorating Simon's room will be its own special penance for my thoughtlessness toward you, ach?"

Maria couldn't help a reluctant laugh, and despite her unease, she soon found herself caught up in their easy, cheerful banter. And thanks to Simon's lessons, as well as her own observations, she now knew which of his weapons were used for what, and which ones he usually took out together, and therefore, which hanging locations would likely be best for each of them.

Salvi and Tristan managed the actual hanging, which turned out to be an arduous process that required shocking amounts of twisting and hammering. But they repeatedly refused Maria and Rosa's help, doggedly hanging one weapon, and then another, until the floor was finally, fully clear. And the room felt so large, suddenly, so open, and Maria twirled in the middle of it, laughing, revelling in the foreign feeling of free movement under her feet.

"Thank you," she said, with a true grin toward them both. "You've been so kind."

They both waved it away, Tristan's face again flushed with red, Salvi's flashing her a warm, wry smile. And then, to Maria's ongoing astonishment, they went off to collect a broom and mop from somewhere—and after yet another flurry of cheerful orc activity, Simon's room was bright, organized, and sparkling clean.

Maria could scarcely wait for Simon's return that night, and it was thoroughly gratifying to see him lurch to stillness in the doorway, his tired eyes blinking blankly at his new room. And despite the fact that he was once again covered with an assortment of mysterious new cuts and bruises, Maria bit back the urge to ask questions, and instead darted over to grasp his hands, and draw him inside.

"Please tell me you like it?" she said, with a hopeful smile. "But if you don't, I will happily put Salvi to work again to fix it."

Simon huffed a loud snort, but he was smiling back down at her, crooked, slow. "Ach, this pleases me," he murmured. "You are surely due a strong reward for this."

His rewards had become something of a formality these past days, perhaps even a game—but Maria certainly wasn't about to refuse. At least, until Simon actually winced as he tossed her onto the bed, and then reached back to do something to his shoulder that made a loud, unnerving *crack*.

And Maria would gain his trust, she *would*—so she again choked down the question, and grasped for him, and nudged him over onto his back. "You can reward me later," she said, twitching a grin toward him. "Ach?"

There was indeed something like relief in his eyes, or perhaps even reverence, as Maria tossed off her tunic, climbed aboard, and slowly seated herself deep upon him. And once he'd howled out his pleasure, pouring her full of his molten heat, he dragged her up to straddle his hungry, licking mouth. Not seeming to care in the least that he was swallowing copious amounts of his own mess, and instead lavishing her with his clever lips and tongue until she was yanking at his hair, and shouting his name to the ceiling.

Afterwards, it was again easy to forget the nagging darkness, to fall asleep in Simon's warm arms. At least, until the next morning, when Maria awoke to find him already dressed and ready to leave again, his gleaming scimitar strapped to his side.

"You seem to have a lot... going on, right now," she ventured, once he'd beckoned her over to the bench, and handed her his shaving-knife. "Is there any other... permanent Enforcing you still need to finish?"

Any other killing, she meant. And it was a sign, perhaps, of just how easy things had become between them, that Simon didn't tense up, or even frown toward her. "No," he said, arching his head sideways, giving her shaving-knife better access to his throat. "I shall no need to,

I ken, before this battle with Ulfarr comes. I have gained nearly all I wished to fulfill amongst my kin."

Right. That. They were now down to six short days—Maria had been counting very carefully—and she tried for a smile as she drew the knife against his jaw. "I'm glad," she said, and she meant it. "But where do you keep getting all these injuries, then? Are you still out there—*maiming*, then? Or fighting?"

Simon shrugged, perhaps a little too casually. "A bit, mayhap," he said. "There is always something, ach? And some sparring, also."

Oh. The heaviness in Maria's belly plunged deeper, and she held her eyes very intently on her work. On the very slight skitter of the knife against Simon's neck, echoing the scraping shouts in her thoughts.

So she truly hadn't gained his trust yet. Not if he still couldn't even tell her the truth of what he was doing each day, while she was kept trapped here alone. And she was trying so hard, she was striving with everything she had to make this work, and it still wasn't good enough? Still?

"Do you think," she ventured, squaring her shoulders, "that I might be able to come with you, while you work today? Even for a while?"

There was an instant's stillness before her, and then the bitter, abrupt truth of Simon standing up and lurching away from her, his back turned. And suddenly there was the ridiculous, irrational urge to weep, and good gods, that was hysteria, she wasn't supposed to *care*—

But then Maria bit her lip, hard, and somehow bit down on that awful trail of thought, too. Because she did care. However it had happened, she did care about Simon, about these orcs, about this mountain. It wasn't hysteria. It *wasn't*.

"Is there—something I could improve?" she asked toward his back, as steadily as she could. "Some way I haven't pleased you? I know we haven't gone back to the Skai common-room yet, but perhaps we could, if you like? Or perhaps you don't really like what I've done to your room after all, and there's some way I could better arrange it to your liking? Or have I accidentally betrayed your confidence somehow, or underperformed at my lessons, or"—she swallowed hard—"is it something I could do better in bed?"

Simon had been strapping on another weapon, his hand catching on his belt, his shoulders square and stiff. And when he finally turned to face Maria again, he just looked tired, his mouth tight, the shadows heavy under his eyes.

"Peace, Maria," he said, with a sigh. "I am most pleased with you, and all you have done. Ach?"

Maria blinked blankly toward him, her eyes still prickling, her mouth quavering—and in two quick strides, Simon was back before her again. Settling both his hands firmly on her shoulders, fixing her with the truth in his weary, glinting eyes.

"You please me, woman," he said, deeper this time. "You must no think any other. You are so ripe, and warm, and eager, and sweet. You are a great gift to me."

Oh. A trickle of heat flicked through Maria's belly, but she couldn't stop searching his face, couldn't stop herself from speaking. "Then why isn't it enough?" her wavering voice asked. "Why haven't I yet earned your trust? Why do I still need to stay trapped here every day without you?"

She winced even as she heard it, because gods, it sounded so plaintive, so pathetic. As if she'd been here pining after Simon for weeks, as if she'd somehow changed all his deeply held preconceptions about humans in a matter of days. And as if he needed to deal with her drama right now, while he was still desperately preparing for his clan's future, and staring down an impending fight to the *death* against his greatest enemy. Six *days*.

"Actually, never mind," she said, with her best attempt at a smile. "I know you're so busy, and you have so much to think about at the moment. You surely don't need me grousing at you on top of everything else. So please, forget I said all this, and go have a productive day. Hopefully without needing to permanently injure anyone."

Her smile twisted into something that felt truer at the end, and she even leaned up, and pressed a quick kiss to his freshly shaved neck. Feeling, oddly, an unexpected tension within it—and then a sudden, swift grasp of his big hand to the back of her head. Holding her there against him, her body snapped still, her breath caught in her lungs.

"Your scent, it—" he said, unusually stilted, and she could hear him swallow, his breath exhaling. "Ach. *Ach.* You are so—sweet, my pretty one."

His voice sounded so strange, his hand curling slack against Maria's neck, and she eased away a little, enough to see his eyes. Enough to study him, to wait for him to speak. To watch, and listen.

"Ach, mayhap I shall bring you, for a spell," he continued finally, heavily. "But I ken this may vex you, ach? This may alter"—he gave a fluid wave between them—"*all.*"

Oh. He was worried about—*upsetting* her? Scaring her, maybe, with all his bone-breaking, and his fighting, and his Enforcing. And suddenly it was such a damned *relief*, rolling bright and giddy through Maria's thoughts, because surely, after everything she'd faced here so far, seeing Simon's work would be the easy part. As long as he was still with her. As long as he truly wanted her there.

"But if you truly want me to know you," Maria answered, her voice smooth, assured, "you'd want me to see your work, too, right? You'd want to give me the chance to watch and listen and learn? To be a true Skai?"

Simon had again stilled before her, his gaze almost arrested on hers—and then his hand rose to her face, and caressed it. So soft, so gentle, and his mouth had twitched up too, into a slow, crooked little smile. Wry, resigned, *approving.*

"Then come with me, wilful woman," he said, "and you shall learn all my truth."

26

Simon's truth, at least at first, proved to be far more mundane than Maria had expected. Consisting mostly of him walking through the Skai wing's maze of twisty black corridors, and... *talking* to people.

"How is your mate, Igull?" he asked one heavily scarred orc, who'd been lounging in a large, unfamiliar room with a group of other orcs. "You have sent the Ka-esh medics to the camp to see her, ach?"

The orc shook his head, his eyes wary. "No wish to send Ka-esh," he grunted back. "Pretty orcs may *steal* sweet mate."

Simon's growl felt like it rumbled the stone all around, his hands clutched to fists. "You no give your mate care, you no deserve to keep her," he hissed back. "You send Ka-esh *today*, or I send hungry Skai brother tomorrow."

The orc visibly paled, and mumbled some kind of uneasy-sounding reply in black-tongue. To which Simon only scoffed, and nudged Maria away, back out into the corridor. Past where Drafli was taking his pleasure with a random orc's mouth, blatant enough that even Simon elbowed him on the way by, before pulling Maria toward another nearby door.

This room proved to be small and quiet, with only a lone orc inside. The orc looked older than any others Maria had seen here so far, and he was thin and white-haired, sitting slumped on a rickety bed, and gazing blankly toward the opposite wall.

"Dufnall," Simon said, his voice low. "What is amiss?"

The orc glanced up, his eyes cloudy and vague—but when he caught sight of Maria, he jolted, and edged further away on the bed. "Hungry," he said mournfully. "Hunted rat to eat. But they *stole.*"

"Who stole?" Simon asked, again soft, surprisingly soothing. "You ken scents, or faces?"

"No," the orc said, as his eyes caught on Maria again, and he slid further away. "*Human* here."

"Ach, she no harm you," Simon replied. "Skai orcs steal your rat? Brothers?"

"Brothers," said the orc, his voice rising. "Young brothers *always* steal rat!"

Simon visibly exhaled, and settled a heavy hand on Dufnall's thin shoulder. "Peace, brother," he said. "I soon bring new rat. Or you go to kitchen, and eat there. You remember this, ach?"

"Want to *hunt,*" Dufnall replied, with a doleful sigh. "Want *new* rat."

Simon nodded and patted the orc's shoulder, again with surprising gentleness, and then turned and stalked out the door. Dragging Maria after him into another new room, this one entirely empty, though she caught sight of a narrow little crevice at the back.

"Stay," Simon ordered her, as he strode for the crevice, and slipped silently behind it. Vanishing for only a few moments before reappearing again, but now with fresh-looking *blood* on his mouth. And clutched in his hand—Maria shuddered—was indeed a dead, dripping-red rat.

"Oh, how *vile,*" Maria said, her stomach roiling—to which Simon snorted, and beckoned her after him back to Dufnall. Who crowed aloud at the sight of the new rat, and instantly began gnawing at it with thoroughly nauseating gusto.

After that, Simon thankfully washed up in the Skai bath, and then stalked into yet another room, this one with three younger-looking orcs wrestling on the floor inside. And after a loud, alarming bellow from Simon in black-tongue, the young orcs scuttled off past them into the corridor, heads bowed, shoulders hunched.

"Rat hunting," Simon said flatly, by way of explanation. "A full day of this ought to teach them to better honour their elders, ach?"

And looking at the grim satisfaction in his eyes, Maria felt the odd, rising urge to throw her arms around him, perhaps to shove him up against the closest wall—but he was already striding out into the corridor again, where he soon proceeded to sniff out several more unnerving situations. Including an accusation of theft, a pair of orcs who were screaming at each other in black-tongue, and an irate trading-room porter who'd refused to serve a certain orc because, apparently, he'd snored too loudly the night before.

And finally, to Maria's rising astonishment, was a cozy, fur-lined room, with two orcs inside. One of the orcs was again Drafli, now leaning against the nearest wall, frowning at Maria with his typical dislike—and the other orc was sitting cross-legged in the middle of the room, holding two small objects in his fingers, and staring up at Maria with wide, fearful black eyes.

It was—a *little* orc. With a smooth, unmarked grey face, and a neat braid winding over his shoulder. And in his hands—Maria studied them again, recognition dawning—were a pair of carved stone figures. *Toys.*

Simon spoke something to the little orc in black-tongue, his voice back to quiet and soothing—but those small, glittering eyes were still fixed to Maria, and tainted with unmistakable fear. "That is human," he said, his voice high-pitched, his tiny claw pointing toward Maria. "It smell funny."

Maria blinked, and beside her Simon actually nodded, his face perfectly impassive. "Ach, humans' scent is no like orcs," he said evenly. "This human is Maria. Maria, this is Bjorn, who is new to our mountain."

Oh. The name sounded vaguely familiar, and wait, *wait*, this was the young orc whose father Simon had *killed* the other day, good gods. And despite the sudden clutch in Maria's belly, she drew in breath, and even managed a little smile down toward him.

"Hi there," she said. "It's so lovely to meet you. I like your toys."

The fear in Bjorn's eyes had given way to something more like suspicion, and he carefully slid the toys behind his back, out of Maria's sight. "What good are you?" he asked her, his nose wrinkling. "What do you do here?"

Maria blinked again, but felt her mouth twitching up, her eyes glancing at Simon's impassive face. "Well," she said, "I mostly hang around Simon's room, and eat his food, and pester him to entertain me. I also fight very badly."

The small orc looked even more suspicious than before, his black brows furrowing. "This is no good. You do no else of use?"

Maria couldn't help her smile this time, quick and true. "I can clean, I suppose. And, well"—she shot another swift glance at Simon—"I used to be able to do a decent jig, if that counts?"

Bjorn looked wholly unconvinced, so without further hesitation, Maria tapped out a beat with her foot, and then launched into a jig. It was one of the most ridiculous ones her father had taught her, consisting of much foot-stomping and arm-flailing—but it was also just as fun as she remembered. And even if both Simon and Drafli were looking at her like she'd grown two heads, that was surely amusement in Bjorn's eyes, and perhaps even an upwards tug at the corner of his mouth.

"This is yet no real use," he said thoughtfully. "But if this please Simon, mayhap it is enough for him to keep feeding you."

The bubble of laughter escaped before Maria could help it, and she grinned at Simon beside her, at the unmistakable trace of warmth in his eyes. "Gods, I hope so," she said lightly. "I'll jig for you any time you like, Simon."

Simon did smile at that, showing just a hint of sharp fang, and then he strode over to the little orc, fishing something out of his trouser pocket. "Here, little brother," he said, handing it over, and Maria realized it was another carved figure, in the shape of a tiny orc. "I bring you more tomorrow, ach?"

Bjorn snatched away the figure with visible eagerness, and immediately set to playing again. And once Simon and Maria were back in the corridor, Maria couldn't seem to stop her arm from circling around Simon's waist, drawing him close. Needing to touch him, somehow, to bury her face in the warm, pulsing heat of his chest.

"I thought you were supposed to be off maiming and killing," she said, muffled, "and here you are helping the elderly, and looking out for women, and giving *toys* to small *children*."

Her voice sounded accusing, because hadn't Simon said he'd been worried about scaring her, in this? Frightening her off? While in this moment, all Maria wanted to do was climb him, and kiss him, and even say, perhaps, that—

"Ach, this is naught, in the midst of all else I have done," he replied, heavy, though his arms had circled around Maria too, his head pressing against her hair. "But I thank you for your kindness to Bjorn. He has no smiled thus since he came here."

Maria only squeezed Simon tighter, his heartbeat jolting in her ear, and it almost felt painful when he pulled away. "Now come," he said, his voice rough. "You shall now learn the rest of it, ach?"

Maria nodded, catching and squeezing his big hand, and then willingly accompanied him through yet more twisty black corridors. These ones darker and narrower than any others she'd encountered so far, and all seeming to tilt steadily downwards, until Simon strode into yet another new room, this one feeling and smelling distinctly different than the rest.

He'd left the lamp outside the door, and peering into the heavier darkness, Maria abruptly realized that this room was—alive. Not with orcs, but with... mushrooms?!

And yes, yes, *mushrooms*. Of an astonishing variety of colours and shapes, scattered thick across the floor, and even growing up the walls. Some had tiny button tops, others flared into strange elaborate fans, others almost looked like honeycomb—and some even glowed into the dark room, giving off a faint, blue-green light.

"This is—*wonderful*, Simon," Maria said, hushed, into the silence. "Is it yours?!"

"Ach, no," came Simon's reply. "It is Joarr's. Are you ready for our match, brother?"

Maria blinked around the seemingly empty room, frowning—and then realized, with a jolt of shock, that Joarr was indeed leaning there against that wall, so still and silent as to be nearly invisible. And in the mushrooms' peculiar greenish light, he looked almost unearthly, his black hair standing on end, his eyes glinting with danger.

And rather than answering Simon, Joarr ducked with astonishing speed, his claws swiping at something below—and suddenly he stood before Simon and Maria, holding out a mushroom in each hand. Simon's was an alarming-looking bright red, and Maria's tiny and brown.

"Thank you, brother," Simon said to Joarr, as he took his mushroom and tossed it into his mouth, and then shot a sidelong glance toward Maria. "He no poison you, ach?"

Maria managed a grateful smile, and then took a careful bite of her mushroom, too. Finding, to her surprise, that it was delicate and sweet, quite unlike anything she'd ever tasted before.

"It is good," she said, with genuine relief. "Thank you."

It was impossible to tell if Joarr was pleased with this, but next he turned to Simon, and began speaking in low, clipped black-tongue. To which Simon nodded, and then shot Maria a swift, unreadable look. "Mayhap you shall wait here, ach?" he said. "This shall no be pretty to watch."

But Maria had already seen Simon spar multiple times now, and she was supposed to be seeing his truth, she was. "I want to see," she said firmly. "I want to know all your truth, Simon."

Simon's mouth tightened, his gaze darting toward Joarr—but Joarr looked almost satisfied, and beckoned them both toward the opposite wall. To where a small crack in the stone turned out to be a steep little staircase, twisting as it sank deeper into the earth.

Simon descended with ease, holding his hand out for Maria to follow. And once she'd scrambled down after him, she found herself in another green-tinged room. But this one filled with a mass of posts and boulders, all looming with strange, shadowy menace.

Joarr had somehow disappeared again, and Simon waved Maria toward a large boulder that was propped beside the wall, with more greenish mushrooms clustered around its base. "You stay," he ordered her, pointing his claw toward it. "And you no move, until I say we are done. Ach?"

His voice sounded slightly slurred, and Maria blinked at him, bemused—but he only jabbed his claw again, more forcefully this time. So she nodded, and awkwardly climbed up atop the boulder. Perching herself on the edge of it, and frowning at the sight of Simon actually swaying on his feet. Like he was dizzy, or—or *drugged*, or...

And without warning, a black blur shot out of the shadows. Flying straight toward Simon's unsteady form, and crashing them both to the earth with a deafening, stone-shuddering thud.

Maria choked back a shout, both hands clapped to her mouth—but Simon had jerked into motion, flailing up beneath what Maria now recognized as Joarr. His spiky-haired body moving almost too swiftly to be real, and wait, those were actual *knives* in his hands, their sharpened blades glinting silver. And they were flashing toward Simon's *neck*, good gods, and Simon was moving far too slowly to possibly avoid them, and, and—

His bellow was sheer agonized rage, red blood spraying wide from his shoulder—and Joarr was still slicing and swinging, striking with impossible speed. Punching Simon straight in the nose with a clenched fist, and then jabbing the knife directly toward his *eye*—

Maria did scream this time, covering her own eyes with her hands—but when she dared another look, Simon had somehow rolled out of the way, and clutched for one of Joarr's arms. And in another spray of blood—from Simon's *hand* now—the knife went flying end over end across the room. While Joarr spat something in black-tongue that might have been a curse, and then leapt to his feet—and landed a vicious, brutal kick straight between Simon's parted legs.

Simon bellowed again, ragged, broken, horrifying. His body curling double as Joarr kicked him again and again, the awful sounds of thudding flesh echoing through the room—and then Joarr's knife was flashing again, aiming for Simon's exposed back this time, and Maria couldn't watch, she couldn't—

But she couldn't look away, either, not even as the knife dragged against bare skin, and Simon roared again. The sound like an explosion in Maria's ears, the blood flying wide—and Joarr *laughed* as he twirled the knife in his fingers, and again plunged it down toward the same wound as before—

Simon's body lurched sideways, somehow, and the knife's blade scraped against the floor, jagged and shrill. And Maria's breath caught, choked, as Simon shoved upwards, blood spraying, his body swaying, and lunged toward Joarr. Just catching him by the arm, jerking him back onto the floor...

And in one more wrenching flash of movement, it was over. Joarr's arm trapped between Simon's, bent back, on the verge of breaking. And Joarr's foot was kicking Simon's leg, three times.

Simon had—*won*.

But as he eased up to his knees, it surely didn't look like he'd won. Blood was streaming from his nose, his back, his shoulder, and there were deep purple bruises blooming on his face and chest. And he still swayed as he pushed to his feet, even as Joarr grasped for his arm, and held him steady.

"No bad," Joarr was saying to Simon, with a shockingly careless shrug. "Could have cut out eye, though."

Simon nodded, wincing at the movement, wiping at his bloody nose with his visibly trembling hand. "Ach," he said, his voice thick, as he shook the blood off his hand. "Shall better watch for this, next time."

Next time. Maria's hands were still clamped over her mouth, her heartbeat still thundering in her ears, and she realized that there was water streaking down her cheeks, betraying her distress, her *terror*. But truly, what the hell was she supposed to do with this, with watching the orc she—she cared about—be beaten, and stabbed, and *defeated*?

And she was supposed to be watching, listening, trying to learn, to understand—but suddenly, nothing was making sense. Not the way Simon was clapping Joarr on the shoulder, just as he often did with Baldr, and *thanking* him.

Joarr only shrugged, and then strode over toward Maria—to where Maria was cringing back, curling up, her eyes wide and terrified on his shadowy face. But he didn't even seem to notice, and instead plucked up another mushroom, and tossed it over toward Simon.

"You still go healer," Joarr told Simon. "Then again tomorrow?"

Simon swallowed the mushroom whole, and then nodded, hard, bracing, his eyes squeezed shut. "Ach," he replied. "Again with Drafli also, ach? You both at once?"

Joarr nodded back, and then strode away, giving a casual wave over his shoulder. And now it was only Maria and Simon, Maria still frozen in place on her boulder, while Simon gulped in dragging breaths, and kept pooling blood on the floor beneath him.

"Come, woman," he said finally, as he took a slow, limping step toward the staircase. "We are done."

Maria's body felt weighted with lead, but she somehow shoved off the boulder, landing on her badly trembling legs. Her eyes still blinking back the water prickling behind them, threatening to pour down her burning cheeks, to mingle with the sticky hot blood under her feet. Why. Why. *Why?*

But she still couldn't seem to speak. Only followed in stilted silence as Simon climbed up the stairs with visible effort, bracing himself on the walls this time, his breaths shuddering through his huge, bloody frame. His pain feeling almost visceral, scraping against Maria's belly, pounding into her madly beating heart.

"Can I," she finally choked out, once they'd reached the glowing upper room again, "*help,* somehow? Is there something—anything—I can do?"

Simon shrugged, wincing, as he shuffled across the room. "I shall heal," he said, his voice still laced with pain. "Efterar shall fix the worst of it."

Efterar. The healing orc. And Maria was staring at Simon again, while multiple disparate memories seemed to twine together in her brain, folding into place. Simon had been doing... *this,* all these days? When he'd gone off to work?

"But—why?" she asked, helpless, pleading. "Why would you *do* this to yourself, Simon?"

And surely he would explain, surely here she would understand—but he only shrugged again. "I must soon fight for the future of all I own, and all my clan, and mayhap all my mountain," he said, hoarse. "You no ken this shall be easy? Or pretty, or fair?"

Wait. Simon was doing this because of—*Ulfarr?* But Ulfarr wasn't supposed to be able to defeat Simon, surely he couldn't, even Simon had said so...

Or had he? *Defeat wears many faces,* Simon had told her, and suddenly Maria remembered that he'd seemed... off, that night. *Afraid.*

And staring at his limping, bloody form, it occurred to Maria, perhaps for the first time, that for Simon, this was—*real.* That he was truly facing his death, with this fight. That this wasn't some kind of distant, far-off boxing-match, fought fair and clean, that he was already sure to win. No. For him, this was *everything.* The loss of everything he owned. The loss of his people's *future.*

The future of orcs like Bjorn. Like Dufnall. His scouts, his friends, his Skai brothers' mates. Himself. And...

"Simon," Maria said, her voice a croak. "If Ulfarr defeats you, what happens to... *me*?"

And Simon... didn't look at her. Kept limping. Kept dragging in those guttural, gasping breaths. While the fear began thudding, rising in Maria's ribs, he'd said he would keep her safe, he'd *promised*...

"I shall keep you safe," he said thickly, his hazy eyes angling toward Maria, as though he'd heard her very thoughts. "I *shall*."

But that wasn't the same as him saying he'd win this fight. It wasn't the same as him saying Maria wasn't supposed to become the victor's spoils, in all this. Or that Ulfarr wouldn't rightfully be able to claim her, if he won. Was it?

"But I thought," Maria said, her voice high-pitched, "that I wasn't really your mate. So I don't—*count*, as yours. I'm just—someone you *bought*."

And Simon wasn't speaking again, only limping, bleeding, his jaw grinding in his cheek. And wait, wait, *wait*. He'd been trying to show his clan a new way, with this. He'd been trying to teach them how this could be done, without the hunt, or the rut. And if he succeeded...

And here, all at once, were the images of all the ways Simon had sought to do this. Parading Maria before his kin in a Skai loincloth. Keeping her safe and content. Showing her as eager to help and serve and please him. Giving her all those lessons. Teaching her his clan's ways. Making her a Skai.

And of course, perhaps most powerful of all, taking her before his clan that day. Proving to them how much she wanted him. How it was... true.

With this, he'd told her, *I have fulfilled all that is required of a Skai and his woman, but for the hunt or the rut. No other Skai shall dare touch you now.*

The walls felt like they were spinning, suddenly, and Maria had to reach out and grip at one, fighting to drag in breaths. *Had* Simon succeeded in making her his mate, before his clan? Had he?

"Simon," Maria said, her voice very far away. "*Am* I your mate now? A... *real* one?"

And gods, the way he looked at her. The pain flaring across his

eyes, blood still streaming down his body, his face so haggard, so...
tired.

"What do you ken?" he asked her. "Are you?"

Was she. And Maria's throat was thick with something she couldn't name, her eyes wide on his bruised, bloody face. Was she? *Was* she?

"I—I'm your *prisoner*," she heard her distant voice say. "We have a contract. I'm barely—barely allowed out of your *room*."

Something flashed in Simon's eyes, dark and angry, and he abruptly staggered away again, limping faster down the corridor. And had Maria said the wrong thing, surely not, it was true, but—

But it was too late, and Simon was turning, lurching into a room. Into a familiar room, the clinic with the beds, with the scarred, ugly healer orc. Efterar.

Efterar had leapt up to his feet, visible surprise flashing through his eyes—but when he strode over toward them, he wasn't looking at Simon's bruised, bleeding form. In fact, it was as though he hadn't even noticed Simon at all, and instead, his eyes were fixed to—Maria.

Or, rather, to Maria's belly. Where they held, unblinking, for far too long, before rising to her face. Speaking of satisfaction, of warmth, of everything changed...

"Why, congratulations, Maria," he said. "You're going to be a mother."

27

She was going to be a mother.

The words sounded foreign, laughable, impossible. Ringing and resonating through Maria's brain, her belly. And suddenly her hands were on her waist, clutching tight against it, while something fierce and desperate began rattling, racing, raging inside her ribs.

She was going to be a mother. After so many years, so much longing. A *mother*. To a tiny, sneezy, pointy-eared *orcling*.

And somehow, her dazed, screaming brain wasn't protesting at that. Not at the fact that her son—her *son!*—would have claws, and fangs, and grey or green skin. That her son would be... an orc.

No. No, it was protesting at something else. At the huge, bloody, blank-faced orc standing beside her. The orc who'd asked her that question, only a moment ago. *Are you?*

Are you?

And wait. Did that mean—Maria stared at Simon's hazy, unreadable eyes—he'd already known about their son? Since... *when?*

Since... that morning, her brain supplied, bleak, true. Since he'd made that odd comment about her scent—and then he'd finally agreed to take her with him while he'd worked. Keeping her close. Keeping her *safe*.

Because now—Maria's hands clutched at her waist, while a swift, sickening comprehension swarmed her thoughts—it wasn't only about her. Because even if *she* didn't really count—even if Simon hadn't succeeded in making her his own—

Her son surely would be.

And Simon had *said*, that day, what felt like years ago. He'd said. *Should I fail to win this fight for my place as Enforcer, I shall lose all. My mate, should I have one. My son.*

This son. Here. *Hers.*

Maria's stomach was violently churning, the room whirling around her, and it took all her effort to stagger for the nearest bed, and sink heavy down upon it, her face buried in her hands.

Gods curse her, how had she not realized. How had she not seen. If she bore Simon a son, their son would become just another pawn in this horrible Enforcer game. More collateral. Something to be envied, plotted against, *stolen* from his dead father's hands.

Simon's son would never be truly safe. *Never.*

Good gods, what had she *done.*

Someone was speaking, distant but close—Efterar, Maria realized, as she blinked up at him with swimming wet eyes. And Efterar was asking, she vaguely registered, if she felt ill, if she would like him to help her sleep for a while—

"No, no, no," she babbled, waving her hands. "Please don't, I'm perfectly fine, we came here so you could help Simon, he's quite horribly injured, *please.*"

Efterar made a sound much like a snort, but accordingly turned away again, and began asking Simon a list of terse, irritated-sounding questions. Things like what Joarr had drugged him with this time, what kind of blade had he used, had he had any help, did any of these blasted Skai realize that repeated kicks to the groin could cause permanent reproductive damage...

Maria almost wanted to laugh at the last bit, but she was too busy wiping at her eyes, fighting at the thoughts screaming in her skull. Gods, what if Ulfarr defeated Simon. What if her son somehow ended up in Ulfarr's hands. What if...

The vision of Bjorn flashed across her brain, sickening enough that Maria had to clap her hand over her mouth—and now here was

Efterar again, his hand settling against Maria's neck. "Deep breaths," he told her, as the worst of the nausea faded. "Are you sure you don't want to rest, Maria?"

Maria could only seem to wave it away, erratic, frantic, and suddenly she couldn't stand to sit here for another instant. She was pregnant, her son was already at risk, and her son's father had known.

He'd *known*, and he'd done it anyway. Because...

She is only woman I buy. You ken I no think of this, when I buy ripe, yielding woman to bear me a son, with no hunt, and no rut?

Because this had always been about Simon's job. His people. His future.

Something seemed to crumple, deep in Maria's chest—and she leapt to her feet, grasped for the lamp, and lurched for the door. Just needing to get away from Simon, away from everything, and she rushed through the corridor, unseeing, unthinking, fighting back the wild, wailing urge to weep.

Simon had said so many lovely things, he'd been so kind lately, so patient. It had almost begun to feel safe, like home, but that was still because—because—

Maria clutched at her belly and ran faster, dodging around the occasional orcs she encountered. Searching desperately for familiar landmarks, yes that corridor, that ridge in the wall, lamps ending and light fading, yes, this was their room, no, Simon's room. And suddenly she couldn't bear to even look inside it, so she rushed a little further, shivering and weeping, and burst into Baldr's room instead.

But gods *damn* it, Baldr wasn't alone, he was with Drafli—and they weren't touching this time. And instead, Baldr was pacing the room, stripped to the waist, and... *shouting*.

"You could at least," he barked at Drafli, his hands clutched in fists at his sides, "have the courtesy to wait until I am out of the wing. Or to avoid the damned *corridor*. Do you not know what that *smells* like?!"

Drafli was standing perfectly still before Baldr, his face set and unreadable, until his clawed hand made a series of stiff-looking gestures. To which Baldr loudly scoffed, and flicked another gesture back.

"I *know* what you do," he retorted. "You need to prove, again and again, to every Skai in this mountain, that you are *not* mated to another orc. That your precious Skai ways are *always* more important to you than I am!"

Drafli's hands snapped out another series of gestures, one of them jerking toward—Maria. And even though she was backing away, stumbling for the corridor again, the damage was surely already done. Baldr's whole body stiffening in place, his red-rimmed eyes darting to her face—and then dropping, too, to her waist. And suddenly his shoulders sagged, and Maria could see the effort it took him to turn away from Drafli, and step closer toward her.

"Maria," he said, his voice thick. "What is amiss? I am sorry I did not"—his throat convulsed—"smell you there."

And shit, *shit*, because behind him Drafli's eyes had dangerously flashed, his lips curling up in a feral-looking snarl. And he swept over too, standing far too close, and Maria was unnervingly aware of his height, his lean coiled strength. Of the sheer *hatred* in his eyes as he looked at her.

And when he turned back to Baldr, Maria could almost taste the derision, the rage—and he again made another series of hand gestures, matched this time by his mouth. Speaking aloud, or so it seemed—but his voice was a hoarse rasp, breathy and strange, quieter than a whisper.

"You only care," it hissed, "until *woman* show up. You *thank* me, someday."

With that, he spun on his heel and strode off, pointed and silent, leaving Maria alone with Baldr. Who was staring after Drafli, his throat convulsing, his face deathly pale—and suddenly Maria felt wretched, awful, the misery bubbling and curdling inside.

"Gods, I'm *so* sorry, Baldr," she gasped. "Please go, work this out with him, I'm *fine*."

But Baldr's brow had creased, the concern shifting in his too-bright eyes. "I can barely *look* at him, when he smells like that," he said, choked. "And you"—he stepped back and inhaled, his chest visibly filling, his gaze dropping again to her waist—"you are due my congratulations, ach? Your son already smells strong and hale, just like Simon. Like *you*."

He flashed Maria a genuine, wavering smile, and though Maria desperately wanted to smile back, she couldn't even seem to make her mouth move. Couldn't seem to make anything move—at least, until she felt the familiar, telling prickle, lingering on her back.

It was as though it had caught her, reeled her around like a fish on a cruel hook. Making her look at the huge, bruised, battered orc standing silently in the doorway, his eyes just as dark and distant as Drafli's had been. *Simon.*

"Leave Baldr be, woman," he said, his voice heavy and deep. "Come."

And gods, it was so—presumptuous, so arrogant, so *infuriating.* For an orc who'd just lied to her all day—who'd perhaps lied to her since she'd come here—to be controlling who she wanted to see, in this moment? When she'd just found out she was *pregnant*? With his son, who would forever be in danger? Because of Simon's horrible job, and his horrible clan's horrible *ways*?!

"No," Maria hissed at him, her voice cracking. "No, Simon. You do *not* get to throw your commands at me, after this. After you *swore* you wouldn't play games with me!"

Something hard and dangerous passed through Simon's eyes, and he shifted in the doorway, his arms folding over his bruised, still-bloody chest. "I *never* play game with you," he growled. "I never speak false to you. I keep you safe. I *honour* you."

The words seemed to suck Maria's breath away, and she stared at his forbidding face, at the sheer fucking *audacity* of that claim. And for a skittering, hanging moment, for the first time in *days*, she was briefly, viciously reminded of her *husband.* Sitting so coolly in his silk sheets, speaking his lies so calmly, so rationally. Making Maria question her own truth.

And that day with her husband, as on so many days with him, Maria had... *hidden.* Concealed her real self under the exterior he'd expected to see. Met him on the terms he'd established. *Enabled* him.

But no. Not anymore. Maria was done with hiding. With lying. With pretending and placating and pasting appropriate expressions on her face, on her heart. She was fucking *done.*

"No, Simon," Maria said, and though her voice wavered, she was saying it, she was. "You didn't tell me how much danger I'm now in, thanks to your *job.* You didn't tell me how much danger our *son* will be in. You didn't tell me you spend your days being drugged and beaten to a *pulp.* You didn't even tell me I was *pregnant* with your *child!*"

Simon's mouth had gone very tight, his jaw grinding in his cheek— but he didn't speak, didn't even try to explain or deny any of this, so Maria stepped closer, her teeth gritted, her hands clenched. "I deserved to know," she hissed at him. "I have tried my very best to honour you, and keep my word to you, and learn and respect your clan's ways. And in return, this is how you treat me? You lie to me about my own safety? My own body? My own *son?*"

Simon's eyes were glittering on hers, his lip curling, his arms flexing against his chest. "I no *lie*," he said flatly. "I only no yet speak of this. I never say I tell you all I think!"

But he was doing it again, bending the truth to suit him again, and Maria shook her head, took a sharp step closer. "More rubbish, Simon," she snarled. "That's called hiding the truth. That's called playing a fucking *game!*"

The fury flashed across Simon's glinting eyes, the anger kindling through the room, and he stepped closer too, towering over Maria, a forbidding wall of strength and disapproval and *threat.* "Ach, and you hold no fault in this, woman?" he snapped at her. "You no hide truth? You play no game with *me?*"

There was something new in his voice, something that caught oddly in Maria's belly, but she kept her glare steady on his, her body straight and stiff. "Of course not," she retorted. "I came here and told you what I wanted, and you *agreed* to it! And here I am"—she gave a frantic, forceful wave toward her waist—"holding up my end of the bargain, and giving you *exactly* what you wanted!"

The darkness seemed to flare deeper in Simon's eyes, and suddenly he *laughed*, cold and harsh and mocking. "Ach, and you ken I should have *chosen* this?" he sneered at her. "You ken I wish to father son thus? Upon woman who *weep* when she learn of his life? Woman who never stop *lying* to me?!"

What? *What?* It was like the world had juddered, pitching sharp and sideways, and Maria felt herself flinching backwards, her eyes snapping wide. Had he just said—he'd just said—wait—

"You—you," she began, and then shook her head, hard, as though to thrust out his words—but they were still there, burrowing deep and deadly and devastating. *You ken I should have chosen this. You ken I wish to father son thus.*

Simon hadn't—*wanted* this? Her, or his—his son?

Maria's body was abruptly shivering, a cold chill racing down her back. And her arms were skittering to her waist, circling tight against it, and she couldn't breathe, why couldn't she breathe...

"*Simon,*" said a low voice, urgent, reproachful—and when Maria's flickering, hazy gaze searched for it, it was Baldr. Still standing there, his face very pale, his eyes intent and surprisingly angry on Simon's face.

"No, brother," Simon's flat voice hissed. "She wish no game, she stop playing game with me. Ach, woman?"

Maria's blurry eyes had whipped back to Simon again, and the panic was suddenly rising, rattling, raging. But the words didn't seem to register, to ring true. *She wish no game, she stop playing...*

"Y-you didn't w-want me?" was all her mouth would seem to say, her arms clutching tighter at her waist. "T-truly, Simon?"

Simon's eyes briefly closed, his hand rubbing against his face—and it was like something was flashing behind Maria's eyes, bright and dizzying and disastrous. All those times he'd asked if she'd truly wanted it, all those times he'd touched her, taken her, *cleansed* her. Gods, just this morning—had it just been this morning?—when he'd said, *You please me, you are a great gift to me...*

"*Simon,*" Baldr hissed again, sharper this time, but Simon still didn't speak, didn't open his eyes. And Maria's panic was wailing now, rioting against her ribs, because what was happening, what had she done. Good gods, was Simon truly saying she'd somehow forced him, she hadn't stopped lying to him, she stop *playing*?! And what the hell could he possibly mean, what kind of power could she possibly have over him, he was perhaps the deadliest orc in the *realm*, and she was...

Oh. Ohhhhhh.

And it was as though a door had slammed, like a punch had landed, like a bell had rung deep inside Maria's skull.

He was right. She'd lied. She'd played a game. And now, once again, she was defeated. Worse than defeated. Destroyed.

"Oh," she whispered, very quiet. "Yes. It's true. I am Anita-Maria Bassala, the second Duchess of Warmisham."

28

Maria's words fell into empty, abject silence. Into the horrible, awful truth of two orcs staring blankly toward her, witnessing her utter devastation.

And in this desolate moment, somehow, Maria was still done with hiding. With lying. With... games. With whatever the hell kind of game she'd been playing, without even realizing it.

She'd deceived them. She had to make it stop. Make it—truth.

"I'm sorry I lied to you," she said to the floor, her voice a whisper. "I didn't think you would accept my offer if you knew. I was desperate, you see, I'd just been impoverished by my husband, and I was beginning to fear"—she swallowed hard, she could say this, face this—"for my health, and perhaps my life."

Her voice was beginning to fray, to scatter, but she gulped in air, wrung her hands together. "I wasn't—thinking of you," she said, "or how this might affect you. I had very strong ideas of what orcs were, at the time, and I"—she swallowed again, squeezed her eyes shut—"I know better now. I'm sorry."

There was only more silence before her, and Maria desperately fought to raise her eyes, to find Simon's face. His blank, entirely unreadable face, his eyes black hollows within it.

You ken I should have chosen this, he'd said. *Woman who never stop lying to me.*

"And I truly regret," she gulped, "if by my falsehood I somehow"—she grimaced, say it, *say* it—"if I took your choice away from you. Or if I misread signals I ought to have caught. I would never, *ever* have wanted to—to—"

Something on Simon's face twitched, but he didn't speak, and Maria had to keep going, had to. "And worst of all, to involve a *child*," she whispered, wretched, her hands again clutching at her waist. "Who perhaps you—you didn't truly want, with me. Or perhaps you did want, but only to make a point to your kin, to gain the future you long for. Or—"

Or wait. *Wait.* Because if Simon had known who she was, this entire time—a powerful duchess, wed to the awful duke who'd so aggressively warred against the orcs—what other motives might the orcs have had, in this? And Maria knew how much Simon cared about his people, about their future. So maybe... maybe...

"Or maybe you only accepted me as a public play against my husband," she continued, wooden, every word a bitter, broken blow. "I suppose that"—she had to wipe at her leaking eyes—"would have been the logical thing to do, wouldn't it?"

And good gods, fucking over her husband was exactly why Maria had come here too, so why did everything feel so empty, suddenly, so hopeless. Why did she feel so sick, like she'd been kicked in the gut, like the one last missing piece had snapped into place.

"And that's why you were willing to put me at such risk in your fight against Ulfarr," she whispered. "That's why you worked so hard to make me truly yours. Because it didn't m-matter. *I* didn't matter. I was just someone you—*bought*. Someone trying to play a *game* with you."

Something had again twitched on Simon's face, something perhaps like disbelief, and Maria's thoughts were scrambling again, skipping backwards and forwards and sideways. "B-but our son," she said, her voice badly trembling. "I—I thought you wanted him. You—you wouldn't truly sacrifice him for my falsehood, would you, Simon? Gods, I"—she gripped her hands together, scraped their cold dampness against her tunic—"I know I signed the contract, I know I said I'd hand him over to you, but could we—could we please make another amendment, for his sake? Please, Simon? *Please*."

But Simon still wasn't speaking. Was only looking at her like that, his face so blank, so distant, somewhere else. And what the hell was Maria supposed to do with this, and finally she turned toward Baldr, her mouth opening, perhaps to beg him to plead her case to his captain, or Lady Norr, or—

But Baldr was—*weeping*. The tears streaking freely down his scarred face, and he was shaking his head, his mouth tight, his dripping eyes fixed on... Simon.

"I cannot," he said to Simon, his voice clipped. "I *cannot*. You selfish Skai *pricks*. You need to sort yourselves out, and fix your precious damned *ways*, and learn how to stop hurting people you claim to care about. I am *finished*."

With that, he turned and strode for the door, hands in fists, shoulders hunched—but then Maria's blurry eyes saw him hesitate, his shoulders sagging. "I am happy to offer whatever help you need, Maria, whenever you are ready," he said over his shoulder, his voice flat, slightly formal. "I assure you that if you had touched any orc but a Skai that first day you came, he should be rejoicing in his bright gift from the gods, and filling your ripe womb with seed and sweetness."

And with those words still ringing through the air, Baldr strode off, without looking back. Leaving Maria standing there alone with Simon, who still hadn't moved, his eyes on her so heavy, so cold, so bleak. So... broken.

And suddenly Maria couldn't bear to look at him, couldn't bear to stay one more instant, and she jerked sideways, toward the door—and found, somehow, that Simon was standing before it. His huge body fully blocking it, his chest heaving, his eyes wide and fixed and far too close.

"Maria," he said finally, his voice a croak. "I—wish for our son. I have wished for naught more in all my days. I"—he cleared his throat—"I shall guard him in this life, and far beyond it. I shall *always* keep him safe, no matter what comes for him, or for me. I swear this to you. Ach?"

And despite everything, the relief swarmed in a rush, powerful enough that Maria slightly staggered, her breath exhaling harsh. And she nodded, again and again, and even felt herself give him a wan little smile.

"Oh," she whispered, her eyes dropping to his feet. "I—I hoped you would. Thank you."

But Simon still wasn't moving, why wasn't he moving, and suddenly she could hear his breaths, in and out. "I shall keep you safe also," he continued, his voice still not sounding like his. "I never *once* think you no matter. I never *once* mean to risk you in this battle against Ulfarr. I never once even *fear* Ulfarr, until this. Until it came clearer"—his breath exhaled, harsh—"all I might lose, in my defeat. Ach?"

Oh. And that should have helped. It should have. Maria hadn't only been part of Simon's game. It had been more, even if only in some small way. Even in the midst of all these secrets and lies.

But the heaviness was still here, dragging on Maria's breath, her eyes, her heart. And she couldn't move, couldn't find a way through the sickening, deadening mess in her thoughts. Defeated. Destroyed.

"Maria," Simon breathed, and in a flick of movement, he was close, so close, his scent swarming, his trembly hand touching her face. Wanting her to see him. And Maria obeyed, had to obey, even now, her bleary gaze catching on his, on that strange arrested stillness in his eyes.

"Maria, I—" he began, and she could see his mouth grimacing, his throat convulsing. "I—met you, when you first came here. I—*chose* this."

He chose this. Maria blinked at him, not at all following, and Simon's chest heaved again, in, out. "Joarr hunted you here," he said, in a rush. "He followed you, when you ran from your husband's house. We watch this house for many moons now, but you surprise us with this, ach? And stronger still when we see where you run. When you seek to come *here*."

Maria kept blinking at him, her brain uselessly whirling, fighting to make sense of this. The orcs had been watching the house, he'd said. Warmisham House. For many moons. They'd been—*targeting her husband?*

They'd love nothing more than to publicly ruin me, her husband had told her that day. *Just like they did to Norr.*

And he'd been... *right?*

"We think, first, that this duke send you," Simon continued, still speaking quickly. "Captain and his mate decide we meet you. Offer you help. Learn more of duke's plan before we choose next path."

The understanding was finally, slowly creeping in, and with it, suddenly, was a deep, dragging shame. Good gods, they'd *all* known who Maria was, all this time. The captain. Lady Norr. Those women. Baldr. Drafli. Joarr. *Ulfarr.* Every orc, perhaps, in this damned cursed *mountain*.

"Joarr ought to have first met you," Simon's voice said, flatter now. "He has long sought a mate, and he hunted you all this way from Preia. By rights of the Skai, you were his to claim, had you wished for this."

Something jolted unpleasantly in Maria's gut, and Simon's eyes seemed to sharpen on her face, his hand rubbing at his mouth. "You ken your first day here," he said, "when Nattfarr speak of this... *bond* to you?"

This bond. Maria did remember, vaguely, and when she nodded Simon's throat convulsed again. "It is no... easy," he said, "for a woman to choose any orc, ach? The first orc to meet her—to put scent upon her—already begin to build this bond. This is no *fate*, the Ka-esh say to me again and again. No *force*. Woman or orc can yet break this. But it makes... *preference*."

He spoke the word carefully, his eyes still heavy and intent on Maria's face. "Joarr," he continued dully, "was to be first orc to meet you. But Joarr is also good brother to me, ach? He watch you for all these days, and he then send word to me. He tell me, *Skai-kesh make this woman for you.*"

Maria's heart was thumping erratically, her gaze frozen on his, waiting—and Simon's mouth twitched up, into something that might have been meant as a smile. "Joarr spoke truth, ach?" he said, and his hand spread against Maria's face, tilting it up. "You are fairest woman ever I set eyes upon. Your scent is so ripe, so sweet. You are hearty and eager and kind. All your strong *feeling* reads true on your scent and your face, and you shall thus *never* play game with me, or hide your truth from me. You are all"—his throat convulsed again—"all an Enforcer should ever wish for, ach?"

Oh. *Oh.* So Simon *had* wanted her, then. He'd *chosen* her. He'd...

come to meet her that day on the road, in hopes of forging a... *bond* with her?

And yes, yes, that was true in his watching eyes, in the weight of his exhale. In the way his hand lingered on her cheek, as though he still craved this touch. This memory of that moment.

"And this was good, ach?" he whispered, fierce. "When I met you. When you touched me. I tasted your hunger for me. I tasted your peace, in my arms. Your *trust* in me."

And despite everything this orc had done, despite her ringing shock at all these words, Maria felt herself... nodding. Agreeing. There had been peace, there, in that moment. Just like the peace she'd found with him afterwards, again and again and again.

"But," Simon continued, his hand dropping, "this was also wrong. Ach? This broke the ways of the Skai. All my kin knew you were no mine to take. I could have led a rut upon you, and rightly gained you thus, but"—he grimaced—"even had I wished for this, I could no have borne it. No after tasting your trust in me thus."

There was something thick in Maria's throat, and she fought to swallow it back as Simon barked a sound that might have been a laugh. "And next, you tell me you wish to *sell* to me," he said, hoarse. "And all breaks apart from this. You say you shall take any orc, even after I put scent upon you. You again and again speak false to me. You fear me. You fight me and shame me when I seek to claim you as mine. I am sure"—his hand again rubbed at his mouth—"you yet serve this husband. This duke. This *war*."

Maria's eyes had closed, pained, because gods, this explained *so much*. Simon thought she'd been a *spy*, this entire time. He'd thought she'd come here not of desperation, or revenge—but to start a *war*.

"B-but," Maria stammered, her thoughts grasping at her scattered memories. "You questioned me. Again and again. And I told you the truth. I *did*."

Her voice cracked on the last, and when she opened her eyes again Simon was nodding. "Ach," he said, quieter. "I ken. You hate husband. You hunger for me, and my cleansing. When husband's war come, you fear this. You fear this as strong as you fear Ulfarr. So why you yet speak false to me? Why you yet hide from me? I seek to learn you, I seek to show you truth and kindness and teach you the deep ways of my clan, and"—she felt his exhale against her skin—"*still* you speak false to me. You hide your deepest truth. You hide who you *are*."

His eyes glittered as he spoke, his claw jabbing toward her chest. And it suddenly felt like he'd peeled her tunic away, and then her very skin. Like those eyes were following the tip of that claw, seeing straight through her ribs, into her heart. Her self.

"B-because," Maria whispered, trapped, exposed, stricken. "I didn't *want* to be that person anymore. I didn't *want* to be a hysterical, unwanted, childless duchess, forever tied to a man I hate. I wanted"— she tried to smile, why couldn't she smile—"I wanted you to cleanse it away. I *wanted* you to Enforce me. I wanted you to turn me into your real mate, a real Skai. I wanted you to make me—into *myself* again."

Something new flashed through Simon's eyes, something that surely spoke of comprehension, or perhaps even pain. "Ach," he said, his voice rough. "Ach. *Now* I ken, woman. But it no work thus, ach? When I Enforce, I seek truth. This must first come to light, ach? And next—*next*—we face what this shows."

Oh. Right. And this truth had shown... what? That Simon had lied to her, all this time. That Maria had lied to him. And that—her brain sifted back, back, wait, had he just said—

"Did you just say, *when* war came?" she whispered. "When my *husband's* war came?"

And there it was, perhaps the worst blow of them all, flaring across Simon's black eyes. Because yes, yes he had said that, he'd meant that, and abruptly Maria was thinking, again, of all the times he'd disappeared to—to *work*, leaving her alone, and then he'd returned, and—

"You've been fighting my husband's war?" she whispered. "For how long?"

Simon's shoulders rose and fell, and suddenly he just looked tired, worn. "Your husband's men followed you here," he said. "He set a bounty upon your return this next day. Bands of men have swarmed our mountain each day since."

Maria couldn't move, couldn't breathe, couldn't stop staring at those empty, resigned eyes. There'd been a war, all this time. A new war against the orcs, because of her. Because despite all her efforts, all her carefully laid plans, Maria had—she had—

She had handed her husband exactly—*exactly*—what he'd

wanted. Proof of the orcs' aggression toward him. Undeniable cause for war.

And now, what was left? Now that Maria was pregnant, and bound to both a duke and an orc? Now that she'd ruined everything—her plans, her freedom, her safety? Whatever this had been, between her and Simon, that had, yes, given her such peace?

There was nothing, nothing but emptiness and defeat. So heavy, so alone, so much to bear—and finally Maria bowed her head under its weight, and wept.

29

Maria didn't know how long she stood there weeping, while Simon stood there and watched. While neither of them spoke a word.

And gods, Maria should have spoken. Should have yelled, begged, railed against him. Should have demanded how someone who hated games so much could play one like this.

But she couldn't speak, couldn't stop, and when she felt that familiar warm strength step closer toward her, she couldn't push it away, either. Couldn't even begin to resist the powerful, painful comfort of those arms plucking her bodily up against him, tucking her whole to his broad chest, her ear against his rapidly thundering heart.

And curse him, but it helped. And so did the movement, the easy silent steps of his feet, as he strode out of Baldr's room, down the corridor, and back into his familiar room again. As he set her down on the soft furs, stealing his warmth away from her, even as his big hands wiped at her wet cheeks with careful, stilted gentleness.

"I fetch—help, ach?" his voice rasped above her. "I come back soon, my brave one."

His *brave* one. But before Maria could follow, blink at that, he abruptly turned and strode away, out the door. And whatever composure Maria had just found somehow fully vanished with him, and the misery flooded her again, even worse than before. He'd lied to her. She'd lied to him. And what happened now, what came next? Her husband had set a bounty, he'd said, men had swarmed the mountain, and she was pregnant with a lying orc's son, and—

And then—Lady Norr strode in. Wearing her men's trousers, her long braid slung over her shoulder, her eyes dark and regretful on Maria's face. And behind her, again, was Simon—but rather than following her into the room, he'd leaned against the doorway, his arms crossed over his chest, his eyes strangely bright in the lamplight.

"Oh, *Maria*," said Lady Norr, and Maria blankly registered her tall, trousered form sinking heavily down onto the bed beside her. "Are you all right? Simon tells me you finally told him—well. Needless to say, we're *so* sorry. Gods, what a *mess*."

It sounded like she meant it, and Maria blinked her bleary eyes at Lady Norr's face. At where she looked like she meant this, too, her head shaking, her mouth grimacing. Because—because she'd known. She'd known who Maria was too, and she'd *lied*.

"I know it's probably no help now," Lady Norr continued, with a sigh. "But we truly believed you were bait. A willing trap. Every single sign—every *scrap* of intelligence we had—pointed to Warmisham sending you here. Him setting up your kidnapping as grounds to finally break our treaty for good, and get his *war*."

Maria couldn't speak, couldn't find words through the blockage in her throat, and Lady Norr sighed again, her hands rubbing against her knees. "He and that damned Council haven't given us a single moment's rest since that treaty was signed," she said. "It's been constant aggression. Constant new laws. Constant pretending his own people's violations of our treaty don't exist, while secretly slipping money to this lord or that, or trying to rouse common folks to attack us. All while pretending he's so far above it all, and would *never* truly worry about being threatened by *orcs*."

The sheer vehemence in her voice was surprising, but Maria still couldn't seem to speak, and Lady Norr kept talking, her frown deepening. "We've had some success playing him and his fellow lords off each other," she said flatly, "and none of them have yet been able to raise enough coin to really wage a proper offense against us—so we've managed to foil the worst of their plans so far. But recently

Warmisham proposed this infuriating new law to the realm's Council—perhaps you knew of it?—that allows him to fund his wars by openly stealing money from anyone he wishes."

Oh. Maria's curdling brain had reflexively flicked back to that day, to her husband speaking so coolly in his silk sheets. "I did know about that," she heard her voice croak, almost inaudible, "because I was the first person he stole from."

"Oh of course, the swine," Lady Norr replied, her voice scathing. "So fucking *typical*. Luckily, however, Warmisham's new law has proven *singularly* unpopular, because no one—most of all Warmisham's wealthy friends and supporters—wants all their coin appropriated for an orc war, right? So for now, rather than actually funding any proper armies, Warmisham's been stuck waving around the promise of a massive bounty for your return. Which means that we've been getting the realm's best hoodlums and mercenaries instead."

She sounded grimly satisfied with this development, and when Maria's still-bleary eyes focused again on her face, she indeed looked almost smug—but then it faded, sinking into something much like regret.

"But *you*," Lady Norr said, with a sigh. "It didn't make sense. Even after questioning you—Nattfarr has a gift of truth-seeking, you see—it was very clear you still had some major ulterior motives. So afterwards"—she grimaced—"Grimarr ordered Simon to keep you here, in the Skai wing. To watch you. To make sure you couldn't communicate with anyone on the outside."

Wait. *Wait.* So Simon's rule about Maria staying here, being his prisoner, earning his trust—that hadn't been entirely his doing? It had been an order from his *captain*?

But in glancing at Simon, Maria could see the truth of it. Written on his harsh face, speaking in the flex of his claws against his taut bicep. In the glare of his black eyes on Lady Norr's face.

"And no, of course Simon didn't approve," Lady Norr added, with a wry glance toward him. "If there's anything the Skai stand united against, it's confinement. But"—she sighed again—"Grimarr made it an ultimatum for your continued presence here, which I will admit, I thought was fair at the time. And Simon didn't want to lose you altogether, so..."

Her voice trailed off, and she ran a hand against her hair. "It's why I haven't been doing more to make you welcome here, either, Maria," she said, "and I do apologize for that. I was *sure* I would give it away at some point—we likely know so many of the same people, and I've met Warmisham multiple times. And I don't mean to offend you, but the man is *vile*, and also *far* cleverer than the rest of them. And"—she exhaled, heavy—"we couldn't risk letting one man's hatred and bigotry ruin our entire future. We *can't*."

Her eyes on Maria's were wide and regretful, almost as if pleading with Maria to understand. And of course Maria did understand, but perhaps she still should have shouted, or raged at the unfairness of it all. At being suspected, conspired against, lied to, ignored. Without even being given a chance to defend herself.

But she just felt... resigned. Tired. So damned tired, still, of secrets and whispers and lies.

"So what happens next," she said, her voice wooden. "With my husband. This war. *Me*."

Lady Norr hesitated, and her eyes angled, brief but telling, toward Simon. "I'm not fully certain," she said slowly. "But from our side, you're welcome to stay, if you like. We're very lucky that none of Warmisham's men actually saw you enter the mountain—they just followed you in this direction—so we've officially told your pursuers, multiple times, that no one of your name or description has ever come here. Thank you for that bit of truth, by the way."

She'd flashed Maria a halfhearted smile, which Maria couldn't seem to return, and Lady Norr cleared her throat, and continued. "And we're not overly bothered by mercenaries—they can't get in, obviously, so it's more of an annoyance than anything else. The real question is whether Warmisham can sway his Council—and public opinion— into fully supporting his wealth-stealing warmongering scheme, so he can pull together a proper army to invade us, and prove that his poor, helpless wife is even *here*."

She shot Maria another wry smile, and Maria did feel her own mouth slightly twitch this time, before the heaviness settled again.

"But my husband *always* gets his way with that Council," she replied, quiet. "Those lords worship at his feet."

"Ah, but do they?" said Lady Norr, a rather militant spark in her eyes. "They're afraid of him, yes. But we've got a few of those lords in our pocket now—Otto and Culthen will both be swayed, if it benefits them—so in truth, it's really only Warmisham and Anton of Dunburg holding the rest of the lot together. So if we can deal with Warmisham—and Anton would be a bonus—we might actually have a chance of real, lasting peace. A chance to focus on the problems in this realm that really matter. Like poverty. Cruelty. Injustice. *Hate*."

Her voice had gone low and fervent, her eyes still sparking on Maria's, and Maria was swiftly, forcefully reminded of Simon's words. Simon's future. Winning wars through words, whispers, perceptions.

And for an instant, there was a brief, flickering glimpse of... hope. Maybe Duke Warmisham could be defeated, after all. Maybe he would never need to know Maria was even here. And then, if Simon could just defeat Ulfarr, and gain her son's safety, as he'd sworn...

Maybe Maria really could... stay. *Stay*?

And even as the vision of that swarmed her thoughts, bringing with it a sudden, churning warmth in her belly, there was still something else. Something nagging at her, dragging at her, drawing her deeper and deeper below...

One last, final blow. Dealt by her own hand, destroying her own future. Ensuring her permanent, inviolable defeat.

"But I wrote letters," she said, her voice blank, broken. "I confessed it all. And once those letters are sent, they'll destroy *everything*."

30

For a silent, horrible moment, both Lady Norr and Simon stared at Maria. Lady Norr with confusion in her eyes, and Simon with... disbelief. *Judgement.*

"What do you mean, you confessed it all in letters?" Lady Norr asked, her brow furrowing. "You can't have sent any letters from here. Can she?"

That question was directed toward Simon, who gave a very slow, very purposeful shake of his head. But his judgement was still there, because he'd already put it together. Already knew. This damned orc, seeing far too much, as always.

"I left the letters with lawyers in Preia," Maria said, grimacing. "Dozens of them. With instructions to send them, at a certain date in the very near future, to a diverse variety of gossips, rebels, columnists, and various enemies of my husband."

Lady Norr blinked, and for a brief instant, she might have looked almost amused. "And can't you just write the lawyers, and ask them not to follow through? We can send messages from here, you know."

But Maria was grimacing again, shaking her head. "No. I did it all in disguise, under a false name. And even if they did suspect who I was, I also instructed them not to change the plan under any circumstances, at any request. Unless it was from me, in person."

The amusement had faded from Lady Norr's eyes, her head cocking sideways. "And what did all these letters say, exactly?"

What did they say. Maria's words were failing her again, vanished, and she dragged in a gulping breath, her gaze angling, reflexively, toward Simon. Simon, who was still looking straight back at her, his eyes dark, clouded, grim. Knowing her words, before she even spoke them.

"These were your vengeance, ach?" he said, his voice very steady. "They heaped shame upon this husband. They sought to disgust him, and mock him, by spreading this truth across the realm. His pretty duchess wife, eagerly bouncing upon a fat orc-prick. Sucking foul orc-seed into empty womb. Bearing disgusting orc *spawn*."

He almost spat out the last word, and it felt like he'd kicked her in the stomach, the nausea surging and roiling. Because as usual, he was right. That had been exactly Maria's intention. The letters had been sordid, scandalous, shocking. They'd been meant to humiliate her husband. To destroy him.

But instead, it was Maria being destroyed, her hands rubbing painfully at her face, her eyes welling with prickling heat. "I didn't want to—to give my husband more cause for the war he wanted so much," she choked out. "So—yes. I went for—*scandal*, instead. Explicit. Obscene. As much fodder for the gossips as possible."

And gods, she couldn't even look at Simon, couldn't bear to face the brunt of his judgement—but Lady Norr, thank the gods, still bore no judgement in her eyes. No shame.

"So you didn't actually accuse us of kidnapping?" she asked, her voice thoughtful. "Or any kind of force, or aggression, against you?"

Maria shook her head, quick and desperate, and heard herself make a sound that might have been a laugh. "I cast myself as an eager, willing accomplice," she said, her voice cracking. "As someone whose husband was so fucking disappointing, that an orc was a welcome change."

A lord, in the prime of his life, cuckolded by an orc.

And gods, how had Maria thought such things. How had she written such things. And no wonder Simon was angry, because she'd meant it as an insult. As mockery. As *judgement*.

The room had fallen utterly silent, and Maria forced out the rest of it, please the last of it, please gods, *please*. "I wanted to deny my husband his war," she croaked, "by framing it as my choice. But if he already thinks I've been kidnapped, and he's set a bounty on me, and sent men here, and made all this public—those letters will only be fuel on the fire in this war, right? They'll be more shit in a horrible mess of it, he'll say I was seduced, he'll say you made me write those things, he'll say I'm foolish, irrational, *hysterical*. And I mean, he was always going to say that anyway, but—"

But gods, she'd been so *stupid*. Of course this had been the stupidest possible plan. Of course her husband would sniff it out, twist it to suit himself, justify his awful war. And of course Maria would be left like this, alone, miserable, broken. Defeated.

"Well," Lady Norr said, in a bracing voice. "That's a lot to unpack, I must say. I'd like to go run it by Grimarr, if you don't mind, and perhaps a few others as well. But"—her hand carefully reached out, and squeezed Maria's—"you're still welcome to stay here, Maria, as long as you like. I know what a piece of work Duke Warmisham is, and I'm impressed you escaped his clutches at all—let alone set up such a clever plan to defeat him. Gods, I wish I'd thought to do that against my own vile husband."

She again smiled at Maria, wry, genuine—and Maria couldn't even smile back. Couldn't speak. Couldn't think, couldn't feel anything, but for the flat, certain dread of an orc's judgement, boring into her from across the room.

"Look, why don't I leave you two for tonight," Lady Norr continued, with another pat at Maria's hand that was surely meant to be reassuring. "And we'll reconvene in the morning to talk through our options. All right?"

Maria somehow managed a nod, blank and empty. And then Lady Norr was gone, and it was only Maria, and the orc she'd betrayed. The orc she'd used, for her revenge. The orc who'd known the truth, from the start.

And he'd lied, too. He'd pretended he hadn't known. He'd signed that fucking contract. He'd dragged her into this deadly game with his clan, his enemy. He'd put her at risk. He'd gotten her pregnant, when he'd known their son would be at risk, too. He'd let her think this war wasn't a threat. He'd let her think Ulfarr wasn't a threat. He'd let her think—oh gods, he'd let her think—

Maria raised her face toward him, toward the truth of that contempt flashing in those eyes, that judgement. And it had been so long since he'd looked at her like that, she'd fought so fiercely to obey him, to honour him, to please him. And he had been pleased, he had been, that *had* to still be true...

But he kept glaring at her, his disapproval a visceral living thing between them. And in the desolation, Maria somehow... smiled back at him. Wan, weak, worthless.

"So are you going to Enforce me now?" she asked, wretched. "Or am I even worth that to you, anymore?"

The contempt flashed higher, so painful and so familiar in his beautiful black eyes, and Maria smiled again, forcibly shoving back the misery, the anguish. "Or was I ever worth that to you at all," she whispered. "Or was that a lie, too?"

Simon's growl was instant, harsh, deep, his body huge and taut in the doorway. "No," he bit back, clipped. "And you shall stop this, woman."

Something flailed in Maria's stomach, and she gripped at the bed beneath her. "Stop what," she choked. "Being so gullible? So stupid? *Hysterical?*"

Simon snarled, the sound shivering down Maria's back. "No. You ken what I mean."

The helplessness was flailing, crashing against the disbelief, the gods-damned injustice of it all. "No, I don't know what you mean!" she shot back, her voice shrill. "I don't know anything anymore. I can't trust anything you say anymore. I feel like I don't even *know* you anymore!"

She was hurling the words at Simon, perhaps wanting something, *anything*, to break that dark, cold judgement in those watching eyes. But it only seemed to flare, to sharpen, as he came a slow, deliberate step closer.

"No," he said again, the word a heavy thud in the small-feeling room. "You know me. And I know *you*, woman."

For a blank, blinking moment, Maria stared at him—and then she laughed, the sound high-pitched, horrible, nearly a scream. "No, I don't!" she shouted. "And you don't! You lied to me and seduced me and trapped me here and played games with me, with my *life*! We know nothing of each other, we *are* nothing to each other, and"—she was shaking, sweating, her body lurching off the bed—"you're just a fucking *orc* and I don't fucking *care*!"

And what was she saying, where the hell was she going, this room was full of orc, of his judgement, his rising, thundering rage. "No," he barked at her, and somehow, suddenly he was here, a breath away, looming huge and bloody and menacing over her. "And when I am done with you, wilful woman, you shall *never again* speak so false to me!"

Maria opened her mouth, about to shout something back, anything, needing to hurt him, to make him feel what this felt like—

When out of nowhere, he *grabbed* her. Massive, powerful clawed hands gripping tight at her waist, and hurling her down onto her back on the bed. Knocking the breath full out of Maria's lungs, and even as she choked and flailed for air, Simon's weight shoved down against her, his huge body pinning her there, his legs roughly knocking hers apart.

"Y-you *bastard*," Maria managed, between dragging breaths—and in return he growled at her, his lips pulled back, baring all his sharp teeth.

"*No*," he bellowed down at her, so loud it rang in her ears. "No more."

But Maria couldn't stop, kicking and writhing up beneath him. Hating him, raging at him, how dare he, he'd ruined everything, she'd ruined everything. "You don't *get* to order me around anymore!" she shouted at him. "You have no right to *Enforce* me, as if I'm one of you shitty, sneaky, lying Skai!"

Simon's bark was almost a roar this time, and one of his huge hands snapped down to circle around Maria's *neck*, oh gods. "You *are* Skai," he snarled at her, "and this, you *know*!"

And Maria did not, he did not, and she twisted and flailed beneath him, lost in the misery, the devastation, the *rage*. The end of her freedom, of all she'd so desperately longed for, and it was his fault, all his fault, her fault, *hysteria*—

And then he was there. That hard, leaking, demanding beast,

shoving up brutal and uncompromising against Maria's splayed-open heat. Jolting all else to utter stillness, her breath snatched from her lungs, the rage so close to bursting, flailing and festering beneath the ferocity of his glittering orc eyes.

"You are *mine*," he spat, slow, grim, the words shuddering in their strength. "You are Skai. You know this. You *want* this. You want *me*. Ach?"

And Maria might have kept fighting it, could have, would have—if not for that damned fucking question at the end. Asking. Fucking *asking*, making her say it, even now, when he knew it was fucking true, he *knew*. And he was such a bastard and Maria hated him more than life and it was fucking *true*—

"Yes," she spat back, biting the word out. "Yes, you lying prick, *yes!*"

One more grunt from his body above her, smug, satisfied. As the beast between Maria's legs swelled, flexed, filled with alarming, breathtaking power...

It slammed inside in a single, devastating plunge, carving Maria in two around it. Impaling her, owning her, and her scream shattered through the room, her body thrashing, pushing him, clutching him, craving him.

And in another swift jerk of movement, Simon had both her wrists caught in one huge hand, slamming them to the bed above her head. While his other hand dropped from her neck, long enough to drag its claws deep down the front of her tunic, shredding it into rags, hurling the pieces aside.

It left Maria fully exposed beneath him, skewered full upon him, wearing only her loincloth and dagger. Her breasts peaked and heaving, her nipples so hard as to be almost painful, and Simon's glinting eyes were pure hungry blackness as he dragged himself out, slow, smooth, torturous...

His slam inside was sheer agony, utter ecstasy. So much to bear, too much to face, and Maria's invaded heat frantically clamped against him, needing him, hating him, please, more, *please*—

"Y-you," she tried again, as he circled his hips against her, vicious and powerful. "You—fucking—"

But the rage only flashed again across those eyes, that beast swelling fuller within her, and one huge hand dropped to pinch at her nipple, hard. "No," he hissed, as his other hand flexed against her wrists, pinning them harder to the bed. "No more, Skai."

And gods, Maria loathed him, the fury and the craving swarming and mashing together, and she had to defeat him, strike back, somehow. "Y-you lied to me!" she gasped. "You played—games with me. R-risked my life, and my—"

Another hard pinch at her nipple broke the words into a howl, her body arching beneath him—but there was only the trampling, cursed need for more, *more*, as strong fingers pinched her again, rolling the peaked, swollen bud between sharp claws.

"No," Simon hissed again, mocking, taunting, his hips again circling, gouging his beast deep inside. "You shall learn."

"I won't learn *anything* from you!" Maria shouted back at him, as she twisted against him, her breath hissing between her teeth. "You lied to me, you used me, you—"

He barked at her again, his eyes blazing, his hand snapping downwards—and wait, wait, that was her *dagger*. Spinning silver in his fingers, the sharpened blade whirling only a breath away from her skin, and what the hell, he wouldn't, he would *not*—

"You wish me to silence you?" he demanded at her. "Teach you to listen?"

And good gods, there should have been only sheer terror, screeching and flashing bright deadly warnings—but the craving was still stronger, all-consuming, *everything*. And somehow, impossibly, Maria felt herself nodding at him, *nodding, needing* this, please—

Simon huffed a grim, satisfied grunt, his invading heat bulging even fuller within her, as his fingers casually shifted on the dagger, dangling it hilt-first over her face. And before Maria could move, shout, *think*, the smooth, rounded steel hilt met her lips, and sank firm and cold between them.

He was putting a *dagger-hilt* in her *mouth*?!

But yes, yes, he was guiding it in gentle, purposeful—and when Maria made to spit, writhe, flail back and forth, he only sank it deeper, until the hilt's blunt end was brushing at her throat, the pommel resting against her quivering lips. *Gagging* her, with her own damned dagger?!

"Better," he gritted out, harsh, taunting, his huge body shifting above her, his hot hand tightening against her wrists. "You be silent. You listen. You *learn*."

Maria could have spat it out, *should* have, the noises and wails now escaping wordless from her blocked mouth—but the craving kept screeching, soaring in relentless, white-hot streams. Needing more, yes, *more*, even as Simon's other hand dropped back to her neck, circling warm and close and deadly.

"No," he hissed again, stern, commanding, utterly in control. "You learn, Skai. You accept your Enforcer's judgement."

Skai. *Your Enforcer.* Those words enough, somehow, to knock Maria nearly back to stillness again. Blinking and quivering beneath a massive, bloody, powerful orc, who had one hand on her wrists, the other on her neck. With his dagger-hilt filling her mouth, the monster at his groin swelling and leaking deep within—and deeper still, the new life he'd already made inside her. Skai. His.

"Mine," he said, so smooth, so sure, the words twining into Maria's belly, into her soul. And he slowly dragged out, all the way, hovering at just the edge—and then slammed back inside, wrenching her whole body beneath him. "Skai."

Maria couldn't think, answer, *breathe*, and Simon's eyes held steady on hers as he did it again. "Mine," he said, dragging out, driving in. "Skai."

And then he did it again, again, again. So intent at first, so deliberate, as if piercing the words into her, writing them with hot flesh and cold merciless steel. But then faster, harder, deeper, railing against her with the stark depth of that truth, slamming against her heart, scraping into her soul. *Mine. Skai.*

Maria's sense was spiralling into darkness, deeper and faster, her helpless moans escaping around the steel in her mouth—but there were no words now, no protests. Only this moment, watching, listening, learning. Sparking and swirling in her Enforcer's eyes, his truth, his judgement. The sheer strength of his determination, desperate and tightly controlled, all of him lost in showing her, teaching her. She was his, she was Skai, and he would do anything, *anything*, to guard that truth. To hold it safe.

His. Skai.

And suddenly Maria needed to hold it too, so urgent it flooded all else. Her hand yanking against his grip on her wrists, just for a moment, please...

But he knew her, he did, he always had. And he released her wrist without question, without hesitation—and in return, Maria's fluttering, tingling hand found his sweaty chest, and spread wide over his furious thundering heart. His. Hers.

Skai.

She nodded, abrupt, desperate, jerking the sharpened dagger-blade toward his face—and it was like he'd instantly uncoiled, sagging against her, his relief thick in the hot, musky air. His grip relaxing on her neck, his hand slipping up, sliding the steel out from between her swollen lips.

"Ach?" he whispered, so hoarse, so tenuous. "Ach, my Maria?"

And Maria was still nodding, but he wanted to hear her say it, needed it—and she coughed, found her breath. Her truth.

"Ach," she whispered back, her voice a croak. "Yours. Skai."

And gods, there was water streaking down her face, dripping into the fur, and Simon's big hand cupped her cheek, cradling it, so soft, so reverent. "Ach," he breathed. "Ach, my love."

His love. His truth. Twisting and clamouring inside, settling against all the rest. Filling her with its power, with the strength still rooted deep in her belly, with the weight of his body finally sinking low and warm and close.

And when he buried his face in her neck, and began rocking once more against her, it was... different. Unlike it ever had been before. Quiet, quivering, with no challenge, no aggression. Not even when Maria felt the unmistakable truth of deadly sharp orc-teeth against her neck, skittering and scraping against smooth untouched skin...

And when those teeth sank deep, breaking the skin, *biting* her, Maria didn't cry out. Didn't resist. Only clutched him closer, gulping for air, her body stilled, her eyes snapped wide. Watching. Learning. Skai.

And in the mingled pain and pleasure, the filling and the taking, the sound of an orc's throat swallowing her very *lifeblood*, there was also... peace. Ecstasy. *Euphoria.* Being claimed, consumed, cleansed. Being one with an orc, filled with orc, lost in his cock and his teeth and his craving, his need, his truth. In his most vulnerable, most powerful parts driving into her again and again, marking her, knowing her, swelling full, locking tight—

And then he reared up, his face smeared with blood, his mouth howling to the sky—and *flooded* her. His hot molten seed spraying and bursting within her, while the screaming relief of her own release clamped and shouted and flared. His. Hers. Skai.

And as they stared at one another, the shocks still rippling through them both, Maria again felt this truth, still fragile and new, but real enough to touch. An Enforcer and his Enforced. An orc and his woman. A Skai... and a Skai.

And in that instant, all was utter, perfect clarity. Cleansed. Whole.

She needed to... run.

31

She needed to run.

And as Maria blinked up at Simon's blood-streaked face, the truth of it seemed to twine tighter, deeper. She had to run. It was the only way.

And it was almost as though Simon saw it, knew it. As though Maria could see it, stealing across his eyes, stilling his breath.

"Now you stay," he said, his voice very low. "You *stay*. I keep you *safe*."

It sounded like pleading, like he was begging Maria to agree, to obey—but she couldn't, she *couldn't*, and it almost hurt to shake her head. To see the disbelief, the *pain*, in his watching eyes.

"I can't," she whispered. "I can't, Simon. I need to stop those letters. And by staying here"—she gulped for air—"I'm only calling down more war upon you. I'm putting your kin's *lives* at risk. I'm giving my awful husband everything he wants. And..."

She bit her lip, not wanting to say it, not now—but Simon was waiting, staring down at her, the darkness swallowing his eyes. As if he already knew, and Maria was speaking her truth. She wasn't hiding anymore. *Skai*.

"And by staying here, I'm still—*yours*," she whispered. "Which means I'm still at risk from Ulfarr. Our son is still at risk. But if we leave, we're no longer yours, right? And therefore—"

But Simon's face, oh gods, it looked suddenly hollow, haggard, broken. Like Maria had somehow struck at him, defeated him. *Destroyed* him.

"Ach," he said, his voice rough. "You no trust me to keep you safe."

Maria swallowed hard, but didn't deny it, couldn't. Not after everything today. And in truth, not after all else she'd seen from Ulfarr, too. As long as orcs like Ulfarr were allowed to walk free—and to make legitimate deadly claims on other living, breathing people—Maria wasn't safe here. Maybe no one was.

Simon's eyes had squeezed shut, his throat convulsing—and his big body abruptly pulled up, drawing away from her. Leaving a chilly, hanging emptiness behind—and when he lurched to his feet, dragging on his trousers, his back purposely turned, it felt like something had shattered in Maria's belly, sharp and brittle and sickening.

"It's not that I don't want to stay," she said to his stiff shoulders. "Or that I don't want to return, after, if you defeat Ulfarr. It's just—"

But Simon's shoulders only hunched higher, his hands now clenched to huge fists at his sides. And there was the understanding, swift and forceful, that he was hurt, angry, insulted. Because Maria had just implied—had she just implied?—that maybe he *wouldn't* defeat Ulfarr. That her loyalty to him was dependent on his ability to defeat Ulfarr. That she would wait out his fight to the death, and *then* pick a side.

And again, perhaps even worse, she'd just reinforced how much she didn't trust him. If she would rather take her chances away from him, on her own, in a world that would surely loathe and fear the son she carried. In a world that would surely attempt to *kill* her son, without question or remorse.

It suddenly felt like Maria's skin was crawling, her eyes fixed to Simon's stiff shoulders—wait, did he think she was throwing away their *son?*—and without thinking, she leapt out of the bed, and staggered toward him. Flinging her arms around his stiff back, pressing her wet face against his warm scarred skin.

"I still want our son, Simon," she whispered. "I'll do everything I can to keep him safe."

The words felt solid and true, pressed into the furious beat of his heart. And for an instant, Maria was sure he would turn, relax, gather her close, find a way through this—

But instead, he—*laughed*. The sound bitter, mocking, *cruel*, ringing through the room.

"Ach, *you* shall keep our son safe?" he sneered at her, and it was like the words were deep dragging daggers, flaying her bare. "You, who have spoken false to me again and again, in the face of all I have borne for you? You, when you even now seek to break your pledge toward me? Your own human words, sworn in *ink*?!"

Sworn in... ink? And even as the truth of that began trickling, unfurling into Maria's churning belly, Simon had already jerked away from her, lunging toward his shelf. His shelf, where that contract had still sat so carefully atop his pile of papers. That contract, in which Maria had sworn... to obey him. To honour him. To remain here, until their son was born. To *stay*.

And as Simon clutched the contract into his clawed fingers, there was another realization, pitching heavy into Maria's gut. He had... *wanted* the contract. He hadn't trusted her to keep her pledge, perhaps—but he'd trusted in the power of these new, foreign human ways. In the power of these... words.

I wish you to seek these new ways with me. Find new future. Find peace.

Maria blinked hard, fighting for air, opening her mouth to speak— but it was too late, too late, Simon gripping the contract in his claws, and... *tearing* it. Ripping it straight down the middle, and then again, and again, and again. Until his clean, bare floor was strewn in shreds of paper, in the broken, bitter remnants of all Maria's empty words.

"Simon," she heard herself say, choked. "Look, I swear, I—"

His bark was loud, grating, furious, and he hurled the last bits of paper to the floor at her feet. "No," he hissed at her. "No more, woman. No more lies. No more games. I can no—"

His mouth snapped closed, hard enough that Maria could hear the clack of his teeth, and his head whipped back and forth, his eyes squeezed shut. "I am Enforcer," he said, and it almost sounded like a prayer, like a refuge, like a final barrier crashing down between them. "I am Enforcer of Orc Mountain. I bear no trap. No game. No more human *lies*!"

And Maria had to speak. Had to salvage this, somehow, make new promises, find new ways—but Simon didn't want her words, her promises, her *lies*. And what could she say, what could she do, what defense did she have, defeated...

And Simon saw it. He knew. And with one last, sneering snarl from his lips, he spun on his heel, and left.

32

I t was an empty, endless night. Spent entirely alone in Simon's room, with no respite, no relief. Even sleep wouldn't come, no matter how Maria tossed and kicked under the fur, no matter how fervently she whispered her truths into the darkness.

She had to run. She had to deal with the letters, with the war, with her husband. Simon had made her Skai, and a true Skai would never sit back and allow war to overtake their kin, their home. They would keep it safe. Defend it to the death.

And—Maria wiped at her eyes, glared up into the empty blackness—she *couldn't* trust Simon. He'd lied to her, too. He'd played his own games. He'd signed that damned contract under false pretenses. He'd put her at risk. He'd yelled at her, overpowered her, Enforced her...

The water kept leaking from her eyes, and Maria dragged in a broken, hitching breath. No. No more lies. She'd wanted that. She'd craved that. It had brought her peace, like it so often had. Like *Simon* so often had. With his teaching, his patience, his... *kindness*.

And even now, lying here alone in the dark, the depth of that kindness kept coming clearer. How he'd *known* she was lying all this time, and how he'd still sought to teach her, to care for her. How he'd sought to make her belong among his clan. How he'd surely had to defend her against his kin, when she'd singlehandedly brought more *war* to their doorstep.

And even how this, here, was the very first night Maria had spent alone in this room. How despite all the hours Simon had left her alone during the days, he had always come back at nights. Had cared for her. Kept her safe.

And now? Maria scrubbed at her face, dragged in more breath. She'd hurt him. She'd insulted him. She'd broken her word. She'd destroyed everything.

And she still had to run. She *had* to.

"Maria?" came a tentative voice from the doorway—and when she twitched up to look, it was Baldr. Standing there holding a lamp, looking just as tired as she felt. "Are you able to come meet with us, for a spell?"

Right. Lady Norr's meeting. Meaning that it must be morning, finally, and Maria silently nodded, and slid out of bed. Not even caring that she was still wearing only her loincloth—at least, until Baldr's hand thrust out what appeared to be... clothes?

"Simon tells us you wish to leave," he said, quiet. "He asked me to give these to you."

Oh. Something else seemed to crack, low in Maria's chest, but she nodded again, and took the clothes, and pulled them on. But gods, she'd gotten so used to the easy movement of Simon's huge tunics, that even these loose-fitting men's garments felt uncomfortably close and constricting. Trapping her into a form and a facade that weren't hers, that she no longer wanted to be hers.

But she kept going, and once she'd finished fastening the trousers over her loincloth, she attempted a smile at Baldr's shadowy-looking face. "Thank you, Baldr. You've been so good to me."

He jerked a shrug, and then raised the lamp, casting its light over the room, over the still-shredded remnants of the contract on the floor. "Is there aught else here that is yours?"

Maria swallowed, about to say that nothing here belonged to her— but then her gaze caught on something, glinting on the floor beside the bed. Her dagger. Hers, Simon had told her.

And surely any decent Skai wouldn't go travelling without at least one weapon, so Maria went to grasp for it, tucking it into its usual place against her hip. And then hesitated, glancing around at this so-familiar room, with its bed, its weapons, its papers and clothes and carvings. Her prison, her *home*.

Her eyes fell on the carving at the front of Simon's little group—his father—and for some reason she lurched toward it, carefully resting her hand on its head, the way Simon had done. "I'm sorry," she whispered to it. "I'm so sorry, Sjovarr. But I *will* keep your grandson safe. I *will*."

The certainty of that statement seemed to settle, heavy and quiet—and somehow, in the midst of all the swirling chaos, it helped. Enough that Maria could raise her eyes again, and seek one more favour of the orc who'd already been so, so generous to her.

"Before the meeting, Baldr, could you please take me to the Skai shrine?" she asked. "Just for a moment?"

Baldr nodded, and accordingly turned, and led her down the corridor. And when they reached the door to the shrine, he didn't step inside, but instead held back, and waved Maria forward. Because, maybe, he wasn't Skai, and she... *was*.

She tried to smile her thanks toward him, but the heaviness had begun sinking again, curdling in her belly. And it was all she could do to choke back a sob as she knelt on the fur-covered bench before Skai-kesh, and bowed her head.

"I'm so sorry," she whispered. "I've fucked this up beyond imagining. I've broken my word, and betrayed the one person I most—care for. All for the sake of my... *revenge*."

But the last word felt strange in her mouth, unfamiliar, almost like it belonged to someone else—and when Maria raised her head, blinking, it was as though the god's glinting black eyes were looking through her, into her. Knowing that word wasn't hers anymore too, and instead searching for her fear, her longing, her blessing. Her truth.

So Maria drew in a quivering breath, held it deep. "For my fear," she began, "I'm afraid I've ruined everything. I'm afraid I've lost all the peace I've found here. I'm afraid I've lost Simon, for good."

And that was true, she felt it, and she dragged in more breath, more courage. "For my longing," she continued, "I long to make it right. To find a way to make amends. To stop this war. To stop my husband. To gain Simon's trust again."

And yes, that was true, too, sinking in alongside the rest. And there was one more to find, to speak. The blessing.

"And I'm so thankful," she whispered, "for all I've learned here. For Simon. And for"—her hands dropped, found her waist, spread wide— "for my son. I've wanted a child for so long, you know. And I can scarce believe he's real, I can't believe I've gained such a gift. And he will be *wonderful*, I know, he'll be so stubborn and patient, he'll probably have a pathological obsession with weaponry, he'll keep his promises and sacrifice *everything* to keep his kin safe, and I just—"

Gods, she was weeping again, the tears streaking down her face, and she dashed them away with shaky fingers. "I can't risk him," she choked out. "I can't. I need to do everything to keep him safe. You must see that. *Please.*"

And blinking up at Skai-kesh's watching eyes, there was the certainty, sudden and simmering, that he did see. That he'd... accepted it. Accepted her.

Mine. Skai.

Maria's exhale was heavy, worn, relieved. Yes. Skai. She would do this. Watch. Listen. Learn. Find new ways. Find... courage.

And when she felt an odd prickle, skittering up her back, she didn't even twitch, and instead turned to look toward it, feeling through the darkness. Toward... Joarr?

But yes, it was Joarr again, leaning casually against the wall, just where he'd been the first time she'd come here. Looking at her with the same glinting watchfulness in his eyes. The same *satisfaction*.

"Come, woman," he told her, pushing off the wall, inclining his head as he strode past. "We speak, and next we go."

We? Maria blinked, but didn't argue, and accordingly followed him out of the room. Toward where Baldr was already waiting, and soon they were striding through the corridor together, their combined foot-falls completely silent on the stone floor beneath them.

And as they walked, Maria realized that they were taking her out of the Skai wing. Beyond the familiar, twisty dark corridors, and into an area that looked different, felt different. The corridors brighter, wider, straighter, with many unfamiliar orcs walking by. Orcs with different kinds of faces, often broader and warmer, even smiling at Maria as she passed.

And on another day, in another reality, maybe Maria would have smiled back, or even looked eagerly around her, drunk up these new and fascinating sights—but instead, she kept her eyes on Joarr's back, her hands spread reflexively against her waist. She had to run. She had to.

Finally Joarr led her into a vaguely familiar-looking room, with a large square table, and a fire crackling at the opposite end. It was the room Maria had met all those orcs in, her very first day here—and even the people looked to be the same. The captain, Lady Norr, Rosa and John, and several more orcs and women whose names Maria didn't even know. Because she'd been their prisoner, all this time. Because they'd thought she was here to *betray* them.

Every face in the room had turned toward her, but suddenly Maria could only see one of them. Simon, leaning beside Drafli against the nearest wall, his arms folded over his chest. And gods, he was—*glaring* at her. Frowning at her. Fixing her with the force of his judgement, almost powerful enough to make her stagger on her feet. Condemning her, perhaps even... *hating* her.

And in this moment, Maria desperately wanted to lunge for him, to touch him, to beg him to understand—but no. No. He clearly didn't want that from her anymore. Maybe didn't even want her anymore.

So Maria held herself still, staring at him, feeling the misery curdle and clang in her chest. "I'm sorry, Simon," she heard her cracked voice whisper, despite all the others watching, judging. "I'm so, *so* sorry."

Something jumped in Simon's jaw, but he didn't move, or speak, or even acknowledge that she'd spoken at all. And Maria felt her eyes dropping, her shoulders sagging, her hands clutching against her waist. Defeated. Destroyed.

Something had gently nudged at her shoulder—Baldr, his eyes narrow and dark—and he waved her toward the table, toward the empty space beside Lady Norr. So Maria nodded, and lurched over to sit. Barely noticing as Joarr silently sank down on her other side, while Lady Norr reached to grasp her hand, squeezing tight.

"We gather today to settle what next comes," said the captain, his deep voice resonating through the room. "Maria, shall you speak your truth to us?"

Maria nodded again, and looked toward the orc with the

unnerving eyes who'd questioned her that first day—Nattfarr, his name had been—but he wasn't even looking at her this time. Instead, he was murmuring something to the scantily clad woman beside him, before glancing back at Maria, brows raised. As if he—they—were just... waiting.

So Maria drew in breath, and spoke. Starting at the beginning, with her father's unexpected inheritance, her parents' deaths, the astonishing attentions from a duke. And then the bitter disappointment of her marriage, the casual cruelty, the whispers, the betrayals, the hysteria.

And next, she told of her husband's new law, and her decision to run. Her letters, her escape, her meeting Simon in the road. The peace she'd found in his arms.

And then, her voice wavering, she spoke of Simon's kindness. His teaching. Of how she'd learned, and changed, and realized all the mistakes she'd made. How she'd wanted to become someone else. A true Skai.

"And a true Skai would never put other people at risk like this," she said, her eyes blinking at the table. "They would seek to make amends for what they'd done, and keep their people safe. They would prove"— she swallowed hard—"their loyalty to someone they love. They would seek to cover the shame they'd brought, and bring honour, instead."

The room had fallen utterly silent, but Maria couldn't bear to look up again, to risk again finding that disapproval in Simon's eyes. Even though she'd sought to honour him in this, making no mention of Ulfarr, no suggestion that she didn't trust Simon to keep her safe. No indication that she was defying him, betraying him, breaking the contract they'd made. Running away with his son.

But maybe the rest of them knew it anyway, judging by the weight of the silence all around, the feel of prickling eyes on Maria's skin. And when someone finally spoke, it wasn't the captain, or Simon—but instead, it was Rosa.

"Did you really just say," she demanded, her voice indignant enough to snap up Maria's chagrined eyes, "that you singlehandedly set up an entire secret *information campaign* against Duke Warmisham, targeting key contacts all across Preia? And no one thought to *inform* us about this *crucial development*?!"

She shot an outraged look toward John beside her, who was also looking unmistakably peeved. And Maria winced, about to speak, to apologize—but wait, their combined disapproving frowns weren't directed toward her, but toward *Simon*.

And when Maria's eyes finally found Simon's face, he was—looking at her. Not judging, not condemning. Just... looking.

"We need to make a plan," Rosa said firmly, her sparkling eyes again fixed to Maria's. "Gods *bless* you, Maria, you've just spared us quite possibly an entire *year* of work, and dumped that sleazy, shit-eating duke right into our hands. Give us a little while to pull this together, and we'll meet where, at the northeast tunnel? By noon?"

To Maria's rising astonishment, Joarr nodded beside her, and then jabbed a sharp-clawed finger across the room, again toward Simon. "You, pack food for mate," he said, voice clipped. "I no waste time cooking for human, ach?"

Wait, what? Surely Maria wasn't still Simon's *mate*, and surely Joarr didn't mean he was truly coming *with* her—right? But now Joarr and Simon were glaring at each other, with something Maria couldn't at all read passing between them—something that ended with Simon giving a jerky, almost imperceptible nod, and Joarr a smug, satisfied smile.

"Excellent," said Lady Norr firmly, her hand squeezing against Maria's. "Who else is going? Baldr?"

Baldr? But wait, he was already nodding too, his eyes flicking an obstinate look toward Drafli's scowling face. "And we shall need Olarr's help also," Baldr added, his gaze sliding to another unfamiliar, craggy-featured orc opposite them. "Gerrard will grant us his aid, ach?"

Gerrard? As in, her husband's top *general*?! Maria was feeling truly bewildered now, but the Olarr orc was curtly nodding, and Lady Norr's mouth had spread into a slow, not-so-nice smile. Her eyes alight on the captain's across the table, and he smiled too, sharp and wicked.

"Just what we were thinking," Lady Norr purred. "Now, let's make a plan, and snag ourselves a duke."

33

A short time later, Maria was ready. Standing in a dark, narrow tunnel, and wearing a heavy pack on her back, sturdy boots on her feet, and a warm cloak over her shoulders.

The supplies had been courtesy of the Skai tailor and storage-room, commandeered under the firm orders of Lady Norr. And as Maria had dressed and packed and submitted to a variety of measurements, she and Lady Norr had continued to work through the plan's details, until Maria's head was spinning, caught somewhere between shock and disbelief and sheer, twirling gratefulness.

"Are you *sure*?" she'd asked doubtfully, but Lady Norr had only waved it away, and drawn Maria back into the corridor again.

"Of course we're sure," she'd said, her eyes alight. "We've been desperate to deal with Warmisham for ages now. You were a gift on a platter, Maria."

She'd softened those words with a wry grin, contagious enough that Maria had almost smiled back—but even despite the activity and the excitement, all of which Maria might have otherwise enjoyed, there was still the misery. Cold, black, empty, dragging heavy against her belly.

She'd broken her word. She was leaving. Maybe—forever.

And as she stood here in this strange corridor, while various strange orcs bustled and chattered all about, she couldn't seem to stop scanning the darkness, the misery deepening with each breath. Was Simon not even going to say goodbye? If not to her, then even to their son?

But Simon had been conspicuously absent these past hours, not in the corridors, or the Skai wing, or even in his room when Maria and Lady Norr had passed. And now, as Joarr and Baldr approached together—Joarr bare-chested and unencumbered, Baldr fully clothed and carrying a massive-looking pack—there was the rising, overpowering urge to ask after Simon, to beg one of them to take her to him, one last time—

Until there was a telling, familiar prickle, shivering up Maria's back. And when she whirled around, peering into the corridor's distant darkness, she could only see shadow, dark and forbidding.

But her heart was pounding, seeking to leap into her throat, and she took one quiet step into the darkness, and then another. Fighting not to think, but only to feel, as her hand reached out, and found warm shifting skin beneath it.

Simon.

Maria couldn't speak, suddenly, over the catch in her throat, but her fingers were spreading wider, feeling the truth beneath them. The deep, forceful thud of his rapidly racing heart.

And surely he was still furious, and perhaps Maria would never change that, and she choked back the surging misery, the rising urge to weep. The desperate need to see his face, to hear him speak, to *know*—

"You shall—stay with Joarr and Baldr, ach?" Simon's voice said, low and gruff, a sheer, painful relief. "You no seek to run from them, ach?"

The misery surged again, clamouring against the relief and the ache. Because gods, clearly all Maria's hopes of gaining Simon's trust had been futile from the start, if he truly still thought she would *run* from Baldr and Joarr, after they'd offered their help with such kindness?

"No, I'll stay with them," she replied, her voice wooden. "I know how skilled they are. I'm very grateful for their generosity and protection."

Her other hand slipped reflexively down to clutch at her waist, and she swallowed hard, her eyes dropping. And maybe that was all Simon had wanted to say, one last barb at how untrustworthy she was, but she still couldn't seem to move, to draw her hand away from the power of his racing heart.

"You ken," Simon continued, abrupt, "I should come with you. Ach? If I were no Enforcer. If I must no—"

Oh. Maria's body twitched to stillness, her eyes blankly blinking. Simon would have come? If not for his work, and for... Ulfarr?

But yes, surely that was what he meant. That fight to the death was now in five short days, and Simon surely couldn't afford to miss that, or slack off on his training. He couldn't risk Ulfarr taking over as Enforcer. He couldn't.

But Maria would miss it. She wouldn't be by his side to support him, to cheer him, to glory in his victory, or grieve his death. She would be gone, and he would be fighting for everything he cared about, and she wouldn't even *know*.

"I—wish you all luck, Simon," Maria said, the truth fervent in her voice. "And all Skai-kesh's blessing. I'll be praying every day for your strength. For your victory."

But there was only more silence in return, stretching out heavy and dark, overpowering even the distant clatter of orcs up the corridor. And Maria needed him to say something, needed to hear his voice for perhaps the last time, please...

And she could try. She could say this. Truth.

"If I can," she whispered, "would you want me to come back here? After?"

And it was a foolish idea to begin with, because gods knew what would happen next with Ulfarr, with her husband—but as the question hung there between them, echoing in the silence, Maria suddenly felt its insult, its gods-damned presumptuousness. Here she was, in the very act of running from Simon, stealing away the son he'd so desperately longed for, leaving him to face his fight to the death alone—and she already wanted his forgiveness? His permission to waltz back in here afterwards, as though nothing had happened at all?

And Simon surely felt it too, his big body utterly still in the darkness, his heart beating its powerful pulse against her fingers. And before he could speak his refusal aloud, Maria jerked away from him, ducking her head, dashing the water from her eyes with a shaky hand. It was done, she was doing it, she had to—

"Maria," came his voice, husky and thick, and with it was a clutch of warm strong fingers, closing around her wrist. Holding her there. Perhaps even not wanting her to leave...

"You are Skai," he continued, very quiet. "You are thus now free to come and go as you wish. Ach?"

But the ache kept crawling, kept dragging, clamping close at her throat. Because it wasn't a yes. It *wasn't*. It was just Simon again keeping his word. Being kind. Giving her yet more generosity that she didn't deserve.

He surely didn't want her anymore. And Maria surely couldn't blame him. Not now.

"Th-thank you," she made herself say, over the obstruction in her throat. "And j-just in case, was there something you"—she dragged in a hitching breath—"wanted to name your son?"

There was a hoarse, unfamiliar noise from Simon, and then, surprisingly, the sounds of his breaths. Thick, heavy, unnaturally loud in the choked silence.

"Arnthorr," he said finally, his voice rough. "Should you wish."

Arnthorr. After his childhood friend, the one carved on his shelf. And the name seemed to settle in the too-taut air, curling itself close, and Maria's hand spread wider against her waist, testing it, tasting its truth. Arnthorr. Their son.

"Arnthorr, then," she said, with a pathetic attempt at a smile. "Of Clan Skai."

But there was no reply this time, no words, only the weight of Simon's breaths. And the weight of Maria's misery, plunging violently into her gut, because this was goodbye, then. She was finally leaving this mountain, she would finally see the sky again, and all she wanted was to curl up on the floor and weep.

"Ready, Maria?" called a voice from up the corridor—Lady Norr—and Maria grimaced, and squared her shoulders. She was doing this. She had to do this.

"Thank you for everything, Simon," she whispered, and before she could stop herself, she'd lurched up, and pressed a quick, furtive kiss to where she knew his cheek to be. "I'll miss you."

There was an odd tinge of salt on Maria's lips, but still no reply, not even his breath. It was goodbye. It was over.

And before Maria could start pleading, or sobbing, she jerked away, and whirled into the darkness.

34

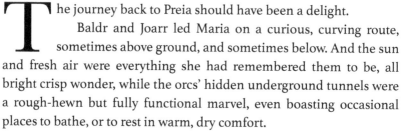

The journey back to Preia should have been a delight.

Baldr and Joarr led Maria on a curious, curving route, sometimes above ground, and sometimes below. And the sun and fresh air were everything she had remembered them to be, all bright crisp wonder, while the orcs' hidden underground tunnels were a rough-hewn but fully functional marvel, even boasting occasional places to bathe, or to rest in warm, dry comfort.

Their route above ground proved to include a few tricky bits as well—fording a rushing river, climbing a sheer wall, walking a narrow bridge over a chasm—but with Baldr's help, Maria managed it all without incident. And while the journey was unquestionably tiring, it still felt far easier than her initial trip to the mountain, without the constant weariness, or the bone-deep exhaustion that had left every limb aching.

They even made astonishing time, thanks to Joarr's insistence on following the most direct possible route to Preia, rather than the usual meandering human roads. Joarr had proved to be an extremely accomplished navigator, tracking their position only via instinct and the sun, while Baldr seemed able to smell almost anything, and at inconceivable distances. Ranging from other humans a league away, to a campfire even further, to a tiny, hidden patch of delicious berries that had been buried beneath the earth.

It should have been a delight. A true joy, after all those days trapped in the bowels of Orc Mountain. But the misery in Maria's belly wouldn't seem to fade, and felt heavier and heavier with each step she took. She'd betrayed Simon. She'd broken her pledge. She was leaving him alone to face his fight to the death.

By the time they stopped that first night, in a cozy little underground room, Maria could scarcely speak for the dread, the constantly curdling regret. She should have told Simon the truth from the start. She should never have signed a contract she wasn't sure she could keep. She should have worked out a plan with him, found a way to hand over his son but somehow still stay in touch, providing any of them survived this at all...

"Are you well, Maria?" Baldr asked, as he rolled out what looked like an actual sleeping-mat onto the stone floor, and then waved her toward it. "Is there aught we can do to help?"

His voice was quiet, his eyes dark in the light of the lamp he'd lit, and as Maria went to sit on the mat, it belatedly occurred to her that Baldr had been unusually subdued today too, despite his consistent kindness toward her. That his smile hadn't come nearly so easy, and that his shoulders looked hunched, his mouth tight and grim.

"No, I'm fine," Maria said reflexively, but then winced, and drew in a thick breath. "I mean, thank you for asking. I just—there's nothing you can do, really. Unless you can make Simon magically appear here, and make him forgive me, and guarantee that he doesn't hate me anymore."

She tried for a smile toward Baldr, but it felt wan and pitiful, and across the room Joarr huffed a loud snort. He was sitting casually against the far wall, his long legs sprawled wide, and he'd begun scraping a knife against a stone, a sight that was twisting Maria's insides even worse than before.

"My brother no hate you, silly woman," he said unexpectedly. "I can no summon him here, but mayhap"—he smirked at Maria, and reached for Baldr's overstuffed pack—"this help you?"

This. A long, solid-looking item that he lightly tossed over into Maria's waiting hands. And as she caught it, blinking down toward it, the weight in her belly wildly shuddered, her face instantly flooding with heat.

It was one of Simon's—*implements*?

But it wasn't one she'd seen before, and it was even larger than all the rest. Large enough, perhaps—she swallowed hard, her fingers compulsively circling its heft—to be on a scale with Simon himself.

"Where," she croaked, "did you get this?"

There was another snort from Joarr, amidst that familiar sound of steel scraping against stone. "Simon send it," he replied, in a tone that suggested this was obvious. "You no ken *I* carve you his prick?"

Wait. Was Joarr suggesting—surely he wasn't suggesting—that *Simon* had made this? That he'd made—*all* of them? Or that—Maria stared down toward the stone in her hand, truly searching this time—this was supposed to be a representation of... *him*?

But her oddly skittering fingers had already traced up the stone again, feeling its familiar length and girth, the blunt power of its rounded head, the width of its flared base. While her memories darted back to the tools in the chest, to the way they'd grown steadily larger, to Simon's constant carving on the bench. *I shall find your fresh scent upon these each day...*

"But—*why*?" she asked, her voice plaintive, her gaze darting to Joarr's watching, glinting eyes. "Why would Simon do that?"

Joarr's spiky-haired head tilted, black brows furrowing. "You are Simon mate," he said, again as though this were obvious. "He wish mate comfort whilst he is apart, ach? Also"—he smirked at her—"he no wish mate womb to shrivel, without his strong ploughing each day."

Maria's disbelief was blessedly drowned by a surge of indignation, and she frowned at Joarr, even as her hands tightened against her precious new implement. "Women do not," she snapped, "*shrivel*."

But Joarr's eyes were unnervingly narrow on hers, the sound of his scraping steel even louder than before. "Ach, and you take Skai prick easy on first try?" he countered. "You take Simon ploughing with no care?"

Maria's face flushed even hotter, the words and the memories tangling tight together—and Joarr was still scowling at her, with what looked like genuine disapproval in his glinting eyes.

"No," Joarr continued, as if Maria had in fact replied, or argued. "My brother take great care with you. He work hard on you, and teach you with no blood or pain. He *honour* you. You wish him forgive you? *You* now honour *him*."

Oh. Maria couldn't quite find an answer to that, but for perhaps the first time today, some of the constant heaviness had seemed to fade. And in its place, there was something small, quiet, flickering. Something almost like... hope.

She could still prove this? Still gain Simon's trust? Still?

But Joarr was nodding, again as if Maria had spoken the words aloud. "Honour him," he said firmly, with a flutter of long fingers toward the tool still clutched in her hand. "He shall know, when next he plough you."

Even more heat had swarmed to Maria's face, but now it was also swirling in her belly, husky and low. *Honour him. He shall know...*

Joarr kept looking at her expectantly, black brows raised—and Maria felt a distant, uneasy awareness dawning. "Wait. Um, you don't mean I should do so... here? *Now?*"

Her voice had come out like a squeak, and the disapproval flashed again across Joarr's watching eyes. "Ach, silly woman," he replied. "You honour Simon here, safe. You ken we no see you in thrall to him before? We no see you spurt and squeal upon him?"

Maria's face was truly smarting now, her chagrined eyes angling toward Baldr—surely he hadn't been witness to such things, too?—but there was an unmistakably wry twist on his mouth. Suggesting, good gods, that he'd spent all this time living next door to them—in a place lacking actual doors—so of course he had.

"Mayhap you shall hide this beneath your cloak," Baldr helpfully suggested, "if that should help you feel more comfortable?"

Maria grimaced at them both, even as she felt her shoulders squaring, her hands clutching tighter at her stone. Simon had given her a chance. A gift. And no matter what, she had to try. She had to honour him. She *had* to.

She flopped back onto the sleeping-mat with a groan, and yanked her heavy cloak over on top—and then, while two orcs blatantly watched, she slipped down her trousers, and brought the new stone close. Fighting back the whispers of shame, of fear, because Simon had given this to her, Simon wanted this, wanted *her*...

She gasped aloud as she felt the stone's rounded head, searching, seeking—and then even louder as it began to breach her, piercing her whole upon it. And gods, it *did* feel like Simon, deep and solid and utterly uncompromising, filling her with its certainty, its strength.

And as it kept driving, kept filling, it was almost as though the small underground room had blinked away. And instead, Maria was in Simon's room, on her back on his furs, quivering and gasping under his huge hovering weight. Filling her breath with his scent, scraping her fingers against his broad back, arching and begging and craving him, needing him, her mate, the father of her son, *hers*.

The pleasure blared bright and wide, flooding Maria with sheer pulsing sensation, with impossible warmth. With her sated body sagging onto the mat beneath her, while something almost like relief settled into her soul.

She could do this. Prove this. Fix this.

And when the room around her slowly slipped into focus again—and with it, Joarr and Baldr—Maria didn't even feel humiliated, or ashamed. At least, not enough to fret over, not with Joarr looking at her with such saucy approval in his eyes, and Baldr with something that might have been... longing?

"Better, ach?" Joarr said crisply, before sliding his dark gaze toward Baldr. "Now next, how we fix *you*, pretty Grisk? Mayhap *you* welcome strong Skai fuck also?"

Joarr's long-fingered hand had brazenly slipped down to clutch at his groin, clearly displaying the swollen bulge beneath. And perhaps it was a sign of just how relaxed Maria felt, or how much time she'd spent with these orcs, that she didn't even feel slightly shocked, and instead rearranged herself and sat up, searching Baldr's shadowed face. Remembering, abruptly, about his fight with Drafli, and how she'd walked in on it, and made it even worse.

You only care, Drafli had growled at him, *until woman show up.*

"No, I had best not," Baldr replied, grimacing, after an instant's silence. "I thank you for the offer, though."

Joarr shrugged and returned to his sharpening, but Maria was still watching Baldr, caught on the almost visceral misery in his eyes. And gods, he'd been so kind to her all this time, and here she'd helped muck up something he clearly cared about. And then she'd gone and entirely forgotten about it, while wallowing in her own miserable fuck-ups?

"Is there anything else we could do to help?" she asked Baldr, echoing his own question toward her earlier. "I truly regret interrupting you and Drafli the way I did. I know I only made it worse."

But Baldr waved it away, and his answering smile was sad, and painfully genuine. "It was not your fault, Maria," he said. "This has been building for some time. I ought never have moved into the Skai wing as I did. This only laid bare all the rifts between us."

And surely it wasn't Maria's place to keep pressing, but suddenly she couldn't bear not to, either. "How so?" she asked. "Shouldn't living closer together be a good thing?"

Baldr winced, and shook his head. "This showed me, stronger than ever, that I shall never be Drafli's mate, or gain his fealty," he said, his voice wooden. "And it showed him the depth of my... ease with you. My help. My... *care.*"

His care. Maria felt briefly struck to her sleeping-mat, her eyes wide on Baldr's face—surely he didn't care for her like *that?*—and thankfully he winced again, and gave another sharp shake of his head.

"Not—*hunger*," he said, too quickly. "Not for *you*, Maria, as lovely as you are. But just"—he made a face—"*women.*"

Oh. Ohhhh. Maria felt herself wincing too, even as Baldr kept speaking, his eyes now on his clenched hands before him. "I was— late, coming to our mountain," he said, in a rush. "Almost fully grown. Until then, I spent the whole of my life with my mother, and I loved her with all my strength, ach? You humans are so soft, so sweet. So *whole.*"

And as Maria considered that, it occurred to her that Simon had spoken like this, too. But instead of the bitterness she remembered in Simon's voice and eyes, Baldr just looked... sad. Alone.

"Well, if it is a woman you truly want," Maria said, into the stilted silence, "perhaps it might be worth pursuing, then, if it would make you happy? And I'm sure, Baldr"—she felt herself smile toward him, small but true—"you would have no trouble at all finding a woman to adore you."

But across the room, Joarr had again snorted, this time pausing his sharpening to smirk at Baldr. "Ach, until she meet Drafli," he said, with gusto. "He send her away screaming, ach? Or better, he take Baldr before her, and make *him* scream her away."

Joarr looked as though he would thoroughly enjoy witnessing such a sight, and in return Baldr actually bared his teeth, a low growl hissing from his throat. "That is *bollocks*, Joarr," he snapped. "You know Drafli would never touch me *again* if I took a woman for a mate."

Joarr barked a laugh, his spiky head shaking. "Ach, Drafli soon overcome this," he said firmly, "when his pretty Grisk pet deny him. Walk around *shrivelling*. Reek only of *human*. You ken you say no, when he fight you down and plough you? Whilst little human watch in fright, and he *laugh* to see her run?"

Baldr glared at Joarr, and opened his mouth—but then closed it again. As if he couldn't argue this rather horrifying little image, and Maria blinked between him and Joarr, her brain fighting to catch up. "So you really *would* choose Drafli, over a woman?" she asked Baldr. "You care about him that much? Even if he's constantly—"

Betraying you, she was about to add, though she cut off the words, just in time. Because surely it wasn't even *slightly* fair to Baldr if Drafli was off blatantly taking his pleasure however he wished, while also demanding Baldr deny himself the mate he clearly longed for? While also possibly planning to *terrify* said mate into oblivion?

But Baldr's nod was slow, weary, almost painful to watch. "Drafli and I have had an—understanding, ach?" he said, quiet. "I know the Skai ways. I thus—agreed to this with him, even if I do not like this. Until all this, it was yet worth—"

He didn't finish, grimacing down at his hands, and across the room Joarr laughed again, and actually *winked* at Maria. "Worth strong Skai ploughing, ach?" he said. "You agree, woman? You have borne much for Skai prick, I ken?"

And gods curse her, but Maria couldn't help a small, twitching smile back, even as Baldr hissed another growl toward Joarr. "It is not just this," he countered. "Drafli is—good to me. *Kind*."

That truly seemed beyond fathoming, to Maria's mind, but Baldr was frowning between her and Joarr, as though he needed to say this, to prove this. "When I came here," he said, "this mountain was not...

safe. Most of all for those who did not belong. And Drafli"—he drew in breath, his voice thickening—"Drafli kept me safe. He taught me to fight, and showed me these strange orc ways. He... *saw* me, when others did not."

Oh. Maria swallowed, the words resonating low in her belly—but Baldr was frowning at Joarr again, his eyes resentful. "In the face of all your damned Skai *ways*," he hissed, "you are good at that, ach? You oft seem so hard and cold, but you watch, and listen, and *know*. And you *never* abandon your own."

Joarr's hands had returned to his sharpening, but he was smiling toward Baldr, placid and smug. "No," he agreed. "And thus, you ken all you do, when you run away from him with pretty Skai woman, ach? Are you *sure* you no wish to add strong Skai ploughing to this? That *sure* send my brother raging, ach?"

Baldr groaned aloud, burying his head in his hands, but Joarr kept grinning, his sparkling eyes flicking to Maria's face. Clearly expecting her to share in the joke, and somehow, she actually did feel her mouth tugging up, the warmth creeping into her eyes.

Because Joarr was saying—again—that there was hope. That the Skai wouldn't give up. That Drafli wouldn't give up. That maybe Simon wouldn't give up.

And she wouldn't give up, either.

That certainty kept rising, even as the three of them settled down to sleep, Maria curled up in her cloak. She would do this. Prove this.

And as the next few days passed, filled with tiring but productive travel, and truly enjoyable companionship, Maria also began to realize that it wasn't just about proving this to Simon, or to her unborn son. It was about proving it to herself. About becoming, finally, the person she wanted to be. Brave. Fierce. Loyal. Unashamed. Someone who would never abandon the people she cared about.

And it kept sinking truer, deeper, as Maria began each day with a prayer to Skai-kesh, begging for Simon's safety, his victory. As she sought to be a helpful fellow traveller to Baldr and Joarr, fetching wood and water, cooking her own meals, staying close and safe. As she worked to learn whatever Joarr and Baldr would teach her, whether about themselves, or the Skai, or orcs in general. And as she ended each day with Simon's gift, imagining his scent, his power, his certainty.

It was early on the fifth day—the same day of Simon's fight against Ulfarr—that they finally crossed the border into Preia. As they crept overland through the forest that encircled Duke Warmisham's sprawling estate, and Maria caught her first glimpse of Warmisham House, looming tall and square and elegant beyond the trees.

And perhaps it was fitting, Maria thought, as she carefully washed and dressed, that she and Simon were each facing their respective enemies on the same day. That even parted, they would fight together for the clan and the people they cared for. The people they loved.

And as Maria strode up the lane, smoothing out the expensive silk of her stylish new dress, she thought of Simon. Of his courage. His certainty. Of all he'd taught her. Of home. Skai.

Her gloved hand rapped on the huge door with resounding sureness, and she stood calmly, quietly, as the door opened. As the butler's jaw dropped, and behind him, a passing housemaid skittered to stillness, her feather-duster falling to the floor with an echoing *thunk*.

"Good afternoon," Maria said, with a smile. "Is my husband at home?"

35

On another day, Maria might have almost enjoyed the chaos her unexpected arrival had created. Drawing the attention of not only Warmisham House's butler and housemaid, but soon the head housekeeper, the cook, several gardeners, and a footman.

"You—you were *kidnapped by orcs*, Your Grace," said the breathless maid, her hand clutched to her heaving bosom. "How did you *possibly* escape?"

Maria's laugh rang out on its own, bright and genuine. "Kidnapped by *orcs*?" she echoed, her voice carrying through the vaulted entry-hall. "That's preposterous. I most certainly was not kidnapped by orcs, but rather"—her eyes flicked to the rear of the hall, to where a familiar silhouette was lurking—"was urgently called away, to manage some family affairs in Sakkin Province."

She gave the still-goggling maid her sweetest smile, and then strode across the hall, her high heels clicking on the marble floor. Her gaze fixed to the tall, well-dressed man standing stock-still at the back of the room, staring at her with blank, shocked *loathing* in his lovely grey eyes.

"Imagine my surprise when I heard a *bounty* had been set for my return," Maria continued loudly, as she closed the space between them. "Upon hearing it, I realized I had best come home at once. Before my devoted husband mistakenly starts an entire *war* to search for me."

She drew to a halt before him, squaring her shoulders, inwardly bracing for the familiar rush of panic, the uncontrollable rage. But as she lifted her eyes to his shocked, smooth, handsome face, there was something sharp and new, curling into her belly. Something much like... contempt.

And as she looked her husband up and down, her gaze lingering on his tailored clothes, his slim shoulders, his impeccably coiffed hair—the contempt only sparked higher, darker. *This* was the man who'd ruined her life for the past six years? *This* was the man who'd been terrorizing the orcs all this time? This little man, with his bulging eyes, and his little pouting mouth, and his slightly knocking knees?

"A private meeting, if you would, husband," Maria said smoothly. "Or would you rather discuss this here?"

She smiled again, not quite so nicely this time, and Warmisham noticeably twitched as he turned his back to her, and strode down the main hallway. Clearly intending Maria to follow, and she willingly did so, glancing around as she went. Perhaps seeing the house with new eyes, too, with all its unnecessary grandeur, all its attempts to over-power and intimidate.

But after spending weeks in Orc Mountain, Maria wasn't intimi-dated. Not even as her husband drew her into the very last room down the hall—well out of noise range of the rest of the house—and then locked the heavy oak door behind them.

Maria looked around with interest—it was his study, warm and cozy, and likely also soundproof. And there was even a lovely fire burning in the grate, and she settled herself comfortably on the nearest opulent chair, while her husband strode to sit behind the desk, fixing her with an absurd little glare.

"You have some nerve, wife," he said, in a voice that was surely meant to be menacing. "You up and vanish for almost a *month*, and then you walk in here and behave like *this*?!"

Maria folded her hands in her lap, and felt her eyebrows rising. "Like what? Like a woman who *lives* here? A woman who's *married* to you?"

Warmisham shot another menacing little glower across the desk, his chest puffing out. "I am not," he huffed, "about to play any more of your foolish, hysterical *games*, wife!"

Something prickled unpleasantly in Maria's gut, but she felt her mouth smiling, her hands reaching to open the reticule she'd been carrying. "Excellent," she replied, "as I have no interest in playing games with you, either. So here"—she snapped down a handful of papers on the desk between them—"is what I want."

Warmisham blinked down at the papers, clearly nonplussed, so Maria reached across the desk, and spread them out before him. "Three contracts, in triplicate," she said, voice crisp. "You will sign them all. The first is the official public dissolution of our marriage, and the full reimbursement of my inheritance. And the second"—she tapped her gloved finger against the little pile—"is your immediate removal of the bounty upon my head, and the payment of the bounty to me."

Warmisham was staring at her, his eyes increasingly incredulous, but Maria ignored him, and tapped the third set of papers. "And this one maintains your public commitment to the peace-treaty you ratified. It calls for an immediate and permanent end to your war against the orcs. Oh, and the end of your horrid new money-stealing law, as well."

There was an instant's startled silence between them, Warmisham's eyes gone very wide—and then he threw back his head, and *laughed*. The movement easy, familiar, contemptuous, designed to daunt, to disconcert, to make people cower before him.

But Maria only watched, and listened, and waited until he was done. "And once you sign them," she continued, as if he hadn't interrupted, "you'll earn my reward. For as long as you keep your word."

Warmisham laughed again, though there was something darker in it, something malicious, malevolent. "You've truly lost it now, wife," he said, between chuckles. "Please *do* tell, what kind of reward you think *you* could possibly offer *me*?"

His grey eyes had flicked purposefully up and down Maria's seated form, as if to say how ugly she was, how undesirable—but suddenly, it seemed utterly preposterous that Maria had *ever* wanted this man, and she felt herself coldly gazing back, her eyes flinty on his mocking face.

"For your reward, I offer you your reputation," she replied, voice clipped. "You must have noticed, just now, how your household reacted to me? It was quite a shock, surely, to see a woman who was supposedly kidnapped and brutalized by orcs, walking around perfectly healthy and safe?"

Warmisham blinked, once, and Maria gave him a chilly, placid smile. "It was almost as though," she said, "you made a grave mistake, *husband*. Almost as though you didn't even know what happened to your own *wife*. Almost as though you're losing your edge."

The mirth had fully faded from her husband's face now, but Maria kept smiling. "I also hear some of your fellow nobles aren't overly pleased about your new wealth-stealing law. Surely they'll be *very* eager to know that you've been trying to appropriate their money under false pretenses? That your intelligence, and your judgement, was wrong? That your entire new *war* was wrong?"

And clearly Warmisham recognized the weight of that threat, because a visible trace of unease flashed through his eyes before he laughed again. Sounding perhaps more forced this time, his fingers clutching against the desk.

"That's your hysteria speaking again, wife," he said, with damnable coolness. "I am one of the most powerful men in the realm, and your own reputation is already *very* deeply compromised. No one is going to believe your baseless blackmail over the word of a duke. *No one*."

Maria felt the first snap of impatience, flicking through her belly, and she sat up straighter, looked him in the eyes. "Wrong again, *husband*," she replied. "You see, I don't need to say anything at all. All I need to do is spend a few days swanning about town, visiting and shopping, and telling everyone I know about my family emergency in Sakkin. I know all too well how gossip travels in our circles, and I know"—she jabbed her finger at the desk between them—"that it's *you* who will suffer from this. It's you who will forever be the man who launched a *war*, because he couldn't figure out where his own damned *wife* went."

Warmisham's mouth betrayed a brief grimace, his eyes narrowing. "Then I tell them I rescued you from the orcs, in a successful secret operation," he said flatly. "And you were just too overwrought to remember. Too hysterical. As usual."

Maria rearranged her skirts, and gave him another brittle smile. "Then I start sharing tales of my *very* interesting time with the orcs," she said coldly. "I'm sure all your friends and colleagues and minions would be *most* intrigued by all the sordid details, don't you?"

And there it was. The faint, unmistakable flare of *fear*, crossing her unfeeling husband's face. A sure confirmation, perhaps, that as misguided as Maria's original plan with the letters had been, that she hadn't been wrong about it, either. That its threat still held real, lasting power over this petty, pathetic, prideful *toad* of a man.

A lord, in the prime of his life, cuckolded by an orc.

"You're *delusional*," Duke Warmisham finally hissed at her. "Do you really think I'm going to let you walk out of this house, after making all these unwarranted threats toward me? Do you really think"—his lips curled into a satisfied sneer—"my staff will defy my orders, once I command them to keep safe my hysterical, runaway wife? Once we lock you up where you belong, and throw away the damned key, *forever*?!"

Good gods, this again, and suddenly Maria was done with him, with this utterly tiresome *absurdity*. "I will *never* be confined again, *ever*," she replied, curt. "And if you even *try*, in addition to your destroyed reputation, you will have an enraged band of orcs overrunning this house by *sunrise*."

Warmisham gaped at her, his eyes bugged wide, his mouth hanging open with gratifying astonishment. "You're *mad*," he spat at her. "You can't possibly do such a thing. You wouldn't. You *couldn't*."

"Couldn't I?" Maria countered. "You don't think I could have brought back a fully armed fighting-band with me, and given them detailed instructions on how to get into your cellar?"

The words rang with power, with truth—because they were, in fact, entirely true. The orcs had been willing to wager their whole peace-treaty on this, because—as Lady Norr had told Maria, with determination blazing in her eyes—there would never be any hope of lasting peace, if that damned Council wasn't dealt with. If this man wasn't dealt with.

Of course, the fighting-band was intended as a last resort, if all else failed—and they'd travelled separately from Maria and Joarr and Baldr, and remained well hidden throughout. Making sure they could be called upon if needed, while not providing this scum with any more fodder for his war.

"You—" Warmisham said now, and his gaze had sharpened on Maria, flicking up and down. Looking more closely this time, and perhaps catching on the new strength filling out her new dress, or even on the still-present trace of teeth-marks against her neck.

"You lying *lunatic*," he gasped, his eyes fixed unblinking to Maria's throat. "The orcs—the orcs *did* get you. They *did!*"

His voice had risen to almost a wail, grating against Maria's clenched teeth, and she reflexively reached into her reticule, and drew out first her dagger, and then a stone. And as Warmisham stared, aghast, she began sharpening the stone, the sound whirring through the room.

"No," she said smoothly, "the orcs got *you*, just as you feared. Now either sign my contracts, or gain a reputation as a warmongering fool, or a cuckold. Or"—she dragged her stone louder, slower—"watch your whole household fall around your feet, while I sit back and *laugh*."

Duke Warmisham's eyes were darting desperately between the contracts, and Maria's face, and her dagger. And she could see his foolish plan forming, his mouth opening, clearly about to scream for help, guards, protection against his hysterical wife—

But before a sound could escape, Maria had lunged around the desk, and thrust her dagger flat against his pale, convulsing throat. And when he flailed and scrabbled against her, she swiftly kneed him in the groin, grabbed him by the hair, yanked his head back, and let him truly feel the freshly sharpened edge of her blade.

"Or, we can do it this way," she said, only slightly out of breath, though her heart was thundering in her chest. "Should I keep going, *husband*?"

Duke Warmisham's eyes were white-rimmed with terror, his body gasping and flailing beneath her—but another swift, purposeful shove of Maria's knee against his groin jerked him back to stillness, his breaths heaving in his chest.

"You will *not* get away with this," he snarled at her. "This is black-mail. This is extortion. This is *illegal!*"

Maria shrugged, and flicked her knife against a bit of grey stubble his valet had clearly missed that morning. "It's no worse than the kind of things you do *every damned day*," she replied flatly. "Creating horrible new laws, stealing money, starting wars, sending people to their *deaths*. Oh, and manipulating an innocent, recently bereaved girl into marrying you, so you could squander her father's money, and then throw her away like yesterday's *rubbish!*"

Her husband's glare at her was pure loathing, though he'd begun looking rather white around the mouth. "I should *never* have married you, witch. Better yet, I should have sent you off to the asylum months ago, where you fucking *belong!*"

The anger was finally bubbling, hissing and skittering in Maria's chest, and she nudged the dagger harder against his throat. "Too late," she snapped at him. "And now we're doing things my way. Are you going to sign, and save your reputation, and make me go away forever? Or would you rather be the weakling duke who lost his own wife, and recklessly started a war? Or better yet"—she smiled viciously—"the fool whose so-called fortress of a house got overrun by orcs, while he wasn't fucking paying *attention*?!"

Warmisham kept spluttering, still protesting, but Maria wasn't listening anymore. Because behind him, there was a window, leading out into the garden beyond—and the sash on the window was slowly, silently sliding up. And clutching it was a clawed grey hand, attached to a familiar, silent grey form.

Joarr leapt in without a sound, flashing Maria a sly grin—and then he smoothly strode around the desk, and dropped himself into the chair. While Warmisham twitched, and then goggled, and then would have shrieked, if Maria hadn't had the forethought to knee him again, and clap her hand over his mouth.

"He's still making up his mind," she told Joarr, over her shoulder, "but he's going to sign. Aren't you, *husband*?"

Warmisham was still gaping toward Joarr, his body trembling beneath Maria's touch. "You—*disgust* me," he croaked at her. "You left your pampered, privileged life as a duchess, so you could be used and ravaged by the likes of *that*?!"

Maria glanced back at Joarr, and again felt her lips pulling up into an icy smile. "Oh, I wasn't ravaged by *him*," she said coolly. "My orc is much, *much* bigger, and far more terrifying. Perhaps next he'll pay you a visit as well, if you need a little extra incentive to keep your mouth shut? I know he'd dearly *love* to meet you."

All the remaining colour had drained from Duke Warmisham's face, and he finally sagged under Maria's grip, his mouth twisting into a petulant little pout. "You're *insane*," he insisted, as though it were the last offense he had left, as though he still held that power over her. "You've lost your *mind*."

"No," Maria said, "I've found it again. And now"—she thrust a nearby quill into his trembly hand—"you've been defeated. For good."

36

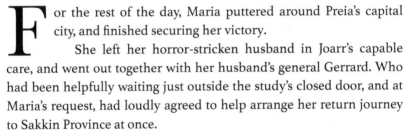

For the rest of the day, Maria puttered around Preia's capital city, and finished securing her victory.

She left her horror-stricken husband in Joarr's capable care, and went out together with her husband's general Gerrard. Who had been helpfully waiting just outside the study's closed door, and at Maria's request, had loudly agreed to help arrange her return journey to Sakkin Province at once.

The servants had been avidly watching and whispering all the while, not that Maria had cared—keeping them quiet was another hurdle her husband would need to sort out, once she was well out of his life. And after a quick stop in the estate's furthest gardening-shed, Maria was once again dressed in disguise—back in her nondescript men's clothing—and ready to face the world.

Of course, it was a significant help to have Gerrard with her, hand-delivering his employer's urgent communications—and as they moved from lawyer to council-hall to yet more lawyers, Maria teased out Gerrard's tale of how he'd been compromised by orcs. Or rather, by one particular orc—the craggy-faced Olarr, of Clan Bautul—after chasing him down in Preia's southern forest.

"Thought I could defeat him in single combat, and take back his head to the duke, and get myself a promotion," Gerrard said, with a wry, wincing grin toward Maria. "Turns out, these orcs aren't so easy to defeat, are they? I paid for my pride, let me tell you."

Maria laughed, but searched his handsome face as they crossed a busy street. "And you... *wanted* to keep supporting the orcs, after?" she asked carefully, her voice dropping. "You *chose* to change your allegiances, and serve as a spy in Warmisham's house?"

Gerrard shrugged, a faint stain of red creeping up his cheeks. "Not right away," he said. "But Warmisham doesn't do a good job of earning loyalty, or taking care of his people, does he? And the more time I spent with Olarr, the more I, well"—he shrugged again—"I started to see things differently. Started wanting to help find a new way."

The new ways again. Through knowledge, and *words*. And Maria fervently nodded as they approached their last stop of the day— another lawyer's establishment, on the very outskirts of town. "This one is mine," she said. "You'll do a circuit again, while you wait?"

Gerrard nodded, and casually kept walking as Maria stepped inside. And after a short wait, followed by a smooth explanation on her part, the lawyer handed over a familiar thick packet of letters. And then accepted an even thicker packet in return, this one featuring Rosa's neat writing across the outermost letter.

"And I'd like to arrange for yet another mailing, in another month's time," Maria told the lawyer, as she slid a small bag of clinking coins toward him. "I'll have the next set of letters delivered to you shortly, as well as further payment."

The lawyer agreed with gratifying eagerness, and even allowed Maria to burn her original letter-packet in his fire-grate. And when she walked out again, it was with a much-lightened step, and a near-giddy relief swirling in her chest.

It was done.

She'd defeated her husband. She'd delivered his incriminating signed contracts into the best possible hands, where they were sure to be immediately acted upon. And while Duke Warmisham would no doubt seek to go back on his word in multiple ways, Maria had most assuredly accomplished the forthcoming dissolution of their marriage, and had already acquired both her bounty and her inheritance, and squirrelled them safely away for future use.

And perhaps most importantly, she'd destroyed her original

letters—and instead, their intended targets would receive a plentiful variety of Rosa's well-written, thoughtfully argued treatises. A new way, with new words, telling the other side of the tales. Telling the orcs' truth.

And throughout it all, Maria had made amends. She'd shown herself a true Skai. She'd honoured her mate, and her clan. She'd proven this, not only to Simon, but to herself.

And as she strode around the corner toward where Gerrard was likely to be, there was an odd, hopeful feeling, settling into her belly. Something almost like... peace?

Until a rough, powerful hand gripped at her arm, and dragged her sideways. Yanking her staggering, flailing body off the main street, and into a narrow, shadowed alley. And when Maria kicked and punched at the foreign force dragging her, it felt hot and hard, familiar but not, because wait, *wait*—

"Silence, woman," hissed a deep, dreadful voice, as a huge hand circled tight against her neck. "Lest you wish to *die*."

37

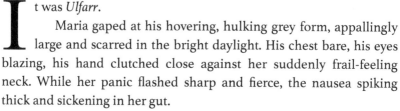

It was *Ulfarr*.

Maria gaped at his hovering, hulking grey form, appallingly large and scarred in the bright daylight. His chest bare, his eyes blazing, his hand clutched close against her suddenly frail-feeling neck. While her panic flashed sharp and fierce, the nausea spiking thick and sickening in her gut.

Ulfarr was here? In the middle of Preia? *Kidnapping* her?!

"What," she gasped, "the *fuck*, Ulfarr!"

Ulfarr's hand on her throat clenched tighter, and he bodily dragged her further down the alleyway. "I said *silence*," he growled, and when Maria kicked and flailed again, there was the distinctive, terrifying feel of pointed claws, digging into her skin. "You are mine now, woman. And you shall *obey*."

The *hell*?! Maria briefly froze against his deadly grip, long enough for Ulfarr to lunge them toward what looked to be a small *hole* in the ground. And in a swift, powerful leap, they were inside it, dropping deep into the earth—

And suddenly, all was blackness. Cold and clammy and far too close, and when Maria wildly kicked and thrashed, her legs only scraped on hard, forbidding rock. While Ulfarr kept dragging her deeper, further from the dwindling light above. No, no, this couldn't be happening, *no*—

The panic was clanging, wailing and writhing against Maria's ribs, but even stronger was the sheer disbelief, the pure pouring rage. After all she'd just done to help the orcs, to help finish that damned war for good, this prick was charging in like this and trying to ruin *everything*?!

"You can't *do* this, Ulfarr!" she shouted at him, her voice shrill. "You can't kidnap a woman from the middle of the street in the middle of a city! What if someone had seen?! Don't you realize you could have just destroyed our whole *peace-treaty* with this stupid stunt?!"

Ulfarr abruptly halted before her, his voice barking something in black-tongue—and then Maria felt the shocking, stinging feel of a *slap*, striking hard across her cheek, snapping her face sideways. "Silence!" he ordered, so close she could feel his spittle on her skin. "You are *mine*, fool woman, and you will *obey*!"

The rage shot deeper, sparking in Maria's hands and feet, thrumming into her bones. "I am not yours, and I will *not* obey!" she spat back. "I am Simon's mate! His! *Not* yours!"

There was an instant's quiet, and then—Ulfarr *laughed*. A bitter, mocking scrape, soaring harsh and terrifying down Maria's back.

"No," he said, slow, deliberate, sure. "You are mine now, woman."

The certainty rang through his voice with brutal, unnerving strength, enough that Maria jolted to stillness, her eyes wide and unseeing in the dark. *You are mine now.* As if Ulfarr had a *right* to say that. As if it were true...

Because—wait. Today had been the day. *That* day. Simon and Ulfarr's fight to the death.

And Ulfarr was here. Alive. While Simon... *wasn't*?

Maria's heart plunged deep into her belly, so forceful that she felt herself stagger sideways, her breath frozen and jagged in her lungs. No. That couldn't be what he meant. It *couldn't*.

"You—didn't," she gasped, "fight Simon today. Did you?"

Ulfarr's laugh was harsh, grating, horrible. "You are *mine*, woman," he repeated, with deadly finality, as his huge hand grasped her wrist, dragging her further into the blackness. "You shall now forget him, ach? *Forever*."

Bile rose in Maria's throat, and she choked it back, while waves of sick misery surged through her suddenly shivering form. No. It wasn't possible. *No.*

"No," she heard herself say, thin, plaintive. "You're lying to me. Simon would *never* fall to the likes of *you.*"

And that was true, it had to be true, Simon was so strong, he'd worked so hard, he would keep his kin safe. And Maria fought for that thread of certainty, clung to it with everything she had, even as the memory of his words burrowed beneath her skin.

Defeat wears many faces. You ken this fight shall be easy, or fair?

The shudders were driving through Maria now, flashing in painful flares, bright enough that she could scarcely hold herself upright. Her eyes desperately blinking in the darkness, toward where she could feel Ulfarr's awful presence, could taste the strength of his scent in the air.

Had he defeated Simon? And was he now defeating her? Their *son?*

The bubbling panic kept blazing higher, threatening to consume Maria whole, because gods, this was bad. Very bad. She clearly had no hope of escaping Ulfarr in the dark, let alone in a tunnel as rough and unfamiliar as this one. And even if Gerrard had noticed her disappearance, he still wouldn't be able to follow without light or support, and a public chase could alert an entire city of humans to the presence of orcs in their midst. And Joarr was back at Warmisham House, fully prepared to wait for however long it took, while Baldr was still stationed in the woods next to the estate. And the band of fighters Lady Norr had sent were waiting on Joarr's orders, and surely they would be nowhere near here, wherever the hell *here* was.

And Simon. If Simon was—if he was—

The vision of his bloody, broken, dead-eyed body flashed across Maria's thoughts, and she heard herself moan aloud, her head frantically shaking. No. She couldn't think of that. *No.* Think of Simon's strength. His teaching. His *approval.*

Listen. Learn. You are mine. Skai.

Maria seized for that truth, clutched it close, sucked back breath after choking breath. Listen. Learn. Skai.

She'd faced her husband. She could face this. She had to.

Her steps had stopped dragging behind Ulfarr, and he accordingly pulled her on faster, deeper into the dark. Surely intending to hurry her away, no doubt far from the city and Baldr and Joarr, from any hope of help. So that he could—what? Seduce her? *Claim* her? Seek to harm her son, or *replace* him?

The bile surged again in Maria's throat, and she gulped it down, gulped for air. She would do this. Skai. Listen. *Learn.*

So she forced her flailing attention to the corridor all around her, rough and rocky and close, occasionally still scraping against her as she passed. It was markedly different than all the other orc tunnels she'd encountered so far, all of which had suggested some level of planning, of maintenance—while this felt stale and unused, perhaps temporary or abandoned. Which surely stood to reason that it couldn't go on forever. Right?

Next Maria forced her focus to Ulfarr, to his pungent scent swarming her lungs, to the memory of his hideous face in her thoughts. To how—*wait*—he hadn't been bloody, or bruised, or broken in any way. Had he?

No, no, he hadn't. No blood, no injuries. And if Ulfarr *had* truly fought Simon today, surely he wouldn't have walked away without a scratch. *Surely.* And if Simon hadn't fought him yet, that meant...

It meant there was hope. Simon wouldn't give up. He *wouldn't.*

So Maria kept watching. Kept waiting, listening, following Ulfarr with careful steps. Feeling the tension in his grip on her wrist, the urgency in his scent, the rapid pace of his breaths. He was rushing. Taking risks. Preoccupied, perhaps. Not paying attention.

And when he finally dragged Maria up and out of the earth, back into dazzling white light, she was ready. Ready to reach for where Ulfarr's huge taut body was already pulling away, about to take her deeper into—her squinting eyes briefly darted around them—a forest. And judging by the position of the sun—something else Maria had begun to take note of, thanks to all those days travelling with Joarr—Ulfarr was planning to take her east. Away from Baldr and Joarr. Away from Orc Mountain.

He was running, then, coward that he was.

"Wait," Maria gasped, as her hand grabbed at Ulfarr's meaty shoulder. "Ulfarr. Please. Just a moment."

Ulfarr whirled around to glare at her, the urgency bright in his narrow eyes—but in return, Maria smiled at him. Hopeful, rueful, with as much warmth as she could possibly manage.

"Look, I realize when I've been defeated, all right?" she said, her voice only slightly wavering. "But I still don't even *know* you. And you don't know me. So before you do this"—she took a step closer—"can't we at least get to know one another first? Like you offered back at the mountain?"

Ulfarr's eyes flared with suspicion, but Maria ignored it, and instead took another step closer, her gaze steady on his, her shoulders as relaxed as she could make them. "Even just a little?" she asked, as she twisted her trembling hand sideways in his still-clutching grip, enough to stroke it against his bare chest. "I will admit, I do like big males. I like"—she drew in breath—"to be filled, you know?"

Ulfarr's heart was floundering under Maria's hand, his still-narrow eyes searching her face—but then his gaze darted, brief but telling, toward the west. Prompting Maria to lurch even closer, into his pungent scent, so that their bodies were almost fully touching. So that she could feel the telltale nudge of swollen heat, rising slow but true beneath his trousers—

"Just for a moment?" she murmured, spreading her fingers wider on the sticky skin of his chest. "I thought you big Skai boys liked to claim your hunts in public places like this? Make us spurt and squeal upon you?"

The suspicion sparked even higher in Ulfarr's eyes, but he wasn't refusing, and that heat at his groin was swelling fuller, larger. Nearly in the same place as Simon's had been, around the same height, and Maria held his eyes, ground herself a little closer against him. Feeling it, learning it, stroking her other hand over her hip toward it...

And in a breath, a desperate prayer to Skai-kesh, her dagger-hilt was in her fingers. Gripped sure and close and familiar, as pure instinct flooded through her body. Steady her feet. Feel the earth, the strength in her torso. Turn the blade. Adjust her aim. And...

The dagger slashed sharp and deep, slicing sheer and powerful against that ridge in Ulfarr's trousers. Flashing first shock across his watching eyes, and then a convulsive, wide-eyed agony, as something hot and sticky spurted onto Maria's fingers. Something that surely wasn't pleasure, but instead reeked of iron and salt. Of *blood*.

Ulfarr's howl tore through the air, the pain and rage contorting his face, his hands clasped to his bloody groin. And when Maria belatedly leapt away, her whole body trembling, he lurched after her, claws swiping between them—but then he bent double again, his hands clutching back to his groin.

"You almost cut it off, you sneaking human *hag*!" he shouted at her, between gasping breaths. "You shall make amends to me for this! You shall writhe and *scream* under my rut, and worship bloody and broken at my *feet*, you—"

But before he could finish, something new shot through the air. Something huge and grey and swinging, crashing straight into Ulfarr's bent-double body, and hurling him whole to the earth.

Simon.

38

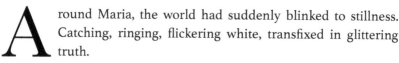

Around Maria, the world had suddenly blinked to stillness.
Catching, ringing, flickering white, transfixed in glittering
truth.

Simon was *here*.

And not just here. Everywhere. *Everything*. Swarming Maria's lungs
with his familiar scent, filling her ears with his roar, flooding her eyes
with the fluid, capable power of his furious fighting form. His fists
flying into Ulfarr's belly and face, spattering blood in a wide arc,
unleashing a yelping, broken howl from Ulfarr's throat.

Ulfarr somehow shoved back against the onslaught, blocking
Simon's next punch, keeping one hand cupped over his still-spurting
groin. But Simon was far too strong, too fast, and Maria clutched her
own bloody hands against her pounding heart as he flew into Ulfarr
again. His fist landing with a sickening crunch against Ulfarr's nose,
his muscular leg driving straight into Ulfarr's bloody groin.

Ulfarr roared and retched and then rounded up again, striking for
Simon's undefended gut with his fists. But there was no pain in
Simon's answering growl, no defeat—only sheer, vicious fury, rippling
raw and deep up Maria's shivering spine. And at Ulfarr's next attack,
Simon landed a pulverizing blow into his belly, hurling him back
against the earth, where he wailed and writhed at Simon's booted feet.

"This shall be a slaughter, ach?" said a cheerful voice beside Maria, making her leap near out of her skin—but it was only *Joarr*, good gods, leaning casually against the nearest tree, flashing her his quick, sly smile. "This was much help," he continued, "when you near cut off Ulfarr prick. Make mate proud."

He jerked his head toward Simon's still-raging form, which was currently driving repeated punches into Ulfarr's bent-double waist. "Um," Maria said, fighting for words, for air. "Good? I think? But how—where did you—*Warmisham*—"

She helplessly flapped her hands around them, and thankfully Joarr seemed to follow without effort. "Duke having happy nap," he said with a wink, as he plucked a tiny mushroom from his pocket, tossed it in the air, and then tucked it away again. "And Baldr has smelt Ulfarr and Simon hunting us for many days now. Only no wished to frighten you with this, ach?"

Wait. Ulfarr had been following them for *days*? And Joarr and Baldr had *known*?! And wait, Joarr was nodding toward Maria's other side—toward where *Baldr* had indeed appeared. Looking briefly sheepish, before his eager eyes flicked back to the still-ongoing brawl before them.

"We knew you wished to focus on facing this duke, Maria," Baldr said. "And you may be sure, you were not once in true danger. Not with Simon tracking Ulfarr thus."

Maria's gaze had darted back to Simon too, watching him kick and punch Ulfarr's cowering form with graceful, ferocious ease. "But Ulfarr—he *kidnapped* me," she managed. "In the middle of the *street!*"

A surprising flare of anger lit up Baldr's eyes as he glanced at her, his arms crossing over his tunic. "Ulfarr is a fool," he said, voice clipped. "As if the Ka-esh do not know all the old ways all over Preia—and as if they should not then share this knowledge with Simon, so we may help keep his mate safe? After Simon has sought to keep the Ka-esh safe also, unlike the other Enforcers before him?"

Maria couldn't stop frowning at Baldr, despite the odd, hitching warmth surging through her chest. "But—you *couldn't* have been there with us," she protested. "Ulfarr didn't even *smell* you!"

Baldr winced, and on Maria's other side Joarr laughed aloud, merry and mocking. "You hide naught from a clever Skai, ach?" he said. "That was Baldr, woman. You ken he gain this place as captain's Left Hand by only his sweetness, or his tight pretty arse?"

Baldr winced again, darting Joarr a dark, reproachful look—which Joarr returned with another laugh, and a meaningful glance behind Baldr. To where—Maria blinked—*Drafli* had also appeared, striding straight toward them.

But Drafli wasn't looking at Joarr or Maria, or even at Simon and Ulfarr's still-brawling bodies beyond. No, he was only looking at Baldr, his eyes glimmering and intent.

And in this moment, for perhaps the first time, Maria's stilted, disordered thoughts could maybe—maybe—see what Baldr saw in Drafli. It was the ease in how he walked, the grace in his lean prowling form, the expressiveness in his speaking black eyes. In the way his long fingers snapped up to flick at Baldr's cheek, quick and light, in a silent question, perhaps even a command. *Look at me*, it meant. *I'm here.*

But Baldr's answering glance toward Drafli was furtive, brief, uncertain. And when he looked away again, his gaze sliding back to Simon and Ulfarr, Maria saw it for the refusal—or even the rejection—it was. A rejection that Drafli clearly saw too, and Maria didn't miss the telltale tightness on his mouth, the hint of bleakness in his glinting black eyes.

A blood-curdling howl from Ulfarr abruptly jerked Maria's attention to Simon again, to where—she winced—Ulfarr's leg was now bent at an unnatural, awful-looking angle. And Simon's huge, fluid form was slamming Ulfarr forcefully to the ground, his hand gripped tight around his neck.

"You shall yield before your kin, Ulfarr," Simon ordered, his deep voice carrying—and Maria realized, with another jolt of shock, that there were somehow more orcs, standing all around. Their tall, still forms almost blending in with the trees, their eyes fixed on the sight before them.

"Never," Ulfarr gasped, hoarse and broken, and Maria could see blood staining his mouth, slipping down his scarred cheek. "Finish it."

Finish it. Because this was—this was a fight to the death. This was Simon defending his place as Enforcer, permanently. This was the victory Simon had fought for. The victory he surely deserved.

"Finish it," Ulfarr gasped again, his voice almost pleading. "Do what you did to my father."

His *father*? But—oh. Right. Of course. Ulfarr's father had been Enforcer, Simon had said, for many summers. Until—

Maria felt her eyes squeezing shut, her body bracing for the impact, for Ulfarr's final croaks, for a dead-eyed emptiness left behind. And despite everything Ulfarr had said and done, suddenly there was a furious, desperate urge to rush forward, to grasp at Simon, to beg and plead, to stop the revenge, the death, the winnowing of his kin, *please*—

"Your father deserved this, for all the harm he brought to our kin," Simon's voice said, powerful, utterly certain—and when Maria's eyes blinked open, it was to the sight of Simon glancing toward... *Tristan and Salvi*? Yes, they had somehow appeared too, standing at the rear of the other orcs, their eyes on Simon's face. And as Maria watched, Salvi slid his arm around Tristan's shoulder, and pulled him close.

"Then finish it," Ulfarr wheezed again. "Do your *job*, Enforcer."

But above him, Simon—*stood*. The movement smooth, sure, just as certain as his voice had been. And as he towered huge and menacing over Ulfarr, he brushed off his hands, flicking drops of blood down onto Ulfarr's convulsing, defeated body.

"Ach, I no ken I shall," Simon replied, cool, clipped. "Salvi, come tend to him, ach? And Efterar, *you* only help if he is near death."

Simon's eyes had angled sideways as he spoke, to where—Maria stared—Efterar and Kesst had also materialized, standing still and silent amidst the circle of watching orcs. And in response to Simon's statement, Efterar accordingly shrugged, while a look of unmistakable satisfaction stole across Kesst's black eyes.

"And no one shall heal *this*," Simon continued, with a dismissive flick of his hand toward Ulfarr's bloody groin, "with no my leave. No until our fallen brother *earns* this reward, ach? Until he works for our clan, and our kin, as one who seeks to be an Enforcer should. Until he again gains my trust."

Something warm and flickery was sparking in Maria's chest, and only bubbled higher when Simon slowly turned. His movements so fluid and careless, his clawed hands easy at his sides, his gaze sweeping over the watching orcs. Settling, oh so briefly, on Maria, before passing by again.

And as Maria followed his eyes, she realized, with a true jolt, that nearly all these orcs were Skai. Apart from Kesst and Efterar, Tristan and Salvi, and Baldr, they were all orcs she'd met over these past days—orcs like Killik and Halthorr and Fulnir, Balgarr and Igull and Argarr. The Skai whose allegiance Simon had worked so hard to gain.

"I am your Enforcer," Simon's voice continued, unwavering. "And this is my judgement, upon an orc who sought to steal a woman his brother has claimed. This is my judgement upon an orc who sought to break the peace our brothers have so fiercely fought for. This is my judgement upon an orc who sought to claim my place, and then *ran* from me, to hunt *my* woman."

No one moved or spoke, beyond Ulfarr's choking breaths, and Simon prowled around him in a circle, again fixing his gaze to his fellow Skai as he passed. "Shall any of you stand against me in this?" he demanded. "Shall any of you spurn my judgement, or back Ulfarr's claim against me as Enforcer?"

There was yet more silence, and more shivery warmth in Maria's belly as Simon held his eyes to hers, and then passed by again. As if she truly were a Skai, able to question him, to challenge him, to freely speak as she wished.

But no one moved, protested, spoke. At least, until Simon had finished another prowling circle, his glittering eyes again catching on Maria, then on Joarr beside her. And this time Joarr laughed aloud, the sound blithe and bright in the stilted silence.

"Ach, no, brother," he said firmly, his voice carrying. "No after a lone human felled him with only a dagger, ach? With *your* dagger. Upon *your* teaching."

Joarr smirked at Maria as he spoke, and she could feel Simon's eyes flicking back toward her too, warm, *approving*. "Ach," Simon said, voice gruff. "My woman has learnt much from her time with the Skai. She has brought me great honour."

Great honour? A hard ripple of heat raced up Maria's back, her disbelieving eyes fixed to Simon's face—but yes, good gods, he'd meant that. Great honour. From *her*?

"Ach," Simon murmured, and it was as though his eyes were

looking into her, through her. "And this woman has taught me much, also."

She had? But Simon was still seeing her, still nodding, still *approving.* "You ken, my brothers," he said, "how this woman tasted, when first I brought her before you? You tasted her shame? Her fear?"

None of the orcs replied, but Maria could suddenly feel the force of their attention on her, their judgement. Their memories of that moment, when she'd stood in her loincloth before them, trembling, terrified.

"Maria came here seeking freedom," Simon continued, his voice flat. "Seeking *peace,* amidst the suffering she had borne. I saw this. I *knew* this. Even as I knew I must lead a rut upon her, to gain her for my own, in the ways of our fathers. Ach?"

Still no one spoke, and Simon started striding again, catching his brothers' eyes as he passed. "I *forsook* this way," he said, "to gain this woman's peace. And in this"—his eyes flicked back to hers, held there—"I have gained much more. I have gained her blade, and her hunger, and her ripe womb. I have gained her willing, eager fealty. Ach?"

There was more silence, watchful and careful, as the orcs' glances kept searching Maria, prickling against her skin. But her own eyes remained fixed to Simon, to his certainty, his strength.

"Thus, in the face of this," he said, "I call the Skai to seek a new way, with this rut our fathers granted us. I no call for an *end* to this, but"—his gaze again swept over the watching orcs—"for a *choice,* for our mates. I call for them to *choose* this rut. To choose when, and where, and *who.*"

And where there might have once been panic, there was instead warmth, spreading wider, burrowing into Maria's belly. While her mate's deadly, powerful eyes once again caught to hers, holding her, knowing her, *approving.*

"I wish to gain our mates' true hunger," Simon said, his voice deepening. "I wish to hear them beg for our strong Skai ploughing, whilst all our clan bears witness. Ach?"

And as Maria looked at him, it was as though the warmth smoked, smouldered, and flashed up into furious, crackling flame. *Wish to gain our mates' true hunger. Wish to hear them beg for our strong Skai ploughing...*

Simon was making a new way. Seeking it, here, with his words, with these orcs' perceptions, with *her*. And now he was tossing it toward her, alight and alive and bursting with power. With *hope*.

And Maria caught it. Held it. Treasured it. Her mate, the father of her son, knowing her. Trusting her. Honouring her. Skai.

"I love you, Simon," she said to his watching, glinting eyes, her voice quiet but clear. "And I would be honoured if you would lead a rut upon me, at any time or place you might wish. But only"—she smiled, warm, rueful—"with you? Please?"

And in the stunned, stilted silence, there was—*peace*. Peace in the way Maria's mate was smiling at her, so slow, so crooked, so true. In the way he prowled closer, his huge hand catching hers within it, and raising it to his mouth. In the way—the craving kindled, exploded—he sucked off her fingers, one by one, his tongue twining and caressing, cleaning off the remnants of Ulfarr's *blood*.

"Ach, my pretty one," he purred. "Then kneel for your Skai, and grant me my prize."

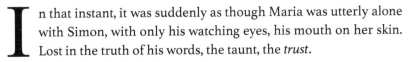

39

In that instant, it was suddenly as though Maria was utterly alone with Simon, with only his watching eyes, his mouth on her skin. Lost in the truth of his words, the taunt, the *trust*.

Kneel, and grant me my prize.

It was a challenge, a chance—and good gods, Maria was taking it. Snatching it, and pelting away with it, and *grinning* at him. Warm, fierce, loyal, brave. Unashamed.

"Of course, Simon," she whispered back, as she slipped her hand out to his chest, spread it against his wildly beating heart. "Whatever you wish."

And with that, she dropped to her knees. Not looking, not thinking, only frantically grasping for the front of her mate's trousers, and yanking them downwards. Freeing the swollen, leaking monster within, already prodding hot and hungry against her parted lips.

Fuck. Maria opened wide, sucked him deep, her eyes furiously fluttering—because oh gods, the *taste* of him, all slick fiery sweetness, exploding on her tongue. And after so long, it was like breath, like *life*, like *everything*. Like there was nothing else to do but drag on it, sucking it out in thick, decadent streams, gulping it down her starving throat. Needing her orc's seed, his approval, his *honour*.

And it was there, surely, in the low rumble from his chest, in the way his clawed hands had carded into her hair. Guiding her hungry mouth back and forth upon him, sliding her up and down his ridged, massive length, while Maria suckled and swallowed, moaning aloud with the longing, the relief, the pure, pulsating *bliss*.

And when her mate grunted, and yanked fully away from her, Maria didn't resist, didn't protest. Only held her mouth open as he grasped his girth in an easy clawed hand, and then—*sprayed* himself out onto her. Spattering hot streams across her tongue, her lips, her cheeks. Even easing it back and forth, so that he might better spread it out over her, marking her with his scent, his claim, his *approval*.

It left Maria blinking, kneeling, and dripping with succulent slippery heat—and as Simon's hand moved to smear the mess on her face, it was sheer instinct to lean into his touch, to trail her hungry tongue against her swollen lips. To take all this orc would give her, to worship with utter devotion at her Enforcer's feet.

And gods, the way he was *looking* at her, his eyes bright, blazing. And when his thumb skated across Maria's bottom lip, she lunged for it, suckling it, biting it—and that was surely a groan, growling from his throat.

"Gods, I want you, Simon," she whispered, before he could ask, against the warmth of his skin. "Take me? Flaunt me? Please?"

And as those eyes shone upon hers, Maria suddenly felt the depth of this moment. Of her pleading, her kneeling, her worship. Creating a new rite, a new way—not only for Simon and his clan, but for Simon and *herself*. Simon had cleansed her, Enforced her, made her a Skai, kept her safe. Kept his word, kept that contract, even after she'd broken it. He was worthy, he was *true*, and right now he was all Maria wanted. Every single craving poured to perfect life, standing here huge and bloody and menacing, blinking down into her soul with beautiful black eyes.

"Please, Simon," she said again, her voice breaking. "Please, take me. Let me honour you in this. Let me *worship* you."

Another rasping groan burned from his throat, those black lashes fluttering—and in a whirl of fluid motion, his hands curved close around Maria, and swept her flat onto her back on the mossy knoll beneath them. Catching her wild eyes with his, his gaze glinting with such meaning, such warmth, such *approval*.

"Ach, my pretty one," he breathed, his voice curling into Maria's belly, into her heart. "I shall grant you my rut. I shall make you spurt and squeal upon me."

Maria frantically, eagerly nodded, and Simon flashed her that grin of his, crooked, true. And in an easy swipe of his hand, he caught both her wrists at once, clenching them together, drawing them up above her head.

"And you shall show me all that is mine," he continued, the softness of his words at sudden, surreal odds with his other hand, catching on the neck of her tunic—and then dragging downwards in a sharp slice, cutting through the fabric with glorious ease. "You shall flaunt my prize before me."

Maria gasped and shivered beneath him, but again, there was only the craving, deep, dark, desperate. And surging still higher when—she moaned aloud—both her bare breasts popped free, jutting up into the cool air, their brown nipples pointing hard and hungry toward the darkening sky.

"Pretty," Simon murmured, as his fingers gently tweaked at one hard peak, and then the other. "I shall take great joy in smearing my seed against these. In seeing them bounce and jiggle as I plough you."

Good *gods*. Maria shuddered again, the warmth and the hunger quavering from her head to her feet, and Simon smiled again, more challenging this time, flashing her a mouth full of sharp, vicious orc-teeth. "Ach, this shall surely please you, my pretty one," he said, as he began tearing again, slicing through more fabric, ripping Maria's trousers apart, yanking off her loincloth and dagger. "It is no every woman who gains only the greatest prick of the Skai, in her rut."

That prompted several answering noises of disapproval, from somewhere very far away, but Simon didn't even seem to notice, his black eyes glittering on hers. "You have sought to keep yourself open for me, ach?" he breathed. "You have used the gift I sent with you, to keep yourself ready for my taking?"

Maria jerked a frantic nod, and that approval again flashed in his eyes. While his hands slid firm and proprietary down her bare front, pausing to caress against the very slight swell at her waist. And then slipping lower as his huge powerful thighs, still wearing trousers, eased between her legs, and thrust them wide apart.

There was no denying Maria's grating gasp, no way to hide the answering throbs of her swollen, exposed heat. And Simon was watching, smiling, *amused*, as he grasped her parted thighs, and spread them even wider, blatant, obscene.

"Ach, mark this," he breathed, boasted, over his shoulder—and Maria could only stare and shiver as she saw several other orcs stepping around to look. Witnessing her bared form, her splayed thighs, the swollen, clenching, dripping-wet heat between them...

One of the orcs laughed, saying something in black-tongue, and Simon answered in kind, the smooth words pooling easy off his tongue. While he shifted his weight between Maria's thighs, using his own legs to open hers wider, so he could drop his hand between, and *stroke* her.

Maria started and moaned, and in return more of the orcs laughed—but not Simon. No, Simon was still stroking, his fingers teasing gently up and down her parted crease, his eyes intent on the sight. On where—Maria jerked again—he was nudging those fingers against her, making her clench and flare upon him, showing the bare truth of her hunger to all these watching orcs—

"Ach, you shall milk me thus, woman," he purred, and Maria's ragged whine escaped on its own, rippling through the clearing all around. Earning more laughter from the watching orcs, but somehow it didn't feel insulting, not with Simon looking at her like this, his lips parted, black lashes fluttering. "You bear a good womb, ach, my pretty one? Wet, ripe. Fat and open. Strong enough to berth a Skai, and bear a hale, hearty son."

Maria nodded again, jerky and fervent, and Simon flashed her another toothy grin, his body shifting forward, *approving*—and oh gods, this was happening, finally, *finally*. That slick, sleek, dripping-wet cockhead just brushing at where his fingers had been, kissing, nudging, *cleansing*.

"Open for your Skai," he ordered her, his hardness now shuddering close against her, seeking its way inside. "Taste me. Milk me. *Suckle*. Ach?"

Maria was writhing, dragging for air, and still nodding. Yes, yes, *gods*, yes, and that slick swelling heft was already pressing forward, driving deeper and deeper, spreading her wider and wider. Feeling even more massive than it ever had before, stretching her around its width, tighter and tighter until he'd slowed to a stop, the pressure wincing and dancing across her fluttering eyes—

"Ach, she is full," said another voice, from far away. "This is all you shall get, with your *great prick*."

There was more laughter from above, and then a thick grunt from Simon, a hard flex of the solid flesh jammed up into Maria's taut heat. "Ach, no," he said, breathless, and Maria felt his invading pole draw out slightly, the faintest of reprieves in the chaos. "I am only gentle with her, ach? She has learnt to suckle my full prick. She has learnt the joy of a Skai, sunk to the bollocks in her fat, ripe womb. She has learnt how to *honour* me. Ach, my pretty one?"

Yes, *yes*, and Maria nodded as she fought to relax, to welcome him. As her hands wrenched out of his gentle grip, fluttering to clutch at his broad back, to yank him closer, harder, please, *now*—

He chuckled, low and indulgent, as his eyes dropped to the sight between them. To his veined, visibly vibrating hardness, swelled larger than Maria had ever seen it, jutting halfway up inside her. Pulsing its slick heat into her, preparing her, easing his way...

And when he bore down again, driving his way inside, Maria smoothly, willingly took it. Gasping and choking at the mingled shock and pleasure, at the jagged sparking streams of warmth, at how the whole world kept curling tighter, wrapping closer, condensing down to this. To her mate's massive pole of a prick, ramming into her, splitting her as wide as she would go. Her body furiously writhing and clamping, punched full of rutting orc, consuming her, owning her, *honouring* her—

And in one last, breathless thrust, he sank all the way home. His huge, bulging bollocks shoved deep into Maria's parted crease, his massive cock seated full and hot within. And Maria was shrieking, howling, arching up beneath him, needing his rut, his power, his *ecstasy*.

"Please, Simon, *please*," she babbled, begged, her prickling fingers yanking him tighter against her. "More. *More*."

His jerky nod was sheer, trammelling relief, his hands shifting to grip at Maria's hips. And then he drew back, dragging himself out, slow, agonizing—and then plunged in again. Skewering her whole upon him, and Maria shouted and kicked and flailed, oh fuck, oh gods, oh please...

He did it again, harder this time, hurling himself against her, his hips slamming, his eyes rolling back. And then again, and again, driving her shouts higher and shriller, taking her, claiming her, owning her, cleansing her, his Skai, his mate, *his*—

And with one more deep, gouging plunge, the proof of it soared, and shattered. Simon's roar rumbling as he spurted out within her, pumping her full of his fierce, fiery approval.

Maria's entire body had curled up with the power of it, clinging to him as the ecstasy swung and swerved—but even lost in the chaos, there was still something else. Something more, in the way Simon was dragging his still-pulsing hardness out of her, and watching the resulting mess with something that might have been satisfaction, or hunger, or both.

"You no ken we are done, ach?" he growled at her, his voice husky and hot. "You no ken a pretty, ripe woman like you escapes a Skai rut with only this?"

There were grunts and hoots of appreciation beyond them, but Maria's full attention was locked on Simon, on that certain challenge in his eyes. "Then give me more," she choked, her hands again clutching and clawing at him, fighting to drag him closer. "Please."

And oh gods, he was already doing it. Already grasping her thighs, tilting them up and back, so that he might better access the next empty part of her. The part of her that was already twitching in anticipation, and soaking wet from the still-streaming slick above it.

"Ach, you shall have more," Simon purred, promised, as that rounded head settled there, slow and purposeful. "Suck me deep into your rump. Milk out more good seed from me. Ach?"

Yes, yes, Maria would, everything, *yes*—and as he once again impaled her flailing, convulsing body upon him, it was almost like rapture, like delirium. Like euphoria had unfurled itself within her, swerving and swiving and shrieking, and all she could do was open wide, welcome it, fly with it into the deep.

And if it was shameful to be ploughed like this, dripping and screaming, struck full of pounding orc, Maria didn't notice. Didn't care. Only arched and wept and begged, while the pleasure pummelled again and again. While her orc once again poured her full of him, his black hair loose around his head now, flying back as he arched and strove and howled his release to the sky.

And when he drew out again, leaving more bubbling slick in his wake, pouring out of both gaping-open places at once—the blaze only shot brighter, the chaos crashing white behind Maria's eyes. Her mouth wailing and pleading, her hands raking at her deadly, rutting orc as he next eased up over her, straddling her waist. As he then gripped both her jiggling breasts with his huge clawed hands, crushing them close together—and then slowly, smoothly, slid his still-dripping heft tight between.

Fuck, *fuck*, the sight of him, the scent of him, so close, hurling Maria ever deeper into the abyss—and when he sprayed out again, painting her neck and her face with yet more of him, there was only pride, primal and raw, so potent that Maria's furious fluttering hands slipped into it, rubbing it against her, coating herself in its truth. Needing more, aching for more, her tongue now frantically licking off her slick fingers—and thank the gods Simon gave her more, easing further up over her, stroking himself with an easy clawed hand. While his other hand slid a finger into Maria's mouth, pulling it wide open, so he could spray even more bounty down into her waiting, eager throat.

Maria gulped back every last drop, even as she begged for more, the chaos wailing and wheeling—but then stuttering as Simon put his hand to her mouth. Holding his fingers there, firm against her sticky lips, in a silent command that she instantly obeyed, her voice breaking to silence, her soaking, reeking, dripping body jittering to stillness under his touch.

"Only once more, my hungry one," he murmured at her. "I must no push you too far, ach? Must no lose you, or break you. Must keep you whole, and *safe*. At peace."

Oh. Something new burned through Maria's trembling body, something that drew yet another hoarse, helpless moan from her mouth. Something that made her tingling hands grasp once more for him, yanking him close—and he came easily this time, without a trace of resistance in his huge, powerful form. Only understanding her, knowing her, as he knelt over her, slipped his legs back between hers, and sank home, one more time.

But it was quiet this time, easy, sweet. It was him once more finding the place he'd already claimed and filled. Him first and last, he'd told her about the rut that day, and Maria desperately clung to him, drinking up this final dropping truth, the whispering certainty amidst the maelstrom. Her mate making her his, in every possible way, before all his clan—and now finishing it. Writing it, swearing it, just as strong as his contract, his Enforcing. His. Skai.

And when his skittering lips found Maria's pulsing neck, she tilted her head, dragged him closer. And then arched up, gasped her relief, as sharp teeth sank deep, his throat convulsing in tandem with the fluid, familiar drive of his hips against her. His. Skai.

The pleasure whirled up steady and smooth this time, spinning Maria around it, securing her in the sheer magnitude of his devotion, his *safety*. Holding her here, drinking her lifeblood in reverent gulps as he eased in and out of her, as though she were something perfect, private, precious. As though this was his vow, sworn with seed and teeth, with an orc on his knees, with the fear and longing and blessing flaring full and fulfilled between them.

The relief flashed like thunder, like a thudding blow into the earth. With Maria once again crying out, arching against her mate, while the spasms shot out in wave after furious wave. While Simon drove deep once more, his huge, rutting beast swelling even fuller, as if locking her there, stretched and skewered and exposed, nearly enough to break—

And then *he* broke. His howl roaring through the trees, his face contorted with vicious pleasure, as his clamped-tight heft seized again and again, pumping Maria full of hot molten ecstasy. Owning her, marking her inside and out, flooding her with his scent, his power, his *victory*.

And then, finally, all was quiet. The earth beneath, the sky above, the witnesses all around. Until finally Simon hauled in a thick, shuddering breath, and carefully drew up and away. His huge body slightly trembling, his mouth smeared with red, his hazy eyes dark and intent on Maria's face.

"You honour me, my Maria," he said, his voice almost painfully soft. "You are a great gift. You bring me such joy."

Maria was still shivering, blinking toward his eyes—but she felt her head jerk a nod, her tingling hand twitching against his chest, finding its place against his thundering heart.

"And you honour me, Simon," she whispered back. "Thank you, for granting this to me."

And in another world, another life, surely Maria would never have *thought* of thanking an orc for such a thing. For baring her like this, flaunting her like this, having his filthy way with her on a dirty forest floor. For drenching her all over with his leavings, coating her with his scent, filling her mouth and her womb and her very *innards* with him...

But instead, Maria felt only relief. *Peace*. Even as Simon abruptly eased up to his feet again, tying his trousers with swift fingers. Standing tall and imperious between her still-sprawled legs, his eyes flicking up and down her pliant, grimy body. Lingering first on her heated face, then her sticky-wet breasts, and then on the dual mess still oozing from between her thighs. Almost as if—as if he were assessing her. *Judging* her.

But lying here at his feet, sprawled and sated and painted in his scent, Maria still felt no fear. No shame. Only watched, waited, while her mate's blood-stained lips slowly, surely, curled up. Smug. Certain. *Approving*.

"Shall any of you Skai stand against me in this?" he said finally, his deep voice rumbling through the trees. "Shall any of you stand against the right of my claim upon this woman, through this rut she has so eagerly borne? Shall any of you say this should no please our Skai fathers? This should no please Skai-kesh?"

He'd waved a casual hand toward Maria's sprawled, dripping form—and suddenly she could feel the weight of the surrounding orcs' eyes. The weight of them watching, learning, seeking truth. Skai.

"Anyone?" Simon demanded, the challenge chilly on his voice. "Shall any of you claim that a woman taken thus—or even an orc taken thus—yet no belongs to the one who has done this?"

Still no one spoke, though Maria could see several of the orcs glancing toward one another, their eyes silently speaking. Judging, perhaps. Weighing this new way. Seeking truth.

And finally it was Joarr who stepped forward, his gaze cool and satisfied on Simon's face. "Ach, no," he said, inclining his spiky head. "I see your gain, Skai, and wish you a strong son."

The words sounded strangely formal, somehow—and now there were more orcs saying it, too. Some speaking in the common-tongue, some in black-tongue, but surely all holding the same meaning. A rite, maybe. A vow.

And even Drafli was agreeing, mouthing the words, making a quick, fluid motion with his hands. And for perhaps the first time since they'd met, his eyes on Maria weren't angry, or contemptuous. Instead, they looked almost... *longing*, as they angled toward Baldr beside him, and then quickly away again.

"I thank you, my kin," Simon replied, once the orcs' voices had fallen silent again. "I welcome you to seek this way also—but only *after* you have gained the trust of the one you would seek to claim. Ach?"

There were some scattered nods from the watching Skai, even a few brief smiles—and then the orcs seemed to melt away again. Fading back into the trees, their forms disappearing into the darkening light.

And when Maria blinked around her again, there were only a few orcs left. Joarr, Baldr and Drafli, Kesst and Efterar. And—she twitched—Tristan and Salvi, both of them bent over *Ulfarr*, good gods. Who'd still apparently been lying there all this time, though he at least appeared unconscious at this point, and didn't even flinch as Salvi pulled his broken leg straight with an awful-looking yank.

"Are we clear, you ken?" Simon said to Joarr, his voice low. "Is there aught more to face? With this duke, mayhap? Or orcs yet sworn to Ulfarr?"

Joarr gave a dismissive shrug, a brief glance northward. "I ken no," he said. "But I shall keep a band here, and send you word, ach? You no fret over this. You fret"—he jerked his head toward Maria, still sprawled in the dirt at Simon's feet—"over your mate, ach?"

Joarr winked at Maria as he spoke, but Simon visibly grimaced, and his eyes flicking up and down Maria's body looked far different than before. Not proud or smug this time, but perhaps... uneasy. Uncertain.

But before Maria could search that, react to that, he'd grabbed for her nearby loincloth and dagger, and then knelt and swept her up into his arms. Not seeming to notice the utter mess of her, and instead tucking her tight and close against his bare chest, against the steady patter of his familiar beating heart.

"Peace, my brave one," he murmured, his breath warm against her hair, and she could feel him striding, carrying her across the clearing. "Efterar, you shall look over her, ach? And Arnthorr, also?"

Arnthorr. Their *son*. As if he were already real, already here, and Maria felt her shaky hand skitter to her waist, her bleary eyes blinking up at Simon's face. She hadn't often dwelled on Arnthorr's presence these past days, let alone the name Simon had given him—in fact, she'd fought very hard not to think of him at all, for reasons she hadn't wanted to consider too closely. But suddenly there was the realization, giddy and oddly staggering, that maybe it was safe to face this again. To see it as real again. To be—*free*?

"You grant your leave for this, Maria?" Efterar asked, and at her answering nod, she felt his cool hand gently touching to her bare back, and then slipping up, and down, and sideways.

"All is well," Efterar said, after a moment. "You bear no tearing or bruising, and your son—Arnthorr, you say?—feels hale, and already large for his days. Now you should rest, and eat, and drink more of your mate's good seed."

This seemed an entirely surreal pronouncement, considering how full Maria's belly currently felt, and beside Efterar Kesst huffed a laugh, his head shaking. "Gods, Eft, if she has any more, she's going to explode, aren't you, sweetheart?" he said lightly. "You positively *reek* of Skai, you must know. How many times did you blow, Simon? Five?"

"Six," Simon corrected him, voice flat. "As if I were a band of five, ach?"

Right. Because the orc leading the rut—the main orc—would have done so twice. And perhaps Maria ought to have been offended at just how calculated that clearly had been, but she was too caught on the look in Kesst's eyes. Wry, rueful, almost *impressed*.

"Well, if you two have truly just managed to rid your clan of that awful practice from the fucking *dark ages*," Kesst said, his voice both scathing and amused, "you have my respect. Maybe Grim won't need to tear into the lot of you after all."

A tenuous warmth was skittering up Maria's spine—had Kesst just spoken as if *she* were a Skai, too?—and here was the feel of Simon's mouth, brushing soft against her forehead. "Ach, it is thanks to my brave mate that we have earned this," he said, hoarse. "And I thank you for your help also, Efterar. And you, Salvi."

He said the last over his shoulder, and Maria caught a hazy glimpse of Salvi waving a bloody hand, dismissing it. "I refuse to clean your filthy room *ever again*, though," he called back. "After this, we are *square*, Simon."

Simon snorted a laugh, and then spun on his heel and strode away. Hoisting Maria's sticky body a little closer as he walked through the trees, deeper and deeper, until she heard the distinctive sound of rushing water. And when Simon settled her down again, it was on a small patch of grass, close beside the surge of a bubbling stream.

"Stay, my brave one," he murmured, "whilst I care for you."

With that, he yanked out a rag—what might have been the remnants of Maria's tattered tunic—and dipped it in the water. And with careful, gentle strokes, he began wiping her clean. Starting with her face, smoothing carefully over her eyes, her cheeks, her mouth, before moving steadily, slowly downwards.

It still felt bizarrely unreal, in a day that had already been full of utter impossibilities, and Maria watched him with dazed, hazy eyes. Drinking up the tenderness in his touch, the faint tremble of his fingers on her skin. The way his head was bowed over her, his long hair still hanging loose, his eyes not quite meeting hers.

"So I take it," Maria finally said, her voice slightly wavering, "you forgive me, then?"

Simon's eyes blinked toward her, almost as if startled, so Maria drew in courage, and kept going. "For lying to you, and breaking our contract, and running away, like I did? And"—she grimaced—"not trusting you?"

Simon's brow had furrowed, his head ducking again, and there was an odd stain of red, creeping up his neck. "Ach, I forgive you," he said, quiet. "I can no fault you for what I also should have done, in your place. For what *any* Skai should have done."

Oh. Something fierce and warm flickered in Maria's belly, and she watched Simon's hand wipe at her shoulders, her collarbones. "I only raged at the truth of this, ach?" he continued, his gaze still not meeting hers. "I swore to keep you safe, and thus I could no even run away with you, no with Ulfarr so hungry to hunt you. I was thus bound to hunt *him*, to guard you, whilst you ran without me. Whilst you faced this cruel duke *alone*."

Wait. So *that* was why Simon hadn't come with her, when she'd left? Not because of his work, or even his fight to the death—but because he'd needed to stay with Ulfarr? To keep Maria *safe*?

"I raged at you, for my own failing," he said, even quieter, his mouth twisting. "This was wrong, ach? It was only easier to rage, than to face the depths of my fear. To face this threat"—his huge shoulders rose, fell—"of losing you, for always."

Oh. It felt like a confession, like an apology, like something he was *ashamed* of. And it didn't make sense, suddenly because he'd said, he'd *said*—

"But when I left," Maria whispered, "you said you didn't care if I came back. That it didn't—*matter*, to you."

Simon's eyes snapped up to hers, his brow furrowed deep. "You are Skai," he said, his voice cracking. "Thus, you were free to make this choice. You are *always* free to make this choice. Even after I have fully claimed you thus."

He waved a jerky hand toward her waist, toward the mess still spattered against it—and the understanding dipped and soared, hurtling across Maria's thoughts. She was no longer his prisoner. She was no longer bound by a contract. She was Skai. She was *free*.

And Simon—Simon's eyes had dropped again, and Maria could see the tension in his jaw, his shoulders, his still-wiping fingers on her skin. "Mayhap you yet wish for this freedom, ach?" he whispered, as though he'd once again read into her soul. "I have no shown myself a good mate to you, in this. I have raged at you. Confined you. Brought you pain. *Wielded* you, against my clan's ways. Even today"—his throat convulsed—"I have done this, with my rut. With my *words*."

Right. Maria's thoughts flicked backwards, to the way Simon had spoken, before all his watching kin. To all his forceful, powerful words. Changing his clan's ways. Changing their future.

And he'd gained that, he'd accomplished that, he should be over-joyed by that—but in this moment, he looked almost regretful. Miserable. *Defeated*.

Something was wildly swerving in Maria's chest, and her tingling hand clutched to his, pressing it tight against her skin. Needing him to look at her, suddenly, and thank the gods he did, those eyes so molten, so uncertain, so *afraid*.

"Simon," she breathed, hoarse. "What you did today was *incredible*. Not only did you keep *me* safe, but you've also granted safety to all the Skai mates after me. And you refused to fight to the death, and showed a new way for Enforcers after you, too. And even before all that"—her fingers spasmed against his—"you taught me to keep *myself* safe, Simon. You gave me confidence. Courage. *Peace*."

Simon blinked at her, and then barked a sound that might have been a laugh. "You yet held all this, my brave one," he whispered. "You only needed to find it again, ach? Since this first day we met, you have been so true. So brave. So *pure*."

Maria's mouth choked a laugh too—*pure* was surely the last way she could describe herself, after having been ravaged and rutted by an orc, six times, in *public*—but Simon's eyes had abruptly narrowed, his claws flexing against her skin.

"You are," he insisted. "You *are*. You spurned your husband, and ran alone across all the realm to me. You bravely met me, and swore to bear me a son, and honour me. And you have done all this, ach? Each day, amidst all I have cast upon you"—his other hand jabbed a finger toward her—"you have done this. You have sought to obey me, and learn from me, and become one of my kin. You sought to *help* me."

His voice was fervent, and his eyes were just the same, glinting bright upon hers. "I meant to Enforce you, and cleanse you," he said. "But in this, you cleansed *me*. With your peace, you gave *me* this peace also."

Oh. Maria's throat felt thick, her eyes prickling, and her free hand numbly, instinctively reached out, and found the furious beat of his heart. Spreading wide over it, knowing it, *hers*.

"And today," Simon continued, his jaw grinding in his cheek. "You defeated this duke. You defeated Ulfarr. And next, you welcome my rut, before all my kin, when I have no even *spoken* of this to you? You watched me, and you learnt me, and you met me, and honoured me, and—"

His voice caught, his head shaking, his finger again jabbing toward her. "I sent you away from me *weeping*," he hissed. "I tasted the vastness of your grief, even as you granted me our son's own *name*. And yet, today you do this? You welcome me thus? You beg for me and my seed, and flaunt your joy in this? You alter *all* for me, and my clan? You gain us our *freedom*, to choose our mates as we wish? To gain our *future*?"

Maria couldn't stop blinking at him, at the way his glittering eyes held hers. "You are so pure, my brave one," he whispered. "You are all I have ever *dreamt* of."

Oh. Something was bubbling in Maria's chest, raw and desperate, and she grabbed at him, dragging his huge form close, burying her face in his fragrant neck. "But *you*, Simon," she gasped, squeezing her eyes shut, inhaling deep. "You *did* cleanse me. You *saw* me. You made me a Skai, made me your mate. And you *destroyed* Ulfarr, and kept me safe, just as you swore you would. As I should have known you would. I should have *trusted* you with that."

Simon's arms had circled tighter around her, and there was a hoarse chuckle, vibrating through his chest. "Ach, but this way, I witnessed my sweet mate near slice off my foe's prick," he murmured back. "You can no *fathom* the pure joy this sight brought me, my pretty one."

Maria laughed too, muffled against his neck, but she could feel a trace of his sharp claws, skittering on her still-sticky skin. "I may yet still kill Ulfarr, you ken," he said, quieter. "Just as we may yet kill this duke, should he betray us. But I wish to yet try these new ways, ach?"

Maria nodded against him, squeezing her arms tighter around his waist. "Thank you," she whispered, "for seeking your new ways, Simon. Thank you for seeking me. For *seeing* me."

His big hand was stroking at her hair, his pulse thudding slow and sure beneath her ear. And when he drew back, his eyes so painfully intent upon her, there was only this. Only peace. Only... hope.

"I see you, my brave mate," he breathed. "And with this, I pledge you my troth. I grant you my sword, and my favour, and my fealty. I shall keep you *safe*, so long as I am able, and so long as you shall wish."

It felt like a vow, a gift, a promise. Like something that could never be unspoken, wrapping its truth around Maria's heart. Making her his, *forever*.

And as she searched his shimmering eyes, there was no expectation, no judgement. Only this offering, willing and open. *You are always free to make this choice.*

And Maria was making this choice. Not just for him, for their clan, for their mountain—but for her. Skai.

"I see you too, Simon," she whispered. "And I pledge you my troth. My sword, and my favour, and my fealty. For as long as I am able, and"—she twitched a smile toward him—"so long as you might wish."

His grin back was slow, genuine, breathtaking. Broader and easier than Maria had ever seen it, his eyes crinkling at the corners, his teeth white and sharp against his lip. "You honour me, my brave one," he said, his voice husky, his eyes bright. "Now, shall you come home with me?"

Home. The word a shining, flashing joy, crashing against all the rest, and Maria clutched for it, held it, marvelled at its truth. *Home.*

"Of course I will," she said. "Let's go."

40

Maria's journey back to Orc Mountain was a true adventure. One full of challenges, and learning, and laughter.

Simon, of course, proved to be a truly delightful and capable travelling-partner, navigating with just as much ease as Joarr had shown. However, he also had no qualms about throwing Maria onto his broad back whenever she was tired, or taking a two-day detour to show her a spectacular waterfall, or patiently answering every last question that happened to pop into her thoughts.

It meant that he was constantly teaching her, showing her a world of Skai ways she'd never before encountered. Things like how to identify and track prey in the forest, how to lie in wait, how to make kills clean and quick. How to make a fire, how to conceal one's tracks from humans, how to find water and shelter. Even how to identify the orcs' hidden underground ways, and navigate them in the dark, and be sure to leave a scent, so other orcs would know they'd passed.

And amidst it all, Simon claimed her, again and again. Taking her against trees, in rushing streams, in the deep underground darkness. Filling her with his power and his scent, in every possible way, until it almost felt like it was an immutable part of her. As though she were forever marked by him, forever claimed by her orc.

Simon's teeth-marks on her neck had begun to feel permanent too, especially since he always bit her in the exact same place. Always with palpable gentleness, and he always licked it extensively afterwards, ensuring there was no infection or pain.

"No wish to blot your wholeness *too* much, ach?" he told her, his eyes rueful, when Maria had asked. "Wish to mark you with care, my pretty one."

He accompanied the words with a gentle flick at Maria's already-hard nipple—and at her answering gasp, he promptly turned her around, yanked up her tunic and loincloth, and sank himself deep inside. Plunging in again and again, until Maria was juddering and flailing upon him, howling her release to the sky.

She was almost disappointed when Orc Mountain loomed close, early on their eighth day of travelling, but Simon's eagerness felt truly infectious, his hand spreading wide against her back. "We shall rest and work here for a spell," he said firmly. "Now that I no must confine you, I shall show you all our mountain. And after this, you shall come out with me again whilst I work, ach? You shall learn more of hunting, and also see our Skai camps, and meet our other Skai women. This shall please you, I ken."

And suddenly Maria did feel pleased, and almost giddy with excitement. And when they finally reached the base of the mountain later that morning, she was astonished to discover that there appeared to be an entire crowd of orcs and humans milling about outside. Almost as if... *waiting* for them?

"Maria!" Rosa crowed, as she bounded over toward them, with John in tow. "Welcome back! I heard what you did to deal with Warmisham, how *marvellous*—and you know, there's a relevant tale I've been meaning to tell you—and *dozens* of our new treatises have already been delivered, and there's been a positive *uproar!*"

She was smiling beatifically toward Maria, her hands clasped over her heart, and Maria laughed aloud, and grinned up at Simon beside her. "I'm so glad to hear it," she replied, "but I had so much help. From Simon, and the Skai, and all of you."

She flapped a helpless wave at the crowd all around, because indeed, suddenly it seemed like everyone was here. Baldr and Drafli, Tristan and Salvi, Kesst and Efterar, Olarr and Gerrard, Joarr and multiple Skai scouts, and of course, the orcs' captain, with a broadly smiling Lady Norr. And in Lady Norr's arms—Maria twitched, because she hadn't caught sight of him since her first day here—was her tiny, green-skinned son. Tengil.

"We've all heard how spectacular you were, Maria," Lady Norr said firmly, as she strode toward them, hoisting Tengil upright. "And word is, Warmisham's kept his mouth shut so far, and has followed through on calling off that wealth-stealing law, and hasn't even begun any further aggressions against us. Which is truly the best outcome we could have ever asked for. Thank you, from all of us."

Maria's face felt very hot, and she attempted what she hoped was a suitable response—at least, until Tengil blinked his big black eyes toward her, and *sneezed*. The sound high-pitched enough to carry over the chatter all around, and Maria couldn't help a peal of laughter, an affectionate rub at his downy little head.

"Are you *still* allergic to me, after all this time?" she demanded at him. "Or is this your sneaky baby way of telling me I need a bath again?!"

It had indeed been a few days since they'd found a suitable stream to wash in, and Joarr—who'd come over to clap Simon on the shoulder—smirked at Maria, darting a telling glance downwards. "Good work, brother," he said to Simon. "I smell her from half-day away, ach?"

Simon's sharp-toothed grin toward Maria was easy, and unmistakably smug. "Ach, it pleases my mate to flaunt my good scent," he purred. "She is a true Skai, ach?"

The warmth swarmed from Maria's head to her feet, so forceful that she felt distinctly light-headed, and thankfully Simon settled his strong arm around her waist, and proceeded to greet the rest of their well-wishers. His big body warm and relaxed beside hers, the smile again coming with surprising ease to his mouth.

As he talked, even more orcs had seemed to arrive—the whole scene had begun to feel rather like a morning party—and soon someone brought out a gigantic platter of food, and some drummers began pounding out a merry rhythm. And then some orcs began a sparring-match, while others began dancing, and Maria even caught sight of Bjorn, standing half-hidden behind one of the drummers, and peering around toward them.

Simon had seemed to catch sight of Bjorn at the same time Maria had, and beckoned him over with a purposeful wave. And to Maria's vague surprise, Bjorn indeed crept toward them, his eyes darting suspiciously at the chaos all around.

"Here, little brother," Simon said to Bjorn, once he was bobbing on his feet before them. "I have brought you more to play with, ach?"

With that, Simon reached into his pocket, and pulled out another handful of little carvings. He'd been making them throughout their journey, Maria knew, mostly while she'd slept—and Bjorn snatched them away with gratifying eagerness, his dark eyes shining briefly on Simon's face before he turned to scurry off again.

But then he hesitated, his gaze darting uncertainly back toward Simon. Almost as if he didn't want to leave yet, and Maria didn't miss that thoughtful, assessing look in Simon's eyes. "You ken, little brother," he said slowly, "that my Maria has much yet to learn of orcs, ach? Thus, for these next moons, I shall oft teach her our ways. Should you wish, I should welcome your help in this."

Bjorn's eyes betrayed another unmistakable flash of eagerness, before narrowing back to suspicion again. "You no need help teach," he said flatly. "You know *all*, Simon."

Simon's shrug was rueful, the warmth genuine in his eyes. "Ach, I know much," he replied. "But I am grown orc, ach? It has been many summers since I was new to our ways. But you are young, and thus closer to all this—and thus, your teaching shall hold great worth, I ken."

The suspicion had somewhat faded from Bjorn's eyes, and Maria felt herself nodding, the smile tugging up her mouth. "I have a *lot* left to learn," she informed Bjorn. "And Simon can be *very* bossy at times. Perhaps you'll go a little easier on me?"

But Bjorn's eyes had narrowed again, his clawed hands clutching tighter at his toys. "I no be *easy*," he said, voice flat. "You are no use, as you are. Why you no even *jig* for Simon yet?"

He jerked his sharp shoulder toward the drummers, his eyes imperious on Maria's face, and it took all her willpower to choke down the bubbling surge of laughter. "Excellent point, Bjorn," she said, her voice slightly wavering. "I know how much Simon enjoys my jigging."

She couldn't even look at Simon as she launched into her jig, bouncing up and down, following the drummers' pulsing beat. Instead, she kept her eyes on Bjorn, who had crossed his arms over his little chest, and was watching with his mouth pursed. Almost as if assessing her. *Judging* her.

And a glance up at Simon—who happened to be in the exact same pose, giving her the exact same look—was almost Maria's undoing, and she had to pause for air, dragging in unsteady breaths. And thankfully Rosa strode up, her eyes alight, her blonde head already bobbing to the beat.

"You know how to jig, Maria!" she exclaimed. "You'll teach us, right? Maybe Simon would like to learn too?"

She shot a hopeful, teasing look toward Simon, who instantly scowled back—but several of the other women had come over, too. And after an extremely belated round of introductions—the jewel-wearing one was Ella of Clan Grisk, and the plump, soft-spoken one was Stella, from Bautul—they followed along while Maria taught the steps, until they were all laughing too hard to continue.

"Did this suitably please you, Simon?" Maria asked him, once she'd tripped back to where he was still standing beside Bjorn. "And you, Bjorn?"

Bjorn gave a curt, commanding little nod before turning and wandering off again, back toward the mountain. While Simon's eyes on Maria weren't quite approving, but instead almost... warm. Affectionate.

"Ach, you ken I am always pleased with you," he murmured. "Now come and bathe with me, ach?"

Maria certainly wasn't about to refuse a bath, especially once Simon escorted her into the mountain, and down an unfamiliar passage to an entirely new room. One that smelled distinctly of sulphur, and boasted huge pools cut into the stone floor, all steaming with hot water.

"Good gods, Simon," Maria gasped, as she slid down into the wonderful, all-encompassing heat, and Simon drew her close into his arms. "What else have you been hiding from me, all this time?"

There turned out to be quite a lot, Maria soon discovered, once she was freshly bathed and dressed, and Simon had begun escorting her on an impromptu tour of Orc Mountain. Showing her a kitchen, a large trading-post, multiple forges and shrines and common-rooms, and even a *library*, presided over by an ever-enthusiastic Rosa.

It was all highly intriguing, but even so, Maria felt herself relaxing as they crossed back into the familiar Skai wing, with its narrower, twisty corridors, its oddly comforting darkness. Almost as if, somehow, over these past weeks, it truly had become home.

And as they walked back into Simon's familiar room, Maria's throat felt strangely choked, her eyes blinking hard. Because not only was the room still exactly the same—still carefully neat, all the weapons still hanging, her chest still there on the bench—but there was also some-thing new on the shelf. A new carved figure, standing close beside Simon's father.

And when Maria stepped closer to look, there was another shock of recognition, because it was *her*. Tall and bare and surprisingly lovely, the curls twisting down her back in carefully carved spirals, her mouth flashing a wide, genuine grin.

Maria truly couldn't seem to speak, and shot a stunned, helpless look toward Simon—to which he rubbed at the stubble on his jaw, and gave a too-casual shrug. "Wished to—remember you," he said. "You are pretty human, ach?"

But that telltale redness was creeping up his neck, and it occurred to Maria that based on what she'd seen of his carvings for Bjorn, this must have taken him more than a few days. Gods, it had surely been *weeks*, and had he been carving this all this time? Perhaps with the full expectation that she would *leave*?!

And without thinking, Maria hurled herself toward him, and threw her arms around his taut waist. Feeling him sag against her touch, his hands settling on her back, his heartbeat slowing under her ear.

"I love it," she whispered. "And I love *you*, Simon."

There was a hitched, twitching silence, a spasm of his fingers against her—and then he drew back, and cupped her face in both his warm hands. Just looking at her, his gaze intent, before he bent down, and pressed a soft, silken kiss to her waiting mouth.

"Wish to reward you," he murmured, a predatory glint flaring in his eyes. "Before my kin. You shall welcome this, ach?"

A furious ripple of heat shot up Maria's spine, and she silently, eagerly nodded—to which Simon grasped for the tunic she'd been wearing, and yanked it off over her head. Leaving her standing there in only her loincloth and dagger, while his glittering eyes flicked up, and down, and up again. Assessing. *Approving.*

And without another word, he shucked his own trousers, clasped Maria's hand in his, and led her out into the corridor. Into *public.* Like this.

But where there might have once been shame or fear, there was only hunger. Pulsing primal and shivery through Maria's half-bared body, whispering of heat, of power, of pride. And her eyes wouldn't seem to stop wandering, drinking up the sight of her huge, prowling, dangerous mate beside her. His steps silent and graceful, his muscles shifting and rippling under his skin, the beast at his groin heavy and half-hard, and fully on display. Fully hers.

And as he guided her into the Skai common-room, and into the sensual chaos of its writhing, hot-blooded orcs, the hunger seemed to flare higher, closer. He was going to flaunt her. Claim her. Show them the sheer force of his favour toward her.

Many of the room's orcs had looked up, their eyes watchful on Maria's bared form—but thankfully, a quick glance over their assembled faces showed no sign of Ulfarr, or any of the orcs who had so blatantly supported him. Indeed, most of them were orcs Maria knew, and she felt herself relaxing even more, her eyes angling up at Simon's face.

But instead of leading her further into the room, Simon had hesitated on the threshold, his gaze catching, oddly, on Drafli. Who this time had no strange orcs touching him, and was standing alone and half-dressed against the wall, his arms crossed, his eyes narrow on Simon's. Almost as though he'd been waiting for something.

And Simon nodded, jerking his head toward the door behind them—to which Drafli pushed off the wall, and strode out of the room. While Simon led Maria to one of the fur-covered benches lining the walls, and drew her down onto his lap.

"You shall be patient a little longer, my pretty one," he purred, as he nuzzled at her hair. "You shall first witness this with me, ach? Grant our favour?"

Maria couldn't fathom what he was talking about, and opened her mouth to ask—but Simon's eyes were purposely fixed on the door. On where Drafli was already striding back in, but this time, pulling a fully dressed, confused-looking Baldr behind him.

Baldr's hesitation was almost palpable, his eyes casting uneasily around the room. Catching, briefly, on Simon and Maria, before glancing back to where Drafli had pulled him to a halt beside a fur-covered table in the middle of the room—the same place, in fact, where Simon had taken Maria, last time they'd been here.

"What are you—" Maria heard Baldr say to Drafli, his voice barely audible despite the rapidly quieting room. "You know I am not—"

But Drafli had snapped up a hand, pressing his fingers firmly to Baldr's mouth, and with his other hand he made a series of quick, forceful gestures. None of which Maria understood, but Baldr surely did, his eyes widening on Drafli's, his body gone utterly still.

"Speak for him, Baldr," Simon called out, his deep voice echoing through the room. "What does he wish."

Drafli's hand had dropped from Baldr's mouth, and Maria could see Baldr's throat visibly bobbing, his gaze still fixed to Drafli's face. "He wants," he began, and then ran a shaky-looking hand against his hair. "Drafli says—he wants—to make me his—"

He couldn't seem to finish, his breaths heaving from his chest, his eyes suddenly narrow and suspicious on Drafli's. "You *cannot*," he said, almost helplessly. "Your Skai *ways*, Draf. You cannot honestly—"

But Drafli was snapping out more gestures, sharp and decisive, several of them pointing toward *Simon*. Simon, who had carefully shifted Maria down onto the bench beside him, and then risen to his feet.

"You all ken we have found a new way, with our rut," he said firmly, his voice carrying through the now-silent room. "Shall any of you stand against me, in granting this to Drafli? Or to any other orc who should wish to take another orc as his mate?"

His eyes had gone dark and chilly as they swept the room, his hands clenched to huge fists, daring another orc to challenge him. And while a few of the watching orcs looked like they might have wished to object, their eyes glancing warily toward one another, no one actually spoke. And after a long, silent moment, Simon flashed the room a swift, dangerous grin, and sank down beside Maria again.

"Then keep on," he said, waving a casual hand at Baldr and Drafli. "Baldr, shall you accept Drafli's rut, and thus become his mate, in the ways of the Skai?"

Baldr blinked toward Simon, and his form had slightly swayed, almost as though if struck—and then he stared back at Drafli, his head tilting, his mouth pressed thin.

"But you know I—" he began, and then squared his shoulders, his gaze darting at the watching orcs all around. "I would want you bound to me. *Only* me. In the ways of the *Grisk*."

And surely that was accusation in his voice, or perhaps even defiance—but Drafli's eyes were just as defiant, his hands snapping out more gestures. The last one just pointing at Baldr's chest, again and again and again. As if to say, *You. You. You.*

And Baldr was staring straight back, his shoulders rising and falling, his sharp teeth biting at his lip. And then his hand twitched up to catch Drafli's, holding it in place, their eyes locked together—until Baldr jerked a quick, fervent little nod. Saying—*yes.*

There was an instant's caught stillness, something flashing through Drafli's eyes—and without warning, he leapt forward, and tackled Baldr down to the table behind him. His clawed hands yanking at Baldr's clothes, hurling them off toward the floor, while his fluid body crouched between Baldr's thighs, spreading them wide apart. While his hand shoved Baldr's head sideways, exposing the line of his quivering, pulsing throat—

And then Drafli's hips drove forward, as his teeth clamped down. As Baldr choked and moaned beneath him, his muscled body arching up, his claws dragging deep red gouges into Drafli's taut, powerful back.

"Fuuuuck," Baldr gasped, his voice breaking, his head angling sideways, almost as if baring his neck even more for Drafli's teeth. "Gods, please, *please*—"

And Drafli was surely obliging him, his hips driving fierce and deep, his throat visibly swallowing. His lithe body moving with feral, fluent ease, while his hand stroked up and down Baldr's flexing flank.

The movements all familiar, proprietary, reverent—and watching them, Maria could almost taste the strength of their joint craving, their furious, frantic relief. As if this was something they'd long been denied, a rite that had always gone empty, unfulfilled, until this moment.

And as Baldr reared up, pierced and helpless and gasping upon his mate's grinding form, Maria felt her own hunger rearing up too, her face flushed and hot. Something that Simon surely noticed, as he reached over, and easily plucked her up onto his lap again.

"Now you ken why we Skai so oft take our joy together here, ach?" he purred, as he shifted her upon him, so that his swollen length nudged tantalizingly against her parted, twitching crease. "You should now welcome my taking, ach?"

Maria couldn't even pretend to argue, not with that delicious hardness teasing so close, and she accordingly wriggled tighter against him, ready to do whatever the hell he wished—but he laughed aloud, low and rolling, as his hands held her still, and he gave a purposeful tweak at her peaked nipple.

"Ach, but no yet, my hungry one," he murmured. "We must wait, and honour this, ach?"

Right. Not that this was a hardship to watch, not with Baldr now kneeling on the floor before Drafli, his long braid wrapped around Drafli's fist, his head tilted back, his heaving chest painted with white. His eyes fluttering as Drafli fed his not-inconsiderable length into his mouth, breath by breath, until Baldr was suckling at the base of him, his throat wildly convulsing.

Simon had huffed a sound that might have been approval, his eyes clearly appreciative—even as his own hand slipped down Maria's front, warm, steady, unhurried. Finding the already-slick heat between her legs, and then opening it wider, and casually trailing his fingers against it. Teasing her, playing with her, while he so coolly watched the shocking scene before them.

And surely it was shameful, depraved, *something*—but Maria could only gasp, and squirm, and spasm against his touch. Moaning aloud as Drafli pumped his liquid pleasure into Baldr's hungry mouth, holding his bottom lip open so that the slick white spilled down Baldr's chin, dripping to the floor. And then, after a sharp, dismissive snap of

Drafli's hand, Baldr accordingly knelt down to lap it off the floor, his face a furious shade of red, while Drafli strode around behind, grasped his bent-over arse, and again drove inside.

Good *gods*. Maria was shivering and whimpering at the sight, but Simon was still watching with visible approval, his finger now nudging deeper between her parted legs. "Ach, there is naught to fear in this," he murmured, close in her ear. "Baldr longs for his mate's strong command, ach? Every orc in this room can taste this, and most of all his mate. It has always been thus, between them."

That did make sense, based on all Maria had seen of them so far, and she shot Simon a grateful, flustered smile before settling in closer against him. Allowing herself to sink into the sight of this, the feel of it, the blazing hunger, the power of Simon's still-teasing touch. One hand playing with her nipples, now, while the other lazily slipped its fingers in and out between her thighs. Making lurid noises with every movement, but he didn't seem to notice, his eyes still fixed appreciatively on Baldr and Drafli's sweaty, writhing bodies before them.

At some point, Baldr had begun fighting back, kicking and flailing against Drafli's fluid strength—a development that only appeared to ramp Drafli's hunger higher. His black hair now flying loose around his face as his graceful body braced against Baldr, hurling him onto his back on the table, pinning him there with his full weight. And then he plunged deep inside again, while Baldr jerked and thrashed, his mouth howling, his neck and torso streaked with red and white, his clawed hands dragging Drafli close—

And as Maria watched, flustered and frantic, Drafli finally bent low, and kissed Baldr on the mouth. Soft, sweet, astonishingly gentle, especially in the light of all else he'd just done—and it was that, somehow, that finally set Baldr shouting against his lips, his curled-up body spraying yet more white between them.

And then, suddenly, it was done. Drafli's sweaty body sagging heavy onto Baldr's, his face again buried in Baldr's neck, while Baldr's arms and legs twined close and careful around him. Again, almost as if it were a rite, a vow, a cleansing.

They stayed there for a long moment, their bodies heaving together—and then Drafli gently disentangled himself, and rose unsteadily to his feet. His glittering gaze sweeping over the watching orcs, the challenge vivid and powerful in his eyes.

And this time, it was Simon who spoke first, drawing a hand away from Maria to press it over his heart. "I see your gain, Skai," he called out, the words weighted with finality. "You have my blessing."

Drafli's eyes flared with bare gratefulness, and he bowed briefly toward Simon, his own hand in a fist against his heart. And as the other watching orcs also spoke, adding their voices to Simon's, it was almost as though Maria could see Drafli's cold bitterness pooling away, the tightness easing from his eyes. And as he reached back toward Baldr, and drew him onto his wobbly feet beside him, his slow smile toward Baldr was astonishingly stunning, enough that Maria surely wouldn't have recognized him, if she'd walked into the room at this moment.

Drafli had flicked a finger at Baldr's cheek, snapping his smoky eyes wide—and then Baldr *laughed*. The sound bright, shivery and warm, his head thrown back, his eyes alight with joy. And beneath Maria she felt Simon chuckle too, the sound purring hot and indulgent through his chest.

"This was good, ach?" he murmured in her ear, as Drafli slid an arm around Baldr's waist, and drew his shaky form over toward their bench. "Any worthy Skai knows how to please his mate, ach?"

He said this with an approving nod up at Drafli, and Drafli nodded back as he silently sank onto the bench beside them. His hands making a purposeful gesture toward Simon, far slower than what he'd done with Baldr, and Simon returned it with a shrug, a companionable bump of his shoulder against Drafli's.

"Ach, you no need to thank me," he said. "You should do the same for me. You *have*. Ach?"

Drafli jerked a shrug too, his eyes sliding up to where Baldr was still standing before him. Looking just as dazed and bemused as Maria currently felt, his skin and hair an utter mess—but Drafli only looked up at him, mouth pursed, before gesturing down between his knees. Meaning for Baldr to sit on the floor at his *feet*, good *gods*—and to Maria's genuine surprise, Baldr instantly obeyed. Dropping to curl up between Drafli's thighs, his head resting almost reverently on his knee.

And in the midst of Maria's own hazy hunger, she suddenly felt an unmistakable indignation, surging against the contentment in her belly. "Seriously?" she heard herself say toward Drafli, her voice thick. "I hope you know how lucky you are. After all the shit you've put him through? You ought to be thanking Skai-kesh that he'll even still *talk* to you. Or that he didn't take up Joarr on his *very* generous offer, while we were away."

She'd twitched her head toward Joarr, who had somehow appeared out of nowhere on Simon's other side, and was currently smirking at Drafli. Earning a furious-looking gesture from Drafli in return, though his narrow eyes were still fixed firmly to Maria's face, his lips curled back in a vicious snarl.

"Ach, Maria," cut in Simon's voice, deep and disapproving. "You no shame another Skai thus. No when he only seek to honour his kin's ways, so he might keep his place serving them."

But Maria couldn't seem to stop glaring back at Drafli, returning his snarl with a sneer of her own. "But you accused Baldr of only caring until a woman showed up!" she hissed at him. "And I can tell you from personal experience that he still very much cared about you while he was helping me, though the gods only know why!"

Drafli looked ready to spit at her, his hand flashing out a series of enraged-looking gestures—and this time, Baldr blinked his hazy eyes up toward Drafli, and reached up to grasp his hand, holding it still.

"No, Draf," he said, his voice husky, surprisingly stern. "You are wrong. I will *not* leave you for a woman, or a son. *Ever.*"

He sounded very sure, his eyes steady on Drafli's face, and Maria could see a slight sag in Drafli's shoulders, his hand slipping down to card into Baldr's hair. Even as he again bared his teeth toward Maria, and she shot him a chilly smile back.

"See?" she demanded, triumphant. "I hope you appreciate him, you *prick.*"

But against her, Simon had made a sound that was half-laugh, half-groan, and he pulled her around to look at him, his eyes glinting. "*Maria,*" he said, the warning heavy on his voice. "You no hear me? You no speak to your kin thus. Now kneel, and cleanse your mouth of this."

He accompanied the words with an imperious snap of his hand toward the floor, not unlike the one Drafli had just used on Baldr. And Maria stared at him, the uncertainty clashing against the wild flaring hunger, as Simon gave the gesture again, his eyes dark, arrogant, dangerous.

"*Now*, woman," he ordered. "You no ken I stop cleansing you once you are my mate? This is only more cause to teach you our ways. Now kneel, and *suckle*."

The heat and the rebellion swarmed with equal, dizzying strength, and after one more impatient jab of Simon's finger, Maria silently nodded, and slid down between his knees. Toward where his monster was already fully swollen, jutting out thick and dripping, oozing its sticky white...

She felt her tongue brushing against her lips, her face flushed painfully hot—but then her gaze darted up, toward where three pairs of orc eyes were watching her. Joarr with palpable amusement, Drafli with a vindictive-looking triumph, and Simon with a brow raised, his hand slipping down to stroke up his full length, displaying it for Maria's rapidly blinking eyes.

"I said, suckle, woman," he told her, his voice low. "You wish for my good cleansing, ach?"

Gods. The hunger flashed higher, sparked by that look in his eyes, that easy command in his voice. And Maria was nodding, furtive and frantic—*fuck*, yes—and in return Simon's lips curled up, his hand sliding down to catch in her hair.

"Good," he murmured, tilting her head back, nudging her mouth open with his other hand—and then, oh hell, he was there. That slick, rounded head slipping between her lips, opening her wide around him, sinking itself full and deep, settling close against her throat.

"Pretty, ach?" he purred, his hand tangling tighter in her hair—and Maria realized, with another jolt of heat, that he wasn't even talking to her. Rather, he was talking to Joarr beside him, and he was even dragging Maria's head back, nearly all the way off his swollen length, as if displaying her stretched mouth and reddened cheeks for Joarr's amused eyes.

"Ach, I knew she should please you," Joarr replied, as Simon drew Maria's head forward again, nestling himself back into her convulsing throat. "You needed one so eager to honour you. One so steadfast, in her worship."

Simon wasn't arguing with this assessment, and his thumb

absently stroked Maria's hot cheek as he slid her backwards again, until he was almost all the way out, pulsing his fiery sweetness onto her tongue. "Ach," he murmured, quiet. "But you no wish you had kept her? You ought to have this, also."

But Joarr waved it away, even as he winked down toward Maria's flushed, suckling face. "Ach, no," he said coolly. "I no need worship, only hard fuck. And this one crave giant prick, and this I no have, you ken? You no saw her wiggle and wail upon your stone, whilst she was parted from you."

With that, Joarr actually reached down, and—somehow—produced the stone in question. The one Simon had sent as a *gift*, oh gods, and Maria felt herself moan at the sight of it, even as she sucked its real version deeper into her mouth. To which both Simon and Joarr laughed, Simon with an affectionate warmth in his eyes, Joarr with a smug, twinkling satisfaction.

"See?" Joarr said, as he dropped the stone into Simon's hand. "And I now have new woman in my scents. *Easier* woman, I ken."

With that, he stood up and strode further down the wall, toward where an unfamiliar orc was bent double over Killik's groin. And with a few swift yanks of Joarr's hands, he was grinding his hips against the orc's bare arse, his head tilted back, his eyes fluttering closed.

Simon had given a pointed tug on Maria's hair, snapping her attention back to where he was still indulgently watching her, his thumb again stroking at her cheek. "When I cleanse you, you shall swallow all," he murmured. "And you shall speak with care to your new kin. And after this"—he ground himself deep and deliberate into her throat—"you shall have my reward. Ach?"

He'd inclined his head toward the middle of the room as he spoke, oh gods—and Maria felt herself frantically nodding, her eyes wide and pleading on his face. Earning a low chuckle in return, his hand guiding her head with more purpose now, easing her back and forth. Taking his pleasure with her, using her mouth as he wished, and she didn't miss the nudge of his shoulder at Drafli beside him. Wanting him to witness this, perhaps, and with a shock of heat Maria realized that Baldr was currently doing this exact same thing to Drafli, both of them kneeling before their sprawled Skai, flaunting their hunger, their worship—

Simon's release surged without warning, flooding with shocking, dazzling power into Maria's mouth. So much that she had to fight to swallow, to keep it all inside, coughing and gagging against his invading strength—but he only kept waiting, brows raised, watching. *Cleansing.*

And when it finally finished, and Maria had somehow choked it all down, Simon drew his spent length from her mouth, and gently tilted her sticky, reddened face toward Drafli. Drafli, who'd been watching this with blank, wholly unreadable eyes, both his hands clutched tight into Baldr's hair.

"Speak, woman," Simon commanded her. "Honour me."

Maria's hunger was still swerving and tingling, and she drew in breath, licked at her swollen lips, held Drafli's watching eyes. "I—I'm sorry I insulted you," she said, hoarse. "And called you names. But you *will* trust Baldr's word, from now on, and take good care of him. Won't you?"

A bright incredulity had flared in Drafli's eyes, and he jerked a sharp nod, his hands clenching tighter in Baldr's hair. And when his gaze flicked back down to Baldr again, Maria could see the bare intensity, the affection, in his glinting black eyes.

"I'm glad," Maria said, her voice quieter than before. "And congratulations, Drafli. I see your gain, and honour this."

Drafli gave another curt nod, his gaze not once leaving Baldr's face as he ground deeper inside—and when Maria glanced back at Simon, that was surely approval in his eyes. And in the way he was patting her cheek, his mouth curving into his warm, crooked smile.

"Good," he said firmly. "Now what do you speak to me, my pretty one?"

And Maria was smiling back, eager, hungry, hopeful. "Thank you for cleansing me, Simon," she murmured. "Now will you finally stop tormenting me, and give me my damned reward?"

His answering grin was almost a reward of its own, stunning and dangerous. "Ach, woman," he said. "Come and scream, whilst I teach you how an orc rewards his mate."

41

Maria trembled all over as Simon finally led her across the Skai common-room. Through the clusters of carousing orcs, drawing their eyes, their gazes prickling on Maria's bared skin.

But there was still no fear. No shame. She was Simon's mate. She was Skai. And they were finally home together, and she was finally, fully free of her old life, of its contracts and obligations and revenge. Free of everything but this heated, heady craving, which had already been simmering for what felt like hours now, and was bubbling dangerously close to the surface, almost about to burst.

And Simon knew it, reading her as easily as he always had—and that was why he was scarcely even touching her now, tilting up her head with a single clawed finger. Enjoying the answering gasp from her mouth, while the smugness flared across his wicked watching eyes.

"You long for me, ach, my pretty one?" he purred. "And you shall again flaunt my prize before all the Skai, ach?"

Maria's nod was frantic, fervent, and Simon's mouth curled up higher, his black tongue flicking against his lips. "Then kneel for me," he ordered, with a wave of his hand toward the fur-covered table behind her. "Show me what is mine."

Oh, gods. Another gasp had escaped Maria's mouth, a shudder

wrenching up her spine—but she instantly obeyed. Clambering up onto the table, and then twitching to turn back toward him, to worship—until his big warm hands caught on her hips, holding her there, facing away from him, on all fours, vulnerable, exposed, shivering.

"Ach, thus," he said, his hands spreading against Maria's hips— and then yanking her slightly backwards, so her knees were nearly at the edge of the table. So he could—Maria choked aloud—flip up her loincloth, and then spread her trembling thighs wide apart. Baring *everything* in between, exposing all her most secret parts to the cool open air of the suddenly silent room.

"Better, ach?" Simon murmured, as she felt his audacious thumb lightly tracing up her quavering crease, teasing, torturous. "But I wish to see more, woman."

More. Maria twitched another nod, and dragged in a bracing breath as she arched her back, angled herself out. Feeling abruptly far more exposed than she had before, and Simon huffed a low, approving laugh as his thumb slipped back down her crease, and then sank deep into her spasming, convulsing heat.

Maria arched and choked, her body clenching tight against him— and in return Simon laughed again, swirling his thumb inside, making her shudder and moan. And then he drew it away, the bastard, leaving her slick and empty and clamping at nothing—until his slippery thumb settled higher, nudging itself against her other secret place, and again sank itself smooth and easy inside.

Maria cried out this time, her exposed body shivering all over, and Simon again swirled his thumb deep, watching this, flaunting this. "Ach, you long for me to fill all your pretty holes," he purred. "You wish to be stretched upon me until you gape open wide, ach?"

Maria's nod was compulsive and desperate, and she again heard Simon's low, approving laugh. "Then beg me, woman. Speak of what you wish for."

His thumb was still circling, opening her even wider upon it, and she moaned again, the sound far too loud in the otherwise hushed room. "I want you, Simon," she gasped. "In me. Stretching me. Filling me. *Please.*"

"Ach, are you sure?" came his taunting, maddening reply. "When you still no yet even show me all that is mine?"

Oh gods, the hunger was shouting and spiralling, and Maria sank her top half downwards to the fur, arching her bottom half up. Opening even more for him, displaying herself for him with brazen shamelessness, and Simon again huffed an approving laugh, his thumb swirling wide and deep.

"Better," he murmured. "You now wish for my prick, hungry woman?"

"Yes," Maria gasped. "Please, Simon. *Gods*, yes."

Another low chuckle, a gentle little slap at her arse—and then, oh hell, something new nudged against her wide-open, dripping-wet heat. Something hard and huge and smooth, but also *cold*—and when Maria whipped her head around to look, it wasn't Simon. It was—his gift. The same size and shape, but not *him*.

But it was still something, please gods, and Maria felt the pleasure spike and swirl as it parted her around it, sinking slow and easy inside. Without even a trace of resistance, steadily splitting her open upon it, deeper and deeper. So fucking good, so fierce and powerful and whole, and her gasp felt almost like a shout when it sank fully within, its wide base pressing flush against her skin.

"Pretty," she heard Simon murmur behind her, soft, as he ground it deep—and then she felt him release the pressure, all at once. So that it smoothly slid out again, despite Maria's desperate attempts to grasp at it, to hold it there. And gods, what must this look like, Simon's stone birthing itself out of her swollen exposed heat, as a room full of orcs watched, and she trembled and moaned, the chaos stuttering higher, closer, please—

She felt the stone fall from her, heard it land in Simon's waiting hand. Heard her empty body still clutching for it, pleading for it, the sounds thick and obscene—and felt Simon's heavy huff of breath as the stone traced up her parted crease, just as his thumb had done. Seeking, swirling, settling in that same other place.

And as huge as it was, it was also slicked all over, and Maria felt herself open for it, for him, for the watching eyes all around. Felt it finding her, easy and gentle, waiting for her to accept it, to welcome it...

And she was, *fuck*, she was. Her arse raised and opened and splayed wide as Simon's gift slowly but surely impaled her, cleaving her open upon it. As the whirling chaos slipped and skittered, winding tighter with every breath, with every slide of the stone driving into her. Until she felt it finally sink all the way home, the base caught firm against her arse, while her body choked and howled and braced against it, oh gods it was so much, too much, she needed more, *more*—

But Simon hadn't moved, perhaps only watching this, seeing the streaks of wetness Maria could now feel slipping from her open, empty heat, down her parted thighs. And the craving was like fire, crackling and burning with agonizing intensity, and suddenly it smashed into the chaos, into an explosion of light and pure flying need—

"More, Simon," Maria's mouth was gasping, begging, all on its own. "More. Please. I beg you. Please, fill me. Now!"

The words rang through the room, bare and surely shameful, but all that mattered was the heavy huff of breath from her mate behind her, the affectionate approval of his laugh. "Hungry woman," he murmured, husky. "You are sure of this?"

And gods curse him, bless him, because he was finally, finally there, his pulsing, powerful warmth prodding against Maria's still-empty heat. And it was everything she needed in this moment, *everything*, and she felt it, revelled in it—and then thrust herself back upon him. Sucking his entire monster deep inside her with one furious, devastating stroke, while her scream rang through the room, his growl scraping hot and low beneath it.

"Wilful woman," he rasped, even as clawed hands clutched her hips closer, impaling her tighter upon him. "It pleases you, to have two of my pricks filling you thus?"

The chaos was screeching, consuming everything, Maria's voice, her thoughts, her thoroughly invaded body still driving back against him, craving his power, his hunger, his approval.

"Yes," she gasped. "Yes, Simon, yes, *yes!*"

He laughed, even as he moaned, his strength swelling even fuller within her, and surely Maria had never been so consumed, so *alive*. And when purposeful hands reached for her upper half, yanking her bodily up against him, it was even stronger, fuller, her back pressed flush to his broad chest, his strength plunged deep inside. Maria's entire heaving front displayed and bared, her breasts jiggling, her heat jammed full, as her mate's head bowed into her neck, teeth scraping sharp, while two powerful fingers slid against her mouth, thrusting deep—

Maria's scream felt like it shook the room, like the pleasure was a living breathing beast, rearing to life inside her. Like Simon's teeth in her neck were her own, her own monster thrashing and raging for escape, flailing against the confines of her skin. And the freedom was here, in the utter perfect invasion of an orc, in his throat gulping her lifeblood, his fingers sunk deep into her gagging throat, his stone strength plunged like a weapon within her. And his living, mighty monster spewing its hot molten fire in a flashing, furious victory, flooding her with pulse after pulse of its flame, its honour, its *conquest.*

But its victory was theirs, his and hers, without a whisper of defeat. It was something to be cherished, like the warm lips kissing gentle where sharp teeth had been, like the secret softness of the beast still curling within her. Like the fragrant musk already seeping between them, the sweet proof of their triumph, made real and alive and true.

And it only seemed fitting that Simon should bend her over the fur again, her arse raised and fully exposed, as the monster retreated. As he also drew out the strength of his still-invading stone, careful and easy. Nudging it free just as more proof of his taking spilled freely out from within her, as he displayed her, flaunted her. His fingers slipping easily into the gaping darkness he'd left behind, his deep voice groaning its low, reverent approval.

"You are mine, my Maria," he whispered, as his hands finally slid away—and in a flare of movement, he'd caught her up against him, her sweaty, sated body curled against his skin. "You are all I have ever longed for, ach?"

Maria couldn't seem to speak, but she clutched herself tighter against him, felt the heat of his exhale as warm lips brushed soft to her forehead. "All I could wish for," he repeated, so quiet, so fierce. "*All,* my pretty, brave, pure one."

He was walking now, and it felt just as lovely as the rest, his strength shifting against Maria, her ear pressed to his wildly beating heart. And when he settled her down again, onto the familiar furs of his bed, that was easy too, especially once his big body curled close, wrapping her up in his powerful arms.

"You are well, ach?" he whispered. "I no harmed you? Caused you shame, or fear, or pain?"

And suddenly Maria needed to see him, squirming against the furs to meet his eyes. To see the unease, and then to sweep it away with a hard shake of her head, an affectionate stroke of her hand along his strong stubbled jaw.

"Nothing of the sort," she whispered back. "It was perfect. It was *victory*."

But Simon's eyes were warm and wry on hers, his head giving a short little shake. "It was mayhap too much," he murmured, "for I ken you are fuck-drunk, my pretty one."

Maria lurched further up to glare at him, even as the room spun, and Simon slid a steadying hand against her head. "I am not," she protested. "It *was* victory. I've defeated my shame, and my fear, and my horrible husband. I've honoured you in every way there is, gained myself a mate and freedom and *home*. Found peace. Found my clan. Found *you*."

She jabbed her finger against his bare chest, making him look at her, holding that glimmering intensity in his eyes. "And you," she continued, quieter. "You've changed your clan's ways. You've kept me safe. You've defeated Ulfarr. You've"—she slid her other hand down to her belly, spread it wide—"gained us a son."

Simon's hand slid down to cover hers, and she could see his throat convulsing, his black lashes fluttering against his cheek. "But you gained all this with me, ach?" he whispered. "None of this should have befallen me, but for you."

Maria's smile back toward him felt strange and quivery, her finger again jabbing into his chest. "And but for your words. Your truth. Your *peace*."

Simon's shoulder jerked a shrug, his eyes briefly darting to Maria's face, and away again. "But mayhap—mayhap this peace is no truth with me, ach?" he asked, so soft, as though it were a confession, shameful and bare. "You ken I rage, I fight, I *kill*. I have whole room full of blades, I find such joy in battle. Even with my sweet mate, I shout, I push you, I flaunt you. I cleanse you, even when you no truly need this. I open all your holes and *laugh* as you scream and beg for me."

He'd been speaking very quickly, his gaze still averted, his claws slightly clenching against her waist. "And added to this," he continued, "it shall no be easy to bear my son, or raise him. It shall *never* be easy with my work as Enforcer. And these rifts with my clan, these *ways*—these shall no pass away, ach? These wars shall no pass away."

His eyes had lifted to hers again, holding there, searching. And in return Maria nodded, and flattened her hand against his chest, his erratic beating heart.

"I know, Simon," she said, quiet, sure. "But we'll learn how to face it together, like true Skai would. We'll hunt and train and play together, and find our own ways. And we'll have such fun with Arnthorr, because I know he'll be brilliant, and you'll be brilliant with him, too. You'll teach him everything, and be ridiculously patient with him, and he'll *adore* you, just as much as I do."

Simon's throat convulsed, his head tilting, and Maria spread her fingers wider against him, felt the steadily slowing beat of his heart. "And," she continued, "I also find myself in possession of a considerable sum of wealth, which we can now dispose of however we please. Maybe I could acquire myself a proper full-sized scimitar, and you could teach me how to use it? Maybe along with Bjorn, too? I'm sure he would even welcome some jigging lessons, between sparring-matches?"

An unmistakable warmth had sparked in Simon's watching eyes, and Maria smiled back, slow. "And do you realize," she added, "despite everything that's happened lately, I still feel better than I have in *years*? And, I never have to look at Warmisham's horrid face ever *again*. And, I'm currently in bed with a clever, delicious, and shockingly well-endowed orc, who even knows how to keep his room clean without my help. So, all in all"—her smile broadened to a full-on grin, bright and jaunty—"success, Simon. *Victory*. We've carried the day, and I can't wait to see what comes next."

Simon's eyes were so soft on hers, glinting with approval, with *hope*. "You are sure, Maria," he breathed. "You are *sure* you wish for all this. For me."

But looking at her deadly, dangerous mate, there was only one answer. The only one, perhaps, there ever had been, since the day Maria had first touched an orc, and found peace in his beating heart.

"Yes, Simon," she said. "I'm sure. *Always*. Now fuck again, ach?"

And there was the smile, crooked, true, *hers*. "Ach, my pretty one," he whispered. "Again."

BONUS EPILOGUE

I t was Maria's favourite kind of day. Bright, warm, with a clear blue sky, and a light whip of breeze on the air. The kind of day that was perfect for hunting, and travelling, and visiting all one's best-loved haunts—including no fewer than three Skai camps, all scattered deep throughout the Sakkin forest.

And also—Maria frowned as she leapt over a brook, slightly slipping in the thick mud—it *might* have been her birthday.

"You are *sure* you are no too weary, woman?" Simon's voice cut in, his big hand snapping out to grip at Maria's elbow. "We no *need* to see Himinn camp today, ach?"

He was eyeing her intently, one hand still holding her steady, the other one supporting a drowsy-looking Arnthorr on his shoulder. Because at seven months old, their son was already big, strong, and stubborn for his age, and he had long ago deduced that clinging to his father—whether to his back, chest, shoulder, or hair—provided the optimal vantage point for hunting, and refused to travel via any other means.

"No, I'm fine, really," Maria replied, angling a sidelong glance toward a suddenly frowning Bjorn beside her. "Really. And Bjorn's been looking forward to Himinn all day, haven't you, Bjorn?"

Bjorn's baleful eyes had promptly transferred from Maria to

Simon, and he crossed his skinny arms over his tunic. "I wait *all day*, Simon," he repeated. "You no *lie* to me, in this?"

Maria had to bite back her smile, but Simon's gaze down at Bjorn was entirely unmoved. "You ken I no lie, little brother," he said, voice firm. "But we four are *pack*, ach? This mean we no risk any of us. This mean we alter plan, if one of us need this. Whether this is me, or Maria, or Arnthorr, or *you*."

His finger jabbed at Bjorn as he spoke, and Bjorn's mouth twisted, his gaze dropping—no doubt recalling the day, several weeks past, when he'd sprained his ankle on a rock, and had needed to be carried home. And he accordingly jerked a sharp little nod, though he looked truly crestfallen, his slim shoulders slumped, his muddy boot tracing a path in the dirt at his feet.

"*Simon*," Maria said, with a pleading half-smile, half-wince up toward him. "I'm fine. Really."

Simon didn't look convinced, his assessing gaze flicking up and down Maria's mud-spattered form. Lingering first on her overfull breasts through her tunic, and then on her face, which was surely flushed and bright with sweat. It had been a full day, no question, and perhaps Maria's legs *did* feel a little trembly—but she didn't want to go back underground yet, either, not on a glorious day like this. *Especially* if it might have been her birthday.

"All right, well how about a short break before we go on, then?" she said, with a hopeful smile at Simon's face. "We're near the Grýtt cave anyway, aren't we? Maybe Bjorn can play with Arnthorr in the field while we rest?"

The flare in Simon's gaze suggested that he perfectly followed her meaning, and beside them the eagerness had returned to Bjorn's eyes, his small body bouncing on his feet. "You listen to our human, Simon," he said triumphantly, jabbing his claw toward Maria. "She knows I am good pack mate. I watch brother, you rest, *then* we go to Himinn."

Simon's mouth was twitching up, a warm tolerance stealing across his eyes—at least, until Arnthorr, who had still been quietly drowsing on Simon's shoulder, snapped his little head up, and instantly began wailing. His big eyes squeezed shut, his chubby arms flailing, his shrill howls echoing through the nearby trees—and before it could escalate into a full-on tantrum, Maria lurched to drag him off Simon's shoulder, pulling his squirmy little body close into her arms.

His wails thankfully subsided, his wet lashes blinking, his little clawed hand reaching up to rest on Maria's cheek. And for a frozen, dangling instant, she was caught in the truth of it, in the exquisite, shimmering ache that still crashed over her when she least expected it. Her very own son, with his expressive grey face, his thatch of messy black hair, his chubby, surprisingly strong body. Her own son, here in her arms, looking up into her soul with beautiful black eyes.

Of course, bearing and raising an orcling hadn't always been easy. The later stages of Maria's pregnancy had been nearly intolerable, and despite the intensive support of Efterar, the Ka-esh, and Joarr's new midwife mate Gwyn, Arnthorr's birth had still been an agonizing, days-long ordeal. Since then, he'd also proven to be viciously stubborn, with a single-minded devotion to his pack, and—Maria laughed as he grabbed for the neck of her tunic with his chubby little hand, and promptly began yanking it downwards—a truly insatiable appetite.

"You're hungry *again*, you little devil?" she demanded at him, tickling her fingers under his chin. "You just ate back in Thistil, remember? Or have you completely forgotten that?"

Arnthorr shot her a distinctively disapproving look, and kept yanking at her tunic, likely hard enough to tear—and Maria laughed again as she grasped his little hand, pulling it safely away. "All right then, I guess we do need to take a break," she said to Simon. "The cave, then?"

Simon had been watching Arnthorr with a look that might have been pain, or affection, or both, and his hand rubbed at his stubbled face. "Ach, the cave," he said. "Bjorn, you shall fill Maria's waterskin at the spring, and find her more to eat, ach? Stay within scent of me?"

Bjorn accordingly snatched the waterskin and darted off, while Maria and Simon and Arnthorr made for the cave. Which was thankfully close by, tucked around and behind a cliff, and soon Maria was curled up on Simon's lap, while Arnthorr nursed loudly and enthusiastically at her breast.

"Ach, it is no wonder you are weary, my pretty one," Simon said behind her, with a sigh. "My son is bent upon taking all you shall give him, ach?"

Maria didn't try arguing that, because by any standard, Arnthorr was an excessively demanding orcling. And even despite the shocking amounts of weight she had gained during her pregnancy, she was now quite possibly the thinnest she'd ever been—other than her swollen breasts, of course, which were emptied with rapid regularity.

"Oh, I don't mind," Maria said, smiling into the cave's darkness as she stroked at Arnthorr's silken hair. "He can't help that he's so hungry—can you, my love? Growing is just such hard work, isn't it?"

She blinked down toward Arnthorr as she spoke, while that glimmering ache flared again in her chest. Gods, she'd never imagined loving another living being so much—and even if motherhood had come with significantly more challenges than she'd expected, it was still something she would never, ever regret. Arnthorr and Simon and Bjorn were her family now. Her *home*.

"Ach, but you must stay well also, my Maria," Simon replied, voice flat. "You ken I no taste your weariness? Or how you seem lost in whatever this is you dwell upon, this day?"

Oh. That. Because of course he'd noticed that, ever-astute orc that he was—and based on the little tinge of hurt in his voice, he'd likely been waiting for her to share it with him, as well. Understandable, because Maria had no interest in keeping secrets from anyone these days, especially him, and she usually had no qualms with telling him whatever was on her mind.

"Oh, it wasn't anything important," Maria said, with a quick smile over her shoulder in the darkness. "I was just thinking—if I've counted the days right—that this might be my birthday."

There was an instant's silence, broken only by Arnthorr's steady gulping, and the sound of Simon's hand as he gently patted Arnthorr's back. "Your *birthday*," Simon finally repeated, as if testing out the word. "What is this?"

Maria shot a surprised look over her shoulder—how had she not realized that orcs didn't do *birthdays*? "It's a human custom, I suppose," she replied. "Where you celebrate the day you were born, and mark the number of years you've passed. If today is really the day, then I should be twenty-eight today."

There was more silence from Simon behind her, and Maria turned to glance up at him again, though he was only a shadow in the dim light. "Do orcs track birthdays at all?" she asked. "Or birth years? I know you've told me you've seen thirty summers before, but beyond that...?"

And it was astonishing, really, that this hadn't come up before— perhaps because of the overall dearth of birthdays in Orc Mountain— and she felt Simon shrug against her. "Ach, thirty, or mayhap now closer to forty," he replied. "And I was birthed in spring, my father said. But I no ken this one *birthday*."

Oh. "Well, if you ever decide you'd like one," Maria said lightly, "we can pick a day, and celebrate you properly. Have all your favourite foods, and give you gifts, suck you off multiple times, that kind of thing."

Simon snorted behind her, and she felt his head angle down, his teeth nibbling lightly against her neck. "I no need special day for sucking," he said. "You shall do this now, if Arnthorr is done, ach? I shall take him to Bjorn now."

Maria couldn't help a laugh, a roll of her eyes toward him—but of course she wasn't about to argue, and Simon gently nudged her off his lap, plucked Arnthorr out of her arms, and strode around and out of the cave. And when he returned, he was already tugging down the front of his trousers, and pulling out his swollen, liberally leaking prick.

Maria's mouth instantly watered at the distinctive musky scent, a hoarse groan escaping her throat—and Simon gave a satisfied grunt as he drew her mouth open with his finger, and slid his slick, dripping cockhead inside. Feeding it deeper and deeper, giving Maria time to adjust, to relax around his heft. She'd been working on sucking him further lately, thanks to some helpful tips from Baldr and Kesst, and she could hear Simon's deep chuckle of approval, could feel his hand carding into her hair.

"Ach, thus, my pretty one," he purred. "I shall feed this first load straight down into your belly, and you shall then suckle out your second, ach?"

Maria moaned, and tried for a frantic nod—to which Simon huffed another laugh, and pumped himself in once, twice. And there it was already, the molten flood of heat pouring and spurting directly down Maria's throat, while the heft in her mouth shuddered in time with Simon's husky groans above her.

He slowly drew back once he'd finished, his powerful length slightly softened between Maria's lips—but she only kept sucking, caressing him just the way he liked best, with lips and tongue and even teeth. Urging him back to hardness again, and revelling in the feel of him smoothly swelling against her, leaking his fiery sweetness onto her tongue.

He indulged her this time, kissing back with that slick head, oozing steady pulses of hot, succulent seed. His groans steadily rising with hers, until his strong hands were buried deep in her hair, and he again sprayed out—this time flooding her mouth with an astonishing quantity of him, thick and sweet and delicious.

"You swallow all, woman," Simon ordered, even as that cock kept pumping out its pleasure. "Each last drop, ach?"

Maria willingly obeyed, frantically gulping until her mouth was clear again, and she was again kissing at his softened head. To which Simon gave another low groan, his hand reaching down to briefly cup at his bollocks—but then he drew fully away, gently patting at her sticky cheek.

"Ach, this is all you shall have for now, my hungry one," he said. "Grant me time to make more for you, ach?"

Again, Maria didn't bother arguing—though she had at first, back when she'd first been pregnant, and Simon had begun insisting that she suck him off multiple times each day. Claiming that it would allow him to properly fatten her up, and help align her body to his, and safeguard her health while she grew his son. All truly laughable claims, or so Maria had thought—at least, until both Efterar and the Ka-esh had defended them with surprising strength. Efterar had in fact informed her, with a perfectly straight face, that she should be sucking Simon off at minimum twice per day, and that the more frequently she did so, the more seed Simon would create to sustain her.

It hadn't been a hardship, of course, and these days Simon's feedings felt as natural to Maria as eating regular food, or drinking milk and water. All of which Simon regularly insisted upon as well, and indeed, he'd already stalked back around to the cave door, where

Bjorn must have left the re-filled waterskin, along with—Maria breathed in deep—what smelled like her favourite berries.

"Eat," Simon ordered her, as he poured them out into her waiting hands. "All, woman."

Maria quickly and meekly obeyed, an action which at least gained Simon's reluctant assent for them to keep travelling on, rather than returning to Orc Mountain. Though as they walked again under the glorious sky, steadily making their way southeast, Maria could feel Simon's eyes frequently catching on hers, his brow vaguely furrowed, as if now he were the one lost in thought.

"This—*birthday*," he said finally, as he steadied Arnthorr's squirming body on his shoulder, and then absently grasped up for the stick Arnthorr had wanted, and put it in his little hand. "You say this should have gifts, and treats? And fucking?"

Maria couldn't help a grin at him, a bump at his arm with her shoulder. "I mean, every good day should have fucking, right?" she said cheerfully. "But that's the idea, yes."

Simon was silent for another long minute, his gaze glowering at Bjorn's scampering form ahead. And far too late, Maria realized the implication of what she'd just said, and she grasped Simon's muscled arm, pulled him to a stop. "I did *not* mean you have to do anything of the sort, Simon," she said. "I mean that. I didn't even remember it, until today."

Simon shrugged, and gave her a hint of his crooked smile—but he remained admittedly distracted as they travelled, and unusually silent. At least, until the Himinn camp came into view, and Bjorn dashed over to grasp both Simon and Maria's hands, pulling them along faster.

"We're here!" Bjorn crowed, his bright eyes lifting to the sky. "Himinn! The Skai Sky Camp!"

It wasn't difficult to become caught in his enthusiasm, because the Skai Sky camp—as Bjorn had fondly christened it—was surely one of the most delightful Skai camps. It was located high above the ground in a dense stand of pine and oak trees, and boasted a twisty maze of interconnected ramps, platforms, ladders, and crooked elevated huts. It wasn't at all the kind of place Maria had envisioned when imagining these mysterious Skai camps, and indeed, most of them had proven to be more like secret little villages, alive with orcs, women, and orclings of all ages.

"There's Galin!" Bjorn cried out, sprinting off to embrace another young, gangly orc about his age. "Race you to the top, brother!"

With that, they dashed toward the nearest tree with astonishing speed, using their claws to climb the rough bark of the trunk. Maria laughed as she watched them go, and then followed Simon around to the closest human ladder, which, while still precarious, was far less deadly to manage.

At the top they encountered a cheerful variety of familiar orcs and humans, all scattered throughout the little tree-houses. Simon had a long conference with his scout Fulnir, who spent much of his time here with his mate and two sons, while Maria and Arnthorr visited with several of the women she'd met here this year. Just sharing news and gossip, and discussing their orclings, and generally enjoying one another's company.

Maria finally ended up back in Fulnir's cozy hut, chatting with his mate Hannah at their table, while Fulnir and Simon finished up outside. At least, until Maria's stomach loudly growled—she'd had to feed Arnthorr twice more during their visit—and Simon promptly appeared from outside the hut, frowning mightily toward her. And after handing off Arnthorr to Fulnir's sons, and shooing the lot of them away, he strode over to Maria, yanked down his trousers, and interrupted her mid-sentence by thrusting his cock into her mouth.

"No," he ordered, at her obvious protest, as he ground into her throat. "You are peaked, woman. You ought to have come to me long before this. *Suckle.*"

Maria couldn't help a frantic glance at Hannah across the table, but thankfully Hannah only looked amused, her sly gaze darting up toward Fulnir—and soon Fulnir was standing before her too, lazily feeding his greenish prick between her sucking lips.

"Does your mate have *birthday*, Fulnir?" Simon asked him, as he sunk his claws into Maria's hair, and moved her faster up and down his length. "You offer gifts, and treats?"

He'd briefly glanced at Fulnir as he spoke, brows furrowed, and Maria could see Fulnir nodding, and plunging deeper into Hannah's mouth. "Offer much seed," he said, in his gravelly accented voice. "Best treat. Eat this out of her womb, also. Make her squeal."

Simon nodded too, frowning back down at Maria's reddened, sucking face. "You no give other gift? New blade, or jewels, or such?"

Fulnir quirked a saucy grin, and then yanked his prick out of Hannah's mouth, in favour of thrusting his swollen bollocks against her lips instead. "She already have good big jewels, ach?" he said. "Suckle your gold, *sæta*."

Hannah shot him a dark look, but didn't even try to refuse, to which both Simon and Fulnir chuckled. And then Simon's eyes fluttered back down to Maria, his pace increasing, until he groaned aloud and sprayed out in her mouth, grinding deep into her convulsing throat.

"Swallow all, my pretty one," he again ordered, husky. "Honour me."

Maria didn't argue—she was far too busy gulping down his delicious seed—and once it was done, she truly did feel markedly better. And she might have even started it all over again, if not for the distinctive sound of Arnthorr's rising wail from beyond the door.

"Ach, we must go, Fulnir," Simon said, with a sigh, glancing toward where Fulnir was in the process of turning Hannah around, and yanking up her skirt. "Until next moon, ach?"

Fulnir nodded, his eyes fluttering closed as he sank inside, while Hannah gave them a shaky-looking wave goodbye. And after another quick bout of Arnthorr-feeding below, Simon and Maria were once again travelling back to Orc Mountain, with Arnthorr again perched on Simon's shoulder, and Bjorn scampering ahead.

But Simon again seemed unusually pensive during their journey, frowning off into the darkness as they walked. And once they'd finally returned to the mountain, and Bjorn had run off to the kitchen, Simon drew Maria into their familiar room, plunked Arnthorr's squirmy body down on the floor, and settled both his heavy hands to Maria's shoulders.

"You ken, woman," he said, "I would have granted you a gift for this *birthday*, had I but known of this. Ach?"

Maria found herself blinking up at him for an instant—had he truly still been thinking about her *birthday*?—and then lurched closer, and threw her arms around his waist. "*Simon*," she said, exasperated, into his chest. "You don't need to do anything. We had such a lovely day together. That was a gift all its own."

She truly meant that, grinning up at his familiar, beloved face— but his brow only furrowed deeper as he looked down at her. "No, wilful woman," he countered. "You have learnt all my ways, and granted me many gifts. You have granted me peace, and joy, and even a *son*. Not only this, but you have eagerly borne hunger and weakness and weariness for many, *many* moons, so you might better serve our son, and grow him strong and hale—and thus you grant me great honour also. Today, you even offer to make me own *birthday*, so you might better honour me, and suckle me, and offer gifts."

Right. Maria winced, thoroughly regretting that she'd ever brought any of this up, and Simon drew away from her, in favour of gently jabbing his claw against her chest. "I am no good mate," he said firmly, "if I then no honour sweet, fierce mate on *birthday*, when she wish this from me. Ach?"

Maria opened her mouth to start arguing, again, but Simon's fingers pressed tight against her lips, his eyes dark. "No, woman," he said. "I shall alter this. But"—his shoulders slightly sagged, his eyes glancing over the room in the candlelight—"I only no knew of this, you ken? And thus, I have naught at hand to grant you. I might have made you a new tool to play with, or mayhap a new likeness"—his hand waved at the shelf with the carvings—"of mayhap Bjorn, or Arnthorr. Or mayhap even your own forebears, if you should welcome this. Or, I might have gained you a new blade—but Argarr is away these coming days, and I no trust another in this."

He was glowering mightily at the opposite wall now, his foot absently nudging at where Arnthorr was now trying to climb his leg. "If you cared for furs or jewels, I should have worked to gain you these," he continued. "Or mayhap one of these wedding-rings my brothers' mates have so oft wished for?"

One of these *wedding-rings*? Maria's head tilted, something skittering in her chest—because they'd talked about this before, multiple times. And each time, she'd roundly dismissed the idea, insisting that a bonded mate was far superior to a husband, and that they surely didn't need to bother with such things. Because surely, Simon wouldn't want to bother with such things.

But for the first time, it occurred to Maria that maybe... maybe Simon *might* actually want that. Maybe he wanted it in the same way he'd wanted their written contract, in the same way he wanted to honour her birthday. Because he knew these human words and ways had their own meaning, their own strength. Their own truth.

"Um," Maria heard herself say. "Is that something *you* would want, Simon?"

He didn't immediately reply, still glaring toward the wall, and Maria cleared her throat and reached for him again, her hand sliding against his warm bare back. "Well, if you truly want to grant something to me today," she said, as lightly as she could, "how would you feel about a little... Enforcing?"

Simon's glare angled down toward hers, his forehead again furrowing. "Enforcing?" he repeated. "For what, woman?"

Maria tried for a casual smile, though she could feel her cheeks rapidly heating. "Um," she said, "well, I completely failed at telling you about my birthday. Or about human birthday customs. Didn't I?"

Simon kept frowning at her, clearly nonplussed, and Maria drew in breath. "And as a result, I've put you in a dreadfully awkward position," she said. "I haven't given you any time to prepare a gift, and therefore obliged you to dishonour me by ignoring my birthday. It was very bad of me. *Terrible* mate behaviour."

The comprehension flared across Simon's face, and Maria felt her own hunger sparking in return, lighting up her eyes, coiling eagerly in her belly. Gods, it had been so *long* since they'd done it like that—between Arnthorr, and work, and travelling, and sleep, even finding time for intimacy at all was a challenge some days. And they were usually obliged to manage it as quickly and furtively as possible, certainly without any shouting or begging, or public displays, or excessive messes... let alone any proper, forceful Enforcing.

But over the past year and a half, the Enforcing was something they'd returned to again and again, most of all whenever things felt most difficult. And in it, Maria had consistently found a different kind of hunger, a different kind of relief. A raw, undeniable reminder, perhaps, that she was still Simon's mate, still Skai, still bound to the deadliest orc in Orc Mountain. Still his to use and judge and fuck as he wished.

But even as Maria's hand was sliding eagerly up Simon's bare chest, his narrow, assessing eyes had flicked down toward Arnthorr, and then up and down her form. "Ach, you are too weary for this today, woman," he countered. "You are weak. You must *rest.*"

Right. That again. Maria felt her own brow furrowing, her mouth opening to argue—but then she choked back the words, her gaze dropping to the floor. If Simon wasn't interested in such things today, she certainly wasn't about to push him, even if his constant concern for her welfare sometimes felt all-consuming. He was her mate, and she adored him, and she'd had such a truly lovely birthday already. She was blessed, and at peace.

"Right then," she said, with her best attempt at a smile toward him, though her eyes felt inexplicably watery. "Rest it is. I'd like that too. And so"—she dragged her eyes down to Arnthorr, who had climbed halfway up Simon's leg, and was currently clinging to his thigh—"are you hungry again yet, my little devil? A snack, and then a nap?"

Arnthorr gurgled his eager agreement, and soon they were curled up together on the bed, while Arnthorr eagerly nursed. And while Simon, oddly enough, kept standing in the middle of the room, his black gaze prickling against Maria's skin.

"Come join us?" she asked him, glancing up, petting the bed beside them—but Simon still didn't move, and his already-disapproving face had deepened into a ferocious scowl. Enough that Maria blinked, studying him, opening her mouth to ask what was wrong—

When Simon abruptly stalked forward, plucked Arnthorr out of her hands, and strode out of the room. Leaving Maria to blink and stare after him, her thoughts frantically churning—until Simon came back in a moment later, this time without Arnthorr, his face still thunderous, his hands in fists.

"You yet wish for Enforcing?" he demanded at her, voice clipped. "Then you fully bare yourself for me, and you *come.*"

He jabbed his finger at the floor beside him, while a furious, shivery chill rippled up Maria's back. And within a breath, she'd leapt off the bed, stripped off her tunic and loincloth, and lurched to stand bare and breathless at Simon's side.

He shot her another dark look, as his big hand snapped up, and grasped for a handful of her *hair*. And then he spun and strode out the door, pulling her after him, without so much as a backwards look.

Another fierce, delicious thrill was hurtling up Maria's spine—yes, finally, *finally*—and she rushed to keep up, her eyes fixed on Simon's face. On where he was scowling ahead down the corridor, not even looking at her, his jaw grinding in his stubbled cheek.

"You ken," he hissed, still without looking at her, "why I now Enforce you, woman?"

Maria could scarcely think over the rising, skittering chaos in her head, and she gulped for breath. "Um," she began, "because I forgot to tell you about my birthday?"

Simon rounded on her, his hand pulling back on her hair, his growl burning from his throat. "No," he snapped. "I do this because you spoke *false* to me, just now. You said you wish to rest, when in truth you wish for hard ploughing from me, for this *birthday*. You hide your truth, because you ken this is what I wished to hear!"

The anger was truly there, sparking in his eyes, and despite Maria's own shivering hunger, she felt a twitch of anger bubbling up, too. "I wasn't lying to you, Simon," she countered. "I was accepting your wishes. *Honouring* you."

It was true, surely it was—but Simon actually snarled at her this time, his eyes flaring. "You no honour me," he said flatly, "when you speak so *false* to me!"

Before Maria could reply, he'd yanked her back to walking again, dragging her through the door of the Skai common-room. Into its now-familiar hum of deep hunger and decadence, into the feeling of multiple orc eyes settling on Maria's bare, prickling skin.

"I wasn't speaking false to you!" she belatedly replied. "I was doing what you wanted. Respecting your wishes. Being a good *mate* to you!"

Simon's answering growl felt like it rumbled the room, his hand yanking back on Maria's hair. "A good mate," he breathed, "no *lie* to her orc, and her Enforcer. Now kneel, and fill your mouth with my good seed, and thus cleanse away these falsehoods!"

Maria's anger was truly snapping now, tangling with the tiredness, the weight of the watching orcs' eyes, the shouting, blaring hunger— and even, perhaps, with the certain, distant truth that Simon was *still* trying to feed her, damn him. "I do *not* need cleansing for that," she retorted, jabbing her finger into his hot chest. "Because I didn't speak any *falsehoods!*"

Something flashed in Simon's eyes, sharp and menacing—and before Maria even saw it, his powerful hands had gripped her, and thrust her flat onto her back on the floor. Not hard, and there were furs here, thank the gods—but still sudden enough to jolt the air from her lungs, her legs flailing and kicking up, shoving him away, what the *hell*—

But he'd yanked his trousers down, his flushed, dripping cock suddenly huge before her eyes—and wait, that was because he was straddling her torso, and leaning forward. And as Maria stared, gulping and breathless—yes, please, *please*—he aimed that thick, leaking cockhead straight for her mouth, and plunged it deep down between her parted, gasping lips.

Oh, *hell.* There was nowhere to go, no possible escape, Maria's mouth plugged full of her mate's massive, delicious orc-prick—*gods*, yes—and when she kicked and flailed and dragged for breath, he only thrust it deeper, his swollen bollocks slamming hard against her chin.

"I said, suckle," he ordered her, as he slightly eased off, and then gouged deep again. "Obey your Enforcer, woman! Every last *drop!*"

Maria was somehow still trying to shout at him around the cock stuffing her face, her body writhing and arching beneath him—and he kept bearing down deeper, so hard she gagged around his prodding heft. To which he barked another harsh growl, and then dragged himself all the way out of her, popping from her mouth with an obscene-sounding noise. Giving her room to breathe, perhaps, to beg for his mercy, to *agree*—

But the rage was still inexplicably curdling with the craving, flashing bright in Maria's eyes, escaping out her swollen lips. "You prick," she spat at him. "I was giving you what you wanted! Just like I *always* do!"

Simon's bark was more of a roar this time, his clawed hand snapping down to clutch at the huge shuddering base of that veined cock—and without warning, he slapped it across Maria's *cheek.* Not hard enough to hurt, but enough to snap her face sideways, her eyes frantically blinking—and then he did it to the other side, oh *gods*, dragging a hoarse, hungry moan from her throat.

"Again you *lie*, woman," he growled, as he yanked her quivering mouth open with his claw, and then slammed his cock back inside. "You no *always* do this. Even now, I have good cause to cleanse your mouth, and yet you *defy* me! You claim you spoke true, and thus dishonour me, and threaten our peace!"

Dishonour him. Threaten their *peace*? Maria was shuddering all over now, her eyes darting around at the room of watching orcs, her mouth still stuffed full of her mate's hunger, his anger, his... *hurt*. And this was supposed to be about the rough birthday fucking, or was it, because yes, that was hurt in his eyes. That was... *fear*?

"You threaten our peace," Simon repeated, quieter, and Maria felt that hardness slightly softening between her lips. "When you no tell me true. When you *hide*. When you show me what you ken I wish to see. When you put away *you*."

His claw had moved down between his still-straddling legs, touching gentle but purposeful to Maria's chest. Because he did mean this, good gods he meant this, and suddenly Maria felt more bared and exposed than she had since those exhausting first weeks after Arnthorr's birth. Hiding from him. Threatening their *peace*.

And then she began suckling on him, as hard and fervent as she possibly could, her eyes bright and intent on his face. Watching his gaze catch and shift, feeling the heft between her lips shudder and swell, growing back into her throat, filling out her cheeks. Yes, *yes*, just like it was supposed to be, and her fluttering tingling hands found his solid rounded arse above her, and yanked him deeper. Needing to feel him gouge and circle inside, just like this, making her gag and convulse upon him. Needing to hear his grunt of approval as he eased out, slow, and slammed back inside—

Yes, yes, *fuck* yes, and Maria sucked him harder, sloppier, deeper. Gulping as much of her Enforcer's cock as he would allow, until his heavy bollocks were again slapping at her face, his slick juices pumping steady down her throat. His breaths heaving, his body stiffening, eyes rolling back, he was close, he was about to—

And though Maria wanted it inside her, craved it so much it ached, she felt her hands shove him back, away. And he went, intuitive orc that he always was, his brow slightly furrowing, his slick cockhead popping free—and as he hovered over her, uncertain, Maria grasped both hands to his slippery, dripping prick, pumping up and down. Again, again, firm and purposeful, until his moan had risen to a roar, his head rearing up, his cock swelling with his seed—

But Maria didn't take it down her throat, like she'd done every other time for so many moons now. Instead, she let it spray out all over her face, catching and streaking against her lips, her cheeks, her eyelids, her hair. Marking her all over with her orc's slick, hot, rugged scent, as her hands eagerly milked it out of him, until she'd wasted every last delicious, nutritious drop.

Simon was staring down at her, his eyes wide and dazed, his chest still heaving—and Maria attempted a smile as she blinked her sticky eyelids at him, and brought up a hand to wipe some of the mess away. "If you truly don't want me to hide from you, my love," she whispered, her voice cracking, "you need to accept what I want, too. Even if it's not always what you think is best for me."

His eyes squeezed shut, his mouth thinning—and something swerved in Maria's chest, her hands fluttering up to stroke at his dear, scarred face. "But right now," she breathed, "I want you to keep going. Give this to me. Enforce me. *Please*."

Simon's eyes blinked back open, searching hers—and Maria flicked her tongue at the mess on her face, gulping it eagerly down her throat. Watching him watch her, seeing that familiar hunger dance back into his blinking eyes.

"Aren't you supposed to be Enforcing me, Simon?" she demanded, far louder this time, teasing him, taunting him before all his kin. "And here you haven't even made me *scream* yet?"

Her mate's answering bark shuddered down her back, and suddenly he was all deadly Enforcer again, huge, looming, menacing. "Wilful woman," he growled at her. "You wish to be stuck and screaming upon your Enforcer's prick?"

With that, his big hands once again grabbed her, this time flipping her over onto her belly, yanking her bare arse into the air, shoving her thighs wide apart. But his hand had somehow fisted into her hair again too, dragging her head up, as his throbbing cock found her splayed clutching heat, and drove inside in one deadly, devastating plunge.

Maria howled, her entire body arching, and Simon huffed a dark laugh behind her as he dragged himself out, and slammed back in. Powerful enough to ram another helpless scream from her throat, and his hand released her hair in favour of digging its claws into her upraised hips as he plunged in again, again, again.

It was harder than he'd used her in many, many moons, so forceful it chattered her teeth, and wildly jiggled her hanging, overfull breasts—and Simon laughed again as he reached down to pinch one, twisting another howl from Maria's mouth. "You wished to scream, wilful woman," he hissed at her, now pinching the other side, his claws possessive, proprietary, leaving red marks against her skin. "Now beg for your Enforcer's good cleansing. Loud. *Now*."

Oh gods, oh *fuck*, and Maria was frantically nodding, her body quivering all over, her invaded heat desperately clamping against his massive, pulsing, still-driving cock. "Yes, Simon," she gasped. "Enforce me. Grant me your good cleansing. Flood me with your good seed. Please. *Please!*"

He kept plunging in faster, harder, his breaths fraying, his claws digging deeper into her hips, and Maria kept begging, kept howling, as the pleasure whirled higher, the chaos rushing black and wild and close. "Please, Simon," she choked, pleaded, wept. "Please fill me. Plough me. Fuck me. I'm yours, yours, *yours!*"

And that was it, fuck that was it, his merciless cock driving in one last time, locking deep—and then blasting out inside her. Flooding her with stream after stream of hot, slick seed, pulsing and spurting, while her own relief clamped, and then ricocheted wide. Screeching through her entire body, baring her whole and pure before all her watching kin, while her claimed, invaded heat desperately milked the cock plunged deep inside it, needing more, more, *more*.

When the rest of the world finally edged back into Maria's vision, it was with the realization, first, that dozens of orcs were avidly looking at her. And second, that she was an utter *mess*, her reddened face still dripping with Simon's spunk, her heavy breasts leaking, and—she reflexively gasped—Simon's softened cock popping out of her, his streaming seed pouring onto the floor below. While Simon, the bastard, gave a light, approving little slap to her arse before pulling away, and then—Maria glanced backward—he rose to his feet, fluid and graceful.

Gods, he looked huge, and menacing, and breathtaking, towering like that over her, holding her blinking gaze steady in his safety, his *approval*. And when one of the watching orcs said something in black-tongue—something about whether a pretty mother really needed Enforcing thus—Simon gave a smug, easy little half-smile, and bent down to pluck Maria's messy, shivery body up into his arms.

"Ach, this day was her *birthday*," he said in common-tongue, his voice careful. "I ken she may need Enforcing each year on this day, so she may well remember who she is, ach? And who she belongs to, also."

With that, he strode for the door, hoisting Maria up strong and close, stroking his big hand against the mess of her hair. And she could only seem to clutch tighter against him, pressing her head to his chest, feeling the familiar thud of his slightly erratic heartbeat.

And it felt good, right, safe. It felt like peace, even if it still trembled a little, fluttering between them. Truth.

"You were right, Simon," Maria said, her voice cracking, as he strode into the cool air of the Skai bath, and settled her down at the edge of the pool. "I suppose I haven't always been entirely honest with you lately. I just—"

The words seemed to catch in her throat, and Simon gently wiped against her cheek with the wet cloth in his hand, smoothing off the mess. "I ken," he said, gruff. "You only seek to please me, and keep all easy between us. And you wish to keep Arnthorr safe, and I have oft wielded this against you also. Ach?"

Maria couldn't seem to reply, and she let her eyes flutter closed as Simon's cloth carefully wiped at her sticky eyes, her hair, her mouth. "You are so sweet, my pure one," he whispered. "I ought no always command you thus, ach? I forget you may no always return my commands with truth. I forget you may no always wish to fight me. I forget I may—push you to *hide* from me."

His cloth had slightly stilled against Maria's shoulder, his eyes distant, his forehead furrowed. "I no wish to be this—*husband*, who so wronged you thus," he said, even quieter. "But mayhap I have yet done this, ach? Mayhap this is why you no wish to wed me, in the ways of your kin?"

Wait, why she didn't want to *wed* him?! Maria blinked blankly at his dark eyes, while something began knocking uncontrollably in her chest. "You think," she somehow managed, "I don't *want* to wed you?"

Simon jerked a curt nod, his gaze still fixed beyond her—and without at all meaning to, Maria flung her arms around his taut body, burying her face in his shoulder. And she was weeping, suddenly, and still somehow laughing, and rubbing irritably at her eyes, while the truth seemed to tumble on its own out her mouth.

"Of course I want to wed you, Simon," she gulped at him. "I just— it's such a big commitment, and you know it hasn't gone well for me before, and what if you change your mind, or regret it, or decide you'd rather someone else instead, and it's just"—she gulped for more air— "safer. Not to. Risk it, I mean."

Simon had gone very still against her, every muscle tight and tense—and he moved away from her, his fingers oddly trembly on her skin. "Maria," he said, snapping her wet eyes to his. "You ken there is naught upon this earth that shall make me regret this. Can you no see all you grant me? All your kindness, all your laughter, your hunger for me, your *peace*. This little Skai *pack* we have made. I never before *dreamt* of finding all this, in this life. And mayhap this is wrong, this is *greedy*, but"—his throat convulsed, his own eyes blinking—"I wish to bind you to me in all ways. In every way. I wish to have you for my mate, and the mother of my son, and my kin, and my Enforced, and my *wife*. And thus, you shall stay with me. *Always*."

His trembly claw had gently touched to Maria's bare chest, his too-bright eyes fixed to hers. "Always," he repeated. "For *every* birthday, until one of us has passed from this earth. Ach?"

Maria was frantically nodding, the sobs still breaking from her throat, and she clutched for him again, dragged him close. "Yes, Simon," she choked into his shoulder. "Yes. *Yes.*"

She could feel him relaxing against her, but for his arms clamping tighter around her back, his claws spreading wide. "Ach," he said, husky. "Thus I shall gain you this ring for your birthday gift after all, my pure one. This shall look so shiny and pretty upon your finger, I ken."

Maria was still nodding and messily gulping for air, dripping from her eyes and nose onto his bare shoulder. And thankfully Simon drew them both into the ice-cold water, and held her shivering body close to his powerful warmth as he scrubbed off the rest of the mess. "And I shall seek to better ask for what you wish," he said firmly, "if you shall seek to better speak true to me? In all ways?"

Maria was still fervently nodding, and Simon's smile toward her was so slow, so crooked, so painfully tender. "Thus, shall you now suckle me?" he whispered. "And swallow all, my pretty one?"

The laugh escaped Maria's throat before she could stop it, the sheer happiness brimming in her chest. She was home. Blessed. At peace.

"Of course, my love," she said. "Every last drop."

∼

THE END

∼

THANKS FOR READING
AND GET A FREE BONUS STORY!

Thank you so much for joining me for this journey among the Skai! I really loved writing this book, and I hope you had fun with it too.

For even more Skai fun, sign up at www.finleyfenn.com for extra content, including gorgeous artwork from *The Duchess and the Orc*, and a free Orc Sworn story. I'd love to stay in touch with you!

FREE STORY: OFFERED BY THE ORC

The monster needs a sacrifice. And she's naked on the altar...

When Stella wanders the forest alone one fateful night, she only seeks peace, relief, escape. A few stolen moments on a secret, ancient altar, at one with the moon above.

Until she's accosted by a hulking, hideous, bloodthirsty *orc*. An orc who demands a sacrifice—not by his sword, but by Stella's complete surrender. To his claws, his sharp teeth, his huge muscled body. His every humiliating, thrilling command...

But Stella would never offer herself up to be used and sacrificed by a monster—would she? Even if her surrender just might grant her the moon's favour—and open her heart to a whole new fate?

www.finleyfenn.com

ACKNOWLEDGMENTS

As always, I am so ridiculously grateful to my readers, and my generous beta readers and advance reviewers. I am truly blessed!

I'm especially thankful to Jesse, Jen R., MK, Ann, Serena, and Erin for all your thoughtful feedback and support. And as usual, all props to my incredible Amy and Jennifer N.—your guidance and enthusiasm have been so, so invaluable to me.

Of course, I must again mention my lovely Facebook group members at Finley Fenn Readers' Den (come join us, they're SUCH a treat!), who kept me going this year with all their warmth, kindness, and delicious orc artwork. Thank you, my loves!

I also remain so deeply grateful to my fellow authors, so many of whom have supported my writing, and freely offered their advice and expertise (up to and including detailed design tutorials!). ;) It's been such an honour to share this journey with you.

Finally, as always, all my love to my own fierce mate, who has spent incessant amounts of time and energy this past year calming me, feeding me, supporting me, and granting me true peace amidst the chaos. I adore you, my brave one.

ABOUT THE AUTHOR

Finley Fenn is "the queen of dark orc romance" (Virgo Reader), and her ongoing Orc Sworn series has been praised as "sexy, romantic, angsty, and captivating ... utter brilliance" (Romantically Inclined Reviews).

When she's not obsessing over her stories, Finley loves reading, drooling over delicious orc artwork, and spending time with her incredible readers on Patreon, Discord, and Facebook. She lives in Canada with her beloved family, including her very own grumpy, gorgeous orc husband.

For free bonus stories and epilogues, special offers, and exclusive Orc Sworn artwork, sign up at www.finleyfenn.com.

Printed in the USA
CPSIA information can be obtained
at www.ICGtesting.com
LVHW041740280124
769859LV00016B/417